THE SONG
OF TROY

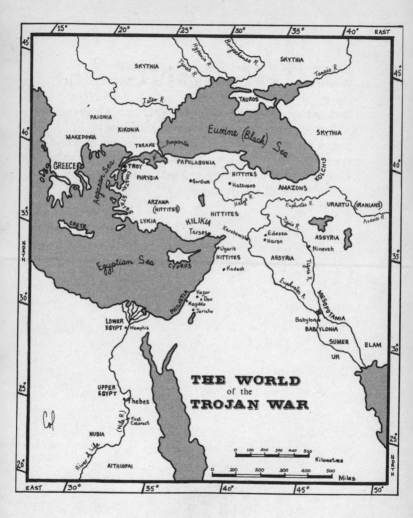

THE SONG
OF TROY

COLLEEN McCULLOUGH

ORION

An Orion Paperback
First published in Great Britain by
Orion Books in 1998
This paperback edition published in 1999 by
Orion Books Ltd,
Orion House, 5 Upper St Martin's Lane,
London WC2H 9EA

A CIP catalogue record for this book
is available from the British Library

ISBN: 0 75281 763 9

Typeset by Deltatype Ltd, Birkenhead, Merseyside
Printed and bound in Great Britain by
Clays Ltd, St Ives plc

For my brother, Carl, who died in Crete
on September 5th, 1965, rescuing some
women from the sea.

πάντα δὲ καλὰ θανόντι περ,
ὅττι φανήῃ.
Death can find nothing to expose in him
that is not beautiful.

Homer, Iliad 22.73

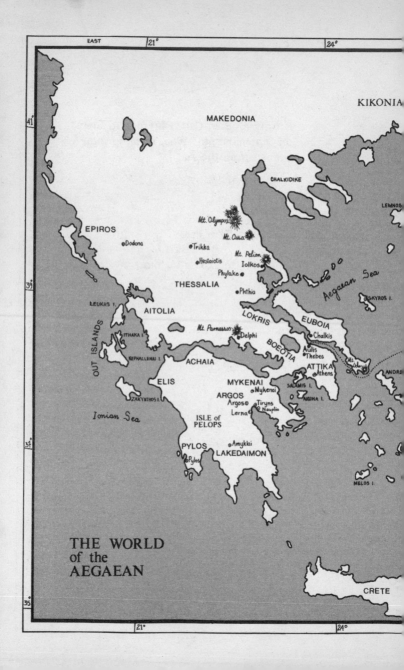

THE WORLD
of the
AEGAEAN

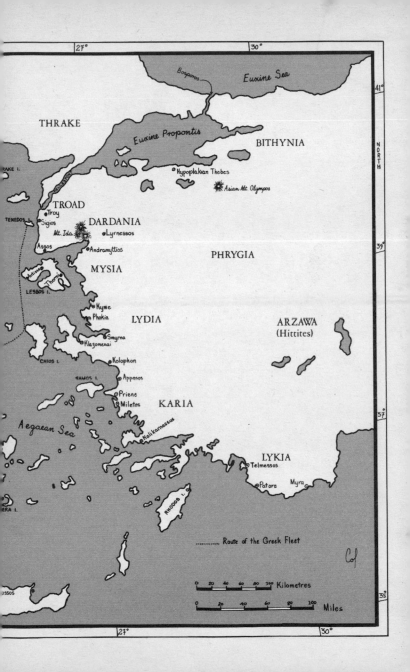

CHAPTER ONE

NARRATED BY
PRIAM

There never was a city like Troy. The young priest Kalchas, sent to Egyptian Thebes during his novitiate, came back unimpressed by the pyramids built along the west bank of the River of Life. Troy, he said, was more imposing, for it reared higher and its buildings housed the living, not the dead. But then, he added, there was an extenuating circumstance: the Egyptians owned inferior Gods. The Egyptians had moved their stones with mortal hands, whereas Troy's mighty walls had been thrown up by our Gods themselves. Nor, Kalchas said, could flat Babylon compete, its height stunted by river mud, its walls like the work of children.

No man remembers when our walls had been built, it was so long ago, yet every man knows the story. Dardanos (a son of the King of our Gods, Zeus) took possession of the square peninsula of land at the very top of Asia Minor, where on the north side the Euxine Sea pours its waters down into the Aegaean Sea through the narrow strait of the Hellespont. This new kingdom Dardanos divided into two parts. He gave the southern section to his second son, who called his domain Dardania and set up his capital in the town of Lyrnessos. Though smaller, the northern section is much, much richer; with it goes the guardianship of the Hellespont and the right to levy taxes upon all the merchants who voyage in and out of the Euxine Sea. This section is called the Troad. Its capital, Troy, stands upon the hill called Troy.

Zeus loved his mortal son, so when Dardanos prayed to his divine father to gift Troy with indestructible walls, Zeus was delighted to grant his petition. Two of the Gods were out of favour at the time: Poseidon, Lord of the Sea, and Apollo, Lord of Light. They were ordered to proceed to Troy and build ramparts taller, thicker and stronger than any others. Not really a task for the delicate and fastidious Apollo, who elected to play his lyre rather than get dirty and sweaty – a way, he explained carefully to the gullible Poseidon, of helping to pass the time while the walls went up. So Poseidon piled stone upon stone while Apollo serenaded him.

Poseidon laboured for a price, the sum of one hundred talents of gold to be deposited each and every year thereafter in his temple at Lyrnessos. King Dardandos agreed; time out of mind the hundred talents of gold had been paid each and every year to the temple of Poseidon in Lyrnessos. But then, just as my father, Laomedon, ascended the Trojan throne, came an earthquake so devastating that it had felled the House of Minos in Crete and blown the island empire of Thera away. Our western wall crumbled and my father hired the Greek engineer, Aiakos, to rebuild it.

Aiakos did a good job, though the new wall he erected had neither the smoothness nor the beauty of the rest of that great, God-begotten encirclement.

The contract with Poseidon (I daresay Apollo hadn't deigned to ask for a musician's wages), said my father, was dishonoured. The walls had not proven indestructible after all. Therefore the hundred talents of gold paid each year to Poseidon's temple in Lyrnessos would not be paid again. Ever. Superficially this argument looked a valid one, save that the Gods surely knew what even I, then a boy, knew: that King Laomedon was an incurable miser, and resented paying so much precious Trojan gold to a temple located in a rival city under the rule of a rival dynasty of blood relations.

Be that as it may, the gold ceased to be paid, and nothing happened for more years than it took me to grow from child to man.

Nor, when the lion came, did anyone think to connect his advent with insulted Gods or city walls.

To the south of Troy on the verdant plains lay my father's horse farm, his one indulgence – though even indulgence had to bring profit to King Laomedon. Not long after Aiakos the Greek finished rebuilding the western wall, a man arrived in Troy from a place so far away we knew nothing of it beyond the fact that its mountains bolstered the sky and its grasses were sweeter than any other grasses. With him the refugee brought ten horses – three stallions and seven mares. They were horses the like of which we had never seen – large, fleet, graceful, long maned and long tailed, pretty faced, demure and tame. Splendid for drawing chariots! The moment the King set eyes on them, the man's fate was inevitable. He died and his horses became the private property of the King of Troy. Who bred from them a line so famous that traders from all over the world came to buy mares and geldings; my father was too shrewd to sell a stallion.

Through the middle of the horse farm ran a worn and sinister track, once used by lions as they travelled north from Asia Minor to Skythia for the summer, and south again to winter in Karia and Lykia, where the sun retained the power to warm their tawny hides. Hunting had killed them off; the lion track became a path to water.

Six years ago the peasants had come running, pallid faced. I will never forget the sight of my father's countenance when they told him that three of his best mares were lying dead and a stallion badly mutilated, the victims of a lion.

Laomedon was not the man to give way to unthinking rage. In a measured voice he ordered a whole detachment of the House Guard to station itself on the track the following spring, and kill the beast.

No ordinary lion, that one! Each spring and autumn he came through so stealthily no one saw him; and he killed far more than his belly needed. He killed for the love of it. Two years after his advent the House Guard caught him attacking a

3

stallion. They advanced on him clashing their swords against their shields, intending to force him into a corner so they could use their spears. Instead, he reared to roar his war cry, charged straight at them, and went through their ranks like a boulder rushing downhill. As they scattered the kingly beast killed seven of them before going on his way unscathed.

One good thing came out of the disaster. A man torn by his claws lived to go to the priests, and told Kalchas that the lion bore the mark of Poseidon; on his pale flank was a black, three-pronged fish spear. Kalchas consulted the Oracle at once, then announced that the lion belonged to Poseidon. Woe the Trojan hand that struck at him! Kalchas cried, for he was a punishment visited upon Troy for cheating the Lord of the Seas of his annual hundred talents' payment. Nor would he go away until it was resumed.

At first my father ignored Kalchas and the Oracle. In the autumn he ordered the House Guard out again to kill the beast. But he had underestimated the common man's fear of the Gods: even when the King threatened his guardsmen with execution, they would not go. Furious but balked, he informed Kalchas that he refused to donate Trojan gold to Dardanian Lyrnessos – the priests had better think of an alternative. Kalchas went back to the Oracle, which announced in plain language that there *was* an alternative. If each spring and autumn six virgin maidens chosen by lot were chained in the horse pasture and left there for the lion, Poseidon would be satisfied – for the time being.

Naturally the King preferred giving the God maidens to gold; the new scheme went ahead. The trouble was that he never really trusted the priests in the matter, not because he was a sacrilegious man – he gave the Gods what he considered their due – but because he detested being bled. So each spring and autumn every virgin maid aged fifteen years was covered head to foot in a white shroud to prevent identification and lined up in the courtyard of Poseidon Maker of Walls, where the priests chose six of these anonymous white bundles for the sacrifice.

The ploy worked. Twice a year the lion passed through, killed the girls as they stood huddled in their chains, and left the horses unmolested. To King Laomedon, a paltry price to pay for the salving of his pride and the preservation of his business.

Four days ago autumn's six offerings were chosen. Five of them were girls from the city; the sixth was from the Citadel, the high palace. My father's most beloved child, his daughter Hesione. When Kalchas came to tell him the news, he was incredulous.

'Do you mean to say that you were idiot enough to leave her shroud unmarked?' he asked. '*My* daughter treated the same as all the rest?'

'It is the God's will,' said Kalchas, calmly.

'It is *not* the God's will that my daughter should be chosen! His will is that he receives six virgin maids, nothing else! So choose another victim, Kalchas.'

'I cannot, Great King.'

From that stand Kalchas would not be budged. A divine hand directed the choice, which meant that Hesione and no other girl would satisfy the terms of the sacrifice.

Though none of the Court was present during this tense and angry interview, the word of it swept through the Citadel from end to end and top to bottom. Favour curriers like Antenor were loud in condemning the priest, whereas the King's many children – including me, his Heir – thought that at last our father would have to break down and pay Poseidon those annual hundred talents of gold.

Next day the King summoned his council. Of course I attended; the Heir must hear the King deliver all his judgements.

He looked composed and undistressed. King Laomedon was a tiny fellow far past the flush of youth, long hair silver, long robe gold. The voice which issues out of him never ceased to surprise us, for it was deep, noble, melodic, strong.

'My daughter Hesione,' he said to the assembled ranks of

sons, near cousins and remote cousins, 'has consented to go to the sacrifice. It has been required of her by the God.'

Perhaps Antenor had guessed what the King would say; I did not, nor did my younger brothers.

'My lord!' I cried before I could stop myself. 'You cannot! When times are hard the King may go to the sacrifice for the sake of the people, but his virgin daughters belong to Virgin Artemis, not to Poseidon!'

He did not care to hear his eldest son chide him before the Court; his lips thinned, his chest swelled. 'My daughter was chosen, Podarkes Priam! Chosen by Poseidon!'

'Poseidon would be happier,' I said through my teeth, 'if one hundred talents of gold were paid to his temple in Lyrnessos.'

At which moment I caught sight of Antenor smirking. How he loved to hear the King and his Heir at loggerheads!

'I refuse,' said King Laomedon, 'to pay good, hard-earned gold to a God who didn't build the western wall strong enough to survive one of his own earthquakes!'

'You can't send Hesione to her death, Father!'

'*I* am not sending her to her death! Poseidon is!'

The priest Kalchas moved, then stilled.

'A mortal man like you,' I said, 'should not blame the Gods for his own failings.'

'Are you saying that I have failings?'

'All mortal men do,' I answered, 'even the King of the Troad.'

'Take yourself off, Podarkes Priam! Get out of this room! Who knows? Perhaps next year Poseidon will ask that heirs to thrones form the sacrifice!'

Antenor was still smiling. I turned and left the room to seek comfort from the city and the wind.

Cold, damp air blowing from the far-off peak of Ida cooled my anger as I strode along the flagged terrace outside the Throne Room and sought the steps, two hundred of them, which led ever upward to the summit of the Citadel. There, far above the plain, I closed my hands on man-made stones; for the Gods had not built the Citadel, Dardanos had done that. Something reached into me from out of those carefully squared bones of Mother Earth, and I sensed in that moment the power residing in the King. How many years, I wondered, would have to pass before I donned the golden tiara and sat on the ivory chair which was the throne of Troy? The men of the House of Dardanos were very long-lived, and Laomedon was not yet seventy.

For a long while I watched the changing march of men and women below me in the city, then looked farther afield to the green plains where King Laomedon's precious horses stretched out their long necks to nudge and tear at the grass. But that was a vista only increased the pain. I looked instead to the western isle of Tenedos and the smear of smoke from fires lit against the chill in the little port village of Sigios. Beyond to the north the blue waters of the Hellespont mocked at the sky; I saw the long greyish curve of the beach which lay between the mouths of Skamander and Simois, the two rivers which watered the Troad and nurtured the crops, emmer wheat and barley, rippling in a soughing, perpetual wind.

Eventually that wind drove me from the parapet to the great courtyard which lay before the entrance to the palaces, and there I waited until a groom brought my chariot.

'Down into the city,' I said to the driver. 'Let the horses lead you.'

The main road descended from the Citadel to join the curve of the avenue which ran around the inside of the city walls. The walls built by Poseidon. At the junction of the two streets stood one of the three gates let into Troy's walls, the Skaian. I could not remember its ever being closed; men said that happened only in times of war, and there was no nation in the world strong enough to make war on Troy.

The Skaian Gate stood twenty cubits tall, and was made of huge logs bolted together with spikes and plates of bronze, too heavy to be swung on the biggest hinges a man could forge. Instead it opened on a principle said to have been devised by

7

Archer Apollo as he lay in the sun watching Poseidon toil. The bottom of the gate's single leaf rested upon a great round boulder set in a deep, curving ditch, and massive bronze chains were cast about the shoulders of the stone. If the gate had to be closed, a team of thirty oxen was harnessed to the chains and pulled the leaf shut fraction by fraction as the boulder ground along in the bottom of the ditch.

As a little boy, burning to see the spectacle, I had begged my father to hitch up the oxen. He had laughed and refused, yet here I was, a man of forty years, husband of ten wives and owner of fifty concubines, still hankering to see the Skaian Gate shut.

Across the top of the gate a corbelled arch connected the walls on either side of it, thus permitting the pathway which ran along the top to be continuous right around the perimeter of the city. The Skaian Square inside the gate lay in permanent shadow from those fantastic, God-built ramparts; they towered thirty cubits above me, smooth and sleek, sheeny in the sun when it bathed them.

I nodded to my driver to move on, but before he could shake the reins I changed my mind, stopped him. A party of men had come through the gate into the square. Greeks. That was manifest in their garb and manner. They wore leather kilts or tight-fitting, knee-length leather breeches; some were bare from the waist up, and others sported tooled leather blouses open to display their chests. The clothes were ornate, decked in gold designs or sporting tassels or rolls of dyed leather; their waists were clipped in narrow by wide belts of gold and lapis-studded bronze; polished crystal beads depended from the lobes of their ears; each throat was girdled with a great gem-encrusted collar; and their very long hair flowed loose in careful curls.

Greeks were taller and fairer than Trojans, but these Greeks were taller, fairer and more deadly looking than any men I had ever seen. Only the richness of their clothes and arms said they were not common marauders, for they carried javelins and longswords.

At their head strode a man who was surely unique, a giant who towered over the other members of the group. He must have stood six cubits high, and had shoulders like dark mountains. Pitch-black and trimmed into a spade, a beard coated his massively jutting lower jaw, and his black hair, though cut short, was wild and unruly above a brow which overhung his orbits like an awning. His only clothing was a huge lion pelt flung over his left shoulder and under his right arm, the head a hood on his back with frightful jaws open on mighty fangs.

He turned and caught me staring. Overwhelmed, I found and looked into his wide still eyes – eyes which had seen everything, endured everything, experienced every degradation the Gods could mete out to a man. Eyes which blazed with intelligence. I felt myself mentally backed up against the house behind me, my spirit a naked scrawn, my mind his for the taking.

But I marshalled my sinking courage and drew myself upright proudly; mine was a great title, mine a gold-embossed chariot, mine a pair of white horses finer than any he had ever seen. Mine, this mightiest city in the world.

He moved through the racket and bustle of the marketplace as if it did not exist, came straight up to me with two of his companions close behind, then put out a hand the size of a ham to stroke the black muzzles of my white horses gently.

'You are from the palace, perhaps of the King's house?' he asked in a very deep voice, though it lacked imperiousness.

'I am Podarkes called Priam, son and Heir of Laomedon, King of Troy,' I answered.

'I am Herakles,' he said.

I stared at him with mouth agape. *Herakles!* Herakles was in Troy! I licked my lips. 'Lord, you honour us. Will you consent to being a guest in my father's house?'

His smile was surprisingly sweet. 'I thank you, Prince Priam.

Does your invitation include all my men? They are of noble Greek houses, they will not shame your court or me.'

'Of course, Lord Herakles.'

He nodded to the two men behind him, a signal that they should step out of his shadow. 'May I present my friends? This is Theseus, High King of Attika, and this is Telamon son of Aiakos, King of Salamis.'

I swallowed. All the world knew of Herakles and Theseus; the bards sang their deeds incessantly. Aiakos, father of the stripling Telamon, had rebuilt our western wall. How many other famous names were there in that little band of Greeks?

Such was the power in that single word Herakles that even my miserly father was moved to put himself out, give the famous Greek a royal welcome. So that night a feast was laid out in the Great Hall, with unlimited food and wine off gold plate, and harpers, dancers and tumblers to provide entertainment. If I had been awed, so too was my father; every Greek in the party of Herakles was a king in his own right. Why, therefore, I wondered, were they content to follow a man who laid no claim to any throne? Who had mucked out stables? Who had been gnawed, bitten and chewed by every kind of creature from gnat to lion?

I sat at the high table with Herakles on my left and the lad Telamon on my right; my father sat between Herakles and Theseus. Though the imminence of Hesione's sacrificial death overshadowed our hospitality, it was so well concealed that I told myself our Greek guests had noticed nothing. Talk flowed smoothly, for they were cultivated men, properly educated in everything from mental arithmetic to the words of the poets they, like us, committed to memory. Only what kind of man was a Greek underneath that?

There was little contact between the nations of Greece and the nations of Asia Minor, which included Troy. Nor, as a rule, did we of Asia Minor care for Greeks. They were notoriously devious people famed for their insatiable curiosity, so much we knew; but these men must have been outstanding even among their own Greek kind, for the Greeks chose their Kings for reasons other than blood.

My father in particular did not care for Greeks. Of late years he had formulated treaties with the various kingdoms of Asia Minor giving them most of the trade between the Euxine and the Aegaean Seas, which meant that he had severely restricted the number of Greek trading vessels allowed to pass through the Hellespont. Not Mysia and Lydia, not Dardania and Karia, not Lykia and Kilikia wanted to share trade with the Greeks, for the simplest of reasons: somehow the Greeks always outwitted them, emerged with better bargains. And my father did his part by keeping Greek merchants out of the black waters of the Euxine. All the emeralds, sapphires, rubies, gold and silver from Kolchis and Skythia travelled to the nations of Asia Minor; the few Greek traders my father licensed had to concentrate their efforts upon fetching tin and copper from Skythia.

Herakles and company, however, were far too well bred to discuss incendiary topics like trade embargoes. They confined their conversation to admiring remarks about our high-walled city, the size of the Citadel and the beauty of our women – though this last they could gauge only from the female slaves who walked among the tables ladling stews, doling out bread and meats, pouring wine.

From women the talk veered naturally to horses; I waited for Herakles to broach the matter, for I had seen those shrewd black eyes appreciating the quality of my white horses.

'The horses which drew your son's chariot today were truly magnificent, sire,' said Herakles at last. 'Not even Thessalia can boast such stock. Do you ever offer them for sale?'

My father's face took on its avaricious look. 'Yes, they are lovely, and I do sell them – but I fear you would find the price prohibitive. I ask and get a thousand gold talents for a good mare.'

Herakles shrugged his mighty shoulders, face rueful. 'I could

11

perhaps afford the price, sire, but there are more important things I have to buy. What you ask is a king's ransom.'

He did not mention the horses again.

As the evening drew on and the light began to fail my father started to sag, remembering that on the morrow his daughter would be led to her death. Herakles put his hand on my father's arm.

'King Laomedon, what ails you?'

'Nothing, my lord, nothing at all.'

Herakles smiled that peculiarly sweet smile. 'Great King, I know the look that worry wears. Tell me!'

And out tumbled the story, though of course Father put himself in a better light than the actual facts dictated: he was plagued by a lion belonging to Poseidon, the priests had ordered the sacrifice of six maidens each spring and autumn, and the choice of this autumn's victims included his most beloved child, Hesione.

Herakles looked thoughtful. 'What was it the priests said? No *Trojan* hand can be raised to oppose the beast?'

The King's eyes gleamed. 'Specifically Trojan, my lord.'

'Then your priests cannot object if a Greek hand is raised against the beast, can they?'

'A logical conclusion, Herakles.'

Herakles glanced at Theseus. 'I have killed many lions,' he said, 'including the one of Nemea whose pelt I wear.'

My father burst into tears. 'Oh, Herakles, rid us of this curse! If you did, we would be very much in your debt. I speak not only for myself, but for my people. They have suffered the loss of thirty-six daughters.'

Pleasurable anticipation crawling through me, I waited; Herakles was no fool, he would not offer to dispose of a God-sent lion without some compensation for himself.

'King Laomedon,' the Greek said loudly enough for heads to turn, 'I will strike a bargain with you. I will kill your lion in return for a pair of your horses, one stallion and one mare.'

What could my father do? Neatly forced into a corner by the public nature of this overture, he had no choice other than to agree to the price, or have word of his heartless selfishness spread throughout his Court – his relatives close and remote. So he nodded in a fair imitation of joy. 'If you succeed in killing the lion, Herakles, I will give you what you ask.'

'So be it.' Herakles sat very still, eyes wide and unseeing; nor did they blink, or notice what went on. Then he sighed, recollected himself, looked not at the King but at Theseus. 'We will go tomorrow, Theseus. My father says the lion will come at noon.'

Even the other Greeks at table with him appeared awed.

Delicate wrists loaded down with golden chains, ankles ringed with golden fetters, dressed in the finest robes and with their hair freshly curled and their eyes painted, the six girls waited for the priests to come in the courtyard fronting the temple of Poseidon Maker of Walls. Hesione my half-sister was among them, calm and resigned, though the little twitch at one corner of her tender mouth betrayed her inner fear. The air was filled with the wailing and keening of parents and relatives, the clink of heavy manacles, the quick breathing of six young and terrified girls. I stayed only to kiss Hesione, then left; she knew nothing of the attempt Herakles was going to make to save her.

Perhaps the reason I did not tell her was because even then I suspected we would not rid ourselves of the curse so easily – that if Herakles did kill the lion, Poseidon Lord of the Seas might replace him with something much worse. Then my misgivings evaporated in the rush of getting from the shrine to the small door at the back of the Citadel where Herakles had assembled his party. He had chosen two helpers only for the hunt: the hoary warrior Theseus and the shaveling Telamon. At the last moment he lingered to have speech with another of his band, the Lapith King Pirithoos; I overheard him telling Pirithoos to take everyone to the Skaian Gate at noon and wait there. He was in a hurry to leave, then, which I understood; the

Greeks were going to the lands of the Amazons to steal the girdle of their queen, Hippolyta, before winter.

After that extraordinary trance in the Great Hall the evening before, no one questioned Herakles's conviction that the lion would come today – though if he did come today, it would be by far his earliest passage south yet. Herakles *knew*. He was the son of the Lord of All, Zeus.

I had four full brothers, all younger than me: Tithonos, Klytios, Lampos and Hiketaon. We accompanied Herakles in our father's escort, and arrived at the appointed spot on the horse farm before the priests appeared with the girls. Herakles paced back and forth for a good distance in each direction, spying out the land; then he returned to us and set up his attacking position, with Telamon on the long bow and Theseus carrying a spear. His own weapon was an enormous club.

While we climbed to the top of a hillock out of wind and eye range, our father remained on the track to await the priests, for this was the first day of the sacrifice. Sometimes the poor young creatures had been obliged to wait many days in their golden chains, with only the ground to sleep on and a few very frightened junior priests to bring them food.

The sun was well up when the procession from the shrine of Poseidon Maker of Walls came into view, the priests shoving the weeping girls ahead of them, chanting the ritual and beating tiny drums with muted sticks. They hammered the chains to staples in the ground under the shade of an elm, and left with as much haste as dignity permitted. My father came scampering up the hillock to our hiding place, and we settled in the long grass.

For a while I watched lazily, not expecting anything to happen until noon. Suddenly the youth Telamon broke cover and ran swiftly to where the girls were crouched, straining at their fetters. I heard my father mutter something about Greek gall as the lad put his arms about my half-sister's shoulders and cradled her head on his bare brown chest. She was a beautiful child, Hesione, enough so to attract the attention of most men, but what folly to venture to her side when the lion might appear at any moment! I wondered if Telamon had acted with Herakles's permission.

Hesione's hands plucked despairingly at his arms; he bent his head to whisper something to her, then kissed her long and passionately, as no man had been allowed to kiss her in all her short life. Then he wiped her tears away with the flat of his hand and ran, unconcerned, back to where Herakles had stationed him. A shout of laughter floated up to us from the three Greeks; I shook with rage. The sacrifice was sacred! Yet they dared to laugh. But when I looked Hesione had lost all her fear, stood proud and tall, eyes shining, even at that distance.

Until late morning Greek hilarity continued, then in an instant they quietened. All we could hear was the restless Trojan wind, forever blowing.

A hand touched my shoulder. Thinking it was the lion, I swung round, my heart racing. But it was Tissanes, a palace servant who worked for me. He leaned over to put his lips to my ear.

'The Princess Hekabe is asking for you sire. Her time is upon her, and the midwives say her life hangs by a thread.'

Why did women always have to choose the wrong time? I signed to Tissanes to sit down and be very quiet, and turned back to watch the path where it dipped down into a hollow from the summit of a small rise in the ground. The birds had ceased to sing and call to each other, the wind fell. I shivered.

The lion breasted the rise and padded down the track. He was the biggest beast I had ever seen, with a light fawn coat and a heavy black mane, his tail tipped with a black brush. On his right flank he bore Poseidon's mark, a three-pronged fish spear. Halfway down and approaching the spot where Herakles lay he stopped in midstep, one paw off the ground, his huge head lifted high, tail lashing and nostrils flaring. Then he saw his victims frozen in terror; the prospect of his enjoyment decided

15

him. Tucking his tail down and gathering in his muscles, he trotted forward with increasing speed. One of the girls screamed, thin and screechy. My sister snarled something to her and she subsided.

Herakles rose up out of the grass, a giant of a man in a lion pelt, his club hanging loosely from his right hand. The lion halted, lips drawn back from yellowed teeth. Herakles shook the club and roared a challenge as the lion compressed himself and leaped. But Herakles leaped too, in under the frightful sweep of those claws, thudding against the lion's black-tufted belly with a force that knocked the beast off balance. The lion reared back on his haunches, one paw up to smite the man down; the club descended. There was a sickening crunch as the weapon came into contact with the maned skull; the paw wavered, the man stepped to one side. Up went the club again, down again, the second sound of impact softer than the first, for the head was already fragmented. No fight at all! The lion lay flat on the worn path, his black mane steaming from the warmth of the blood flowing over it.

While Theseus and Telamon danced out cheering, Herakles drew his knife and cut the beast's throat. My father and brothers started to run down to the jubilant Greeks, my servant Tissanes sneaking in their wake, while I turned to commence the journey home. Hekabe my wife was in childbed and her life was in danger.

Women were not important. Death in childbirth was common among the nobility, and I had nine other wives and fifty concubines as well as a hundred children. Yet I loved Hekabe as I loved none of the others; she would be my Queen when I ascended the throne. Her child didn't matter. But what would I do if *she* died? Yes, Hekabe mattered, for all that she was a Dardanian and had brought her brother Antenor with her to Troy.

When I reached the palace I found that Hekabe was still in labour; since no man could be in the presence of women's mysteries I spent the rest of the day on my own business, which consisted of those tasks the King was reluctant to deal with.

After it grew dark I began to feel unsettled, for my father had not contacted me, nor were there noises of rejoicing anywhere within that mighty palace complex atop Troy's hill. No Greek voice, no Trojan voice floated to me. Just silence. Odd.

'Highness, Highness!'

My servant Tissanes stood there ashen, eyes bulging in terror, trembling uncontrollably.

'What is it?' I asked, remembering that he had lingered on the lion track to watch.

He fell to his knees, clasped my ankles. 'Highness, I dared not move until a short time ago! Then I ran! I have spoken to no one, I have come straight to you!'

'Get up, man! Get up and tell me!'

'Highness, the King your father is dead! Your brothers are dead! Everyone is dead!'

A great calm flowed into me. King at last. 'The Greeks too?'

'No, sire! The Greeks killed them!'

'Speak slowly, Tissanes, and tell me what happened.'

'The man called Herakles was pleased with his kill. He laughed and sang as he flayed the lion, while the ones called Theseus and Telamon went over to the girls and struck off their chains. Once the lion pelt was spread out to dry, Herakles asked the King to escort him to the horse yards. He wanted, he said, to choose his stallion and mare straight away because he was in a hurry to leave.' Tissanes stopped, licked his lips.

'Go on.'

'The King grew very angry, Highness. He denied that he had promised Herakles anything. The lion was sport, he said. Herakles had killed it for sport. Even when Herakles and the two other Greeks grew equally angry, the King would not relent.'

Father, Father! To cheat a God like Poseidon of his due is one thing – the Gods are slow and deliberate in their reprisals. But

17

Herakles and Theseus were not Gods. They were Heroes, and Heroes are far deadlier, far swifter.

'Theseus was livid, Highness. He spat on the ground at the King's feet and cursed him for a lying old thief. Prince Tithonos drew his sword, but Herakles stepped between them and turned back to the King. He asked him to capitulate, to make the agreed payment of one stallion and one mare. The King answered that he was not going to be bled by a parcel of common Greek mercenaries out for what they could get, then he noticed that Telamon was standing with his arm about the Princess Hesione. He walked over and struck Telamon across the face. The princess began to weep – the King struck her too. The rest is terrible, Highness.' My servant used one shaking hand to wipe the sweat from his face.

'Do your best, Tissanes. Tell me what you saw.'

'Herakles seemed to grow to the size of an aurochs, Highness. He picked up his club and crushed the King into the ground. Prince Tithonos tried to stab Theseus, and was run through on the spear Theseus still held. Telamon picked up his bow and shot Prince Lampos, then Herakles plucked Prince Klytios and Prince Hiketaon off the ground and squashed their heads together like berries.'

'And where were you during all this, Tissanes?'

'Hiding,' the man said, hanging his head.

'Well, you are a slave, not a warrior. Continue.'

'The Greeks seemed to come to their senses ... Herakles picked up the lion pelt and said there was no time to find the horses, they would have to leave immediately. Theseus pointed to the Princess Hesione and said in that case she would have to do as their prize. They could give her to Telamon, since he was so smitten with her, and Greek honour would thus be satisfied. They left at once for the Skaian Gate.'

'Have they gone from our shores?'

'I asked on my way in, Highness. The Skaian gatekeeper said that the afternoon was still young when Herakles appeared. He did not see Theseus, Telamon or the Princess Hesione. All the Greeks went down the road to Sigios, where their ship lay.'

'What of the other five girls?'

Tissanes hung his head again. 'I do not know, Highness. I thought only of reaching you.'

'Rubbish! You hid until twilight because you were afraid. Find the steward of my father's house and tell him to search for the girls. There are also the bodies of my father and brothers to bring in. Tell the steward all that you have told me, and command in my name that everything be attended to. Now go, Tissanes.'

All Herakles had asked for were two horses. Two *horses*! Was there no cure for greed, no point at which prudence dictated generosity? If only Herakles had waited! He could have appealed to the Court in assembly for justice – we had all heard my father make the promise. Herakles would have got his fee.

Temper and greed had won instead. And I was King of Troy.

Hekabe forgotten, I went down to the Great Hall and struck the gong which summoned the Court to an assembly.

Eager to know the result of the encounter with the lion – and fretting because the hour was so late – they came quickly. Now was not the moment to sit upon the throne; I stood to one side of it and stared down at the small sea of curious faces: faces belonging to my half-brothers, my cousins of all degree, the high nobility not related to us save through marriage. There was my brother-in-law Antenor, eyes alert. I beckoned to him to draw near, then rapped my staff upon the red-flagged floor.

'My lords of Troy, Poseidon's lion is dead, killed by Herakles the Greek,' I announced.

Antenor kept glancing at me sidelong, wondering. As a Dardanian he was no friend to Troy, but he was Hekabe's full brother, so for her sake I tolerated him.

'I left the hunt then, but my servant remained. Just now he came home to tell me that the three Greeks murdered our King

19

and my four brothers. They sailed too long ago to pursue them. With them they took the Princess Hesione as a rape.'

It was impossible to continue in the face of the ensuing uproar; I sucked in my breath, debating how much I could safely tell them. No, nothing about King Laomedon's denial of a solemn promise; he was dead and his memory should be appropriately kingly, unmarred by such a paltry end. Better to say that the Greeks had intended this outrage all along as a reprisal for his policy barring Greek traders from the Euxine Sea.

I was the King. Troy and the Troad were mine. I was the guardian of the Hellespont and the keeper of the Euxine.

When I struck the floor again with my staff, the noise fell away at once. What a difference, to be King!

'Until the day I die,' I said, 'I pledge you that I will never forget what the Greeks have done to Troy. Every year on this day we will go into mourning and the priests will chant the sins of Greek mercenaries throughout the city. Nor will I tire in my search for appropriate ways to make the Greeks rue this deed!

'Antenor, I appoint you my Chancellor. Prepare a public proclamation: henceforth not one Greek ship will be allowed to pass through the Hellespont into the Euxine. Copper can be obtained in other places, but tin comes from Skythia. And copper and tin combined make bronze! No nation can survive without bronze. In future the Greeks will have to buy it at exorbitant cost from the nations of Asia Minor, as they will have the tin monopoly. The nations of Greece will decay.'

They cheered me deafeningly. Only Antenor frowned; yes, I would have to take him aside and tell him the truth. In the meantime I handed him my staff and hurried back to my palace, where, I suddenly remembered, Hekabe lay at death's door.

A midwife waited for me at the top of the stairs, her face dripping tears.

'Is she dead, woman?'

The old hag grinned toothless through her grief. 'No, no! I mourn for your dear father, sire – the news of it is everywhere. The Queen is out of danger and you have a fine, healthy son.'

They had returned Hekabe from the childing stool to her big bed, where she lay, white and weary, with a swaddled bundle in the crook of her left arm. No one had told her the news, and I would not until she was stronger. I bent to kiss her, then looked at the babe as her fingers spread the linen about his face apart. This fourth son she had given me lay quiet and still, not writhing or screwing up his features as newborn babes usually did. He was quite strikingly beautiful, skin smooth and ivory instead of red and wrinkled. Black, curly hair covered his scalp in masses, his lashes were long and black, his black brows finely arched above eyes so dark I could not tell their colour, blue or brown.

Hekabe tickled him beneath his perfect chin. 'What will you call him, my lord?'

'Paris,' I said instantly.

She flinched. '*Paris*? "Married to death"? It is an ominous name, my lord. Why not Alexandros, as we had planned?'

'His name will be Paris,' I said, turning away. She would learn soon enough that this child was married to death on the day of his birth.

I left her higher on her pillows, the bundle cradled feebly against her swollen breasts. 'Paris, my wee man! You are so beautiful! Oh, the hearts you will break! All women will love you. Paris, Paris, Paris ...'

CHAPTER TWO

NARRATED BY
PELEUS

When my new kingdom of Thessalia was in order and I could trust those I left behind me in Iolkos to deal properly with my affairs, I went to the isle of Skyros. Weary, I craved the company of a friend, and as yet I had no friend in Iolkos who could rival King Lykomedes of Skyros. He had been lucky: he had never been banished from his father's realm, as I had; nor fought tooth and nail to carve another kingdom for himself, as I had; nor gone to war to defend it, as I had. His forefathers had ruled his rocky island since the beginning of time and Gods and men, and he had succeeded to his throne after his father died lying in his own bed, surrounded by his sons and daughters, his wives and concubines; for the father of Lykomedes had adhered to the Old Religion, as did Lykomedes – no monogamy for the rulers of Skyros!

Old Religion or New, Lykomedes could look forward to the same kind of death, whereas my chances were not so assured. I envied him his tranquil existence, but as I walked with him in his gardens I realised that he had entirely missed a great many of life's pleasures. His kingdom and his kingship meant less to him than mine did to me; he carried out his work thoroughly and conscientiously, being both a softhearted man and an able ruler, but he lacked utter determination to hang onto what was his because no one had ever threatened to take anything off him.

I knew in full the meanings of loss, of hunger, of desperation. And loved my hard-won new kingdom of Thessalia as he could never love Skyros. Thessalia, my Thessalia! I, Peleus, was High

King in Thessalia! Kings owed me allegiance, I, Peleus, who had not set foot north of Attika until a few years ago. I ruled the Myrmidons, the Ant People of Iolkos.

Lykomedes intruded. 'You think of Thessalia,' he said.

'How can I keep my thoughts away?'

He waved a white, languid hand. 'My dear Peleus, I am not endowed with your powerful enthusiasms. Whereas I smoulder sluggishly, you burn bright and clear. Though I am content to have it so. Were you in my shoes, you would not have stopped until you owned every isle between Crete and Samothrake.'

I leaned against a nut tree and sighed. 'Yet I'm very tired, old friend. I'm not as young as I once was.'

'A truth so obvious it doesn't bear mentioning.' His pale eyes surveyed me pensively. 'Do you know, Peleus, that you have the reputation of being the best man in Greece? Even Mykenai has to notice you.'

I straightened and walked on. 'I am no more and no less than any other man.'

'Deny it if you must, but it is true all the same. You have everything, Peleus! A fine big body, a shrewd and subtle mind, a genius for leadership, a talent for inspiring love in your people – why, you even have a handsome face!'

'Continue praising me like this, Lykomedes, and I will have to pack up and go home.'

'Be still, I'm done. Actually I have something I want to discuss with you. The paean of praise was leading up to it.'

I looked at him curiously. 'Oh?'

He licked his lips, frowned, decided to plunge into troubled waters without further ado. 'Peleus, you are thirty-five years old. You are one of the four High Kings in Greece, and therefore a great power in the land. Yet you have no wife. No queen. And, ah – given that you subscribe absolutely to the New Religion, that you have elected monogamy, how are you going to ensure the succession in Thessalia unless you take a wife?'

I could not control my grin. 'Lykomedes, you fraud! You have a wife picked out for me.'

He looked cagy. 'I might. Unless you have other ideas.'

'I think of marriage often. Unfortunately I don't fancy any of the candidates.'

'I know a woman who might appeal to you strongly. She would certainly make a splendid consort.'

'Go on, man! I'm listening avidly.'

'And with your tongue in your cheek. However, I do mean to go on. The woman is high priestess to Poseidon on Skyros. She was instructed by the God to marry, but she has not. I cannot force so exalted a prelate to obey, yet for the sake of my people and my isle I must persuade her to marry.'

By this time I was staring at him in astonishment. 'Lykomedes! I am an expedient!'

'No, no!' he exclaimed, face wretched. 'Hear me out, Peleus!'

'Poseidon has ordered her to marry?'

'Yes. The oracles say that if she does not marry, the Lord of the Seas will break the earth of Skyros open and take my isle down into the depths as his own.'

'Oracles in the plural. So you've consulted many?'

'Even the Pythoness at Delphi and the oak grove at Dodona. The answer is always the same – marry her off, or perish.'

'Why is she so important?' I asked, fascinated.

His face became awed. 'Because she is the daughter of Nereus, the Old Man of the Sea. As such she is half divine by blood – *and* divided in her loyalties. Her blood heritage belongs to the Old Religion, yet she serves the New Religion. You know what a state of flux our Greek world has endured since Crete and Thera toppled, Peleus. Take Skyros! We were never as dominated by the Mother as Crete or Thera or the kingdoms of the Isle of Pelops – men have always ruled by right here – but the Old Religion is strong. Yet Poseidon is of the New Religion, and we lie under his thumb – he is not only Lord of the Seas which surround us, he is also the Earth Shaker.'

'I take it,' I said slowly, 'that Poseidon is angered that a woman of the Old Religion is his high priestess. Yet he must have sanctioned her appointment.'

'He did sanction it. But now he is angry – you know the Gods, Peleus! When are they ever consistent? Despite his earlier consent, he is now angry, and says that he will not have his altar served by a daughter of Nereus.'

'Lykomedes, Lykomedes! Do you honestly believe these God-begotten tales?' I asked incredulously. 'I had thought better of you! A man or woman claiming a God for parent is usually born a bastard – and mostly by courtesy of the herdboy or undergroom into the bargain.'

He flapped his arms like an agitated fowl. 'Yes, yes, yes! I know all this, Peleus, yet I *believe*! You have not seen her, you do not know her. I have, and I do. She is the strangest creature – ! One look at her, and you will know beyond all doubt that she comes from the Sea.'

By this time I was offended. 'I can hardly credit my ears! Thank you for the compliment! You want to palm some strange, mad woman off on the High King of Thessalia? Well, I won't have her!'

Both his hands went out to clasp my right forearm. 'Peleus, would I serve you a trick like that? I put it badly – I meant you no insult, I swear it! It's just that as soon as I set eyes on you after so many years, I seemed to know in my heart that she is the woman for you. She doesn't lack noble suitors, every well-born bachelor on Skyros has offered for her. But she will have none of them. She says she waits for one whom the God has promised to send with a sign.'

I sighed. 'All right, Lykomedes, I'll see her. However, I commit myself to nothing, is that understood?'

Poseidon's sacred precinct and altar – he had no temple as such – lay on the far side of the island, the less fertile and more sparsely inhabited side; a rather peculiar location for the principal shrine of the Lord of the Seas. His favour was vital to any isle, surrounded on all sides by his watery dominions. His moods and his grace determined whether prosperity or famine prevailed; nor was he the Earth Shaker for nothing. I myself had seen the fruits of his rage, whole cities laid flatter than gold under a smith's hammer. Poseidon was quick to anger and very jealous of his prestige; twice within knowledge Crete had come crashing down beneath his vengeance, when its Kings had grown so puffed up with their own importance that they forgot what they owed him. So it had been with Thera too.

If this woman whom Lykomedes wished me to see was rumoured to be the offspring of Nereus – who had ruled the seas when Kronos ruled the world from Olympos – I could understand the oracles' demanding her removal from office. Zeus and his brothers had no time for the old Gods whom they had overthrown – well, who could easily forgive a father who *ate* one?

I came to the precinct alone and on foot, clad in ordinary hunting garb and leading my offering on a length of rope. I wanted her to deem me humdrum, not to know that I was the High King of Thessalia. The altar was perched on a high headland overlooking a little cove; I made my way softly through the sacred grove of trees in front of it, my mind dizzy with the silence and the heavy, suffocating holiness. Even the sea in my ears was muted, though the waves rolled in slowly and crashed down in white bubbles on the rocks at the scarred base of the precipice. The eternal fire burned before the square, plain altar in a golden tripod; I came closer to it, stopped and drew my offering to my side.

Almost reluctantly she emerged into the sunlight, as if she preferred dwelling in a cool and liquid filtration of day. Fascinated, I stared at her. Small, slender and womanly, she yet owned some quality that was not feminine. Instead of the customary dress with all its frills and embroidery she wore a simple robe of the fine, transparent linen the Egyptians weave, and the colour of her skin showed clearly through it, pale and bluish, streaky because the material was inexpertly dyed. Her lips were full but only faintly pink, her eyes changed colour through all the shades and moods of the sea – greys, blues, greens, even wine-dark purple, and she wore no paint on her face save for a thin black line drawn around her eyes and extended outward to give her a slightly sinister look. Her hair was no colour at all, ashen white, with a gleam to it that almost made it seem blue in the dimness of a room.

I advanced, leading my offering. 'Lady, I am a visitor to your island, and I come to offer to Father Poseidon.'

Nodding, she extended her hand and took the rope from me, then inspected the white bull calf with an expert eye. 'Father Poseidon will be pleased. It is a long time since I have seen such a fine beast.'

'As horses and bulls are sacred to him, lady, it seemed proper to offer him what he likes best.'

She stared intently at the altar flame. 'The time is not auspicious for a sacrifice. I will offer later,' she said.

'As you wish, lady.' I turned to leave.

'Wait.'

'Yes, lady?'

'Who shall I tell the God offers to him?'

'Peleus, King of Iolkos and High King of Thessalia.'

Her eyes changed rapidly from a clear blue to dark grey. 'Not an ordinary man. Your father was Aiakos, and his father was Zeus himself. Your brother Telamon is King of Salamis, and you are of the Royal Kindred.'

I smiled. 'Yes, I am son of Aiakos and brother of Telamon. As to my grandsire – I have no idea. Though I doubt he was the King of the Gods. More likely a bandit who fancied my grandmother.'

'Impiety, King Peleus,' she said in measured tones, 'leads to divine retribution.'

'I fail to see that I am impious, lady. I worship and offer with complete faith in the Gods.'

'Yet you disclaim Zeus as your grandsire.'

'Such tales are told, lady, to enhance a man's right to a throne, as was certainly true of my father, Aiakos.'

She stroked the white bull calf's nose absently. 'You must be staying in the palace. Why did King Lykomedes leave you to come here alone and unheralded?'

'Because I wished it, lady.'

Having tethered the white bull calf to a ring on the side of a pillar, she turned her back on me.

'Lady, who accepts my offering?'

Looking at me over her shoulder, she showed me eyes of a cool and neutral grey. 'I am Thetis, daughter of Nereus. *Not* by mere hearsay, King Peleus. My father is a great God.'

Time to go. I thanked her and left.

But not to go very far. Careful to keep out of sight of any watcher from the sanctuary, I slithered down the snakepath to the cove below, dumped my spear and sword behind a rock and lay down in the warm yellow sand, shielded by an overhanging cliff. Thetis. Thetis. She definitely did have a look of the sea about her. I even found myself wanting to believe that she was the daughter of a God, for I had gazed too deeply into those chameleon eyes, seen all the storms and calms which affected the sea, an echo of some cold fire defying description. And I wanted her for my wife.

She was interested in me too; my years and tally of experience told me so. The crux of the matter was how strong her attraction might be; within myself I felt a warning of defeat. Thetis would no more marry me than she would any of the other eligible suitors who had asked for her. Though I was not a man for men, I had never cared overmuch for women beyond satiation of an urge even the greatest Gods suffer as painfully as men do. Sometimes I took a woman of the house to sleep with me, but until this moment I had never loved. Whether she knew it or not, Thetis belonged to me. And as I upheld the New Religion in all aspects, she would have no rival wives to contend with. I would be hers alone.

The sun beat down on my back with increasing strength. Noon came; I stripped off my hunting suit to let the hot rays of

Helios seep into my skin. But I could not lie still, had to sit up and glare at the sea, blaming it for this new trouble. Then I closed my eyes and sank upon my knees.

'Father Zeus, look favourably upon me! Only in the moments of my greatest abandon and need have I prayed to you as a man might seek the succour of his grandsire. But so I pray now, to that part of you kindest and most beneficient. You have never failed to hear me because I never plague you with trivialities. Help me now, I beg! Give Thetis to me just as you gave me Iolkos and the Myrmidons, just as you delivered the whole of Thessalia into my hands. Give me a fitting queen to sit on the Myrmidon throne, give me mighty sons to take my place when I die!'

Eyes closed, I stayed on my knees for a long time. When I rose I found nothing had changed. But that was to be expected; the Gods do not work miracles to inculcate faith in the hearts of men. Then I saw her standing with the wind blowing her flimsy gown behind her like a banner, her hair crystal in the sun, her face uplifted and rapt. Beside her was the white bull calf, and in her right hand she held a dagger. He walked to his doom tranquilly, even settled himself across her knees when she went down on them in the edge of the lapping waves, and never struggled or cried out when she cut his throat, held him while bright ribbons of scarlet coursed over her thighs and her bare white arms. The water about her became a fainter red as the shifting currents sucked the calf's blood into their own substance and consumed it.

She had not seen me, did not see me as she slid further out into the waves, dragging the dead calf with her until she was deep enough to sling his body around her neck and strike out. Some distance offshore she shrugged her shoulders to release the calf, which sank at once. A big, flat rock jutted out of the water; she made for it, climbed out of the sea onto its top and stood silhouetted against the pale sky. Then she lay down upon her back, pillowed her head on her arms folded behind her, and seemed to sleep.

An outlandish ritual, not one condoned by the New Religion. Thetis had accepted my offering in the name of Poseidon, then had given it instead to Nereus. *Sacrilege!* And she the high priestess of Poseidon. Oh, Lykomedes, you were right! In her lie the seeds of destruction for Skyros. She is not giving the Lord of the Seas his due, nor does she respect him as Earth Shaker.

The air was milky and calm, the water limpid, but as I walked down to the waves I trembled like a man with the ague. The water had no power to cool me as I swam; Aphrodite had fastened her glossy claws hard enough in me to lacerate my very bones. Thetis was mine, and I would have her. Save poor Lykomedes and his isle.

When I reached the rock I fastened my hands in a ledge on its side and jerked myself upward with an effort that cracked my muscles; I was crouching above her on the stone before she realised I was any nearer than the palace above Skyros Town. But she was not sleeping. Her eyes, a soft, dreamy green, were open. Then she scrambled away and looked at me black-eyed.

'Don't you touch me!' she said, panting. 'No man dares touch me! I have given myself to the God!'

My hand flashed out, stopped barely short of her ankle. 'Your vows to the God are not permanent, Thetis. You're free to marry. And you'll marry me.'

'I belong to the God!'

'If so, which God? Do you pay lip service to one and sacrifice his victims to another? You belong to me, and I dare all. If the God – either God! – requires my death for this, I will accept his judgement.'

Mewing a note of distress and panic, she tried to slide off the rock into the sea. But I was too quick for her, grasped her leg and dragged her back, her fingers clawing at the gritty surface, her nails tearing audibly. When I took hold of her wrist I let go of her ankle and hauled her to her feet.

She fought me like ten wildcats, teeth and nails, kicking and biting silently as I clamped my arms around her. A dozen times she slipped through them, a dozen times I captured her again, both of us smothered in blood. My shoulder was sheared, her mouth split, hanks of our hair blew away in the rising wind. This was no rape, nor did I intend that it be; this was a simple contest of strength, man against woman, the New Religion against the Old. It ended as all such contests must: with man the victor.

We fell to the rock with an impact that knocked the breath out of her. Her body pinned beneath me and her shoulders held down, I looked into her face.

'You are done fighting. I have conquered you.'

Her lips trembled, she turned her head to one side. 'You are he. I knew it the moment you came into the sanctuary. When I was sworn to his service, the God told me that a man would come out of the sea, a man of the sky who would dispel the sea from my mind and make me his Queen.' She sighed. 'So be it.'

I installed Thetis in Iolkos as my Queen with honour and pomp. Within our first year together she became pregnant, the final joy of our union. We were happy, never more so than during those long moons waiting for our son. Neither of us dreamed of a girl.

My own nurse, Aresune, was appointed chief midwife, so when Thetis began her labour I found myself utterly powerless; the old crone exercised her authority and banished me to the other end of my palace. For one full circuit of Phoibos's chariot I sat alone, ignoring the servants who begged me to eat or drink, waiting, waiting ... Until in the night marches Aresune came to find me. She had not bothered to change out of her birthing robe, its front smeared with blood, just stood huddled within it all withered and bent, her seamed face webbed with pain. So sunken in her head that they were two black sockets, her eyes oozed tears.

'It was a son, sire, but he never lived long enough to breathe air. The Queen is safe. She has lost blood and is very tired, but her life is not in danger.' The skinny hands wrung together.

31

'Sire, I swear I did nothing wrong! Such a big, fine boy! It is the will of the Goddess.'

I could not bear her to see my face in the lamplight. Too stricken to weep, I turned and walked away.

Several days passed before I could bring myself to see Thetis. When finally I did enter her room, I was amazed to find her sitting up in her big bed looking well and happy. She said all the correct things, toyed with words expressing sorrow, but none of it was *meant*. Thetis was pleased!

'Our son is dead, wife!' I burst out. 'How can you bear it? He will never know the meaning of life! He will never take my place on the throne. For nine moons you carried him – for nothing!'

Her hand came out, patted mine a little patronisingly. 'Oh, dearest Peleus, do not grieve! Our son has no mortal life, but have you forgotten that I am a Goddess? Because he had not breathed earthly air, I asked my father to grant our son *eternal* life, and my father was delighted to do so. Our son lives on Olympos – he eats and drinks with the other Gods, Peleus! No, he will never rule in Iolkos, but he enjoys what no mortal man ever can. In dying, he will never die.'

My astonishment changed to revulsion, I stared at her and wondered how this God thing had ever been allowed to take such hold of her. She was as mortal as I and her babe was as mortal as both of us. Then I saw how trustingly she gazed up at me, and could not say what I itched to say. If it took the pain out of her loss to believe such nonsense, well and good. Living with Thetis had taught me that she did not think or behave like other women. So I stroked her hair and left her.

Six sons she gave me over the years, all born dead. When Aresune told me of the second boy's death I went half mad, could not bear to see Thetis for many moons because I knew what she would tell me – that our dead son was a God. But in the end love and hunger always drove me back to her, and we would go through that ghastly cycle all over again.

When the sixth child was stillborn – how *could* he be when he had gone to full term and looked, lying on his tiny funeral car, so strong despite his dark blue skin? – I vowed that I would dower Olympos with no more sons. I sent to the Pythoness at Delphi and the answer came back that it was Poseidon who was angry, that he resented my stealing his priestess. What hypocrisy! What lunacy! First he doesn't want her, then he does. Truly no man can understand the minds or the doings of the Gods, New or Old.

For two years I did not cohabit with Thetis, who kept begging to conceive more sons for Olympos. Then at the end of the second year I took Poseidon Horse Maker a white man foal and offered it to him before all the Myrmidons, my people.

'Lift your curse, bless me with a living son!' I cried.

The earth rumbled deep in its bowls, the sacred snake shot from beneath the altar like a flash of brown lightning, the ground heaved, spasmed. A pillar toppled to earth beside me as I stood unmoving, a crack appeared between my feet and I choked on the reek of sulphur, but I held my position until the tremor died away and the fissure closed. The white man foal lay on the altar drained and pathetically still. Three moons later Thetis told me that she was pregnant with our seventh child.

All through those weary times I had her watched more closely than a hawk watches the ground bird's chicks; I made Aresune sleep in the same bed every night, I threatened the house women with unspeakable tortures if they left her alone for an instant unless Aresune was there. Thetis bore these 'whims', as she called them, with patience and good humour; she never argued or tried to defy my edicts. Once she made my hair stand on end and my flesh prickle when she began to sing a strange, tuneless chant out of the Old Religion. But when I ordered her to cease she obeyed, and never sang so again. Her time grew imminent. I began to hope. *Surely* I had always lived in proper fear of the Gods! *Surely* they owed me one living son!

I had a suit of armour belonged to Minos once; it was my most treasured possession. A wondrous thing, it was sheeted in gold atop four separate layers of bronze and three of tin, inlaid with lapis and amber, coral and crystal depicting a marvellous design. The shield, of similar construction, was as tall as the average man and looked like two round shields joined together one above the other, so that it had a waist. Cuirass and greaves, helmet and kilt and arm guards were made to fit a bigger man than me, so I respected the dead Minos who had worn it as he strode about his Cretan kingdom confident that he would never need it to protect himself, only to show his people how rich he was. And when he did fall it was no use to him, for Poseidon took him and his world and crushed them because they would not subscribe to the New Religion. Mother Kubaba, the Great Godesss of the Old Religion, Queen of Earth and All High, always ruled in Crete and Thera.

With the armour of Minos I had placed a spear of ash from the slopes of Mount Pelion; it had a small head fashioned from a metal called iron, so rare and precious that most men thought it a legend, for few had seen it. Trial had proven that the spear flew unerringly to its target yet felt a feather in my hand, so after I ceased to need to employ it in war I put it with the armour. The spear had a name: Old Pelion.

Before the birth of my first son I had unearthed these curios for cleaning and polishing, sure my son would grow to be a man big enough to wear them. But as my sons continued to be born dead I sent them back to the treasure vaults to live in a darkness no blacker than my despair.

About five days before Thetis expected to be confined with our seventh child I took a lamp and trod the ragged stone steps leading into the palace's bowels, threading my way through the passages until I came to the great wooden door which barred off the treasury. Why was I there? I asked myself, but could find no satisfactory answer. I opened the door to peer into the gloom and found instead a pool of golden light on the far side of the huge chamber. My own flame pinched out, I crept forward with my hand on my dagger. The way across was

cluttered with urns and chests, coffers and stored sacred gear; I
had to pick my path carefully.

As I drew nearer I heard the unmistakable sound of a woman
weeping. Aresune my nurse was sitting on the floor cradling
the golden helm which had belonged to Minos within her
arms, its fine golden plumes streaming over her crinkled hand.
She wept softly but bitterly, moaning to herself and breaking
into the mourning song of Aigina, the island from which she
and I originally came, kingdom of Aiakos. O Kore! Aresune was
already weeping for my seventh son.

I could not leave her unconsoled, could not creep away and
pretend I had never seen, never heard. When my mother had
ordered her to give me her breast she had been a mature
woman; she had reared me under my mother's disinterested
gaze; she had trailed through a dozen nations in my wake as
faithful as my hound; and when I had conquered Thessalia I
raised her high in my household. So I went closer, touched her
very gently on the shoulder and begged her not to weep.
Taking the helmet from her, I gathered her stiff old body close
and held her, saying many silly things, trying to comfort her
through my own suffering. At last she fell quiet, bony fingers
plucking at my blouse.

'Dear lord, why?' she croaked. 'Why do you let her do it?'

'Why what? Her? Do it?'

'The Queen,' she said, hiccoughing.

Afterwards I realised that her grief had sent her a little mad;
otherwise I could not have prised it out of her. Though she was
dearer to me by far than my mother had been, she was always
conscious of the difference in our stations. I gripped her so
hard between my fingers that she writhed and whimpered.

'What about the Queen? What does she do?'

'Murders your sons.'

I rocked. 'Thetis? My sons? What *is* this? Speak!'

Her frenzy dwindling, she stared at me in dawning horror as
she grasped the fact that I knew nothing.

I shook her. 'You had better go on, Aresune. How does my wife murder her sons? And why? *Why?*'

But she folded her lips one over the other and said nothing, eyes in the flame terrified. My dagger came out; I pressed its tip against her loose, slippery old skin.

'Speak, woman, or by Almighty Zeus I swear that I will have your sight put out, your nails ripped from their beds – anything I need to do to unstopper your tongue! Speak, Aresune, speak!'

'Peleus, she would curse me, and that is far worse than any torture,' she quavered.

'The curse would be evil. Evil curses rebound on the head of the one who casts them. Tell me, please.'

'I was sure you knew and consented, lord. Maybe she is right – maybe immortality is preferable to life on earth, if there is no growing old.'

'Thetis is mad,' I said.

'No, lord. She is a Goddess.'

'She is not, Aresune, I would stake my life on it! Thetis is an ordinary mortal woman.'

Aresune looked unconvinced; I did not sway her much.

'She has murdered all your sons, Peleus, that is all. With the best of intentions.'

'How does she do it? Does she take some potion?'

'No, dear lord. Simpler by far. When we put her on the childing stool she drives all the women from the room except me. Then she makes me put a pail of sea water under her. As soon as the head is born she guides it into the water and holds it there until there is no possibility that the child can draw breath.'

My fists closed, opened. 'So that's why they're blue!' I stood up. 'Go back to her, Aresune, or she will miss you. I give you my oath as your King that I will never divulge who told me this. I will see she has no opportunity to do you harm. Watch her. When the labour begins, tell me immediately. Is that clear?'

She nodded, her tears gone and her terrible guilt drained away. Then she kissed my hands and pattered off.

I sat there without moving, both lamps foundered. Thetis had murdered my sons – and for *what*? Some crazed and impossible dream. Superstition. Fancy. She had deprived them of their right to be men, she had committed crimes so foul I wanted to go to her and run her through on my sword. But she still carried my seventh child within her body. The sword would have to wait. And vengeance belonged to the Gods of the New Religion.

On the fifth day after I had spoken to Aresune the old woman came running to find me, her hair streaming wild in the wind behind her. It was late afternoon and I had gone down to the horse paddocks to watch my stallions, for mating season was close and the horse masters wanted to give me the schedule of who would service whom.

I loped back to the palace with Aresune perched upon my neck, something of a steed myself.

'What are you going to do?' she asked as I lowered her outside Thetis's door.

'Come in with you,' I said.

She gasped, squealed. 'Sire, sire! It is forbidden!'

'So is murder,' I said, and opened the door.

Birth is a women's mystery, not to be profaned by any masculine presence. It is a world of earth owning no sky. When the New Religion overcame the Old, some things did not change; Mother Kubaba, the Great Goddess, still rules the affairs of women. Especially everything having to do with the growing of new human fruit – and the plucking of it, whether immature, at perfect ripeness or withered with age.

Thus when I entered no one saw me for a moment; I had the time to watch, to smell, to hear. The room stank of sweat and blood, other things foreign and appalling to a man. Labour had clearly progressed, for the house women were in the act of conducting Thetis from her bed to the childing stool while the midwives hovered, instructed, fussed. My wife was naked, her grotesquely swollen abdomen almost luminous with distension. Carefully they arranged her thighs on the hard wooden surface to either side of the wide gap in the stool's seat designed to free the birth canal's termination, the place where the baby's head would appear and its body follow.

A wooden bucket slopping water stood on the floor nearby, but none of the women spared it a glance because they had no idea what it was there for.

They saw me and flew at me, faces outraged, thinking that the King had gone mad, determined to drive him out. I swung a blow at the closest which knocked her sprawling; the rest cowered back. Aresune was hunched over the bucket, muttering charms to ward off the Evil Eye, and did not move when I chased the women out and dropped the bar on the door.

Thetis saw everything. Her face glistened with sweat and her eyes were black, but she controlled her fury.

'Get out, Peleus,' she said softly.

For answer I shoved Aresune aside, walked to the pail of sea water, picked it up and tipped the water upon the floor. 'No more murders, Thetis. This son is mine.'

'Murder? *Murder?* Oh, you fool! I've killed no one! I am a Goddess! My sons are immortal!'

I took her by the shoulders as she sat, bent over, atop the childing stool. 'Your sons are dead, woman! They are doomed to be mindless shades because you offered them no chance to do deeds great enough to win the love and admiration of the Gods! No Elysian Fields, no heroic status, no place among the stars. You are *not* a Goddess! You are a mortal woman!'

Her answer was a shrill scream of torment; her back arched and her hands gripped the stool's wooden arms so strongly that their knuckles gleamed silver.

Aresune came to life. 'It is the moment!' she cried. 'He is about to be born!'

'You will not have him, Peleus!' growled Thetis.

She began to force her legs together against all the instinct which drove her to open them wide. 'I'll crush his head to pulp!' she snarled, then screamed, on and on and on. 'Oh, Father! Father Nereus! He tears me apart!'

The veins stood out on her brow in purple cords, tears rolled down her cheeks, and still she fought to close her legs. Though demented with pain, she strained every last fibre of will and brought her legs inexorably together, crossed them and twined them about each other to lock them in place.

Aresune was down on the sopping floor, head beneath the stool; I heard her shriek, then whinny a chuckle. 'Ai! Ai!' she screeched. 'Peleus, it is his foot! He comes breech, it is his foot!' She crabbed out, got up and swung me round to face her with the strength of a young man in her ancient arm. 'Do you want a living son?' she asked.

'Yes, yes!'

'Then unlock her legs, sire. He is coming out feet first, his head is unharmed.'

I knelt and put my left hand upon Thetis's top knee, slid my right beneath it to grasp her other knee, and pulled my hands apart. Her bones creaked dangerously; she reared her head up and spat curses and spittle like a corrosive rain, her face – I swear it as I looked at her and she looked at me – her face gone to the scales and wedge of a snake. Her knees began to separate; I was too strong for her. And if that did not prove her mortality, what could?

Aresune dived under my hands. I closed my eyes and hung on. Came a sharp, short sound, a convulsive gasp, and suddenly the room was filled with the wail of a living infant. My eyes flew open, I stared incredulously at Aresune, at the object she was holding head downward from one hand – a grisly, wet, slippery thing jerking and threshing and howling to the roof of the heavens – a thing with penis and scrotum bulging beneath the envelope of membrane. A son! I had a living son!

Thetis sat quietly, her face empty and still. But her eyes were not on me. They were focused upon my son, whom Aresune was cleaning, tying off the cord, wrapping in fresh white linen.

'A son to delight your heart, Peleus!' laughed Aresune. 'The biggest, healthiest babe I have ever seen! I drew him out by his little right heel.'

I panicked. 'His heel! His right heel, old woman! Is it broken? Is it deformed?'

She lifted the swathes of cloth to display one perfect heel – the left – and one swollen, bruised foot and ankle. 'They are both intact, sire. The right one will heal and the marks fade.'

Thetis laughed, a weak and shadowed sound. 'His right heel. So that was how he breathed earthly air. His foot came first ... No wonder he tore at me so. Yes, the marks will fade, but that right heel will be his undoing. One day when he needs it firm and sinewy, it will remember the day of his birth and betray him.'

I ignored her, my arms outstretched. 'Give him to me! Let me see him, Aresune! Heart of my hearts, core of my being, my son! My son!'

I informed the Court that I had a living son. The exultation, the joy! All Iolkos, all Thessalia had suffered with me through the years.

But after everyone had gone I sat upon my throne of pure white marble with my head between my hands, so weary I could not think. The voices gradually died away in the distance, and the darkest, loneliest webs of the night began a-spinning. A son. I had a living son, but I should have had seven living sons. My wife was a madwoman.

She entered the faintly illuminated chamber with her feet bare, dressed once more in the transparent, floating robe she had worn on Skyros. Face lined and old, she crossed the chill flagged floor slowly, her walk speaking of her body's pain.

'Peleus,' she said from the bottom of the dais.

I had seen her through my hands, and took them now from my head, lifting it.

'I am going back to Skyros, husband.'

'Lykomedes won't want you, wife.'

'Then I will go somewhere I am wanted.'

'Like Medea, in a chariot drawn by snakes?'

'No. I shall ride upon the back of a dolphin.'

I never saw her again. At dawn Aresune came with two slaves and got me to my feet, put me into my bed. For one full circle of Phoibos's endless journey around our world I slept without remembering one single dream, then woke remembering that I had a son. Up the stairs to the nursery, Hermes's winged sandals on my feet, to find Aresune taking him from his wet nurse – a healthy young woman who had lost her own babe, the old woman chattered. Her name was Leukippe: the white mare.

My turn. I took him into my arms and found him a heavy weight. Not surprising in one who looked as if he was made from gold. Curling golden hair, golden skin, golden brows and lashes. The eyes which surveyed me levelly and without wandering were dark, but I fancied that when they acquired vision they would be some shade of gold.

'What will you call him, sire?' Aresune asked.

And that I didn't know. He must have his own name, not someone else's. But which name? I gazed at nose, cheeks, chin, forehead, eyes, and found them delicately formed, more in the mould of Thetis than me. His lips were his own, for he had none; a straight slit in his lower face, fiercely determined yet achingly sad, served him for a mouth.

'Achilles,' I said.

She nodded, approving. 'Lipless. A good name for him, dearest lord.' Then she sighed. 'His mother prophesied. Will you send to Delphi?'

I shook my head. 'No. My wife is mad, I take no credence in her predictions. But the Pythoness speaks true. I do not want to know what lies in wait for my son.'

CHAPTER THREE

NARRATED BY

CHIRON

I had a favourite seat outside my cave, carved out of the rock by the Gods aeons before men came to Mount Pelion. It was on the very edge of the cliff, and many were the moments I spent sitting on it, a bear skin spread to shield my old bones from the hard caress of its stone, looking out over the land and sea like the king I never was.

I was too old. Never more so than in the autumn, when I felt the aches begin, harbingers of winter. No one remembered how old I actually was, least of all myself; there comes a time when the reality of age is frozen, when all years and all seasons are but one long day's wait for death.

The dawn promised a day of beauty and peace, so before the sun rose I performed my scant domestic duties, then went outside into the cold grey air. My cave was high on Pelion, almost at the summit on its southern side, and it hung over the edge of a vast precipice. I sank into my bear skin to watch for the sun. The aspect before me never wearied me; for countless years I had gazed out from the top of Pelion over the world below me, the coast of Thessalia and the Aegaean Sea. And while I watched the sun rise I fished a piece of dripping honey-in-the-comb from my alabaster box of comfits and sank my toothless gums into it, sucking hungrily. It tasted of wild blossoms and zephyr breezes and the tang of pine woods.

My people, the Kentaurs, had dwelled upon Pelion for more time than men could record, serving the Kings of Greece as tutors for their sons, for we were unrivalled teachers. I say 'were' because I am the last Kentaur; after me my race will be no more. In the interests of our work most of us had chosen celibacy, nor would we mate with women other than our own; so when the Kentaur women grew tired of their unimportant existence, they packed their possessions and departed. Fewer and fewer of us were born, for most of the Kentaur men could not be bothered making the journey to Thrake, where our women went to join the Maenads and worship Dionysos. And gradually a legend came into being: that Kentaurs were invisible because they were afraid to show men their persons, half man and half horse. An interesting creature if it had existed, but it did not. Kentaurs were simply men.

Throughout Greece my name was known; I am Chiron, and I have taught most of the lads who grew up to be famous Heroes: Peleus and Telamon, Tydeus, Herakles, Atreus and Thyestes, to mention but a few. However, that had all been long ago, and I had no thought of Herakles or his breed as I witnessed the sunrise.

Pelion abounds in forests of ash, taller and straighter than other ash, a shimmering sea of bright yellow at this time of the year because every bright and dying leaf shivered and shuddered in the slightest wind. Below me was the sheer drop of rock, five hundred cubits of it bare of even the smallest touch of green or yellow, and below that again the ash forest growing up to the sky, and many birds calling. I never heard the sounds of men, for no other mortal stood between me and the pinnacles of Olympos. Spread far beneath me and reduced to the size of an ant kingdom was Iolkos – not a farfetched description. They called the people of Iolkos the Myrmidons, the ants.

Alone among all the cities of the world (save for those in Crete and Thera before Poseidon levelled them), Iolkos had no walls. Who would dare invade the home of the Myrmidons, warriors without peer? I loved Iolkos the more for that. Walls horrified me. In the old days when I travelled I could never bear to be shut inside Mykenai or Tiryns for more than a day or two. Walls were structures built by Death from stones quarried in Tartaros.

I flung the honeycomb away and reached for my wineskin, dazzled by the sun crimsoning the great reaches of the Bay of Pagasai, glancing off the gilded figures on the palace roof, brightening the colours of the pillars and walls of temples, palace, public buildings.

A road wound up from the city into the fastness of my retreat, but it was never used. That morning was different, however; I heard a vehicle approaching. Anger dispelled contemplation and I rose to my feet, hobbled to confront the presumptious interloper and send him packing. He was a nobleman driving a fast hunting car with two matched Thessalian bays harnessed to it, and he wore the insignia of the royal household on his blouse. Eyes clear, bright, smiling, he jumped down with a grace only youth could own and walked towards me. I backed away; the smell of a man was disgusting to me these days.

'The King sends greetings, my lord,' the young man said.

'What is it, what is it?' I demanded, discovering without any pleasure that my voice cracked and rasped.

'The King has commanded me to bring a message to you, Lord Chiron. Tomorrow he and his royal brother will come to give their sons into your keeping until they are young men. You are to teach them all that they ought to know.'

I stood rigid. King Peleus knew better! Too old to be bothered with rowdy boys, I no longer taught, not even the scions of a House as illustrious as Aiakos. 'Tell the King that I am displeased! I do not wish to instruct his son or the son of his royal brother Telamon. Tell him that if he climbs the mountain tomorrow he will be wasting his time. Chiron is retired.'

Face a study in dismay, the young man looked at me. 'Lord Chiron, I dare not give him that message. I was commanded to tell you that he is coming, and I have done so. I was not charged to bring an answer.'

When the hunting car had disappeared I went back to my

chair to find that the view had gone behind a veil of scarlet. My rage. How dared the King presume that I would teach his offspring – or Telamon's, for that matter? Years before, it had been Peleus himself who sent heralds throughout the kingdoms of Greece announcing that Chiron the Kentaur was retired. Now he broke his own ordinance.

Telamon, Telamon ... He had many children, but two favoured ones only. The elder by two years was a bastard by the Trojan princess Hesione, Teukros by name. The other was his legitimate heir, Ajax by name. On the other hand, Peleus had but one child, a son by Thetis his queen miraculously born alive after six had died at birth. Achilles. How old would Ajax and Achilles be? Little boys, certainly. Smelly, snotty, scarcely human. Ugh.

All my joy evaporated, my rage in smoking ashes at the back of my mind, I returned to my cave. There was no way out of the task. Peleus was High King of Thessalia; I was his subject and had to obey him. So I looked about my large and airy retreat dreading the days and years to come. My lyre lay on a table at the back of the main chamber, its strings coated with dust from long disuse. I regarded it sullenly, reluctantly, then I picked it up and blew away the evidence of my neglect. Every string was flaccid, I had to tighten each one to the proper pitch; only after that could I play.

Oh, and my voice! Gone, gone. While Phoibos rode his sun car from east to west I played and sang, coaxing my stiffened fingers into suppleness, stretching my hands and my wrists, la-la-la-ing up and down the scale. Since it was a very bad thing to have to get into practice in front of my pupils, I would have to be proficient before they arrived. Thus only when my cave was a gloom and the black silent shadows of bats flittered through it to their haven somewhere deeper inside the mountain did I cease, weary beyond expression, cold and hungry and ill-tempered.

Peleus and Telamon came at noon, travelling together in the

royal chariot, followed by another chariot and a lumbering ox cart. I went down the road to meet them and stood with bent head. It was years since I had seen the High King, but longer by far since I had seen Telamon. My temper improving, I watched them approach. Yes, they were Kings, those two men who radiated strength and power. Peleus as big as ever, Telamon as lithe as ever. Both had seen their troubles melt away, but only after long periods of strife, war, worry. And those forgers of the metal in the souls of men had left their indelible mark. The gold was dying out of their hair before silver's invasion, but I saw no signs of decay in their sturdy bodies, their hard stern faces.

Peleus got down first and came up to me before I could back away; my flesh crawled when he embraced me affectionately, then I found my revulsion tempered by his warmth.

'Sooner or later, Chiron, I suspect it is impossible to look any older. Are you well?'

'All considered, sire, very well.'

We strolled a little way from the cars. I gave Peleus a mutinous look.

'How can you ask me to teach again, sire? Haven't I done enough? Is there no one else capable of dealing with your sons?'

'Chiron, you have no peer.' Gazing down at me from his great height, Peleus gripped my arm. 'You must surely know how much Achilles means to me. He is my only son, there will be no others. When I die he must take both thrones, so he must be educated. I can do much myself, but not without a proper basis. Only you can instil the rudiments, Chiron, and you know it. Hereditary Kings are precariously positioned in Greece. There are always contenders waiting to pounce.' He sighed. 'Besides, I love Achilles more than life itself. How can I deny him the education I had?'

'That sounds as if you spoil the boy.'

'No, I think he is incorruptible.'

'I do not want this task, Peleus.'

His head went to one side, he frowned. 'It's foolish to flog a dead horse, but will you at least see the boys? You might change your mind.'

'Not even for another Herakles or Peleus, sire. But I will see them if you wish it.'

Peleus turned and beckoned to two lads who stood by the second chariot. They approached slowly and one behind the other; I could not see the boy who brought up the rear. Scant wonder. The boy in the lead was certainly eye-catching. Yet a true disappointment. Was this Achilles, the cherished only son? No, definitely not. This one had to be Ajax; he was too old to be Achilles. Fourteen? Thirteen? Already as tall as a man, his great arms and shoulders rippled with muscle. Not an ill-looking lad, but not distinguished either. Just a big adolescent with a slightly snub nose and stolid grey eyes which lacked the light of real intellect.

'This is Ajax,' said Telamon proudly. 'He's only ten, though he appears much older.'

I waved Ajax aside.

'This is Achilles?' My voice sounded constricted.

'Yes,' said Peleus, trying to sound detached. 'He's big for his age too. He turned six last birthday.'

My throat felt dry. I swallowed. Even at that age he owned some personal magic, some spell he used unknowing which bound men to him and made them love him. Not so heavily built as his first cousin Ajax, but a tall, strongly formed child nonetheless. For so young a boy he stood in a very relaxed manner, his weight distributed on one leg, the other gracefully forward a little, his arms loose by his sides but not awkward looking. Composed and unconsciously regal, he seemed made of gold. Hair like Helios's rays, winged brows gleaming like yellow crystal, polished gold skin. Very beautiful, save for the lipless mouth – straight, slitlike – heartbreakingly sad yet so determined that I quailed for him. He looked at me gravely out of eyes the colour of the late dawn, yellow and cloudy; eyes filled with curiosity, pain, grief, bewilderment and intelligence.

CHIRON

I signed away seven of my dwindling store of years when I heard myself say, 'I will teach them.'

Peleus beamed and Telamon hugged me; they had not been sure.

'We won't stay,' said Peleus. 'The cart holds all the boys will need, and I've brought servants to look after you. Is the old house still standing?'

I nodded.

'Then the servants can use it as their lodging. They have orders to obey your least command. You speak in my name.'

Shortly afterwards they drove away.

Leaving the slaves busy unloading the cart, I went to the boys. Ajax stood like the mountain itself, impassive and docile, his eyes unshadowed; that thick skull would have to be pounded before the mind within became aware of its rightful function. Achilles was still looking down the road after his father, his big eyes bright with unshed tears. This was a parting of great importance to him.

'Come with me, young men. I will show you your new home.'

They followed silently as I led them to my cave and showed them how comfortable such an odd dwelling place could be. I pointed out the soft furry skins upon which they would sleep, the area in the main chamber where they would sit with me and learn. Then I took them to the edge of the precipice and sat down in my chair with one of them on either side.

'Are you looking forward to your schooling?' I asked, more to Achilles than to Ajax.

'Yes, my lord,' said Achilles courteously; his father had at least given him lessons in good manners.

'My name is Chiron. You will call me that.'

'Yes, Chiron. Father says I must look forward to this.'

I turned to Ajax. 'On a table in the cave you will find a lyre. Bring it to me – and make sure you do not drop it.'

The hulking lad regarded me without rancour. 'I never drop anything,' he said, quite matter-of-fact.

My brows rose; I felt a slight twinkle of amusement, but it kindled no answering spark in the grey eyes of Telamon's son. Instead he went to do as I had asked, the good soldier obeying his orders without question. That was the best I could do for Ajax, I reflected. Mould him into a soldier of perfect strength and resource. Whereas the eyes of Achilles mirrored my own mirth.

'Ajax always takes you at your exact word,' he said in the firm and measured, pleasing voice I already liked to hear. He stretched out a hand to indicate the city far below. 'Iolkos?'

'Yes.'

'Then that must be the palace up there on the hill. How small it looks! I always thought it dwarfed Pelion, yet from Pelion it is just another house.'

'All palaces are, if you can get far enough away from them.'

'Yes, I see that.'

'You miss your father already.'

'I thought I might cry, but it has passed.'

'You'll see him again in the spring, and the time between now and then will fly. There will be no chance to be idle, and it is idleness which breeds discontent, mischief, malice, pranks.'

He drew a breath. 'What must I learn, Chiron? What do I need to know to be a great king?'

'Too much to detail, Achilles. A great king is a fountain of knowledge. Any king is the best man, but a great king understands that he is the representative of his people before the God.'

'Then learning cannot come too soon.'

Ajax came back with the lyre in his hand, holding it off the ground carefully; it was a big instrument more akin to the harps the Egyptians play, formed from a huge tortoise carapace which glowed all browns and ambers, and it had golden pegs. I laid it across my knee and stroked the strings with a feather touch which produced a pretty sound, not a melody.

49

'You must play the lyre and learn the songs of your people. The greatest sin is to appear uncultured or uncouth. You will commit to heart the history and the geography of the world, all the wonders in nature, all the treasures beneath the lap of Mother Kubaba, who is the Earth. I will teach you to hunt, to kill, to fight with all manner of weapons, to make your own weapons. I will show you the herbs curing sicknesses and wounds, teach you to distil them for medicines, school you in splinting broken limbs. A great king sets more store by life than death.'

'Oratory?' asked Achilles.

'Yes, of course. After learning from me, your oratory will draw the hearts of your listeners out of their breasts in joy or sorrow. And I will show you how to judge what men are, how to frame laws and execute them. I will teach you what the God expects of you because you are Chosen.' I smiled. 'And that is just the beginning!'

I took up the lyre then and set its base upon the ground, drew my hand across its heartstrings. For a few moments only I played, the notes increasing in power, then, on the climax, as the last chord died away into stillness, I began to sing.

'He was alone, at every turn was enmity.
Queen Here brooding spread her hands,
And Olympos shook its golden rafters
As she turned restless to watch him.
Implacable her divine rage! King Zeus
Powerless in all the reaches of his sky
Because he promised glorious Here this,
His son into groaning bondage on earth.
Eurystheus her minion cold and pitiless,
Smiling as he counted those runnels,
His sweat that Herakles gave in payment.
For the children of the Gods must atone
Because the Gods are above retribution,
And that is the difference between men

And the Gods who prey on them as victims.
Bastard child without that drop of ichor,
Herakles took up the price of passion.
In agony and degradation did he pay,
While Here laughed to see mighty Zeus weep ...'

It was the Lay of Herakles, not dead so many years, and as I sang I watched them both. Ajax listened intently, Achilles with his body tensed, leaning forward with his chin propped on his hands, both elbows on the arm of my chair, his eyes only a thread away from my face. When at last I put the lyre from me he dropped his hands with a sigh, exhausted.

So it began, and so it went on as the years rolled by. Achilles forged ahead in everything, Ajax plodded doggedly through his assignments. Yet Telamon's son was not a fool. He had a courage and a determination that any king mighty envy, and he always managed to keep up. But Achilles was my boy, my joy. Every single thing I told him was stored up with jealous care – to be used when he was a great king, he would say with a smile. He loved learning and excelled in all its branches, as good with his hands as he was with his mind. Even now I have some of his clay bowls and little drawings.

But above all scholarship, Achilles was born to action, to war and to mighty deeds. Even in the physical sense he outstripped his cousin, for he was quicksilver on his feet and took to handling weapons like a greedy woman to a casket of jewels. His aim with a spear was unerring, nor could I see the sword once he drew it. Swish, slash, chop. Oh yes, he was born to command! He understood the art of war without effort, by instinct. A natural hunter, he would come back to my cave dragging a wild boar too heavy to carry, and he could run down a deer. Only once did I see him in trouble, when, after his quarry at full tilt, he came crashing down so hard that it was some time before he recovered his full senses. His right foot, he explained, had given way.

51

CHIRON

Ajax could flare into violent rage, but I never saw Achilles
lose his temper. Neither shy nor withdrawn, he yet possessed
an inner quiet and restraint. The thinking warrior. How rare. In
only one respect did that gash of a mouth reveal the other side
of his nature; when something did not suit his sense of fitness
he could be as cold and unbending as the north wind bearing
snow.

I enjoyed those seven years more than all the rest of my life put
together, thanks not only to Achilles, but to Ajax too. The
contrast between the first cousins was so marked and their
excellences so great that welding them into men became a task
filled with love. Of all the boys I have taught, I loved Achilles
most. When he drove away for the last time I wept, and for
many moons afterwards my will to live was a gnat as persistent
as the one which tormented Io. It was a long time before I
could look out from my chair and see the golden trim on the
roof of the palace shining in the sun without a mist hovering
before my eyes that made the gilding and the tile dissolve one
into the other like ore in a crucible.

CHAPTER FOUR

NARRATED BY
HELEN

Xanthippe gave me a rough tussle; I came from the field panting and exhausted. We had gathered a large audience, and I gave the circle of admiring faces my most radiant smile. No man was interested in congratulating Xanthippe for winning the bout. They were there to see *me*. Crowding about me, they sang my praises, used any excuse to touch my hand or my shoulder, a few of the bolder ones jokingly offering to wrestle with me anytime. It was no effort to dodge their sallies; crude, unsubtle stuff.

In years I was still counted a child, but their eyes denied that; their eyes told me things about myself that I already knew, for there were mirrors of polished copper in my rooms, and I too had eyes. Though they were all nobles of the Court, none of them was of great import in the scheme of things. I shook them off like water after a bath, snatched a linen towel from my woman and wrapped it about my bare, sweating limbs amid a chorus of protests.

Then I saw my father at the back of the crowd. *Father* had watched? How extraordinary! He never came to see the women play at their parodies of masculine sport! My expression caused some of the barons to turn; in an instant they had all melted away. I went to my father and kissed him on the cheek.

'Do you always have such an enthusiastic audience, child?' he asked, frowning.

'Yes, Father.' I preened. 'I am much admired, you know.'

'So I see. I must be getting old, losing my powers of observation. Luckily your elder brother is neither old nor blind.

He told me this morning that it might be prudent for me to drop in on the women's sports.'

I bristled. 'Why should Kastor bother with me?'

'A poor state of affairs if he did not!'

We reached the door to the Throne Room.

'Wash off your dirt, Helen, dress, and then return to me.'

His face told me nothing, so I shrugged and ran off.

Neste waited for me in my rooms, clucking and scolding. I let her unwrap me, looking forward to the warm bath, the tingle of the scraper on my skin. Chattering away, she threw the towel into a corner and undid the strings of my loincloth. But I was not listening. Skipping across the cold flags, I leaped into the bath and splashed merrily. Such a delicious sensation to feel the water lap around me, caress me, cloud enough to permit me to caress myself without Neste's beady eyes detecting it. And how pleasant afterwards to stand while she rubbed me with a fragrant oil, rub a little of it in myself. There could not be too many moments in one day to caress, to rub, to give myself those shocks and thrills girls like Xanthippe seemed not to care about nearly as much as I did. Perhaps that was because they had not had a Theseus to teach them.

One of my other women shook my skirt into circles on the floor so that I could step into its middle. They drew it up over my legs and fastened it about my waist. It was heavy, but I was used to the weight by now, for I had been wearing a woman's skirt for two years, ever since my return from Athens. My mother had deemed it too ridiculous to put me back into a child's shift after that episode.

Then came my blouse, laced below my breasts, and the wide belt and apron which could be fastened only while I sucked in my breath. A woman coaxed my curls through the hole in the gold coronet, another looped a pretty pair of crystal earrings through my pierced ears. I held out my bare feet one at a time and let them slip little rings and bells on all my ten toes, held out my arms for dozens of jingling bracelets, fingers for rings.

When they were done I went across to my biggest mirror and

surveyed myself in it critically. The skirt was the nicest one I possessed, all frills and fringes from waist to ankles, weighed down with beads of crystal and amber, amulets of lapis and beaten gold, golden bells and pendants of faience, so that every move I made was accompanied by music. My belt was not laced tightly enough; I made two strong women pull it in.

'Why can't I paint my nipples gold, Neste?' I asked.

'No use complaining to me, young princess. Ask your mother. But save such artifice for when you need it – after you've borne a child and your nipples have turned dark brown.'

I decided she might be right. I was one of the lucky ones; my nipples were a good rose in colour and furled in on themselves like buds, my breasts were high and full.

What had Theseus said? Two plump white puppies with pink noses. My mood changed the moment I thought of him; I flounced away from my image in a tinkle of spangles. Oh, to lie in his arms again! Theseus, my beloved Theseus. His mouth, his hands, the way he tormented my body until it raged to be fulfilled ... Then they had come and taken me away, my estimable brothers Kastor and Polydeukes. If only he had been in Athens when they arrived! But he had been far away on Skyros with King Lykomedes, so no one dared to oppose the sons of Tyndareus.

I allowed my women to trace a line of dissolved black powder around my eyes and paint their lids gold, but refused the carmine for my cheeks and lips. No need of it, Theseus had said. Then I went down to the Throne Room to see my father, who was sitting in an easy chair by one window. He rose at once.

'Come here to the light,' he said.

I did as I was told without question; he was my indulgent father, yes, but he was also the King. While I stood in the harsh, unfiltered sun he stepped back a few paces and looked at me as if he had never seen me before.

'Oh yes, Theseus had a more discerning eye than anyone in

HELEN

Lakedaimon! Your mother is right, you are grown up. Therefore
we must do something with you before another Theseus comes
along.'

My face burned. I said nothing.

'It is time you were married, Helen.' He considered for a
moment. 'How old are you?'

'Fourteen, Father.' Marriage! How interesting!

'It is not too soon,' he said.

My mother came in. I avoided her eyes, feeling peculiar
standing in front of my father while he looked at me with
the eyes of a man. But she ignored me, went to his side and
assessed me too. Then they exchanged a long, purposive look.

'I told you, Tyndareus,' she said.

'Yes, Leda, she needs a husband.'

My mother laughed the high, musical laugh which (so
rumour had it) had so entranced almighty Zeus. She had been
about my age when they found her with her naked limbs
wrapped about a great swan, moaning and keening in pleasure:
she had thought quickly. Zeus, Zeus, the swan is Zeus, he has
ravished me! But I, her daughter, knew better. How would
those delicious white feathers feel? Her father had married her
to Tyndareus three days later, and she had borne two sets of
twins to him: Kastor and Klytemnestra first, then, some years
after, Polydeukes and me. Though now everyone seemed to
think Kastor and Polydeukes were the twins. Or that all four of
us were born together, quadruplets. If so, which of us belonged
to Zeus, and which to Tyndareus? A mystery.

'The women of my house mature early and suffer greatly,'
Leda my mother said, still laughing.

My father did not laugh. He just said, rather dourly, 'Yes.'

'It won't be hard to find her a husband. You will have to fend
them off with clubs, Tyndareus.'

'Well, she's highborn and richly dowered.'

'Rubbish! She's so beautiful it wouldn't matter if she had no
dowry at all. The High King of Attika did us one favour – he
spread praise of her beauty from Thessalia to Crete. It isn't

every day a man as old and jaded as Theseus becomes so besotted he abducts a twelve-year-old child.'

My father's lips tightened. 'I would prefer that *that* subject is not mentioned,' he said stiffly.

'A pity she is more beautiful than Klytemnestra.'

'Klytemnestra suits Agamemnon.'

'A pity then that there are not two High Kings of Mykenai.'

'There are three other High Kings in Greece,' he said, beginning to look practical and efficient.

I moved surreptitiously away from the light, not wanting to be noticed and dismissed. The subject – myself – was too interesting. I liked to hear people call me beautiful. Especially when they went on to say I was more beautiful than Klytemnestra, my older sister, who had married Agamemnon, High King of Mykenai and High King of all Greece. Though I had never liked her, she used to awe me when I was little, sweeping round the halls in one of her famous tempers, her flame hair stiff with fury, her black eyes blazing. I grinned. What a merry dance she must lead her husband with her tantrums, High King or not! However, Agamemnon looked as if he was capable of controlling her. He was just as domineering as Klytemnestra.

My parents were debating my marriage.

'I had best send heralds to all the Kings,' said Father.

'Yes – and the sooner, the better. Though the New Religion frowns on polygamy, many of the Kings have not taken queens. Idomeneus, for instance. Imagine! One daughter on the throne at Mykenai, the other on the throne of Crete. What a triumph!'

Father demurred. 'Crete is not the power it used to be. The two positions are not equivalent.'

'Philoktetes?'

'Yes, a brilliant man, destined for great things, they say. However, he is a king in Thessalia, which means he owes Peleus homage as well as Agamemnon. I'm thinking more of Diomedes, just back from the Thebes campaign and covered in wealth as well as glory. I like the idea of Argos, it's just down the road. If Peleus had been a younger man he would have been my automatic choice, but it is said he refuses to marry again.'

'No use dwelling on those who are unavailable,' my mother said briskly. 'There's always Menelaos.'

'I haven't forgotten *him*. Who could?'

'Send invitations to everyone, Tyndareus. There are heirs to thrones as well as kings. Odysseus of Ithaka is King there now that old Laertes is senile. And Menestheus is a far more stable High King of Attika than Theseus was – thank all the Gods that we do not have to deal with Theseus!'

I jumped. 'What do you mean?' I asked, skin prickling. In my heart I had been hoping that Theseus would come for me, claim me as his bride. Since my return from Athens I had heard no mention of his name.

My mother took my hands in hers and held them firmly. 'Well, best you find out from us, Helen. Theseus is dead, exiled and killed on Skyros.'

I wrenched away from her and ran from the room, my dreams in ashes. Dead? Theseus was *dead*? Theseus was dead and a part of me was forever cold.

Two moons later my brother-in-law Agamemnon arrived with his own brother, Menelaos, in his train. When they walked into the Throne Room I was present – a novelty for me, but an exhilarating one; suddenly I was the pivot upon which all discussion turned. Messengers had come from the palace gate to warn us, so the High King of Mykenai and all Greece entered to the blare of horns, a cloth of gold spread for his imperial feet.

I could never make up my mind whether I liked him or not, yet I did understand the awe he inspired. Very tall and as straight and disciplined as a professional soldier, he walked as if he owned the world. His jet black hair was faintly sprinkled with grey, his snapping black eyes could become menacing, his nose was beaked haughtily, his thin lips curled at the corners in permanent contempt.

Men so dark were unusual in Greece, a land of big, fair men, but instead of being ashamed of his darkness, Agamemnon flaunted it. Though the fashion was for a cleanshaven chin, he sported a long, curling black beard forced into regular screws by ribbons of gold, and he did his hair in the same way. He was dressed in a full-length robe of purple wool embroidered all over in a complicated design of gold thread, and in his right hand he carried the imperial sceptre of solid gold, swinging it as easily as if it were made of chalk.

My father came down from his throne and knelt to kiss his hand, doing him the homage which all the Greek Kings owed to the High King of Mykenai. My mother moved forward to join them. For the moment I was ignored, which gave me time to turn my attention to Menelaos, my prospective suitor. Oh, oh! Eager anticipation gave way to shocked disappointment. I had become quite used to the idea of marrying a replica of Agamemnon, but this man was no Agamemnon. Was he truly a full brother to the High King of Mykenai, son by Atreus out of the same womb? It did not seem possible. Short. Stocky. Legs so thick and shapeless they appeared ridiculous in the tight breeches he affected. Round stooped shoulders. A mild and apologetic man. Ordinary features. Hair the same flaming red as my sister's. I might have been more taken with him if his hair had been a different colour.

My father beckoned. I stumbled forward and gave my hand into his. The imperial visitor transferred his gaze to me, a hot and admiring look. For the first time I experienced a phenomenon which would become very familiar in the days to come: I was no more and no less than a prize animal put up for auction to the highest bidder.

'She's perfect,' said Agamemnon to my father. 'How do you manage to produce such beautiful children, Tyndareus?'

My father laughed, his arm about my mother's waist. 'I am only half of it, sire,' he said.

They turned then and left me to converse with Menelaos, but not before I heard the High King's final question.

'What is the truth behind the Theseus interlude?' he asked.

And my mother breaking in quickly to say, 'He kidnapped her, Agamemnon. Luckily the Athenians deemed it the feather which tipped the load. They drove him out before he could deflower her. Kastor and Polydeukes brought her away untouched.'

Liar, liar!

Menelaos was staring at me; I preened.

'You have never been to Amyklai before,' I said.

He mumbled something, hung his head.

'What was that?' I asked.

'Nuh-nuh-nuh-no,' he managed audibly.

He stammered!

The suitors assembled. Menelaos was the only one permitted to reside within the palace itself, thanks to his relationship with our family – and his brother's clout. The rest were accommodated among the house barons and in the guest house. One hundred of them. The most cheering discovery I made was that none was as boring or as unattractive as the red-haired, stammering Menelaos.

Philoktetes and Idomeneus arrived together, big and golden Philoktetes bursting with energy, haughty Idomeneus stalking in with the conscious arrogance of one born into the House of Minos and destined to rule as High King of Crete after Katreus.

When Diomedes strode in, I saw the best of them. A true king and warrior. He wore the same air of worldly experience Theseus had owned, though he was as dark as Theseus had been fair; as dark as Agamemnon. *Handsome!* Tall and lithe, a black panther. His eyes flashed with impudent humour, his mouth seemed always to be laughing. And I knew in that first instant that I would choose him. When he spoke to me his glance ravished me; a quick thrust of want forked through me, my sex ached. Yes, I would choose King Diomedes from Argos-down-the-road.

As soon as the last of them had come my father held a great feast. I sat on the dais like a queen, pretending not to notice the glances continually flung up at me from a hundred pairs of ardent eyes, my own flickering whenever they dared to Diomedes. Who suddenly turned his attention from me to a man threading his way through the benches, a man whose advent was greeted by cheers from some and scowls from others. Diomedes sprang up and swung the stranger round in a hard embrace. Some quick talk passed between them, then the stranger clapped Diomedes on the back and continued to the dais to greet my father and Agamemnon, both of whom had risen to their feet. *Agamemnon* rising? The High King of Mykenai did not rise for any man!

He was different, the newcomer. A tall man, he would have been considerably taller if his legs had been in proportion to the rest of him. But they were not. They were abnormally short and inclined to be bandy; his muscular frame seemed too large by far to be perched atop such stunted supports. In face he was a truly beautiful man, fine featured and owning a very large pair of luminous grey eyes, brilliant and speaking. His hair was red, the brightest and most aggressive red I had ever seen; Klytemnestra and Menelaos paled to nothing beside it.

When his eyes rested upon me I felt his power. Shiver stuff. *Who was he?*

My father gestured impatiently to a servant, who placed a kingly chair between him and Agamemnon. *Who was he*, to be so honoured? And to be so unimpressed by the honour?

'This is Helen,' my father said.

'No wonder I see most of Greece here, Tyndareus,' he said cheerily, picking up a leg of fowl and sinking his white teeth deeply into it. 'I now believe what the gossip says – she *is* the most beautiful woman in the world. You'll have trouble with this pack of hotheads, to please only one and disappoint so many.'

Agamemnon looked ruefully at my father; they both laughed.

'Trust you to state the problem in a nutshell within one instant of your arrival, Odysseus,' said the High King.

My surprise and wonder vanished, I felt a fool. Odysseus, of course. Who else would dare to speak to Agamemnon as to an equal? Who else would warrant a special chair on the dais?

I had heard much of him. His name cropped up whenever there was talk of laws, of decisions, of new taxes, of war. My father had once undertaken the dreary journey to Ithaka just to consult him. He was held the most intelligent man in the world, more intelligent even than Nestor and Palamedes. And not only was he intelligent; he was also wise. Little wonder then that in my imagination Odysseus had been a venerable old greybeard, all bent with the cares of a century of living, as ancient as King Nestor of Pylos. When Agamemnon had important matters to discuss he sent for Palamedes, Nestor and Odysseus, but it was usually Odysseus who decided the thing.

So much had been whispered about the Ithakan Fox, as men called him. His kingdom consisted of four rocky, barren little islands off the west coast, a poor and pitiful domain as kingdoms went. His palace was modest, he was a farmer because his barons could not contribute enough taxes to support him; yet his name had made Ithaka, Leukas, Zakynthos and Kephallenai famous.

At the time he came to Amyklai and I first saw him he was not much more than twenty-five years old – and may have been younger than that, if wisdom has the power to age a man's face.

They continued to talk, perhaps forgetting that I was on my father's left hand and able to eavesdrop without appearing to do so. As I had Menelaos on my other side, no conversation occurred to divert me.

'Do you intend to ask for Helen, my wily friend?'

Odysseus looked mischievous. 'You perceive me, Tyndareus.'

'Indeed I do, but why? I had not thought you angling for a raving beauty, though she does have a dowry.'

He pulled a face. 'My curiosity – think of my curiosity! Could you see me missing a show like this?'

Agamemnon grinned, but my father laughed aloud.

'Show is right! What am I to do, Odysseus? Look at them! One hundred and one Kings and Princes all snarling at each other and wondering who is going to be the lucky one – and determined to dispute the choice, no matter how logical or politic.'

This time Agamemnon spoke. 'It has developed into a kind of contest. Who is most favoured by the High King of Mykenai and his father-in-law Tyndareus of Lakedaimon? They know Tyndareus must take my advice! All I can see emerging from this situation is enduring enmity.'

'Absolutely. Look at Philoktetes, arching his proud neck and snorting. Not to mention Diomedes and Idomeneus. Menestheus. Eurypylos. And so on.'

'What should we do?' the High King asked.

'Is that a formal request for advice, sire?'

'It is.'

I stiffened, beginning to realise how insignificant my part was in all this. Suddenly I wanted to weep. *I* choose? No! *They* would choose, Agamemnon and my father. Though, I understood now, it was Odysseus who held my fate in the palm of his hand. And did he care? At which moment he winked at me. My heart sank. No, he didn't care. There was not one scrap of desire in those beautiful grey eyes. He hadn't come to sue for my hand; he had come knowing his advice would be sought. He had come only to enhance his own standing.

'As always, I'm pleased to be able to help,' he said smoothly, his gaze going to my father. 'However, Tyndareus, before we tackle the problem of getting Helen safely and politically married, I have a small favour to ask.'

Agamemnon seemed offended; out of my depth, I wondered what subtle bargaining was going on.

63

'Do you want Helen for yourself?' Father asked baldly.

Odysseus flung back his head and laughed so uproariously that for a moment the hall stilled. 'No, no! I wouldn't dare ask for her when my fortune is negligible and my kingdom penurious! Poor Helen! My mind boggles at the vision of such beauty cooped up upon a rock in the Ionian sea! No, I do not want Helen for my bride. I want another.'

'Ah!' said Agamemnon, mollified. 'Who?'

Odysseus preferred to address his reply to my father. 'The daughter of your brother Ikarios, Tyndareus. Penelope.'

'That shouldn't be difficult,' said my father, surprised.

'Ikarios dislikes me, and there have been much better offers for Penelope's hand.'

'I will see to it' from my father.

And from Agamemnon, 'Consider it done.'

Such a shock for me! If they understood what Odysseus saw in Penelope, I certainly did not. I knew her well; she was my first cousin. Not ill looking and a great heiress into the bargain, but *boring*. Once she had caught me allowing a house baron to kiss my breasts – I definitely would not have let him do more! – and served me a homily to the effect that desires of the flesh were unintellectual and demeaning. I would do better, she had pronounced in that measured, unemotional voice of hers, to fix my attention upon the real feminine skills like *weaving*. I had stared at her as if she were mad. *Weaving!*

Odysseus began to speak; I abandoned my thoughts about Cousin Penelope and listened intently.

'I have a fair idea whereabouts you intend to bestow your daughter, Tyndareus, and I understand your reasons. However, who you choose is irrelevant. What *is* relevant is that you safeguard your own and Agamemnon's interests – safeguard your relations with the unlucky one hundred after you announce your choice. I can achieve that. Provided that you do exactly as I say.'

Agamemnon answered. 'We will.'

'Then the first step is to return all the gifts the suitors have tendered, accompanied by graceful thanks for the intention. No man must call you greedy, Tyndareus.'

My father looked chagrined. 'Is that really necessary?'

'Not necessary – imperative!'

'The gifts will be returned,' said Agamemnon.

'Good.' Odysseus leaned forward in his chair, the two Kings following him. 'You will announce your choice at night, in the Throne Room. I want the place dim and holy, so night helps. Have all the priests present. Burn incense copiously. My aim is to oppress the suitors' spirits, and that can only be done through ritual. You cannot afford the name of your choice greeted by flaring warrior tempers.'

'As you wish,' Father sighed. He disliked minutiae.

'That, Tyndareus, is merely the beginning. When you speak, you will inform the suitors how much you adore your precious jewel of a daughter, and how hard you have prayed to the Gods for guidance. Your choice, you will tell them, has been approved in Olympos. The omens are auspicious and the oracles clear. But almighty Zeus has demanded a condition. Namely, that before any man – save you – knows the name of the lucky winner, *every* man must swear an oath to uphold your choice. But more than that. Every man must also swear to give Helen's husband wholehearted aid and co-operation. Every man must swear that Helen's husband's welfare is as dear to him as the Gods are. That, if needs be, every man will go to war to defend the rights and entitlements of Helen's husband.'

Agamemnon sat silent, staring into space, chewing his lips and visibly burning with some inner fire. My father just looked stunned. Odysseus sat back picking at his fowl, obviously pleased with himself. Suddenly Agamemnon turned to grasp him by both shoulders, knuckles pale under the fierce pressure of his hold, his face ominous. But Odysseus, unafraid, looked back tranquilly.

'By Mother Kubaba, Odysseus, you are a genius!' The High King twisted to stare at my father. 'Tyndareus, do you realise

HELEN

what this means? Whoever marries Helen is assured of permanent, irrevocable alliances with almost every nation in Greece!
His future is certain, his position raised a thousandfold!'

My father, though immensely relieved, frowned. 'What oath
can I administer?' he asked. 'What oath is so awful that it will
bind them to something they will abominate?'

'There is only one,' said Agamemnon slowly. 'The Oath of
the Quartered Horse. By Zeus the Thunderer, by Poseidon Earth
Shaker, by the Daughters of Kore, by the River and the Dead.'

The words fell like drops of blood from the head of Medusa;
Father shuddered, dropped his face into his hands.

Apparently unmoved, Odysseus changed the subject
abruptly. 'What will happen in the Hellespont?' he asked
Agamemnon chattily.

The High King scowled. 'I don't know. Oh, what ails King
Priam of Troy? Why is he blind to the advantages of Greek
traders in the Euxine Sea?'

'I think,' said Odysseus, choosing a honey cake, 'that it suits
Priam very well to exclude traders. He gets fat on the
Hellespont tolls anyway. He also has treaties with his fellow
kings of Asia Minor, and no doubt he takes a share of the
exorbitant prices we Greeks are charged for tin and copper if –
as we have to – we buy from Asia Minor. The exclusion of
Greeks from the Euxine means more money for Troy, not less.'

'Telamon did us a bad turn when he abducted Hesione!' said
my father angrily.

Agamemnon shook his head. 'Telamon was in the right of it.
All Herakles asked was rightful payment for a great service.
When that miserable old skinflint Laomedon denied him, a
mindless idiot could have predicted the outcome.'

'Herakles has been dead these twenty years and more,' said
Odysseus, watering his wine. 'Theseus is dead too. Only
Telamon still lives. He would never consent to be parted from
Hesione, even if she'd be willing to go. Abduction and rape are
old tales,' he went on blandly, apparently having never heard a
single whisper about Helen and Theseus, 'and they do not have

much if anything to do with policy. Greece is rising. Asia Minor knows it. Therefore what better policy can Troy and the rest of Asia Minor adopt than to deny Greece what it must have – tin and copper to turn into bronze?'

'True,' said Agamemnon. He pulled on his beard. 'So what will come of Troy's trade embargo?'

'War,' said Odysseus peacefully. 'Sooner or later there must be war. When we feel the pinch hard enough – when our merchants scream for justice in every Throne Room between Knossos and Iolkos – when we can no longer scrape up enough tin to bronze our copper and make swords and shields and arrowheads – then there will be war.'

Their talk grew duller still; well, it no longer concerned me. Besides, I was heartily sick of Menelaos. Wine was beginning to affect the gathering, fewer faces were turned up to me to worship. I slipped my feet out from under the table and stole away through the door behind my father's chair. Down the passage which paralleled the dining hall, wishing I wore something more silent than my jangling skirt. The stair to the women's wing was at the far end where the passage branched off to other public rooms; I reached it, ran up it without being called back. Now I had only to get past my mother's apartments. Head bent, I pulled at the curtain.

Hands fastened upon my arms halted me, and my cry of alarm was muffled by a hand across my mouth. Diomedes! Heart pounding, I stared at him. Until this moment I had had no opportunity to be alone with him, nor conversed with him beyond salutations.

The lamplight gleamed upon his skin and polished it to amber, a cord beat very fast in the column of his throat; I let myself meet his dark, hot gaze, and felt his hand fall from my mouth. How beautiful he was! How much I loved beauty! But never in anything as much as I did in a man.

'Meet me outside in the garden,' he whispered.

I shook my head violently. 'You must be mad! Let me go and

I will not mention how I encountered you outside my mother's rooms! *Let me go!*'

His teeth flashed white, he laughed silently. 'I will not move from this spot until you promise to meet me in the garden. They'll be in the dining hall for a long while yet – no one will miss either of us. Girl, I want you! I care nothing for their decisions or delays, I want you and I mean to have you.'

My head was still fogged from the heat of the dining hall; I put my hand to it. Then, apparently of its own volition, it nodded. Diomedes let me go at once. I fled to my rooms.

Neste was waiting to disrobe me.

'Go to bed, old woman! I will undress myself.'

Used to my moods, she went gladly, leaving me to tug at my laces with trembling fingers, tear off my bodice and my blouse, struggle free from the skirt. I stripped off the bells, bracelets and rings, found my linen bathrobe and wrapped it about me. Then out into the corridor, down the back stairs into the night air. The garden, he had said: I found the rows of cabbages and edible roots, smiling. Who would look for us among the vegetables?

He was naked beneath a laurel tree. Off came my bathrobe, far enough from him to let him see me in the rain of moonlight. Then he was beside me, spreading it for our bed, holding me against himself flat on Mother Earth, from whom all women gather strength and all men lose it. Such is the way of the Gods.

'Fingers and tongues, Diomedes,' I whispered. 'I will go to my marriage couch with hymen intact.'

He smothered his laughter between my breasts. 'Did Theseus teach you how to be a virgin?' he asked.

'No one needed to teach me that,' I said, stroking his arms and shoulders, sighing. 'I am not very old, but I know that my head is the price of losing my maidenhead to any save my husband.'

By the time he left me he was, I think, satisfied, if not as he had anticipated. Because he loved me truly he honoured my conditions, just as Theseus had. Not that I was very concerned about how Diomedes felt. *I* was satisfied.

Which showed the next night when I sat beside my father's throne, had there been any eyes to note it. Diomedes sat with Philoktetes and Odysseus in the throng, too far from me in the dimness to see how he looked. The room, bright with frescoes of dancing warriors and scarlet-painted columns, had sunk to dark and flickering shadows. The priests came, thick and cloying fumes of incense rose, and without fuss or fluster the atmosphere took on the solemn, burdensome holiness of a shrine.

I heard my father speak the words Odysseus had prepared; the oppression settled down like a living thing. Then came the sacrificial horse, a perfect white stallion with pink eyes and no hair of black on him, his hooves slipping on the well-worn flags, his head snaking back and forth in the golden halter. Agamemnon picked up the great double-headed axe and swung it expertly. The horse went down, it seemed, so very slowly, mane and tail floating like wisps of weed in water currents, his blood spurting.

While my father informed the company of the oath he required, I watched in sickened horror as the priests hacked the lovely beast into four quarters. Never shall I forget that scene: the suitors stepping forward one by one to balance their two feet on four limp pieces of warm flesh, swearing the terrible oath of loyalty and allegiance to my future husband. The voices were dulled and apathetic, for power and masculinity could not survive that awful moment. Pale and sweating faces waxed and waned in the torchlight as it wavered; from somewhere a wind was blowing, hallooing like a lost shade.

Finally it was done. The steaming carcase of the horse lay ignored, the suitors from their places looked up at King Tyndareus of Lakedaimon as if drugged.

'I give my daughter to Menelaos,' Father said.

There was a great sigh, nothing else. No one shouted a quick protest. Not even Diomedes leaped to his feet in anger. My eyes found his as the attendants went about kindling the lamps; we said our farewells across half a hundred heads, knowing we were beaten. I think the tears ran down my cheeks as I looked at him, but no one remarked on them. I gave my numbed hand into the damp clasp of Menelaos.

CHAPTER FIVE

NARRATED BY
PARIS

I returned to Troy on foot and alone, my bow and quiver across my shoulders. Seven moons I had spent among the forests and glades of Mount Ida, yet not one trophy did I have to show for them. Much as I loved hunting, I could never bear to see an animal stumble under the impact of an arrow; I preferred to see it as well and free as I was. My best hunting moments concerned more desirable quarry than deer or boar. For me the fun of the chase was in going after the human inhabitants of Ida's woods, the wild girls and shepherdesses. When a girl sank down, defeated, no arrows pierced her save the one Eros shot; there was no stream of blood or dying moan, only a sigh of sweet content as I took her into my arms still gasping from the ecstasy of the chase, and ready to gasp with another kind of ecstasy.

I always spent my springs and summers on Ida; Court life bored me to the point of madness. How I hated those cedar rafters oiled and polished to richest brown, those painted stone halls and pillared towers! Being shut in behind huge walls was to suffocate, to be a prisoner. All I wanted was to run through leagues of grass and trees, lie exhausted with my face pillowed against a perfume of fallen leaves. But each autumn I had to return to Troy and spend the winter there with my father. That was my duty, token though it was. After all, I was his fourth son among many. Nobody took me seriously, and I preferred that.

I walked into the Throne Room at the end of an assembly on a wild, bleak day, still in my mountain clothes, ignoring the pitying smiles, the lips pursed up in disapproval. Dusk was already dimming to the gloom of night; the meeting had been a very long one.

My father the King sat upon his gold and ivory chair high upon a purple marble dais at the far end of the hall, his long white hair elaborately curled and his tremendous white beard twined about with thin strings of gold and silver. Inordinately proud of his old age, he was best pleased when he sat like an ancient god upon a tall pedestal, looking out over everything he owned.

Had the room been less imposing, the spectacle my father presented might not have been so impressive, but the room was, they said, bigger and grander even than the old Throne Room in the palace of Knossos in Crete. Spacious enough to hold three hundred people without seeming overcrowded, its lofty ceiling between the cedar rafters was painted blue and bedewed with golden constellations. It had massive pillars which tapered to relative slenderness at their bases, deep blue or purple, round plain capitals and plinths gilded. The walls were purple marble without relief to the height of a man's head; above that they were frescoed in scenes of lions, leopards, bears, wolves and men at hunt – black-and-white, yellow, crimson, brown and pink against a pale blue background. Behind the throne was a reredos of black Egyptian ebony wood inlaid with golden patterns, and the steps leading up to the dais were edged in gold.

I slid off my bow and quiver, handed them to a servant and worked my way through the knots of courtiers until I arrived at the dais. Seeing me, the King leaned forward to touch my bowed head gently with the emerald knob of his ivory sceptre, the signal to rise and approach him. I kissed his withered cheek.

'It is good to have you back, my son,' he said.

'I wish I could say it is good to be back, Father.'

Pushing me down to sit at his feet, he sighed. 'I always hope that this time you will stay, Paris. I could make something of you if you would stay.'

I reached up to stroke his beard because he loved that. 'I want no princely job, sire.'

'But you *are* a prince!' He sighed again, rocked gently. 'Though you are very young, I know. There is time.'

'No, sire, there is not time. You think of me as a boy, but I am a man. I am thirty-three years old.'

He was not listening to me, I fancied, for he raised his head and turned away from me, gesturing with his staff to someone at the back of the crowd. Hektor.

'Paris insists he is thirty-three, my son!' he said when Hektor arrived at the bottom of the three steps. Even so, he was tall enough to look into our father's face at the same level.

Hektor's dark eyes surveyed me thoughtfully. 'I suppose you must be, Paris. I was born ten years after you, and I've been twenty-three for six moons now.' He grinned. 'You certainly don't look your age, however.'

I laughed back. 'Thank you for that, little brother! Now you *do* look my age. That's because you're the Heir. It ages a man to be the Heir – tied down to the state, the army, the crown. Give me the eternal youth of irresponsibility any day!'

'What suits one man doesn't necessarily suit another' was his tranquil reply. 'I have far less taste for women, so what does it matter if I look old before my time? While you enjoy your little escapades in the harem, I enjoy leading the army on manoeuvres. And while my face may wrinkle prematurely, my body will be fit and spare long after yours sports a pot belly.'

I winced. Trust Hektor to find the vulnerable spot! He could gauge a man's fatal weakness in the twinkling of an eye and pounce like a lion. Nor was he frightened to use his claws. Being the Heir had matured him. Gone was the exuberant, irritating youth of yesteryear, his undeniable powers safely channelled into useful work. Still, he was big enough to take it. I was no weakling, but Hektor towered over me and bulked twice as large. He dressed very plainly – and therefore with a certain compelling dignity – in a leather kilt and shirt, with his long black hair braided, tied back in a neat queue. All of us who were sons of Priam and Hekabe were famous for our good looks, but Hektor had something more. Natural authority.

The next moment I was jerked to my feet and removed from our father's vicinity; old Antenor was peevishly indicating that he wished to speak to the King before dimissal. Hektor and I slipped away from the dais without being called back.

'I have a surprise for you,' my young brother said with quiet pleasure as we began to traverse the seemingly endless passages which connected the wings and minor palaces comprising the Citadel.

The Heir's palace was right next door to our father's, so the walk was not an unduly long one. When he led me into his big reception room I propped and stared about in astonishment.

'Hektor! Where *is* she?'

What had been a warehouse cluttered with spears, shields, armour and swords was now a room. Nor did it stink of horses, though Hektor loved horses. I could not remember ever seeing enough of the walls to know how they were decorated, but this evening they glowed with curling trees in jade and blue, purple flowers, black-and-white horses gambolling. The floor was so clean its black-and-white marble tiles gleamed. Tripods and ornaments were polished, and beautifully embroidered purple curtains hung on golden rings from doorways and windows.

'Where is she?' I asked again.

He blushed. 'She's coming,' he growled.

She entered on the echo of his words. I looked her over and had to commend his good taste; she was extremely handsome. As dark as he, tall and robust. And equally awkward with the social graces; she took one look at me, then looked anywhere else she could find.

'This is my wife, Andromache,' said Hektor.

I kissed her on the cheek. 'I approve, little brother, I approve! But she's not from these parts, surely.'

'No. She's the daughter of King Eetion of Kilikia. I was down there in the spring for Father, and brought her back with me. It wasn't planned, but it' – he drew a breath – 'happened.'

She spoke at last, bashfully. 'Hektor, who is this?'

The crack of Hektor's slapping his thigh in exasperation made me jump. 'Oh, when will I ever learn? This is Paris.'

Something that I didn't like showed for a moment in her eyes. Ah! The girl might be a force to be reckoned with once discomfort and strangeness dissipated.

'My Andromache has great courage,' said Hektor proudly, one arm about her waist. 'She left her home and family to come with me to Troy.'

'Indeed,' I said politely, and left it at that.

Soon I became inured to the monotony of life within the Citadel. While the sleet pattered against tortoiseshell shutters or the rain cascaded in sheets from the top of the walls or snow carpeted the courtyards, I sniffed and prowled among the women for someone new and interesting, someone a tenth as desirable as the least of Ida's shepherdesses. Wearying work without challenge or good hard exercise. Hektor was right. Unless I found a better way to keep myself trim than skulking up and down forbidden corridors, I would develop a pot belly.

Four moons after I returned Helenos came into my rooms to settle himself comfortably into a cushioned window seat. The day was cheerful – quite warm for a change – and the view from my quarters was a fine one, down across the city to the port of Sigios and the isle of Tenedos.

'I wish I had your clout with Father, Paris,' Helenos said.

'Well, you are very junior, even if you are an imperial son. The view comes later in life.'

Not yet shaving, he was a beautiful youth, dark haired and very dark of eye, as were all of us who owned Hekabe for mother and called ourselves imperial. A twin, he occupied a curious position; very strange things were said about him and his other half, Kassandra. They were seventeen years old, which made him too much my junior for any real intimacy to have developed. Besides which, he and Kassandra had the Second Sight. An aura hung about them which rendered others, even

PARISих

their brothers and sisters, uncomfortable. This air was not so marked in Helenos as it was in Kassandra – as well for Helenos, really. Kassandra was crazy.

They had been consecrated to the service of Apollo as babes, and if either of them ever resented this arbitrary settling of their destinies, they never said so. According to the laws laid down by King Dardanos, the Oracles of Troy had to be held by a son and daughter of the King and his Queen, preferably twins. Which had made Helenos and Kassandra automatic choices. At the moment they still enjoyed a certain amount of liberty, but when they turned twenty they would be formally handed into the care of the trio who ruled the worship of Apollo in Troy: Kalchas, Lakoon and Antenor's wife, Theano.

Helenos wore the long, flowing robes of the Religious. With his dreamy expression allied to so much beauty he was sufficiently arresting to hold my attention as he sat surveying the city from my window. He liked me better than he did any of his other brothers – be they by Hekabe, by another wife, or by a concubine – because I had no taste for war and killing. Though his stern ascetic nature could not condone my philandering, he found my conversation much to his liking, more pacific than martial.

'I have a message for you,' he said without turning.

I sighed. 'What have I done now?'

'Nothing deserving censure. I was merely told to bid you to come to a meeting tonight after supper.'

'I can't. I have a prior engagement.'

'You had better break it. The message comes from Father.'

'Bother! Why me?'

'I have no idea. It's a very small group. Just a few of the imperial sons, plus Antenor and Kalchas.'

'An odd assortment. I wonder what's the matter?'

'Go, and you'll find out.'

'Oh, I will, I will! Are you invited?'

Helenos did not answer. His face had twisted, his eyes taken on the peculiar inward gaze of the mystic. Having seen this visionary trance before, I recognised it for what it was, and stared in fascination. Suddenly he shuddered, looked normal again.

'What did you see?' I asked.

'I could not see,' he said slowly, wiping sweat from his brow. 'A pattern, I sensed a pattern … The beginning of a twisting and turning that will go to an inevitable end.'

'You must have seen something, Helenos!'

'Flames … Greeks in armour … A woman so beautiful she must be Aphrodite … Ships – hundreds and hundreds of ships … You, Father, Hektor …'

'*Me?* But I'm not important!'

'Believe me, Paris, you are important,' he said in a tired voice, then got up abruptly. 'I must find Kassandra. Quite often we see the same things, even when we are not together.'

But I too felt a little of that dark, webbed Presence, and shook my head. 'No. Kassandra will destroy it.'

Helenos was correct in that the group was very small. I was the last to arrive, took a place on the end of the bench whereon sat my brothers Troilos and Ilios – why them? Troilos was eight years old, Ilios only seven. They were my mother's last two children, both named for the shadow man who had taken the throne from King Dardanos. Hektor was there. So too was our eldest brother of all, Deiphobos. By rights Deiphobos ought to have been named the Heir, but everyone who knew him – including Father – understood that within a year of ascending the throne he would bring everything down. Greedy, thoughtless, passionate, selfish, intemperate – those words were used of Deiphobos. How he hated us! Especially Hektor, who had usurped his rightful place – or so he saw it.

The inclusion of Uncle Antenor was logical. As Chancellor he attended every meeting of any sort. But why Kalchas? A very disturbing man.

Uncle Antenor was glaring at me, and not because I arrived last. Two summers ago on Ida I had loosed an arrow at a target pinned to a tree just as a wind boiled up out of nowhere; it deflected my dart far off to one side. I found it lodged in the back of Uncle Antenor's youngest son by his most beloved concubine; the poor lad had been hiding to spy on a shepherdess bathing naked in a spring. He was dead, and I guilty of involuntary murder. Not a crime in the true sense, but still a death which had to be expiated. The only way I could do that was to journey abroad and find a foreign king willing to undertake the ceremonies of purification. Uncle Antenor had not been able to demand vengeance, but he had not forgiven me. Which reminded me that I still had not taken that journey abroad to find that foreign king. Kings were the only priests qualified to conduct the rites of purification from accidental murder.

Father rapped the floor with the butt of his ivory sceptre, its round head flashing green because it contained a huge and perfect emerald. 'I have called this meeting to discuss something which has gnawed at me for many years,' he said in his firm, strong voice. 'What brought it to the forefront of my mind was the realisation that my son Paris was born on the very day it happened, thirty-three years ago. A day of death and deprivation. My father Laomedon was murdered. So too were my four brothers. My sister Hesione was abducted, raped. Only the birth of Paris saved it from being the darkest day of my life.'

'Father, why us?' Hektor asked gently. Of late, I had noticed, he had take it upon himself to bring our sire back to the subject when his mind wandered; it was beginning to display a tendency to do that.

'Oh, didn't I tell you? You because you are the Heir, Hektor. Deiphobos because he is my oldest imperial son. Helenos because he will hold the Oracles of Troy. Kalchas because he caretakes the Oracles until Helenos comes of age. Troilos and Ilios because Kalchas says there are prophecies about them. Antenor because he was there that day. And Paris because he was born on it.'

'Why are we here?' Hektor asked then.

'I intend to send a formal embassage to Telamon in Salamis as soon as the seas are safe,' Father said, it seemed to me with proper logic, though Hektor frowned as if the answer troubled him. 'That embassage will request that Telamon return my sister to Troy.'

A silence fell. Antenor went to stand between my bench and the other, then turned to my father on the throne. Poor man, he was bent almost double from a painful disease of the joints he had suffered time out of memory; everyone thought that its ravages were the reasons for his notoriously short temper. 'Sire, this is a silly venture,' he said flatly. 'Why spend Troy's gold on it? You know as well as I do that in all the thirty-three years of her exile, Hesione has never once indicated that she mourns her fate. Her son, Teukros, may be a bastard, but he stands very high in the Salaminian Court and acts as friend and mentor to the Salaminian Heir, Ajax. You will get no for an answer, Priam, so why go to the trouble?'

The King jumped to his feet, furious. 'Are you accusing me of stupidity, Antenor? It's news to me that Hesione is content in her exile! No, it's Telamon prevents her asking us for help!'

Antenor shook his gnarled fist. 'I have the floor, sire! I insist on the right of speech! Why do you go on thinking it was us wronged all those years ago? It was Herakles who was wronged, and in your heart you know it. I would also remind you that if Herakles had not slain the lion, Hesione would be dead.'

My father was trembling from head to foot. There was little love lost between him and Antenor, though they were brothers-in-law. Antenor remained a spiritual Dardanian, the enemy within.

'If you and I were young men,' my father said, biting off his words, 'there would be some point to our continuous warring. We could take up shields and swords and make an end. But you are a cripple and I am too old. I repeat: I am sending an embassage to Salamis as soon as I can. Is that understood?'

Antenor sniffed. 'You are the King, sire, the decision is yours. As for duels – you may like to call yourself too old, but how dare you assume that I am too crippled to make mincemeat of you? Nothing would give me greater pleasure!'

He walked out on the echo of his words; my father resumed his seat, chewing his beard.

I stood up, surprised that I did, but even more surprised by what I proceeded to say. 'Sire, I will volunteer to lead your embassage. I have to go abroad to seek purification for the death of Uncle Antenor's son anyway.'

Hektor laughed, clapped. 'Paris, I salute you!'

But Deiphobos scowled. 'Why not me, sire? It *ought* to be me! I am the eldest.'

Helenos entered the fray in Deiphobos's favour; I could hardly believe my ears, knowing how much Helenos detested our oldest brother.

'Father, send Deiphobos, please! If Paris goes, I know in my bones that Troy will weep tears of blood!'

Tears of blood or no, King Priam's mind was made up. He gave the task to me.

After the others had gone I lingered with him.

'Paris, I am delighted,' he said, stroking my hair.

'Then I am rewarded, Father.' Suddenly I laughed. 'If I cannot bring back my Aunt Hesione, perhaps I can bring back a Greek princess in her stead.'

Chuckling, he rocked back and forth in his chair; my little joke sat well with him. 'Greece abounds in princesses, my son. I admit it would twist the Greek tail perfectly if we made it an eye for an eye.'

I kissed his hand. His implacable hatred of Greece and all things Greek was a byword in Troy; I had made him happy. What matter if the pleasantry was empty, provided it made him chuckle?

Since it seemed the mild winter was going to end early, I went down to Sigios several days later to discuss the marshalling of a fleet with the captains and merchants who would comprise it. I wanted twenty big ships with full crews and empty holds; as the state was paying the bill, I knew I would have a host of eager applicants. Though I had not understood at the time what daimon prompted me to volunteer, I now found myself excited at the prospect of this adventure. Soon I would see places far away, places a Trojan did not hope ever to see. Greek places.

After the conference was over I strolled outside the harbour master's cottage to breathe in the sea-tanged, sharply cold air and watch the activities of that busy beach, the ships drawn up on the shingle during winter now swarming with teams of men whose duty was to inspect their pitched sides and ensure that they were seaworthy. A huge scarlet vessel was manoeuvring close to shore, the eyes upon its prow trying to stare me down, the figurehead tipping the curving cowl of its stern obviously my own special Goddess, Aphrodite. What shipwright had seen her in which dream, to have delineated her so marvellously?

Finally the master of the vessel found enough space to beach its heavy sides in the pebbles; down went the rope ladders. At which moment I noticed that the ship bore a royal standard in its bow, scarlet-encrusted and fringed with solid gold – it carried a foreign king! I walked forward slowly, twitching my cloak into elegant folds.

The royal person descended carefully. A Greek. That was evident in the way he dressed, the unconscious superiority which even the least Greek possessed when he encountered the rest of the world. But as the royal person drew closer I lost my initial awe. Such an ordinary-looking man! Not particularly tall, not particularly handsome, and *red-haired*. Yes, he was definitely a Greek. Half of them seemed to have red hair. His leather kilt was dyed purple and embossed with gold, the fringe hemming it was gold, his wide belt was gold studded with gems, his purple blouse was cut away to reveal a meagre chest, and around his neck he wore a great collar of gold and jewels. A very rich man.

When he saw me he altered his course.

'Welcome to the shores of Troy, royal sir,' I said formally. 'I am Paris, son of King Priam.'

He took my proffered arm and wrapped his fingers about it. 'Thank you, Highness. I am Menelaos, King of Lakedaimon and brother to Agamemnon, High King of Mykenai.'

My eyes widened. 'Would you ride to the city in my car, King Menelaos?' I asked.

My father was conducting his daily audiences and business. I whispered to the herald, who sprang to attention and flung the double doors open.

'King Menelaos of Lakedaimon!' he roared.

We went in together to face a crowd stilled to immobility. Hektor was standing at the back with his hand extended and his mouth open on an unuttered word, Antenor was half turned towards us, and my father was sitting bolt upright on his throne, his hand wrapped so tightly about his staff that the whole of it shook. If my companion got the idea that a Greek was not welcome here, he betrayed no sign of it; after I grew to know him better, I decided that he probably had not noticed. His glance around the room and its furnishings was unimpressed, which set me to wondering what Greek palaces were like.

My father came down from the dais, hand extended. 'We are honoured, King Menelaos,' he said. Pointing to a big couch strewn with cushions, Father took the visitor's arm. 'Would you care to sit down? Paris, join us, but first ask Hektor to join us too. And see refreshments are brought.'

The Court was very quiet, eyes speculative, but the talk at the couch was inaudible two paces away.

The politenesses completed, my father spoke. 'What brings you to Troy, King Menelaos?'

'A matter of vital importance to my people of Lakedaimon, King Priam. I know that what I seek is not in Trojan lands, but Troy seemed the best place to start my enquiries.'

'Ask.'

Menelaos leaned forward, turned side on so that he could look at my father's expressionless face. 'Sire, my kingdom is lashed by plague. When my own priests could not divine the cause of it, I sent to the Pythoness at Delphi. She told me that I must go in person to seek the bones of the sons of Prometheus and fetch them to Amyklai – my capital. They must be reinterred in Amyklai. Then the plague will cease.'

Ah! His mission had nothing to do with Aunt Hesione, or the scarcity of tin and copper, or trade embargoes in the Hellespont. His was a more mundane mission by far. Very common. Contending with plague called for extraordinary measures; there was always some King or other wandering the seas and shores looking for some object the Oracles said he must bring home. Sometimes I wondered if the whole purpose behind such an oracle was to ship the King off elsewhere until natural attrition brought disease to its inevitable end. A way of protecting the King from retribution; if he stayed at home he was likely to die of the same plague or find himself ritually lynched.

Of course King Menelaos had to be accommodated. Who knew whether next year it might be King Priam sent by the Oracle to ask help of King Menelaos? The Royal Kindred, no matter what their differences or nationalities, stuck together in certain situations. So while King Menelaos was made free of the city, my father's scouts went out to locate the bones of the sons of Prometheus, and learned that they resided in Dardania. King Anchises of Dardania protested bitterly, but that came to nothing. Whether he liked it or not, the designated relics would leave him.

I got the job of looking after Menelaos until he could journey in state to Lyrnessos and claim the bones. Which led to my offering him a customary courtesy: his choice of any woman he fancied provided she was not royal.

He laughed, shook his head emphatically. 'I need no other woman than my wife, Helen,' he said.

83

My ears pricked. 'Really?'

Face glowing, he looked besotted. 'I am married to the most beautiful woman in the world,' he said solemnly.

Though I looked polite, I managed to let my incredulity show, 'Really?'

'Yes, really, Paris. Helen has no peer.'

'Is she more beautiful than my brother Hektor's wife?'

'The Princess Andromache is dim Selene compared to the splendour of Helios,' he said.

'Tell me more.'

He sighed, flapped his arms. 'How can one describe Aphrodite? How can one paint visual perfection in mere words? Go down to my ship, Paris, and look at the figurehead. That is Helen.'

My eyes closed, remembering. But all I could envision was a pair of eyes as green as an Egyptian cat's.

I *had* to meet this paragon! Not that I believed him. The figurehead was bound to be superior to the model for it. No statue of Aphrodite I had ever seen could rival the figurehead's face (though, truth to tell, sculptors were a poor lot who would persist in endowing statues with fatuous smiles, stiff features and even stiffer bodies).

'Sire,' I said impulsively. 'Shortly I have to lead an embassage to Salamis, to see King Telamon and ask after the welfare of my Aunt Hesione. But while I am in Greece I also have to seek purification from an accidental killing. Is it far from Salamis to Lakedaimon?'

'Well, one is an island off the Attic shore and the other within the Isle of Pelops, but – no, it's a feasible journey.'

'Would you undertake to purify me, Menelaos?'

He beamed. 'Of course, of course! It is the least I can do to repay your kindness, Paris. Come to Lakedaimon in the summer and I will perform the rites.' He looked smug. 'You doubted me when I spoke of Helen's beauty – yes, you did! Your eyes gave you away. So come to Amyklai and see her for yourself. After which I expect an apology.'

We sealed the pact with a draught of wine, then became absorbed in planning the journey to Lyrnessos, there to dig up the bones of the sons of Prometheus under the indignant gaze of King Anchises and his son, Aineas. So Helen was as beautiful as Aphrodite, eh? I wondered how Anchises and Aineas would stomach *that* comparison when Menelaos came out with it, as he surely would. For everyone knew that in his youth Anchises himself had been so beautiful that Aphrodite stooped to make love to him. Then she went away and bore him Aineas. Well, well! How the follies of one's youth do return to haunt one.

CHAPTER SIX

NARRATED BY
HELEN

When the bones of the sons of Prometheus went into the ground of Amyklai surrounded by precious artefacts, each skull's grin shielded by a mask of gold, the plague began to diminish. How wonderful it was to be able to drive once more through the town, join the hunts in the mountains, watch the sports in the arena behind the palace! Wonderful too to see the people's faces wreathed in smiles, to hear them bless us as we moved among them. The King had cured the plague and all was well again.

Except with Helen. Menelaos lived with a shade. As the years passed I grew ever quieter, even graver – worthy and dutiful, always. I bore Menelaos two daughters and a son. He slept in my bed every night. I never refused him access to my apartments when he knocked. And he loved me. In his eyes I could do no wrong. Which was the reason why I remained a worthy and dutiful wife; I could not resist being treated like a goddess. There was another reason too; I liked my head joined to my shoulders.

If only I had been able to keep my body remote and cold when he came to me after our wedding! But I could not. Helen was a creature of the flesh, not proof against the touch of any man, even one as dreary and fumbling as my husband. Any man better than none.

Summer came, the hottest in living memory. The rains ceased and the streams dried up, the priests muttered ominously from the altars. We had survived plague; was famine to be next on the list of our human agonies? Twice I felt Poseidon Earth Shaker groan and move the bowels of the land, as if he too were restless. The people began to whisper of omens and the priests lifted their voices higher when the emmer wheat fell earless on the parched ground and the hardier barley threatened to follow.

But then as summer reached a peak of unrelenting heat, the sable-browed Thunderer spoke. On a breathless, suffocating day he sent his messengers the storm clouds, piling them up and up in the white metal sky. In the afternoon the sun went out, the gloom thickened; Zeus erupted at last. Roaring his might in our deafened ears, he flung his lightning bolts down to earth with a ferocity that made the Mother shiver and shrink, each shaft falling in a column of pure fire from his terrible hand.

Shaking with terror, sweating, praying in a babble, I huddled on a couch in the little room I used near the public areas and stoppered my ears while the thunder cracked and wild white light came and went. Menelaos, Menelaos, where are you?

Then in the distance I heard his voice, speaking with unusual animation to someone whose Greek was warped and lisping – someone foreign. I made a dash for the door and ran for my apartments, not wanting to incur displeasure; like all the ladies of the palace, I had taken in the heat to wearing a shift of transparent Egyptian linen.

Just before the dinner time Menelaos came to my rooms to watch me step into my bath. He never tried to touch me; this was his opportunity to do no more than look.

'My dear,' he said, clearing his throat, 'we have a visitor. Would you wear your state robes this evening?'

I stared, surprised. 'Is he so important?'

'Very. My friend Prince Paris from Troy.'

'Oh yes, I remember.'

'You must look your best, Helen, because I boasted of your beauty to him while I was in Troy. He was sceptical.'

Smiling, I rolled over, water slopping. 'I will look my best, husband, I promise.'

Which I was sure I did when I came into the dining hall a little before the Court assembled to take the last meal of daylight with the King and Queen. Menelaos was already there, standing near the high table talking to a man who had his back to me. A very interesting back. Much taller than Menelaos, he had a mane of thick, curly black hair falling halfway down his back, and he was bare from the waist up in Cretan style. A big collar of gems set in gold encircled his shoulders, both his powerful arms were clasped by cuffs of gold and crystal. I eyed his purple kilt, his well-shaped legs, and felt a stirring in me I had not experienced for many years. From the back he looked good; but probably, I thought wryly, he would be horse faced.

When I brushed my flounces to make them chime both men turned around. I looked at the visitor and fell in love. It was that simple, that easy. I fell in love. If I was the perfect woman, he was surely the perfect man. I gazed at him quite stupidly. No fault. Absolute perfection. And I was in love.

'My dear,' said Menelaos, coming to me, 'this is Prince Paris. We must extend him every courtesy and attention – he was an excellent host to me in Troy.' He looked at Paris, brows up. 'And, my friend, do you still doubt me?'

'No,' said Paris. And again, 'No.'

His evening made, Menelaos beamed.

A nightmare, that dinner! The wine flowed freely, though (being a woman) I could not partake of it. But what mischievous God put it into Menelaos's head to guzzle it when he was usually so abstemious? Paris was seated between us, which meant I could not get close enough to my husband to gentle him away from his goblet. Nor did this Trojan Prince behave with circumspection. Of course I had seen the attraction flare in his black eyes the moment they settled upon me; but many men reacted similarly, then afterward became timid. Not Paris. Throughout the meal he paid me outrageous compliments, his glances unashamedly intimate, apparently oblivious to the fact that we sat at the high table being watched by a hundred men and women of the Court.

In a tumult of fear and distraction, I tried to make it seem to those observers (more than half of whom were Agamemnon's spies) that nothing untoward was going on. Trying to be civil and offhand, I asked Paris what life was like in Troy – did all the nations of Asia Minor speak a kind of Greek? – how far away from Troy were places like Assyria and Babylon? – did those countries know Greek too?

No fool with women, he answered easily and with authority while his wicked eyes roamed and roved from my lips to my hair, from my fingertips to my breasts.

As the interminable meal wore on Menelaos grew slurred in speech, seemed to see nothing beyond the brimming contents of his cup. And Paris grew bolder. He leaned so close to me that I could feel his breath on my shoulder, smell its sweetness. I moved until I encountered the end of the bench.

'The Gods are cruel,' he whispered, 'to give so much beauty into the keeping of one man.'

'My lord, mind what you say! I beg you, be discreet!'

For answer, he smiled. My chest caved in, I pressed my knees together on a sudden hotness.

'I saw you this afternoon,' he went on as if I had not said anything, 'fleeing away from us in your gauzy gown.'

The scarlet flooded up beneath my skin; I prayed no one on the floor of the hall noticed.

His hand dropped and found my arm. I jumped, the touch unbearable, the sensation coursing through me akin to what I felt when the Thunderer spoke.

'My lord, *please*! My husband will hear you!'

As he laughed he put his hand back on the board, but so abruptly that the goblet at his elbow tumbled over; the red wine in it spread in a lake across the pale wood. Even as I beckoned to a servant to clean it up, he was leaning towards me.

'I love you, Helen,' he said.

89

Had the servants heard? Why were their faces always so impassive while they waited on their betters? I glanced at Menelaos; he sat staring sleepily at nothing, very drunk.

Too drunk to come to me that night. His men carried him to his own apartments and left me to find my way alone to mine. For a long time I sat on the window seat in my parlour, thinking. What to do? How to get through the next however many days this dangerous man would be here? After a single meal in his company I was undone. He stalked me fearlessly, deeming my husband too big a fool to catch him out. But that was the wine, and I knew tomorrow's dinner would see Menelaos sober. Even the most foolish of men has his share of vigilance; besides which, one of the house barons was bound to say something to him. They were paid by Agamemnon to notice everything. Let even one of them decide that I was unfaithful, and Agamemnon would know within a day. Trojan Prince or no, Paris would lose his head. So would I. *So would I!*

Torn between fear and longing, I writhed. Oh, how much I loved him! But what kind of love came so suddenly, without any warning? Pure lust I could resist; I had learned that over the course of my marriage. Love, on the other hand, was irresistible. I yearned to be with Paris for every reason. I yearned to spend my life with him. I wanted to know how he thought, how he lived, how he felt, how he looked while he slept. The arrow had pierced me, the arrow which had driven Phaidra to kill herself, Danai to step into a box her father flung into the sea, Orpheus to brave the kingdom of Hades in search of Eurydike. My life was not my own; it belonged to Paris. I would die for him! Yet … What ecstasy to be able to *live* for him!

Menelaos came into my bedroom a few moments after I had climbed wearily into my bed, while the cocks were crowing raucously and the rim of the eastern sky was pale amid mist. Looking sheepish, he refused to kiss me.

'My breath stinks of wine, beloved, I would offend you. Odd, that I drank so much. There was no need.'

I drew him down to sit beside me. 'How are you this morning, aside from your breath?'

He grinned. 'A little unwell.' Amusement fled; a frown arrived. 'Helen, I have a problem.'

My mouth went dry; I felt myself lick my lips. One of the house barons had told him! Words! I *must* find words! 'A problem?' I croaked.

'Yes. A messenger from Crete woke me. My grandfather Katreus has died there, and Idomeneus is delaying the funeral until either Agamemnon or I can come. Naturally he expects to see me. Agamemnon is tied to Mykenai.'

I sat up, mouth fallen open. 'Menelaos! You cannot go!'

My vehemence surprised him, but he took it as a compliment. 'There is no alternative, Helen. I have to go to Crete.'

'Will you be away long?'

'Half a year at least – I wish you knew more geography. The autumn winds will blow me down, but I will have to wait for the summer winds to blow me back.'

'Oh,' I said, and sighed. 'When must you leave?'

He squeezed my arm. 'Today, my dearest. I'll have to go to Mykenai to see Agamemnon first, and since I'll sail from Lerna or Nauplia, I won't be able to return here before I sail. Such a pity,' he rambled, delighted at my consternation.

'But you can't go, Menelaos. You have a house guest.'

'Paris will understand. I'll perform the purification rites this morning before I leave for Mykenai, but I'll also make sure he feels at liberty to remain here as long as he likes.'

'Take him to Mykenai with you,' I said, inspired.

'Helen, really! In such a hurry? Of course he should go to Mykenai, but at his leisure,' said my foolish husband, anxious to please his guest but blind to the peril his guest represented.

'Menelaos, you cannot abandon me with Paris here!' I cried.

He blinked. 'Why not? You're well chaperoned, Helen.'

'Agamemnon may not think so.'

My hand was wrapped about his forearm; he leaned to kiss it, smooth my hair. 'Helen, rest easy. Your concern is charming, but unnecessary. I trust you. Agamemnon trusts you.'

How could I explain that I did not trust myself?

That afternoon I stood at the foot of the palace steps and said farewell to my husband. Paris was nowhere to be seen.

Once the chariots and carts had disappeared into the far distance I went to my rooms and stayed there. My meals were brought to me. If Paris did not set eyes on me he might grow tired of the game he played, take himself off to Mykenai or Troy. Nor would the house barons have any opportunity to see us together.

But when night fell I could not sleep. Up and down the bedroom I prowled, pacing, then went to the window. Amyklai lay in utter darkness, no lamp burning anywhere, and the mountains were anonymous humps against the starstruck sky. A full moon hung huge and silver, silently pouring delicate light into the Vale of Lakedaimon. Drawing all this in with deep breaths of pleasure, I leaned my head out of the opening to let the stillness invade my bones. And with that enchantment still in me I sensed him behind me, watching the beauty of the heavens over my shoulder. I neither cried out nor turned round, but he knew the moment in which I became aware of his presence. His hands cupped my elbows, he drew me gently to rest against him.

'Helen of Amyklai, you are as beautiful as Aphrodite.'

My body went limp, I moved my head a little under his cheek. 'Do not tempt that Goddess, Paris. She dislikes rivals.'

'She doesn't dislike you. Don't you understand? Aphrodite has given you to me. I belong to her, I am her darling.'

'Is that why they say you have never sired a child?'

'Yes.' His hands at my waist moved in slow circles, unhurried, as if he had all the days of the world in which to make love to me. His lips found my neck. 'Helen, have you never longed to be out there in the night, in the deep forest? Have you never craved the fleetness of a deer? Have you never wished to run free as the wind, fall exhausted under the body of the only man?'

My sinews leaped in response, but I said, mouth dry, 'No. I never dream of things like that.'

'I do. About you. I can see your long pale hair streaming in your wake, your long limbs striving to keep ahead of me in the chase. I should have met you so, not in this empty, lifeless palace.' He parted my gown; the palms of his hands rested light as feathers against my breasts. 'You have washed away the paint.'

And that was the breaking point. I turned then into his arms and forgot everything save the fact that he was my natural mate. That I loved him, truly loved him.

His willing slave, I lay in his arms as limply as my little daughter's rag doll, and wished the dawn away.

'Come back to Troy with me,' he said suddenly.

I raised myself to see his face, saw my own love returned in those wonderful dark eyes. 'That is madness,' I said.

'No, it is good sense.' One hand lingered on my belly, the other toyed with my hair. 'You don't belong with an unfeeling clod like Menelaos. You belong to me.'

'I am born of this land, I am born of this very room. I am the Queen. My children are here.' I brushed my tears away.

'Helen, you belong to Aphrodite, just as I do! Once I swore a solemn oath to her, to give her everything – I abrogated Here and Pallas Athene in her favour if she would grant me whatever I asked. And all I ask of her is you.'

'I *cannot* leave!'

'You cannot stay. *I* will not be here.'

'Oh, I love you! How can I live without you?'

'There's no question of living without me, Helen.'

'You ask the impossible,' I wept, tears falling ever faster.

'Nonsense! What's so difficult? Leaving your children?'

That gave me pause; I answered honestly. 'Not really. No.

The trouble is, they're so plain! They take after Menelaos, right down to their hair. And they're *freckled*.'

'Then if it's not your children, it must be Menelaos.'

Was it? No. Poor, downtrodden, dominated Menelaos, ruled with a hand of iron from Mykenai. What did I owe him after all? I had never wanted to marry him. I owed him no more than I owed his beetle-browed brother, that forbidding man who used us like pieces in some monumental game. Agamemnon cared nothing for me – my wants, my needs, my feelings.

I said, 'I will come to Troy with you. There is nothing for me here. Nothing.'

CHAPTER SEVEN

NARRATED BY
HEKTOR

The harbour master at Sigios sent word to me that Paris's fleet had returned from Salamis at last; when I joined the day's assembly I sent a page to whisper the news to my father. It was the usual wearisome, leisurely audience – disputes over property, slaves, land and so forth – an embassage from Babylon to be received – a complaint about grazing rights from our noble relatives in Dardania, put forward as always by Uncle Antenor.

The Babylonian embassage had been dealt with and dismissed and the King was about to deliver judgement on some trifling matter when the horns blared and Paris strutted into the Throne Room. I could not help smiling at his appearance; he had gone Cretan with a vengeance. The complete dandy, from his bullion-fringed purple kilt to his jewels and curls. He looked very well and very pleased with himself. What mischief had he been up to, to look like a jackal getting to the kill ahead of the lion? Of course our father was gazing at him with doting favour – how could a man wise enough to sit upon a throne be so blinded by mere charm and beauty?

Paris strolled down the length of the hall to the dais and was already settling himself on the top step as I drew near. That incurable stickybeak Antenor was also edging up within hearing distance. I went to stand openly beside the throne.

'Have you good news, my son?' the King asked.

'Not about Aunt Hesione,' said Paris, shaking his head, his ringlets bouncing. 'King Telamon was courteous to me, but made it very clear that he will not give up Aunt Hesione.'

The King stiffened dangerously. How deep did that old hatred go? Why, even after so many years, did Father continue to be implacably turned against Greece? The hiss of his indrawn breath silenced the whole room.

'How dare he! How dare Telamon insult me! Did you see your aunt, have the chance to speak with her?'

'No, Father.'

'Then I curse them all!' He reared his head at the roof and closed his eyes. 'O mighty Apollo, Lord of Light, Ruler of Sun and Moon and Stars, grant me the chance to bring down Greek pride!'

I leaned over the throne. 'Sire, calm yourself! Surely you expected no other answer?'

Twisting his head to see me, he opened his eyes. 'No, I suppose not. Thank you, Hektor. As always you draw my attention to cold reality. But why should the Greeks have it all, tell me that? Why should they be able to kidnap a Trojan princess?'

Paris put his hand on Father's knee, tapped it gently. Gazing down at him, the King's face softened.

'Father, I have fittingly punished Greek arrogance,' said Paris, eyes brilliant.

I had been about to move away, but something in his tone arrested me.

'How, my son?'

'An eye for an eye, sire! An eye for an eye! The Greeks stole your sister, so I have brought you a prize out of Greece greater by far than any fifteen-year-old girl!' He jumped to his feet, so full of himself that he couldn't bear to sit at King Priam's feet a moment longer. 'Sire,' he cried, his voice ringing round the rafters, 'I have brought you Helen! Queen of Lakedaimon, wife to Menelaos the brother of Agamemnon and sister to Agamemnon's queen, Klytemnestra!'

I reeled in shock, unable to find words. That was a tragedy, for it gave Uncle Antenor the chance to get in first. He leaped forward, the swollen joints of his hands making them seem like huge, misshapen claws.

'You stupid, ignorant, meddling fool!' Antenor roared. 'You pansy-faced philanderer! Why didn't you really make it worth your while, kidnap Klytemnestra herself? The Greeks lie down meekly enough under our trade embargoes and their own shortages of tin and copper, but do you expect them to lie down under this as well? *You fool!* You've handed Agamemnon the opportunity he has waited years for! You've plunged us into a conflagration that will be the ruin of Troy! You brainless, conceited idiot! Why didn't your father expose you? Why didn't he stop your profligate career before it started? By the time that we have reaped all the consequences of this, no Trojan will utter your name without spit!'

Half of me applauded the old man silently; he voiced my sentiments exactly. Yet I cursed Uncle Antenor too. What might my father have decided if he had held his tongue? Where Antenor found fault, the King inclined to favour. No matter what Father thought privately, Antenor had pushed him onto Paris's side.

Paris was standing thunderstruck. 'Father, I did it for you!' he beseeched.

Antenor sneered. 'Oh, yes, of course you did! And have you forgotten the most famous of all our oracles? *"Beware the woman taken out of Greece as a prize for Troy!"* Doesn't that speak for itself?'

'No, I did not forget it!' my brother shouted. 'Helen is no prize! She came with me willingly! She wasn't the victim of an abduction, she came with me willingly because she wants to marry me! And as evidence of that, she brought a great treasure with her – gold and jewels enough to buy a kingdom! A dowry, Father, a dowry!' He giggled. 'I did the Greeks a far worse insult than to kidnap a queen – I *cuckolded* them!'

Antenor looked done. Shaking his white thatch slowly, he slunk back into the ranks of the Court. Paris was gazing at me urgently, imploringly.

'Hektor, support me!'

'How can I do that?' I asked through my teeth.

He turned, slipped to his knees and wrapped both arms about the King's legs. 'What harm can possibly come of it, Father?' he wheedled. 'When has the voluntary flight of a woman ever meant war? Helen comes of her own free will! Nor is she a green girl! Helen is twenty years old! She has been married for six years – she has children! And can you imagine how terrible her life must have been, to leave a kingdom and her children behind? Father, I love her! And she loves me!' His voice broke pathetically, the tears began to fall.

Tenderly the King touched Paris's hair, stroked it, patted it. 'I will see her,' he said.

'No, wait!' Antenor came forward again. 'Sire, before you see this woman, I insist that you hear me! Send her home, Priam, send her home! Send her back to Menelaos sight unseen – send her back with sincere apologies, all the treasure she has brought with her, and a recommendation that her head be separated from her neck. She deserves nothing less. *Love!* What kind of love can leave children behind? Doesn't that say something? She brings Troy a great treasure, but not her children!'

My father wouldn't look at him, but he must have known how the rest of us were feeling, for he made no attempt to stop the tirade. So Antenor swept on.

'Priam, I fear the High King of Mykenai, and so should you! Surely last year you heard the selfsame Menelaos prattle about how Agamemnon has welded the whole of Greece into an obedient vassal of Mykenai? What if he should decide on war? Even if we beat him, he will ruin us. Troy's wealth has increased for time immemorial for one reason – Troy has avoided going to war. Wars bankrupt nations, Priam – I have heard you say so yourself! The oracle states that the woman out of Greece is our downfall. Yet you ask to see her! Take heed of our Gods! Listen to the wisdom of their oracles! What are oracles, except the God-given chance for mortal men to see into the future pattern on the loom of time? You have taken the work of your father, Laomedon, and worsened it – whereas he merely restricted the number of Greek merchants allowed into the Euxine, you have stopped them altogether. The Greeks *starve* for sufficient tin! Yes, they can get copper from the West – at immense cost! – but they cannot get tin. Which does not negate the fact that they are wealthy and powerful.'

Face streaming tears, Paris lifted his head to the King. 'Father, I have told you! Helen is not a prize! She comes of her own free will! Therefore she cannot be the woman of the oracles – she cannot!'

This time I managed to get in ahead of Antenor, and came down from the dais to do so. '*You* say she comes of her own free will, Paris – but is that what they will say in Greece? Do you think Agamemnon will tell his subject Kings that his brother is that most ridiculous of all men, a cuckold? Not Agamemnon, with his pride! No, Agamemnon will give it out that she was abducted. Antenor is right, Father. We are poised on the brink of war. Nor can we view a war with Greece as something affecting us alone. We have allies, Father! We are a part of the Asia Minor federation of states. We have treaties of trade and friendship with every coastal nation between Dardania and Kilikia, as well as inland as far as Assyria, and north into Skythia. The coastal lands are rich and underpopulated – they haven't the manpower to fend off Greek invaders. They aid us in our blockade and they have grown fat off selling tin and copper to the Greeks. In the event of war, do you think Agamemnon will confine himself to Troy? No! It will be war everywhere!'

Father regarded me steadily; I looked back without fear. Only a short while ago he had said, 'Always you draw my attention to cold reality.' But now, I thought in despair, he had abandoned reality. All Antenor and I had managed to do was set his back up.

'I have heard all I care to,' he said icily. 'Herald, send in Queen Helen.'

We waited, the hall as still and silent as a tomb. I glared at my brother Paris, wondering how we had let him become such a fool. He had turned on the dais (though he kept one hand on our father's knee, caressing it) and was staring fixedly at the doors, his mouth curved into a smug grin. Clearly he thought we were in for a surprise, and I remembered Menelaos's saying that she was a beautiful woman. But I always had my reservations when men called queens or princesses beautiful. Too many of them inherited that epithet along with their titles.

The doors swung open, she stood on the threshold a moment before she commenced to walk towards the throne. Her skirt chimed with a delicate tinkling as she moved, turned her into a living melody. I found I was holding my breath, had to force myself to exhale. She truly was the most beautiful woman I have ever seen. Even Antenor was gaping.

Shoulders back and head imperiously level, she walked with dignity and grace, neither shamed nor shy. Tall for a woman, she had the most superb body Aphrodite had ever lavished on any female creature. Tiny waist, graciously swelling hips, long legs thrusting at her skirt. No, there was nothing about her did not please. Her breasts! Bare in the immodest Greek way, high and full, they owed nothing to artifice save that their nipples were painted gold. Time elapsed before any of us got as far as that swanlike neck, her face above it. Superlatives, too many superlatives! As I remember her on that day, she was just ... *beautiful*. Masses of pale gold hair, dark brows and lashes, eyes the colour of springtime grass rimmed with kohl drawn outward in the manner of Cretans and Egyptians.

But how much of it was actual, how much of it a spell? That I will never know. Helen is the greatest work of art the Gods have ever put upon Mother Earth.

For my father she was Fate. Not so far gone in old age that he had forgotten the pleasures to be had in the arms of a woman, he looked at her and fell in love with her. Or in lust. But because he was too old to steal her from his son, he chose instead to take it as a compliment to himself that a son of his could lure her from her husband, her children, her own lands. Swelling with pride, he turned his wondering eyes upon Paris.

They were certainly a striking pair: he as dark as Ganymede, she as fair as Artemis of the forest. Without doing more than take a little stroll, Helen won the silent room completely over. No man there could continue to blame Paris for his foolishness.

The moment the King dismissed the assembly I went to his side, deliberately mounting the dais at its far end and approaching the throne slowly, three steps higher up than the elopers and taller by far than my father's gold and ivory chair. I did not usually parade my pre-eminence, but Helen set my teeth on edge; I wanted her to know exactly whereabouts Paris stood – and where I stood. As she watched me she raised her strange, fathomless green eyes to my face.

'My dear child, this is Hektor, my Heir,' said Father.

She inclined her head gravely and regally. 'It is a great pleasure, Hektor.' Her eyes grew coquettishly round. 'My, what a *big* man you are!'

It was said to provoke, but not to provoke want in me; her taste obviously ran to pretty milksops like Paris, not to massive warriors like me. Just as well. I wasn't sure I could resist her.

'The biggest in Troy, lady,' I said stiffly.

She laughed. 'I do not doubt it.'

'Sire,' I said to my father, 'will you excuse me?'

He crackled. 'Aren't my sons magnificent, Queen Helen? This one is the pride of my heart – a great man! One day he will be a great king.'

Eyeing me thoughtfully, she said nothing; but behind her lustrous gaze the mind clearly wondered whether it might not be possible to unseat me as Heir, put Paris in my place. I let her wonder. Time would teach her that Paris wanted no part of any responsibility.

I was already at the door when the King called after me, 'Wait, wait! Hektor, send Kalchas to me.'

A puzzling command. Why did the King want that repulsive

man, if he did not also want Lakoon and Theano? There were many Gods in our city, but our own special deity was Apollo. His cult was peculiarly Trojan, which made his special priests – Kalchas, Lakoon and Theano – the most powerful prelates in Troy.

I found Kalchas walking sedately in the shadow of the altar dedicated to Zeus of the Courtyard. Nor did I question why he was there; he was the kind of man no one presumed to question. For a few moments I watched him unobserved, trying to divine his true nature. He wore long, flowing black robes embroidered with strange symbols and signs in silver, and the sickly white skin of his completely bald head shone dully in the last light of day. Once I discovered a nest of pure white snakes far underground in the palace crypt, when I had been a boy and up to all kinds of mischief. But after encountering those blinded, attenuated creatures of Kore I never ventured into the crypt again. Kalchas aroused exactly the same feelings in me.

It was said that he had travelled the length and breadth of the world, from the Hyperboreans to the River of Ocean, to lands far east of Babylon and lands far south of Aithiopai. His mode of dress came from Ur and Sumer, and in Egypt he had witnessed the rituals which had been handed down the ranks of those illustrious priests since the beginning of Gods and men. Other things were whispered of him: that he could preserve a body so well it looked as fresh a hundred years later as it did the day it was interred; that he had participated in the awful rites of black Set; even that he had kissed the phallus of Osiris, and so gained supreme insight. I could never like him.

I emerged from the pillars, walked out into the yard. He knew who approached, though he never once looked my way.

'You seek me, Prince Hektor?'

'Yes, holy priest. The King wants you in the Throne Room.'

'To interview the woman out of Greece. I will come.'

I preceded him – as was my right – for I had heard tell of priests who came to fancy themselves powers behind thrones; I wanted no such hope to enter Kalchas's mind.

While Helen regarded him with uneasy revulsion, he kissed my father's hand and awaited his pleasure.

'Kalchas, my son Paris has brought home a bride. I want you to marry them tomorrow.'

'As you command, sire.'

Next the King dismissed Paris and Helen. 'Go now and show Helen her new home,' he said to my stupid brother.

They went out hand in hand. I averted my eyes. Kalchas stood unmoving, silent.

'Do you know who she is, priest?' my father asked.

'Yes, sire. Helen. The woman taken as a prize out of Greece. I have been expecting her.'

Had he? Or were his spies as efficient as always?

'Kalchas, I have a mission for you.'

'Yes, sire.'

'I need the advice of the Pythoness at Delphi. Go there after the wedding ceremony and find out what Helen means to us.'

'Yes, sire. I am to obey the Pythoness?'

'Of course. She is the Mouth of Apollo.'

And what exactly was all that about? I wondered. Who was fooling whom? Back to Greece for the answers. It always seemed to go back to Greece. Was the Delphic Oracle the servant of Trojan Apollo or Grecian Apollo? Were they even the same God?

The priest gone, I was alone with Father at last.

'You do a sorry thing, sire,' I said.

'No, Hektor, I do the only thing I can.' His hands went out. 'Surely you see that I cannot send her back? The damage is done, Hektor. It was done the moment she left her palace at Amyklai.'

'Then don't send all of her back, Father. Just her head.'

'It is too late,' he answered, already drifting away. 'It is too late. Too late ...'

CHAPTER EIGHT

NARRATED BY

AGAMEMNON

My wife stood at the high window, bathed in sunlight. It touched her hair with the blaze of new copper, as burning and brilliant as she was herself. She did not have Helen's beauty, no, but for me her attractions were more interesting, her sex stronger. Klytemnestra was a living font of power, not a simple ornament.

The view always drew her, perhaps because it spoke of the exalted position Mykenai owned. Above all other citadels. It looked down the Lion Mountain to the Vale of Argos, green with crops, then up to the ranges all about us, heavily forested with pine above the olive groves.

A commotion began outside; I could hear the voices of my guards protesting that the King and Queen did not wish to be disturbed. Frowning, I got up, but had not taken a step before the door burst open and Menelaos stumbled in. He came straight to me, put his head against my thighs and sobbed. My eyes flew to Klytemnestra, staring at him in astonishment.

'What is it?' I asked, pulling him from his knees and settling him in a chair.

But all he could do was weep. His hair was matted and dirty, his clothing unkempt, and he wore a three days' beard. Klytemnestra poured a full goblet of unwatered wine and handed it to me. When he had drunk he calmed a little, ceased to sob so wildly.

'Menalaos, what is the matter?'

'Helen is gone!'

Klytemnestra sprang away from the window. '*Dead?*'

'No, gone! Gone! She has gone, Agamemnon! Left me!' He sat up, made an effort to compose himself.

'Tell me slowly, Menelaos,' I said.

'I returned from Crete three days ago. She wasn't there ... She's run away, brother – gone to Troy with Paris.'

We gaped at him, mouths open.

'Gone to Troy with Paris,' I repeated when I was able.

'Yes, yes! She took the contents of the treasury and fled!'

'I don't believe it,' I said.

'Oh, I do! The stupid, lusting harpy!' Klytemnestra hissed. 'What more could we expect, when she ran off with Theseus? Slut! Harlot! Amoral bitch!'

'Hold your tongue, woman!'

She showed me her teeth, but she obeyed.

'When was this, Menelaos? Surely not five moons ago!'

'Almost six – the day after I left for Crete.'

'That's impossible! I admit I haven't been to Amyklai in your absence, but I have good friends there – word of it would have been sent to me at once.'

'She put the Evil Eye on them, Agamemnon. She went to the Oracle of Mother Kubaba and induced it to say that I had usurped her right to the throne of Lakedaimon. Then she induced Mother Kubaba to put a curse on my barons. No one dared to tell.'

I crushed my rage. 'So they still lie under the thumb of the Mother and the Old Religion in Lakedaimon, do they? I'll soon fix that! Over five moons gone ...' I shrugged. 'Well, we won't get her back now.'

'*Not get her back?*' Menelaos leaped to confront me. 'Not get her back? Agamemnon, you are the High King! You must get her back!'

'Did she take the children?' Klytemnestra asked.

'No,' he said. 'Just the contents of the treasury.'

'Which shows you whereabouts her priorities lie,' my wife snarled. 'Forget her! You're better off without her, Menelaos.'

He went down on his knees, weeping again. 'I want her back!

AGAMEMNON

I want her back, Agamemnon! Give me an army! Give me an army and let me sail for Troy!'

'Get up, brother! Take hold of yourself.'

'Give – me – an – army!' he said through his teeth.

I sighed. 'Menelaos, this is a personal thing. I can't give you an army for the purpose of bringing a whore to justice! I admit every Greek has good reason to hate Troy and Trojans, but none of my subject Kings would deem the voluntary flight of Helen sufficient reason to go to war.'

'All I'm asking for is an army made up of your troops and mine, Agamemnon!'

'Troy would chew them up. Priam's army is said to number fifty thousand soldiers,' I said reasonably.

Klytemnestra's elbow dug me sharply in the ribs. 'Husband, have you forgotten the Oath?' she asked. 'Raise an army on the Oath of the Quartered Horse! A hundred Kings and Princes swore it.'

I opened my mouth to inform her that women were fools, then shut it with the words unsaid. The Throne Room was not far away; I walked to it and sat myself down on the Lion Chair, grasped its pawed arms and thought.

Only the day before I had received a deputation of kings from all over Greece, wailing to me that continued closure of the Hellespont had brought them to such a pass that they could no longer afford to buy tin and copper from the states of Asia Minor. Our reserves of the metals – particularly tin – had sunk to nothing; ploughshares were being made of wood and knives of bone. If the nations of Greece were to survive, Troy's policy of deliberate exclusion from the Euxine could not be allowed to continue. To north and west the barbarian tribes were massing, ready to pour down and exterminate us, just as we had once poured down and exterminated the original Greeks. And where would we find the bronze to make the millions more of weapons we would need to fend them off?

I had listened, then promised to find a solution. Knowing that there was no solution short of war – but knowing too that

106

many among the Kings who had made up that deputation would sheer away from the most desparate of measures. Now today I had the means. Klytemnestra had shown me how. I was a man in my prime and I had seen my fair share of war, been good at it too. I could lead an invasion of Troy! Helen would serve as my excuse. Sly Odysseus had foreseen it seven years ago when he had told dead Tyndareus to demand an oath of Helen's suitors.

If my name was to endure after my death, I had to leave great deeds behind me. What greater deed than to invade and conquer Troy? The Oath would yield me close to a hundred thousand soldiers – enough men to do the job in ten days. And with Troy in ruins, what was to stop my turning my attention to the coastal states of Asia Minor, reduce them to satellites in a Greek empire? I thought of the bronze, the gold, the silver, the electrum, the jewels, the lands to be had. Mine for the taking if I invoked the Oath of the Quartered Horse. Yes, it lay in my power to carve out an empire for my people.

My wife and brother stood regarding me from the floor of the hall; I sat up straight and looked stern.

'Helen was kidnapped,' I said.

Menelaos shook his head miscrably. 'I wish she had been, Agamemnon, but she wasn't. Helen needed no coercion.'

I suppressed a strong inclination to drub him as I had when we were boys. By the Mother, he was a fool! How had our father, Atreus, sired a fool like Menelaos?

'I don't care what *really* happened!' I snapped. 'You will say that she was abducted, Menelaos. The slightest hint that her flight was voluntary would ruin everything, surely you can see that? If you obey my orders and follow me without argument, I will undertake to raise an army on the strength of the Oath.'

One moment extinguished, the next on fire; Menelaos glowed. 'Yes, Agamemnon, yes!'

I glanced at Klytemnestra, who smiled sourly. Both of us had fools for siblings, and both of us understood that.

A servant hovered too far away to eavesdrop; I clapped my hands to bring him closer. 'Send Kalchas to me,' I said.

The priest entered a few moments later to prostrate himself. I stared down at the back of his neck, wondering again what had really brought him to Mykenai. He was a Trojan of the highest nobility, who until a short time ago had been high priest of Apollo at Troy. When he went on a pilgrimage to Delphi, the Pythoness had instructed him to serve Apollo in Mykenai. He had been ordered not to return to Troy, nor to serve Trojan Apollo again. After he presented himself to me I sent to Delphi to check his story; the Pythoness confirmed it unequivocally. Kalchas was to be my man in future because the Lord of Light willed it so. Certainly he had given me no cause to suspect him of treachery. Endowed with the Second Sight, he had told me only a few days ago that my brother would come in great trouble.

His appearance was unpleasant, for he was that rarity of rarities, a true albino. His head was hairless, his skin white as the belly of a sea-dwelling fish. The eyes were dark pink and very crossed in a large round face which bore a permanent expression of blank stupidity. Misleading; Kalchas was far from stupid.

As he straightened I tried to plumb his mind, but there was nothing to see in those clouded, blind-looking eyes.

'Kalchas, when exactly did you leave King Priam's service?'

'Five moons ago, sire.'

'Had Prince Paris returned from Salamis?'

'No, sire.'

'You may go.'

He stiffened, outraged at being dismissed so summarily; it was plain that he was used to more deference in Troy. But Troy worshipped Apollo as All High, whereas in Mykenai the All High was Zeus. How it must gall him, a Trojan, to be obliged by Apollo to serve where he could not give his heart.

I clapped my hands again. 'Send in the chief herald.'

Menelaos sighed, reminding me that he still stood before me;

though I had not forgotten for one instant that Klytemnestra was still standing there.

'Take heart, brother. We'll get her back. The Oath of the Quartered Horse is unbreakable. You'll have your army in the spring of next year.'

The chief herald came.

'Herald, you will send messages to every King and Prince in Greece and Crete who swore the Oath of the Quartered Horse to King Tyndareus seven years ago. The clerk of oaths has their names in his memory. Your messengers will recite what I dictate, which is as follows: "King – Prince, lord, whoever – I, your suzerain, Agamemnon King of Kings, command that you come at once to Mykenai to discuss the oath you swore at the betrothal of Queen Helen to King Menelaos." Have you got that?'

Proud of his verbatim memory, the chief herald nodded. 'I have, sire.'

'Then get on with it.'

Klytemnestra and I got rid of Menelaos by telling him that he needed a bath. Off he went happily; big brother Agamemnon had the situation well in hand, so he could relax.

'High King of Greece is a mighty title,' said Klytemnestra, 'but High King of the Greek Empire sounds even mightier.'

I grinned. 'So I think, wife.'

'I like the idea of Orestes's inheriting it,' she mused.

And that summed Klytemnestra up. In her savage heart she was a leader, my Queen, a woman who found it galling to have to bow to the will of one even stronger than she was herself. I was quite aware of her ambitions; how much she longed to sit in my place, revive the Old Religion and use the King as nothing more than a living symbol of her fertility. Send him to the Axe when the land groaned under misfortune. The cult of Mother Kubaba was never far from the surface in the Isle of Pelops. Our son, Orestes, was very young, and came after I had despaired of one. His two sisters, Elektra and Chrysothemis, were already in the throes of puberty when he was born. The male child was a blow to Klytemnestra; she had hoped to rule through Elektra, though of late she had transferred her affections to Chrysothemis. Elektra adored her father, not her mother. However, Klytemnestra was extremely resourceful. Now that Orestes, a strong babe, seemed sure to succeed me, his mother hoped that I would die before he came of age. Then she would rule through him. Or through our youngest girl, Iphigenia.

Some of the men who had sworn the Oath of the Quartered Horse arrived in Mykenai before Menelaos returned from Pylos with King Nestor. It was a long way from Mykenai to Pylos, there were kingdoms much closer at hand. Palamedes the son of Nauplios came quickly, and I was glad to see him. Only Odysseus and Nestor exceeded him in wisdom.

I was speaking to Palamedes in the Throne Room when a stir erupted among the small cluster of lesser Kings on the floor of the hall. Palamedes stifled a laugh.

'By Herakles, what a colossus! It must be Ajax the son of Telamon. What does he come for? He was a child when the Oath was taken, and his father never swore it.'

He plodded over to us, the biggest man in all Greece, head and shoulders above everyone else in the room. Because he belonged to a group of youths who adhered to a strictly athletic regimen, he scorned the customary blouse; at all times of the year and in all weathers he went shoeless and shirtless. I could not take my eyes from the massive barrel of his chest, the bulging muscles owning not one speck of fat. Each time he planted one huge foot on my marble flags I fancied the walls shook.

'They say his cousin Achilles is almost as big,' said Palamedes.

I grunted. 'That need not concern us. The lords of the north never come to pay their respect to Mykenai. Thessalia is, they think, strong enough to be independent.'

'Welcome, son of Telamon,' I said. 'What brings you here?'

His childish grey eyes surveyed me placidly. 'I come to offer the services of Salamis, sire, in lieu of my father, who is ill. He said it would be good experience for me.'

I was well pleased. A pity the other Aiakid, Peleus, was so arrogant. Telamon knew his duty to his High King, whereas I would look in vain for Peleus, Achilles and the Myrmidons.

'We thank you, son of Telamon.'

Smiling, Ajax lumbered off in the direction of some of his friends, signalling to him frantically. Suddenly he stopped and swung back to me. 'I forgot, sire. My brother Teukros is with me. He swore the Oath.'

Palamedes was still laughing behind his hand. 'Are we about to open a school for babes, sire?'

'Yes, a pity he's such a lubber, Ajax. But the troops of Salamis are not to be despised.'

By dinner, late that afternoon, I had Palamedes, Ajax, Teukros, the other Ajax from Lokris usually called Little Ajax, Menestheus the High King of Attika, Diomedes of Argos, Thoas of Aitolia, Eurypylos of Ormenion, and several others; much to my surprise, more than one who came had not sworn the Oath. I told them that I intended to invade the Trojan peninsula, take the city of Troy itself and free up the Helles-pont. For the sake of my absent brother I dwelled a trifle too long on Paris's perfidies, perhaps, but that didn't delude any of them; they knew the real reasons for this war.

'All of us have merchants screaming in our ears to reopen the Hellespont. We have to obtain more tin and copper. The cannibal barbarians of the north and west are casting eyes our way. Some of us are ruling states grown too populous, with all the concomitants of that – poverty, trouble, riots and plots.' I looked at them sternly. 'Make no mistake, I am not going to war merely to get Helen back. This expedition against Troy and the states of coastal Asia Minor has the potential to do far more than accumulate wealth and give us unlimited cheap bronze. This expedition offers us the chance to colonise our surplus citizens in rich and underpopulated territories not too far away. The world around the Aegaean already speaks Greek of one form or another. But think now of the world around the Aegaean as *absolutely* Greek. Think of it as the Greek Empire.'

Ah, how they liked that! Every last one of them took the bait greedily; in the end I had no need to invoke the Oath, and was glad of it. Avarice was a better taskmaster than fear. Of course Athens was with me all the way; I had never doubted that Menestheus would back me. So, when he came, would Idomeneus of Crete, the third High King. But the fourth – Peleus – would not. The best I could hope for were some of his subject Kings.

Several days later Menelaos came back with Nestor. I had the old man brought to me at once. We sat in my private parlour with Palamedes, though I dismissed Menelaos; prudence dictated that he should go on believing Helen was the sole reason for war. The inevitable outcome of her recapture had not yet occurred to him, a good thing. Once she was back in our hands, she would have to part with her head.

I had no idea how old the King of Pylos was. Even when I was a boy he was ancient and white-haired. His wisdom was legion, his grasp of a situation no less acute today than it had been then; there was no sign of senility in his keen, bright blue eyes, no tremor in his beringed fingers.

'Now what is this all about, Agamemnon?' he demanded. 'Your brother grows sillier, not saner! All I learned from him was some wild tale about Helen's being abducted – hah! First time I ever knew *that* young woman needed force! And never tell me you've been gulled into indulging his whims!' He snorted. 'War over a woman? Really, Agamemnon!'

'We go to war for tin, copper, trade extensions, free passage through the Hellespont and Greek colonies along the Aegaean shore of Asia Minor, sire. Helen's absconding with the contents of my brother's treasury is the perfect excuse, that's all.'

'Hmmm.' He pursed his lips. 'I'm glad to hear you say that. How many men do you hope for?'

'Present indications say about eighty thousand soldiers, with sufficient noncombatant helpers to bring the total up to more than one hundred thousand. We should launch a thousand ships next spring.'

'An enormous campaign. I hope you're planning it well.'

'Naturally,' I said haughtily. 'However, it will be a very short business – so many men will overrun Troy within days.'

His eyes widened. 'Do you think so? Agamemnon, are you sure? Have you ever been to Troy?'

'No.'

'You must have heard tales about the Trojan walls.'

'Yes, yes, of course I have! However, sire, no walls in existence can keep out a hundred thousand men.'

'Perhaps ... But my counsel is that you wait until your ships are beached at Troy, when you can better judge the situation. Troy, they tell me, is no Athens, with a walled citadel and a single wall running down to the sea. Troy is completely enclosed by bastions. I believe you can win your campaign. But I also believe it will be a long one.'

'We will have to agree to differ, sire,' I said firmly.

He sighed. 'Be that as it may, neither I nor any of my sons swore the Oath, but you can have us. If we do not break the power of Troy and the Asia Minor states, Agamemnon, we – and Greece! – will fade away.' He examined his rings. 'Where is Odysseus?'

'I've sent a messenger to Ithaka.'

He clicked his tongue. 'Tch! Odysseus won't come to that.'

'He must! He swore the Oath too.'

'What do oaths mean to Odysseus, of all men? Not that any of us can accuse him of sacrilege – but he *devised* the scheme! He probably swore it backwards under his breath. At heart he is a peaceful man, and I gather he's settled into a contented rut of domestic bliss. He has quite lost his old zest for intrigue, I am informed. Happy marriage does that to some men. No, Agamemnon, he will not want to go. But you must have him.'

'I realise that, sire.'

'Then go and get him yourself,' said Nestor. 'Take Palamedes with you.' He chuckled. 'A thief to catch a thief.'

'Should I take Menelaos too?'

His bright eyes twinkled. 'Definitely. That will prevent his hearing too much about economics and too little about sex.'

We journeyed overland and took ship in a little village on the west coast of the Isle of Pelops to sail the windy strait to Ithaka. As we beached I surveyed the island dourly – small, rocky, a trifle barren – hardly a fitting kingdom for the greatest mind in all the world. Picking my way up the bridle path to the single town, I cursed the fact that Odysseus had not even thought to furnish his only suitable beach with transportation. In the town, however, we managed to find a few fleabitten donkeys; profoundly glad that none of my courtiers was present to witness his High King perched on an ass, I rode to the palace.

Though it was small, the palace came as a surprise; it was rich looking, with lofty pillars and the best paints indicating that its interior would be sumptuous. Of course his wife had come dowered with huge lands, chests of gold and a king's ransom in jewels – how her father, Ikarios, had protested at giving her to a man who couldn't win a footrace without using trickery!

I expected to see Odysseus waiting in the portico to greet us; word of our advent would have flown from the town. But when we clambered gratefully off our ignoble steeds we found the place silent, deserted. Not even a servant appeared. I led the way inside – Zeus, what frescoes! – magnificent! – feeling more puzzled than offended, to discover that from one end to the other the place was devoid of life. Not even that cursed hound, Argos, which Odysseus took everywhere, bayed at us.

A pair of wondrous bronze doors told us where the Throne Room was; Menelaos pushed them open. We stood on the threshold amazed, taking in the quality of the art, the perfect poise of the colours, and the sight of a woman crouched weeping on the bottom step of the throne dais. Her head was muffled in her cloak, but when she raised it we knew well enough who she was, for her face was tattooed in a web of blue with a crimson spider on her left cheek: the insignia of a woman dedicated to Pallas Athene in her guise of Loom Mistress. Penelope spun.

She leaped to her feet, then dropped to her knees to kiss the hem of my kilt. 'Sire! We did not expect you! To greet you with such an exhibition – oh, sire!' Whereupon she burst into a fresh flood of tears.

I stood looking and feeling ridiculous, an hysterical woman wound about my ankles. Then I caught the eye of Palamedes, and had to smile. Why expect the usual when one dealt with Odysseus and his own?

Palamedes leaned over her to whisper in my ear. 'Sire, I may find out more if I scout a little. May I?'

I nodded, then lifted Penelope to her feet. 'Come, cousin, calm yourself. What is the matter?'

'The King, sire! The King has gone mad! Absolutely mad! He doesn't even recognise *me*! He's down there now in the sacred orchard, gibbering like a lunatic!'

Palamedes had returned in time to hear.

'We must see him, Penelope,' I said.

'Yes, sire,' she said, hiccoughing, and led the way.

We emerged from the back of the palace to look down on farm lands spreading away in all directions; the centre of Ithaka was more fertile than its rim. As we were about to descend the steps an old woman appeared from nowhere, holding a babe.

'Lady, the Prince is crying. It is past his feeding time.'

Penelope took him instantly, cradling him in her arms.

'This is Odysseus's son?' I asked.

'Yes, this is Telemachos.'

I brushed his fat cheek with my finger, then moved onward; the fate of his father was of far greater moment. We walked through a grove of olive trees so old their tortured trunks were thicker than a bull, and found ourselves in a walled area containing more bare soil than it did fruit trees. At which moment we saw Odysseus. Menelaos muttered something in a choked voice, but I could only gape. He was furrowing the ground with the oddest team I have ever seen hitched to a plough – an ox and a mule. They hauled and jerked in opposite directions, the plough heaved and went sideways, the furrow was as crooked as Sisyphos. On his red head Odysseus wore a peasant's felt cap, and threw something haphazardly over his left shoulder.

'What is he doing?' asked Menelaos.

'Sowing salt,' said Penelope stonily.

Babbling senselessly to himself, laughing insanely, Odysseus ploughed and sowed his salt. Though he must have seen us, no light of recognition came into his eyes; they shone instead with the unmistakable glare of madness. The one man we needed above all others was beyond our reach.

I couldn't bear to watch. 'Come, let us leave him,' I said.

The plough was close to us now, its team growing angrier, harder to control. And without warning Palamedes leaped. While Menelaos and I stood paralysed, Palamedes snatched the child from Penelope's arms and set him down almost under the ox's hooves. Screaming shrilly, she tried to go to the babe, but Palamedes held her back. Then the team came to a halt; Odysseus ran in front of the ox and picked up his son.

'What is it?' asked Menelaos. 'Is he sane after all?'

'As sane as a man can be,' said Palamedes, smiling.

'He *feigned* madness?' I asked.

'Of course, sire. How else could he avoid honouring the Oath he swore?'

'But how did you know?' from Menelaos, bewildered.

'I found a talkative servant just outside the Throne Room. He told me that Odysseus was given a house oracle yesterday. It appears that if he goes to Troy, he must remain away from Ithaka for twenty years,' said Palamedes, enjoying his little triumph.

Odysseus gave the child to Penelope, who wept in earnest now. Everyone knew Odysseus was a great actor, but Penelope could act too. Fitting mates, that pair. His arm was about her and his grey eyes were fixed upon Palamedes. Their expression was not pleasant. Palamedes had incurred the hatred of one who could wait a lifetime for the perfect opportunity to be revenged.

'I am found out,' said Odysseus impenitently. 'I take it you need my services, sire?'

'I do. Why so reluctant, Odysseus?'

'War against Troy will be a long and bloody business, sire. I want no part of it.'

Yet another who insisted it would be a long campaign! But how could Troy possibly withstand a hundred thousand men, no matter how high its walls?

I returned to Mykenai with Odysseus in my train, having put him in full possession of the facts. No use trying to tell *him* that Helen had been kidnapped. As usual he was a mine of advice and information. Not once had he turned back to see Ithaka fade across the waters; not once had I seen evidence that he would miss his wife – or she him, for that matter. They were controlled and stuffed with secrets, Odysseus and Penelope of the webbed face.

When we reached the Lion Palace I found that my cousin Idomeneus of Crete had come. He was very willing to join in any expedition against Troy – for a price, of course. He asked the co-command, and I gave it to him readily. Co-command or not, he would bow to me. He had been very much in love with Helen and took her defection (I had to tell him the truth too) badly.

The roll call was almost complete, clerks committed this and that and another to memory, every shipwright in Greece was hard at it. Luckily we Greeks built by far the best ships and owned vast forests of tall straight pines and firs to fell, as much pitch from their resin as we needed, sufficient slaves to donate hair to mesh it with, enough cattle for the hide sails. No need to commission ships elsewhere, betray our plans. The total was even better than I had anticipated: twelve hundred ships had been promised, and over a hundred thousand men.

As soon as the fleet was under construction I called the inner council into session. Nestor, Idomeneus, Palamedes and Odysseus sat with me while we reviewed everything thoroughly. After which I asked Kalchas to conduct an augury.

'Good thinking,' Nestor approved. He liked to defer to the Gods.

'What does Apollo say, priest?' I asked Kalchas. 'Will all be well with our expedition?'

He did not hesitate. 'Only, sire, if your expedition contains Achilles, the seventh son of King Peleus.'

'Oh, Achilles, Achilles!' I cried, grinding my teeth. 'No matter which way I turn, I hear that name!'

Odysseus shrugged. 'It's a great name, Agamemnon.'

'Pah! He's not even twenty years old!'

'Even so,' said Palamedes, 'I think we ought to hear more about him.' He turned to Kalchas. 'On your way out, priest, ask Ajax the son of Telamon to join us.'

He didn't like being ordered about by Greeks. But he went, the cross-eyed albino. Was he aware that I was having him watched day and night? Just a precaution.

Ajax appeared shortly after Kalchas departed.

'Tell me about Achilles,' I said.

This simple request unleashed a spate of superlatives I for one found hard to sit through. Nor did it tell us anything we did not already know. I thanked the son of Telamon and dismissed him. What a lubber.

'Well?' I asked my council then.

'Surely what we *think* doesn't matter, Agamemnon,' Odysseus said. 'The priest says we have to have Achilles.'

'Who will not come in answer to a summons,' said Nestor.

'Thank you, I know enough to know that!' I snapped.

'Hold your temper, sire,' the old man said. 'Peleus is not young. He didn't swear the Oath. Nothing compels him to assist us, nor has he offered assistance. Yet think, Agamemnon, think! What could we do if our army contained the Myrmidons?'

His voice strengthened on that magical name; a heavy silence fell which he broke himself. 'I would rather have one Myrmidon at my back than half a hundred others,' he said.

'Then,' I said, determined that some of them there should suffer, 'I suggest, Odysseus, that you take Nestor and Ajax to Iolkos and ask King Peleus for the services of Achilles and the Myrmidons.'

CHAPTER NINE

NARRATED BY
ACHILLES

I was close to him now, I could smell his rankness and his rage. Spear steady in my hand, I crept down on him in the thicket. Came his snuffling breath, the ground tearing as he raked it with a foot. Then I saw him. He was as big as a small bull, his bulk rolling on short and powerful legs, his black coat bristling, his long cruel lips drawn back around the curved and yellowed tusks. His eyes were the eyes of one doomed to Tartaros; he saw the phantom Furies already, and he was filled with the terrible wrath of a mindless beast. Old, coarse, a mankiller.

I shrieked aloud to tell him that I was there. At first he did not move, then slowly he turned his massive head to look at me. The dust rose as he raked, as he bent his snout and lifted a clod of earth on his tusks, gathering power for the charge. I came into the open and stood with Old Pelion my spear poised, daring him to come. The sight of a man facing him boldly was new to him; he seemed uncertain for a moment. Then he broke into a lumbering, ground-shaking trot that built into a headlong gallup. Amazing, that such a huge thing could run so fast.

I gauged the level of his charge and stayed where I was, Old Pelion in both hands, its point a little upwards, its base down. Closer now. Impelled by all the weight he carried on his bones, he could have bored straight through a tree trunk. When I saw the red flash of his eyes I crouched, then stepped forward and buried Old Pelion in his chest. He embraced me; we went down together, the steaming gush of his life pouring over me. But then I found my feet and dragged his head up with me to ride out his threshing with my hands wrapped about the spear shaft, my feet slipping in his blood. And so he died, astonished at meeting one mightier than he. I pulled Old Pelion out of his chest, cut out his tusks – they were a rare prize to adorn a war helmet – and left him lying there to rot.

Nearby I found a little cove, and descended a snakepath to its back reaches, where a brook meandered down to meet the sea. Ignoring the sparkling invitation of the rivulet, I loped through the sand to the edge of the lapping waves. There I cleansed the boar's blood off my feet and legs, my hunting suit and Old Pelion, then waded out to spread everything on the sand to dry. After which I swam lazily before joining my stuff lying in the sun.

Perhaps I slept for some time. Or perhaps the Spell had come upon me even then. I do not know as I try to remember, only that cognisance faded. When it returned, the sun was slipping towards the tree tops and there was a faint coolness in the air. Time to go. Patrokles would be anxious.

I got up to fetch my things, and that action was the end of sanity. How to explain the inexplicable? To me it afterwards became the Spell, a period during which I was cut off from what was real, yet not cut off from some sort of world. A foetid smell I associated with death invaded my nostrils and the beach shrank to minute size while a shrine on the headland above suddenly zoomed to such an immensity that I fancied it was going to tip over and crash down on top of me. That world was a thing of contradictions, this grown large and and that diminished.

While brackish brine flowed from the corners of my mouth I sank to my knees overcome with terror, consumed by a lonely wilderness of tears and deprivation; nor could I do anything in all my youth and strength to banish the mortal dread I felt. My left hand began to shake, the left side of my face twitched, my spine stiffened, arched. Yet I hung onto consciousness, willing myself not to let that awful jerking march go further. How long the Spell lay upon me I have no idea, save that when I regained my strength I saw that the sun was gone and the sky flushed pink. The air was still, filled with bird songs.

Trembling like a man in the grip of the ague, I got to my feet, the taste of something foul in my mouth. I did not stop to gather up my things or think of Old Pelion. All I wanted was to get back to camp, to die in the arms of Patrokles.

He was there and heard me coming, ran to me, shocked, and put me down on a bed of warm skins by the fire. Once I had drunk a little wine I began to feel ordinary life steal into my bones; I lost the last of my confused panic and sat up, listening with boundless thanks to the thudding of my heart.

'What happened?' Patrokles was saying.

'A spell,' I croaked. 'A spell.'

'Did the boar wound you? Did you suffer a fall?'

'No, I killed the boar easily. Afterwards I went down to the sea to wash off his blood. That was when the Spell came.'

He sank into his heels, eyes wide. 'What spell, Achilles?'

'Like death coming to me. I smelled death, I tasted it in my mouth. The cove shrank, the shrine grew giantic – the world twisted and reshaped itself like something Protean. I thought I was dying, Patrokles! I have never felt so alone! And I was stricken with the palsy of old age, the fear of a craven. But I am neither old nor a craven. So what happened to me? What was that Spell? Have I sinned against some God? Have I offended the Lord of the Skies or the Lord of the Seas?'

His face loomed worried and apprehensive; later he told me that I did indeed look as if I had given death the kiss of welcome, for I had no colour, I shook like a sapling in the wind, I was naked and covered in scratches and cuts.

'Lie down, Achilles, let me cover you from the cold. It may not have been a spell. Perhaps it was a dream.'

'Nightmare, not dream.'

'Eat a little and drink some more of the wine. Some farmers came with four skins of their best pressing in thanks for the killing of the boar.'

I touched his arm. 'I would have gone mad had I not found you, Patrokles. I couldn't bear the thought of dying alone.'

He clasped my hands, kissed them. 'I am far more your friend than your cousin, Achilles. I will always be with you.'

Drowsiness came, a gentle sensation with no fear in it. I smiled, reached out to ruffle his hair. 'You for me, and I for you. So it has always been.'

'And so it always will be,' he answered.

In the morning I was perfectly well. Patrokles had woken before me; the fire was going, a rabbit spitted over the flames for us to break our fast. And there was bread too, brought by the farm women as their thanks for the killing of the boar.

'You look quite yourself,' said Patrokles with a grin, handing me roast rabbit on a bread platter.

'I am,' I said, taking the food.

'Do you remember as vividly as you did last night?'

That provoked a shiver, but bread-and-rabbit banished the fear in remembering. 'Yes and no. A Spell, Patrokles. Some God spoke, but I did not understand the message.'

'Time will solve the mystery,' he said, moving about, dealing with all the tiny tasks he took upon himself to ensure my comfort. Try though I did, I could never break him of this serving habit.

He was five years older than I. King Lykomedes of Skyros had adopted him as his heir when his own father, Menoetes, died of illness in Skyros. A long time ago. He was my cousin on the left hand, Menoetes being the bastard of my grandfather Aiakos; we felt the blood link keenly, both of us only sons and minus any sisters. Lykomedes thought very highly of him, which was little wonder. Patrokles was that rarity, a truly *good* man.

Our fast broken and the camp packed up, I donned a kilt and sandals, put on a bronze dagger and found another spear. 'Wait for me here, Patrokles. I won't be long. My clothes and trophy are still on the beach. So is Old Pelion.'

123

'Let me come with you,' he said quickly, looking afraid.

'No. This lies between the God and me.'

His eyes dropped; he nodded. 'As you command, Achilles.'

Finding the way easier this time, I went over the ground as fast as a lion can travel. The cove looked innocent as I ran down the snakepath to collect my clothes, the tusks, Old Pelion. No, the cove was not the source of the Spell. At which moment my eyes, roving the clifftop, fell upon the shrine. My heart began to beat heavily. My mother was an unofficial priestess of Nereus somewhere on this side of the island – was this her domain? Had I stumbled into her pavilions by mistake, profaned some mystery of the Old Religion, and been struck down for it?

I climbed slowly back to the summit and approached the shrine, now remembering how huge it had loomed while the Spell had been upon me. Oh yes, this was my mother's domain. And hadn't King Lykomedes warned me never to stray here, where my mother, defying him, had set up residence?

She was waiting in the shadows beside the altar. Suddenly I found I needed to use Old Pelion as a staff; my legs had lost their strength, I could hardly stand upright. Mother! My mother whom I had never seen.

So tiny! She came not far above my waist. Her hair was blue-white, her eyes dark grey, and her skin so transparent I could see every vein beneath it.

'You are my son, the one Peleus denied immortality.'

'I am he.'

'Did he send you to seek me?'

'No. I came by chance,' I said, leaning feebly on old Pelion.

What ought a man to feel when he meets his mother for the first time? Oedipoas had felt lust, had taken her as his wife and queen, bred by her. But I, it seemed, had no Oedipoas in me, for I felt no pang of lust, no flicker of admiration for her beauty or her apparent youth. Perhaps what I felt is best summed up as wonder, as discomfort, as – yes, rejection. This odd little woman had murdered my six brothers and betrayed my father, whom I loved.

'You hate me!' she said, sounding outraged.

'Not hate. Dislike,' I said.

'What did Peleus name you?'

'Achilles.'

She eyed my mouth, nodded contemptuously. 'Very appropriate! Even fish have lips, but you have none. Lack of them turns your face from a thing of beauty to a thing unfinished. A bag with a slit in it.'

She was right. I did hate her.

'What are you doing on Skyros? Is Peleus with you?'

'No. I come alone each year for six moons. I am the son-in-law of King Lykomedes.'

'Married *already*?' she asked, nastily.

'I've been married since I was thirteen years old. I am almost twenty now. My son is six.'

'What a fiasco! And your wife? Is she a child too?'

'Her name is Deidamia and she is older than me.'

'Well, it's all very convenient for Lykomedes. Peleus too. They harnessed you, and quite painlessly.'

Finding nothing to answer, I said nothing. Nor did she. The silence stretched interminably. I, so well trained by my father and Chiron always to defer to my elders, would not break it because I could not break it politely. Pehaps she was truly a goddess, though my father denied it each time the wine got the better of him.

'You should have been immortal,' she said finally.

That made me laugh. 'I want no immortality! I am a warrior, I enjoy the things of men. I do homage to the Gods, but I've never hungered to be one of them.'

'Then you haven't thought on what mortality entails.'

'What can it entail, except that I must die?'

'Exactly,' she said softly. 'You must die, Achilles. And doesn't the thought of death frighten you? You say you're a man, a warrior. But warriors die early, before men of peace.'

125

I shrugged. 'Whichever way it goes, death is my lot. I'd rather die young and gloriously than old and ignominiously.'

For a moment her eyes became misty blue and her face took on a sadness I had not thought her capable of feeling. A tear trickled down her translucent cheek, but she wiped it away impatiently and became again a creature devoid of pity. 'It's too late to argue the point, my son. You *must* die. But I can offer you a choice, because I can see into the future. I know your fate. Soon men will come to ask you to join in a great war. But if you go, you'll die. If you don't go, you'll live to be very old and enjoy much happiness. Young and gloriously, or old and ignominiously. The choice is yours.'

I blinked, laughed. 'What kind of choice is that? None! I elect to die young and gloriously.'

'Why not think on death a little first?' she asked.

Her words sank into me barbed with venom. I stared down into her eyes to see them swim and dissolve, to see her face become shapeless, the sky above her melt and flow beneath her tiny feet. When she grew in height until her head penetrated the clouds I knew the Spell was upon me again – and who cast it. Brine spilled from the corners of my mouth, the stench of corruption filled my nostrils, terror and loneliness drove me to my knees before her. My left hand began to jerk, the left side of my face to twitch. But this time she took her Spell further. I lost consciousness.

When I woke she was beside me on the ground, rubbing sweetly scented herbs between her palms.

'Stand up,' she commanded.

Unable to order my thoughts, enfeebled in body as well as in mind, I got up slowly.

'Achilles, listen to me!' she barked. '*Listen to me!* You are going to swear an oath of the Old Religion, and that is a far worse oath than any under the New. To Nereus, my father, the Old Man of the Sea – to the Mother, for she bears us all – to Kore, queen of horror – to the rulers of Tartaros, place of torment – and to me in my Godhead. You will swear it now, understanding that it cannot be broken. If you do break it, you will go mad for ever and ever, and Skyros will sink below the waves just as Thera did after the great sacrilege.' She shook my arm, her grip hard. 'Do you hear me, Achilles? Do you?'

'Yes,' I mumbled.

'I have to save you from yourself,' she said, breaking open a leathery old egg upon greasy blood and letting the blood splatter over the altar. Then she took my right hand and squashed it down upon the mess, held it there firmly. 'Now swear!'

I repeated the words she dictated. 'I, Achilles, son of Peleus, grandson of Aiakos and great-grandson of Zeus, do swear that I will return at once to the palace of King Lykomedes and assume the dress of a woman. I will remain within the palace for the space of one year, always dressed as a woman. Whenever any persons come asking to see Achilles, I will hide in the harem and have no contact with them, even through intermediaries. I will let King Lykomedes speak for me in everything and abide by what he says without argument. And all this I do swear by Nereus, by the Mother, by Kore, by the rulers of Tartaros and by Thetis, who is a Goddess.'

The moment those awful words were finished, my confusion lifted; the world resumed its true colours and contours, and I could think clearly again. But too late. No man could take such a terrible oath and forswear it. My mother had bound me hand and foot to her will.

'I curse you!' I cried, beginning to weep. 'I curse you! You've made me into a woman!'

'There is woman in all men,' she smirked.

'You've stripped me of my honour!'

'I've prevented your going to an early death,' she answered, and gave me a push. 'Now return to Lykomedes. You won't need to explain anything to him. By the time you get to the palace, he'll know it all.' Her eyes went blue again. 'I do this out of love, my poor, lipless son. I am your mother.'

*

127

ACHILLES

I said not one word to Patrokles when I found him, simply picked up my share of our gear and started back to the palace. And he, attuned as always to my mind, did not ask me one single question. Or perhaps he already knew what Lykomedes certainly knew when he came through the gates into the courtyard. He was waiting there, looking shrunken and defeated.

'I've had a message from Thetis,' he said.

'Then you know what is required of us.'

'Yes.'

My wife was sitting at the window when I came into her room. At the sound of the door she turned her head and opened her arms wide, smiling sleepily. I kissed her on the cheek and stared out the window, down on the harbour and the little town.

'Is that all the welcome you have for me?' she asked, but not indignantly; Deidamia was never put out.

'You surely know what everyone knows,' I said, sighing.

'That you have to dress as a woman and hide in Father's harem,' she said, nodding. 'But only when there are strangers here, and that won't be often.'

The shutter under my hand began to splinter, so great was my anguish. 'How can I do it, Deidamia? The humiliation! What a perfect way to be revenged! She mocks my manhood, the cow!'

My wife shivered, put up her right hand in the sign which wards off the Evil Eye. 'Achilles, don't anger her further! She's a Goddess! Speak of her with respect.'

'Never!' I said between my teeth. 'She has no respect for me, for my manhood. How everyone will laugh!'

This time Deidamia shuddered. 'It is not a laughing matter,' she said.

CHAPTER TEN

NARRATED BY

ODYSSEUS

The winds and currents were always more favourable than the long, tortuous land route, so we sailed to Iolkos, hugging the coast. As we drew into harbour I stood on the deck with Ajax; this was my first visit to the home of the Myrmidons, and I thought Iolkos beautiful, a crystal city shimmering in the wintry sun. No walls. At the back of the palace Mount Pelion towered, wreathed in pure white snow. Wrapping my furs closer about my shoulders, I blew on my hands and looked sideways at Ajax.

'Will you go over the side first, my colossus?' I asked.

He nodded tranquilly; verbal play was lost on him. One massive leg went over the rail, found the top rung of the rope ladder, and the rest of him rapidly disappeared. He was wearing no more than when I had seen him in the halls of Mykenai: a kilt. Nor did his fine skin betray a sign of cold. I let him descend to the beach, then called down to him to locate a conveyance of some kind. Well known in Iolkos, he would have his choice of whatever was available.

Nestor was busy packing his personal belongings in the shelter built on the afterdeck.

'Ajax has gone to find us a car. Do you feel well enough to descend to the beach, or would you rather wait here?' I asked him, tongue in cheek. I enjoyed making Nestor bristle.

'And what makes you think I'm in my dotage?' he snapped, leaping to his feet. 'I'll wait on the beach, of course.'

Still muttering to himself, he went out onto the deck briskly;

impatiently slapping at a sailor's helping hand, he shinnied down the ladder as nimbly as a boy. Old horror.

Peleus bowed us into his home personally. When I had been a youth and he a man in his prime I had met him often, but not since. An elderly man now, he was still erect and proud, kingly. A handsome man, and a wise one. A pity he had only the one son to follow him; owning Peleus as sire, the young Achilles had a reputation to live up to.

Seated comfortably before the big tripod of fire, mulled wine at our elbows, I broached the reason for our coming. Despite Nestor's seniority I had been elected spokesman; if there were any mistakes he could bow out nicely, the reprobate.

'We're sent by Agamemnon at Mykenai to beg a favour, sire.'

His shrewd eyes surveyed me. 'Helen,' he said.

'News travels swiftly.'

'I expected an imperial courier, but none came. My ship-wrights have never seen such business flow into their yards.'

'As you didn't swear the Oath of the Quartered Horse, Peleus, Agamemnon could send no courier. Nothing obliges you to aid the cause of Menelaos.'

'Just as well. I'm too old to go to war, Odysseus.'

Nestor decided I was being too convoluted. 'Actually, my dear Peleus, it isn't you we seek,' he said. 'We've come to see if we can enlist the services of your son.'

Thessalia's High King seemed to shrivel. 'Achilles ... Well, I hoped against it, but I expected it. I've no doubt that he'll accept Agamemnon's offer with alacrity.'

'We're free to ask him, then?' from Nestor.

'Of course,' said Peleus.

I smiled, relaxed. 'Agamemnon thanks you, Peleus. And I personally thank you. From my heart.'

He looked at me long and steadily. '*Have* you a heart, Odysseus? I fancied it's only mind you possess.'

Something stung momentarily at the back of my eyes: I thought, Penelope, and then her image faded. I gave him back his stare. 'No, I have no heart. Why should a man need one? A heart is a severe liability.'

'Then what men say of you is true.' He picked up his goblet from the tripod table, a very fine piece of Egyptian workmanship. 'If Achilles elects to go to Troy,' he said then, 'he'll lead the Myrmidons. They've been spoiling for a hard campaign these twenty years and more.'

Someone entered; Peleus smiled and held out his hand. 'Ah, Phoinix! Gentlemen, this is Phoinix, my friend and comrade of many years. We have very prestigious guests, Phoinix – this is King Nestor of Pylos and this King Odysseus of Ithaka.'

'I saw Ajax outside,' said Phoinix, bowing low. In years he was somewhere between Peleus and Nestor, a very erect and soldierly fellow with a Myrmidon look – fair, big, fit.

'You'll go with Achilles to Troy, Phoinix,' Peleus said. 'Look after him for me, protect him from his fate.'

'At the price of my life, sire.'

Which was all very well and good, I thought, growing a trifle impatient. 'May we see Achilles for ourselves?' I asked.

The two Thessalians looked blank.

'Achilles isn't in Iolkos,' said Peleus.

'Then where is he?' asked Nestor.

'In Skyros. He spends the six cold moons there every year – he's married to Deidamia, daughter of Lykomedes.'

I slapped my thigh in vexation. 'So we have yet another winter voyage to make.'

'Not at all,' said Peleus warmly. 'I'll send for him.'

But somehow I knew that unless we saw to it ourselves, we would never see Achilles draw up Iolkan ships on the sands at Aulis. I shook my head.

'No, sire. Agamemnon would deem it more fitting that we ask Achilles in person.'

And so we came once more into harbour and made our way from town to palace; the difference was that this second palace was little more than a large house. Skyros was not rich.

Lykomedes made us welcome, but as we sat down to eat and drink a minor repast, I found myself prickling. Something was wrong, and not merely with Lykomedes himself. A peculiar tension hung over the place. Servants – all male – slid and skipped without looking at us, Lykomedes wore the mien of one labouring under a heavy burden of fear, his heir Patrokles came in and went out so quickly I almost thought him a figment of my imagination, and – most disquieting of all – I heard not one feminine sound. No woman, even in the distance, laughed, or whined, or screeched, or howled in tears. How alien! Women did not participate in the affairs of men, no, but they were fully aware of their importance in the scheme of things, and they enjoyed liberties no man would dare to deny them. They had, after all, ruled under the Old Religion.

My prickling skin had turned into pins and needles, my nose twitched at the old, familiar smell of danger; I caught Nestor's eye. Yes, he had sensed it too. His brows lifted at me, and I sighed. I was not mistaken, then. We had a problem.

The handsome young man Patrokles returned. I looked him over more thoroughly, wondering what his significance might be in this strange situation. A tender and gentle fellow, not lacking in fight or courage, but possibly very one-sided in his affections – affections which did not, I decided, extend to women. Well, that was his right. No one would think ill of him because he preferred men. This time he actually sat down, looking unhappy.

I cleared my throat. 'King Lykomedes, our mission is very urgent. We seek your son-in-law, Achilles.'

There was a queer, intangible pause; Lykomedes almost dropped his goblet, then got up awkwardly. 'Achilles isn't in Skyros, royal gentlemen.'

'Not here?' asked Ajax, dismayed.

'No.' Lykomedes seemed embarrassed. 'He – he quarrelled violently with his wife – my daughter – and left for the mainland vowing never to return.'

'He's not in Iolkos,' I prompted gently.

'I confess I didn't think he would be, Odysseus. He was talking about Thrake.'

Nestor sighed. 'Dear, dear! It seems as if we are fated never to meet this young man, doesn't it?'

The question was directed at me, but I didn't reply at once, too conscious of a sudden curious lightness, a vast relief. All my instincts were right. Something was seriously amiss, and Achilles was the centre of it. I got up. 'Since Achilles is not here, I think we must leave at once, Nestor.'

I waited, knowing that Lykomedes had to extend the proper courtesies or sin in the eyes of Hospitable Zeus. And while I waited, I turned so that only Nestor could see my face, then shot him a venomous glare of warning.

Lykomedes made the obligatory offer. 'Stay with us overnight at least, Odysseus. King Nestor should rest a while.'

As well I glared at him; instead of snapping that he was quite capable of declaring war on Olympos, he subsided into a pathetic, huddled heap of ancient misery. Old villain.

'Thank you, King Lykomedes!' I cried, looking relieved. 'Only this morning Nestor was saying how tired he is. The winter gales at sea make him ache all over.' I dropped my eyes. 'I do hope our presence won't inconvenience you.'

It did inconvenience him. He had not dreamed that I would accept his formal invitation when our mission was a failure, when we had to get back to Mykenai and break the news to Agamemnon. He put a good face on his disappointment, however. So did Patrokles.

Later I sought Nestor in his chamber and sat on the arm of a chair while he reposed in a steaming bath as an elderly servant – male, how extraordinary! – scraped the salt and grime from his withered hide. The moment Nestor was standing on the floor all swaddled in linen towels, the man departed.

'What do you think?' I asked Nestor then.

'This is a house under a shadow,' he said positively. 'I

suppose if Achilles had quarrelled with his wife and taken himself off to Thrake it might provoke a reaction like this, yet I do not think so. Whatever is wrong, it is not that.'

'I think Achilles is here within the palace.'

His eyes widened. 'No! Hidden, yes, but not here.'

'Here,' I insisted. 'We've heard enough of him to know he's as impulsive as he is warlike. Were he located at any distance from Lykomedes and Patrokles, they'd fail to control him. He's here in the palace.'

'But *why*? He didn't swear the Oath, nor did Peleus. There'd be no dishonour in refusing to go to Troy.'

'Oh, he wants to go! Desperately. It's others who don't want him to go. And somehow they've bound him.'

'What should we do, then?'

'What do you think?' I countered.

He grimaced. 'That we have to wander everywhere within this little building. Preferably I during daylight. I can pretend to be senile. When everyone is asleep, you can wander. Do you truly think they're holding him prisoner?'

But that I could not believe. 'They wouldn't dare, Nestor. If Peleus got word of it, he'd tear this island apart better than Poseidon could. No, they've bound him with an oath.'

'Logical.' He began to dress. 'How long before dinner?'

'Some time yet.'

'Then go and sleep, Odysseus, while I prowl.'

He came to wake me in time for dinner, looking peevish. 'Plague take them!' he growled. 'If they have him hidden here, I can't find where. I've stumbled into every single corner from the roof to the vaults without a sign of him. The only place I couldn't enter was the women's quarters. There's a guard.'

'Then that's where he is,' I said, getting up. 'Hmmm!'

We went down to dinner together, wondering if Lykomedes had gone so Assyrian that he forbade his women the dining hall. A male servant as bath attendant? No women anywhere? A guard on the door of their quarters? Very fishy. Lykomedes didn't want us hearing gossip, so he had to keep his women away from us.

But the women were there, admittedly all thrust into the farthest, darkest corner. I had thought Lykomedes would have to produce them for the main meal; the size of his kitchens and his palace would have made it impossible for him to feed them in their quarters without creating culinary chaos for his royal guests.

No Achilles, however. Not one of those indistinct female forms was anything like large enough to be Achilles.

'Why are the women segregated?' Nestor asked when the food arrived and we sat at the high table with Lykomedes and Patrokles.

'They offended Poseidon,' said Patrokles quickly.

'And?' I asked.

'They're forbidden congress with men for five years.'

I raised my brows. 'Even sexually?'

'That is allowed.'

'Sounds more like something the Mother would demand than Poseidon,' Nestor remarked, swigging wine.

Lykomedes shrugged. 'It came from Poseidon, not the Mother.'

'Through his priestess Thetis?' the King of Pylos asked.

'Thetis is not his priestess,' said Lykomedes uneasily. 'The God refused to take her back. She serves Nereus now.'

After the food went out (along with the women), I settled down to talk to Patrokles, leaving Lykomedes at Nestor's mercy.

'I'm very sorry to have missed Achilles,' I said.

'You would have liked him,' said Patrokles tonelessly.

'I imagine he would have jumped at the chance to go to Troy.'

'Yes. Achilles was born for war.'

'Well, I have no intention of combing Thrake to find him! He'll be sorry when he finds out what he's missed.'

'Yes, very sorry.'

'Tell me what he looks like,' I said invitingly, having learned one thing about Patrokles: it was Achilles to whom he had given his love.

The young face lit up. 'He's a little smaller than Ajax ... So – so *graceful* when he moves! And he's very beautiful.'

'I heard he had no lips. How can he be beautiful?'

'Because – because –' Patrokles searched for words. 'You'd have to see him to understand. His mouth moves one to tears – so much pain! Achilles is beauty personified.'

'He sounds too good to be true,' I said.

He nearly fell for it. Nearly told me that I was a fool to doubt him, that he could produce his paragon for my inspection. Then he closed his lips tightly, the hot words unuttered. Though they may as well have been. I had my answer.

Before we retired I held a little council with Nestor and Ajax, then went to bed and slept soundly. Very early the next day I made my way with Ajax down to the town. I had billeted my cousin Sinon there; it was never wise to display all one's treasures at once, and Sinon was a treasure. He listened impassively as I told him what to do, gave him a bag of gold from the little hoard Agamemnon had given me to defray our expenses. What was mine I hung on to grimly; one day it would be my son's. Agamemnon was well able to pay for Achilles.

The Court was still sleeping when I returned to the palace, though Ajax did not accompany me. He had work to do outside. Nestor was awake and packed; we did not intend to keep Lykomedes in suspense. Of course he made all the proper protests when we announced that we were sailing, egged us to stay longer, but this time I declined politely, to his huge relief.

'Where is Ajax?' Patrokles asked.

'Wandering around the town asking people if they have any idea where Achilles went,' I said, then turned to Lykomedes. 'Sire, as a small favour, would you assemble your entire free household here in your Throne Room?'

He looked startled, then very wary. 'Well ...'

'I'm under orders from Agamemnon, sire, otherwise I wouldn't ask. I'm bidden – just as I was in Iolkos! – to tender the High King of Mykenai's thanks to every free person at the Court. His orders stipulate that *everyone* be present, female as well as male. There may be a ban upon your women, but they still belong to you.'

On the echo of my words some of my sailors entered, bearing great armloads of gifts. Women's trinkets, these: beads, shifts, flasks of perfume, jars of oil, unguents and essences, fine wools and gauzy linens. I asked for tables to be brought forward so that the men could dump their burdens down in careless heaps. More sailors came in, this time with gifts for the men: good bronze-skinned arms, shields, spears, swords, cuirasses, helmets and greaves. These I had placed on more tables.

Greed warred with caution in the King's eyes, when Patrokles put a warning hand on his arm he shrugged it off and clapped for his steward.

'Summon the entire household. Have the women stand far enough away to observe Poseidon's ban.'

The room filled with men, then the women arrived. Nestor and I searched their ranks fruitlessly. None could be Achilles.

'Sire,' I said, stepping forward, 'King Agamemnon wishes to thank you and yours for your help and hospitality.' I indicated the heaps of women's things. 'Here are gifts for your women.' I turned to the weapons and armour. 'And here, gifts for your men.'

Both sexes murmured in delight, but no one moved until the King granted his permission. Then they clustered about the tables to pick the things over happily.

'This, sire,' I said, taking an object wrapped in linen from a sailor, 'is for you.'

Face alight, he stripped the shroud from it until it was revealed as a Cretan axe, its double head bronze, its shaft oak. I held it out for him to take it; beaming with pleasure, he extended his hands.

At that precise moment there came from outside a shrill, high squeal of alarm. Someone sounded a horn, and in the far distance we all heard Ajax bellow a war cry from Salamis. Came the unmistakable clang of armour being strapped on; Ajax yelled again, closer now, as if he retreated. The women shrieked and began to flee, the men broke into confused questions, and King Lykomedes, deathly pale, forgot his axe.

'Pirates!' he said, not seeming to know what to do.

Ajax howled once more, louder and much closer, a war cry from the slopes of Pelion that only Chiron taught. In the rooted stillness suddenly gripping us all I changed my hold on the axe, grasped its shaft in both hands and lifted its head.

One other moved also, erupting into the Throne Room with such force that the terrified women, clustered in the doorway, were flung about like spools of yarn. A sort of a woman. Easy to see why Lykomedes had not dared display her! Impatiently stripping off the linen robe swathed about her to reveal a chest so well muscled that I stared in admiration, she strode to the table where the arms were piled. Achilles at last.

He swept the contents of one table to the floor with a crash, took a shield and spear and towered there at his full height, every fibre of him ready to fight. Axe extended, I walked up to him.

'Here, lady, use this! It looks more your size.' I flourished it, my arms creaking under the strain. 'Do I address Prince Achilles?'

Oh, but he was odd! What should have been beautiful was not, despite the paeans of Patrokles. Though it was not the mouth negated beauty. That actually lent him some much-needed pathos. His lack of beauty, I have always thought, came from within himself. The yellow eyes were full of pride and high intelligence; this was no lubber Ajax.

'My thanks,' he cried, laughing back at me.

Ajax came into the room still holding the arms he had used to create the panic outside, saw Achilles standing with me, and roared. The next moment he had Achilles in his grasp, was

138

hugging him with a force that would have crushed my rib cage. Achilles shook him off without seeming to be impaired, and flung an arm across his shoulders.

'Ajax, Ajax! Your war cry tore through me like a shaft from a longbow! I had to answer, I couldn't stand idle a moment longer. When you yelled old Chiron's war cry you were summoning me – how could I resist?' He spied Patrokles and held out one hand. 'Here, with me! We go to war against Troy! My dearest wish has been granted, Father Zeus has answered my prayers.'

Lykomedes was beside himself, weeping, wringing his hands. 'My son, my son, what will happen to us now? You've broken the oath you swore to your mother! She'll rend us limb from limb!'

Silence fell. Achilles sobered in an instant, his face grim. I raised my brows at Nestor; we both sighed. Everything was explained.

'I can't see how I broke it, Father,' Achilles said at last. 'I answered a reflex, I responded without thinking to a call instilled in me when I was a boy. I heard Ajax and I answered. I broke no oath. Another man's guile destroyed it.'

'Achilles speaks the truth,' I said loudly. 'I tricked you. No God could deem you guilty of breaking your vow.'

They doubted me, of course, but the damage was done.

Achilles spread his arms above his head in exultation then reached for Patrokles and Ajax, hugged them. 'Cousins, we go to war!' he said, smiling fiercely, then looked at me with grateful eyes. 'It is our destiny. Even in the midst of her vilest spells my mother could never convince me otherwise. I was born to be a warrior, to fight alongside the greatest men of our age, to win everlasting fame and undying glory!'

What he said was probably true. I gazed wryly at them, that splendid trio of young men, remembering my wife and son, all the endless years which must elapse between the beginning of my exile and my homecoming. Achilles would win his everlasting fame and undying glory before Troy, but I would cheerfully have traded my share of those two vastly overrated commodities for the right to return home tomorrow.

In the end I did manage to return to Ithaka, on the pretext that I had to form up my contingent for Troy in person. Agamemnon was far from pleased to see me leave Mykenai; he could perform his own part more easily if I were there to lean on.

I spent three precious moons with my web-faced Penelope, time we hadn't counted on having, but eventually I could delay no longer. While my small fleet weathered the stormy rim of the Isle of Pelops, I made the journey to Aulis by land. I went swiftly through Aitolia, not breaking my progress by night or by day until I reached mountainous Delphi, where Apollo, Lord of the Prophetic Mouth, had his sanctuary, and where his priestess, the Pythoness, gave out her infallible Oracles. I asked her if my house oracle had been right in saying that I would spend twenty years away from my hearth. Her answer was simple and straightforward: 'Yes.' Then she added that it was the will of my protectress, Pallas Athene, that I should be away from home for twenty years. I asked why, but got no answer beyond a giggle.

Hopes dashed, I pressed on to Thebes, where I had arranged to meet Diomedes coming up from Argos. But the ruined city was deserted; he had not dared to tarry. Nor was I sorry for the solitude as I put my team on the last short stage of my journey, jolting over the rutted track which led down to the Euboian Strait and the beach at Aulis.

The whereabouts of the expedition's start had been long and carefully debated; a thousand or more ships took up some leagues of room, and the waters had to be sheltered. Therefore Aulis was a good choice. The beach was over two leagues long, shielded from the wildest winds and seas by the island of Euboia, not far offshore.

Last to foregather, I breasted the top of the rise above the beach and looked down. Even my horses seemed to sense something ominous in the air, for they stopped, balked and began to rear, as horses do when commanded to approach carrion. My driver had to fight to control them, but finally managed to coax them on.

Endless they ranged before my eyes! There on the beach in two rows stood those high-prowed, red-and-black ships, each of them built to carry at least a hundred men, with room for fifty on the oars and fifty to lie at rest amid the gear, each with a tall mast to swing the sail upon. I wondered how many trees had crashed to earth to create those thousand and more ships, how many splashes of sweat had soaked into their pitched sides before the last bolt had been driven home and they could ride lightly upon the water. Ships and ships and ships, small from where I stood atop the rise. Enough ships to convey eighty thousand troops and thousands more of noncombatants to Troy. Mentally I applauded Agamemnon. He had dared, and he had succeeded. If he never got those two ranks of vessels any further than the beach at Aulis, it was nonetheless a splendid achievement. The beauty of the land was lost on me; mountains were dwarfed, the sea reduced to a passive instrument for the use of Agamemnon, King of Kings. I laughed aloud and shouted, 'Agamemnon, you have won!'

I drove through the little fishing village of Aulis at a swift trot, ignoring the multitudes of soldiers thronging its single street. Beyond the houses I paused, at a loss. Amid so many ships, whereabouts were headquarters? I hailed an officer.

'Which way to the tent of Agamemnon King of Kings?'

He surveyed me slowly, picking his teeth as he took stock of my armour, my helmet shingled with rows of boar's tusks, the mighty shield which had belonged to my father.

'Who asks?' he queried impertinently.

'A wolf who has devoured bigger rats than you.'

Taken aback, he swallowed and answered civilly. 'Follow the road for a while yet, lord, then ask again.'

'Odysseus of Ithaka thanks you.'

Agamemnon had established temporary quarters only, pitching good leather tents of a fair size and comfort. He had built nothing solid or lasting aside from a marble altar beneath a lone plane tree, a poor tattered thing struggling against salt and wind to produce springtime buds. Handing my team and driver to one of the imperial guards, I was escorted to the biggest tent.

All who mattered were inside: Idomeneus, Diomedes, Nestor, Ajax and his namesake called Little Ajax, Teukros, Phoinix, Achilles, Menestheus, Menelaos, Palamedes, Meriones, Philoktetes, Eurypylos, Thoas, Machaon and Podalieros. The albino priest, Kalchas, was sitting quietly in a corner, his red eyes flickering from man to man, calculating, surmising; their crossedness did not fool me. For a few moments I watched him undetected, trying to plumb him. I did not care for him, not only because of his repulsive exterior, but also because something less tangible in his makeup inspired an intense sensation of mistrust. I knew Agamemnon had felt the same in the beginning, but after moons of having the man watched, he had come to the conclusion that Kalchas was loyal. I was not so sure. The man was very subtle. And he was a Trojan.

Achilles called out joyfully. 'Odysseus, what kept you? Your ships arrived half a moon ago!'

'I came overland. Business to attend to.'

'Timely withal, old friend,' said Agamemnon. 'We are about to hold our first formal council.'

'So I really am the last?'

'Among those who matter.'

We took our seats. Kalchas issued out of his nook to hold the gilded Staff of Debate slackly in one paw. Despite the sunny spring weather outside, lamps were burning, for the only light percolated in through the tent flap. As befitted a formal council of war, we were clad in full armour. Agamemnon was wearing a very pretty set of gold inlaid with amethyst and lapis; I hoped he had a more workmanlike set for battle. Taking the Staff of Debate from Kalchas, he faced us proudly.

'I've called this first council to discuss the sailing rather than the campaign, of course. But rather than issue orders, I think it better to answer questions. Strict debate isn't necessary. Kalchas will hold the Staff. However, if any one of you wants to speak at length, take it.' Looking content, he gave the Staff to Kalchas.

'When do you plan to sail?' asked Nestor placidly.

'At the next new moon. I've delegated the chief part in organisation to Phoinix, the most experienced sailor among us. He has already detailed a special squad of officers to depute the order of sailing – which contingents are the fastest, which the slowest – those ships with indispensable troops aboard and those carrying horses or noncombatants. Rest assured, there will be no chaos when we land.'

'Who is the chief pilot?' from Achilles.

'Telephos. He'll sail with me on my flagship. Each ship's pilot is under orders to keep his vessel within sight of at least a dozen others. This will ensure that the fleet remains intact – in good weather, that is. Storms will make things difficult, but the time of year is with us, and Telephos is coaching all the pilots carefully.'

'How many supply ships have you?' I asked.

Agamemnon looked a little huffy; he had not expected to be asked such mundane questions. 'Fifty are fitted up as supplies, Odysseus. The campaign will be short and sharp.'

'Only fifty? For over one hundred thousand men? They'll eat the food out in less than a moon.'

'In less than a moon,' the High King of Mykenai stated, 'we will enjoy all the food Troy has in store.' His face spoke more volumes than his words; he had made up his mind and would not be budged. Oh, why on this point – the most tenuous point, the most unpredictable point? But he was like that sometimes, and then nothing Nestor, Palamedes or I could say would sway him.

Achilles stood up and took the Staff. 'This worries me, King Agamemnon. Surely you should pay as much attention to our supply lines as you should to embarkation, sailing, even battle tactics? Over one hundred thousand men will eat over one hundred thousand dippers of grain a day, over one hundred thousand pieces of meat, over one hundred thousand eggs or cheeses a day – and will drink over one hundred thousand cups of watered wine a day. If the supply lines aren't properly established the army will starve. Fifty ships, as Odysseus said, will last less than a moon. What about keeping those fifty ships in constant transit between Greece and the Troad, bringing more? And what if it turns out to be a long campaign?'

If Nestor, Palamedes and I could not sway him, what chance did a young pup like Achilles have? Agamemnon stood with lips compressed, a red spot burning in each cheek. 'I appreciate your concern, Achilles,' he said stiffly. 'However, I suggest you leave such worries to me.'

Unrepentant, Achilles handed the Staff to Kalchas and sat down. As he did so he said, apparently to no one in particular, 'Well, my father always says it is a silly man doesn't care for his soldiers himself, so I think I'll carry additional supplies for my Myrmidons in my own ships. And hire a few merchantmen to carry more.'

A message which sank in; I saw quite a few of the others deciding to do the same.

So too did Agamemnon see it. I watched his brooding dark eyes rest on the young man's vivid, eager face, and sighed. Agamemnon was jealous. What had been going on at Aulis in my absence? Was Achilles gathering adherents at Agamemnon's expense?

The following morning we assembled and drove out to inspect the army. Awe-inspiring. It took most of the day to tour the beach from end to end; my knees shook from standing in my car's wicker stirrups bearing the weight of full armour. Two rows of ships towered above us, tall vessels with red sides striped in black seams of pitch, their beaked prows daubed in blue and pink, the big eyes on their bows staring at us expressionlessly.

The army stood in the shadows they cast across the sand,

each man fully armoured, shield and spear at the ready; interminable ranks of men, all loyal to a cause they knew nothing about, save that there were spoils in the offing. No one cheered, no one rushed forward to get a better look at their Kings.

At the very end of the line stood the ships of Achilles and the men we had heard so much about, yet never seen: the Myrmidons. I was experienced enough not to expect them to look any different, but they did look different. Tall and fair, their eyes gleamed uniformly blue or green or grey beneath their good bronze helms, and they were fully clad in bronze rather than in the customary leather gear of common soldiers. Each man held a bundle of ten spears instead of the usual two or three; they carried heavy, man-high shields not that much inferior to my own veteran, and their arms were swords and daggers, not arrows or slingshots. Yes, these were front-line troops, the best we had.

As for Achilles himself, Peleus must have spent a fortune equipping his only son for war. His chariot was gilded, his horses by far the best team on parade – three white stallions of the Thessalian breed, their harness glittering with gold and jewels. Wherever the armour he wore had come from, I knew of only one suit better, and that reposed in my own strongbox. Like Agamemnon's dress suit it was gold-plated, but backed by a weight of bronze and tin that probably only he or Ajax could have carried. It was wrought all over with sacred symbols and designs, and embellished with amber and crystal. He bore one spear only, a dull and ugly thing. His cousin Patrokles drove him. Oh, cunning! When something ahead caused the parade of the Kings to halt for a moment, the horses of Achilles began to talk.

'Greetings, Myrmidons!' cried the near one, tossing his head until his long white mane floated.

'We will carry him bravely, Myrmidons!' issued from the lips of the middle horse, the steady one.

'Never fear for Achilles while we draw his car!' said the off one, his voice more neighing than the others'.

The Myrmidons stood grinning, dipping their clusters of spears in salute, while Idomeneus in the chariot ahead of Achilles stood with jaw dropped, shivering.

But I had seen the trick, following close behind that golden car. Patrokles was talking for them, keeping his lip movements to a minimum. Clever!

The weather continued sunny, the breeze a light zephyr; all the omens spoke of an uneventful sailing and a clear passage. But on the night before the launching I could not sleep, had to get up to pace long and restlessly beneath the stars. I was contemplating the profile of a nearby ship when someone came through the dunes.

'You cannot sleep either.'

No need to peer to see who it was. Only Diomedes would seek out Odysseus in preference to any other. A good friend, my war-scarred comrade, the most battle hardened of all the great company going to Troy. He had fought in every campaign of any size from Crete to Thrake, and he had been one of the second Seven Against Thebes, who took that city and razed it when their fathers could not. He possessed a ruthless passion I lacked, for though I owned the ruthlessness, I did not have the passion; my spirit was forever tempered by the ice inside my mind. As on other occasions, I felt a stab of envy, for Diomedes was a man who had sworn to build a shrine out of the skulls of his enemies and actually kept the vow. His father had been Tydeus, a very famous Argive king, but the son was the better man by far. Diomedes would not fail at Troy. He had come from Argos to Mykenai with all the fiery eagerness his heart could marshal, for he had loved Helen to distraction, and like poor Menelaos he refused to believe she had run away of her own accord. He held me in high esteem, an emotion I sometimes felt was close to hero worship. Hero worship? *Me?* Strange.

'It will rain tomorrow,' he said, lifting his long throat and looking into the depths of the sky.

'There are no clouds,' I objected.

He shrugged. 'My bones ache, Odysseus. I remember that my father always said that a man broken on the rack of battle many times, his frame cracked or shattered by spears and arrows, aches with the coming of rain and cold. Tonight the pain is so great that I cannot sleep.'

I had heard of this phenomenon before, and shuddered. 'For all our sakes, Diomedes, I hope that just this once your bones are wrong. But why seek me out?'

He grinned. 'I knew the Ithakan Fox would not sleep until he felt the waves beneath his ship. I wanted to speak to you.'

Throwing my arm across his broad shoulders, I turned him in the direction of my tent. 'Then let us talk. I have wine, and a good fire in the tripod.'

We settled down on couches with the tripod holding the fire between us, full goblets at our hands. The tent was dim and warm, the seats plumped with pillows, the wine unwatered in the hope it would induce sleep. No one was likely to disturb us, but to make sure, I drew the curtain across the tent flap.

'Odysseus, you're the greatest man in this expedition,' he said earnestly.

I couldn't help laughing. 'No, no! Agamemnon is that! Or, failing him, Achilles.'

'*Agamemnon?* That stiff-rumped, pigheaded autocrat? No, never him! He may get the credit, but that's because he's the High King, not because he's the greatest man. Achilles is only a lad. Oh, I grant you there is potential for greatness there! He has a mind. He may prove formidable in the future. But at this moment he's untried. Who knows? He might turn tail and run at sight of blood.'

I smiled. 'No, not Achilles.'

'All right, I concede that. But he can never be the greatest man in our army, because you are, Odysseus. You are! It will be your work and none other's that delivers Troy into our hands.'

'Rubbish, Diomedes,' I said gently. 'What can intelligence do in ten days?'

'Ten days?' He sneered. 'By the Mother, more like ten years! This is a real war, not a hunt.' He put his empty cup on the floor. 'But I didn't come to talk about wars. I came to ask for your help.'

'*My* help? You're the skilled warrior, Diomedes, not I!'

'No, no, it has nothing to do with battlefields! I know my way around them blindfolded. It's in other things I need your help, Odysseus. I want to watch you work. I want to learn how you hold your temper.' He leaned forward. 'You see, I need someone to watch over this accursed temper of mine, teach me to keep my daimon inside instead of letting it loose to my cost. I thought that if I saw enough of you, some of your coolness might rub off on me.'

His simplicity touched me. 'Then call my quarters yours, Diomedes. Draw up your ships next to mine, deploy your troops next to mine in battle, come with me on all my missions. Every man needs one good friend to bear with him. It is the only panacea for loneliness and homesickness.'

He extended his hand across the bright flames, not seeming to notice how they licked about his wrist. I wound my fingers around his forearm; thus we sealed our pact of friendship, shared our loneliness, and made it less lonely.

Somewhere in the middle marches of the night we must have slept, for I woke in the dawn light to the howl of a rising wind, singing in the shrouds of all those ships, crying loud and vicious about their prows. On the other side of the blackened, guttered fire Diomedes was stirring, breaking off the supple beauty of his arousal with a grunt of pain.

'My bones are worse this morning,' he said, sitting up.

'With good reason. There's a gale outside.'

He got cautiously to his feet and went to the curtained flap of the tent, peered outside and returned to his couch.

'It's the father of all storms come down out of the north. The

wind's still in that quarter, and I can feel the breath of snow.
No launching today. We'd all get blown to Egypt.'

A slave came wheeling a tripod with a fresh fire upon it,
made up the couches and brought us hot water to wash in.
There was no need to hurry; Agamemnon would be so put out
he would call no council before noon. My woman fetched
steaming honey cakes and barley bread, a sheep's cheese and
mulled wine to finish the repast. It was a good meal, the more
so because it was shared; we lingered warming our hands over
the fire until Diomedes went back to his tent to change for the
council. I donned a leather kilt and blouse, laced on high boots
and flung a fur-lined cloak about my shoulders.

Agamemnon's face was as dark and stormtossed as the sky;
fury and chagrin warred in his rigid features, all his plans
collapsed around his golden feet. He had a sneaking feeling he
would yet look ridiculous, his grand venture disbanded before
it so much as got started.

'I've summoned Kalchas to an augury!' he snapped.

Sighing, we made our ways out into the unwelcome teeth of
the gale, pulling our mantles close. The victim lay with all four
legs strapped upon the marble altar beneath the plane tree.
And Kalchas dressed in purple! *Purple?* What had been happen-
ing in Aulis before I arrived? Agamemnon must think the world
of him, to permit him to wear purple.

The coincidence was just too much to swallow, I thought as
I waited for the ceremony to begin; two moons of perfect
weather, then on the very day the expedition was to have
sailed, all the elements combined against it. Most of the Kings
had elected to return to their quarters rather than suffer the
freezing wind and sleet that staying to witness the augury
meant. Only those senior in years or authority remained to
bolster Agamemnon: myself, Nestor, Diomedes, Menelaos,
Palamedes, Philoktetes and Idomeneus.

I had never seen Kalchas at work before, and had to admit
that he was very good. With hands trembling so much they
could hardly lift the jewelled knife, his face waxen, he cut the

victim's throat jerkily, almost upsetting the great golden chalice as he held it to catch the blood; when he poured the scarlet stream out upon the cold marble it seemed to smoke. Then he slit open the belly and began to interpret the multiple folds of entrails according to the practice of priests trained in Asia Minor. His movements were rapid and dysrhythmic, his breathing so stertorous that I could hear it whenever the wind died for a moment.

Without warning he spun about to face us. 'Listen to the word of the God, O Kings of Greece! I have seen the will of Zeus, the Lord of All! He has turned away from you, he refuses to give this venture his blessing! His motives are clouded by his wrath, but it is Artemis who sits upon his knee and begs him to remain obdurate! I can see no more, his fury overwhelms me!'

About what I had expected, I thought, though the mention of Artemis was a deft touch. However, to give him his due, Kalchas really did look like a man pursued by the Daughters of Kore, a man stripped of all save his life in a single flake of time. There was genuine agony in his eyes. I wondered about him anew, for he obviously believed what he said, even if he had worked it all out beforehand. Any man who possesses the power to influence others interests me, but no priest ever interested me as Kalchas did.

And no, you have not yet concluded your performance, I thought; there is more to come.

At the foot of the altar Kalchas wheeled and flung his arms wide, his huge sleeves flapping soaked in the sleety wind, his head far back, the line of its tilt revealing that he looked at the plane tree. I followed his gaze to where the branches were still bare, wormy buds not yet unfurled. A nest was tucked into one fork, and on it sat a bird, hatching. An ordinary brown bird of some indiscriminate kind.

The altar snake was writhing along the branch with greed in his cold black eyes. Kalchas drew in his arms, still upraised, until both hands pointed at the nest; we watched with bated breath. A large reptile, he opened his jaws to take the bird, swallowing her whole until she was a series of tattoos thrusting at his rich brown scales. Then one by one he devoured her eggs: six, seven, eight, nine, I counted. The mother and all nine of her eggs.

The meal over, like all his kind he stopped in his tracks, curling about the thin branch as if graven from stone. His eyes were riveted on the priest without the shadow of an expression; no human blinks fractured the frigid penetration of his stare.

Kalchas twisted as if some God had driven an invisible stake clean through his belly, moaning softly. Then he spoke again.

'Listen to me, O Kings of Greece! You have witnessed the message of Apollo! He speaks when the Lord of All refuses! The sacred snake swallowed the bird and her nine unhatched young. The bird herself is this coming season. Her nine unborn children are the nine seasons as yet unborn of the Mother. The snake is Greece! The bird and her young are the years it will take to conquer Troy! Ten years to conquer Troy! Ten years!'

The silence was so profound it seemed to vanquish the storm. No one moved or spoke for a long time. Nor did I know what to think of that stunning performance. Was this foreign priest a true seer? Or was this an elaborate charade? I looked at Agamemnon, wondering which would win: his certainty that the war would end in a few days, or his faith in the priest. The struggle was a violent one, for he was by nature a religiously superstitious man, but in the end his pride triumphed. Shrugging, he turned on his heel. I left the last of all, never taking my eyes from Kalchas. He was standing stock still, gazing at the High King's back, and there was malice in him, outrage because his first real exhibition of power had been ignored.

The days dripped onward into high spring, tortmented by strong winds and deluges of rain. The sea was lashed into waves as high as the decks of the ships; there could be no hope of sailing. Each of us settled down to wait in characteristic fashion. Achilles drilled the Myrmidons pitilessly, Diomedes paced up and down my poor tent floor with increasing impatience, Idomeneus dallied in the arms of the courtesans he had brought with him from Crete, Phoinix clucked like a demented hen over his fleet, Agamemnon chewed his beard and refused to listen to any kind of advice, while the troops idled and diced, quarrelled and drank. No easy business, either, to bring sufficient food across the rain-soaked leagues to keep the army eating.

I felt little. It was all one to me which way I spent the beginning of twenty years in exile. Only a few of us gathered each day at noon to witness the reading of the omens. None of us expected a positive reason from Kalchas as to why the Great God had turned against us. The new moon waxed to full and waned to nothing without a pause in the tempest; it began to seem a serious possibility that we would not sail at all. If another moon went by the winds would be more unpredictable, and by the end of summer Troy would be closed to us until next year.

More because of my fascination with Kalchas himself than in any real hope that the God would draw back his veil and let us see his purpose, I never missed the noon ritual. Nor did this particular day prompt any prickles that it would turn out to be different. I simply went in my role of Kalchas watcher. Only Agamemnon, Nestor, Menelaos, Diomedes and Idomeneus arrived to keep me company. I had noticed in passing that the altar snake had long since emerged from his gluttonous hibernation and had taken up residence in his niche again.

But today was different. In the midst of his probing into the victim's entrails Kalchas whipped around and pointed one long, bony, bloodied finger straight at Agamemnon.

'There stands the one who prevents the sailing!' he shrilled. 'Agamemnon King of Kings, you have denied the Archeress her due! Her long-dormant anger has roused, and Zeus, her divine father, has heard her pleas for justice. Until you give Artemis what you promised her sixteen years ago, King Agamemnon, your fleet will never sail!'

Not a wild guess. Agamemnon stood swaying on his feet, his face ghastly. Kalchas *knew* what he was talking about.

The priest stalked down the steps, stiff with outrage. 'Give Artemis what you denied her sixteen years ago, and you may sail! Not otherwise. Almighty Zeus has spoken.'

Covering his face with his hands, Agamemnon shrank away from the purple-clad figure of doom. 'I cannot!' he cried.

'Then disband your army,' said Kalchas.

'I cannot give the Goddess what she wants! She has no right to demand it! If I had dreamed what the outcome would be – oh, I would never have promised! She is Artemis, chaste and holy. How can she demand such a thing of me?'

'She demands her due, no more. Give it to her and you may sail,' Kalchas repeated, voice cold. 'If you continue to refuse your sixteen-year-old vow, the House of Atreus will sink into obscurity and you yourself will die a broken man.'

I stepped forward and forced Agamemnon's hands down. 'What did you promise the Archeress, Agamemnon?'

Eyes full of tears, he clung to my wrists like a drowning man to a spar. 'A stupid, unthinking vow, Odysseus! *Stupid!* Sixteen years ago Klytemnestra was at full term with our last child, but her labour dragged on for three days without fruit. She couldn't bring forth the child. I prayed to them all – the Mother, Here the Merciful and Here the Throttler, the Gods and Goddesses of the hearth, of labour, of children, of women. None of them answered me – none of them!'

The tears were falling, but he struggled on. 'In desperation I prayed to Artemis, even though she is a virgin with her face turned away from fecund women. I begged her to help my wife give birth to a fine and unblemished child. In return, I promised her the most beautiful creature born that year in my kindom. Not many moments after I made the promise, Klytemnestra was brought to bed of our daughter, Iphigenia. And at the end of the year I sent couriers through Mykenai to bring me all the offspring they considered most beautiful. Kids, calves, lambs, even birds. I saw them all and offered them all, though in my heart I knew they would not satisfy the Goddess. She rejected every sacrifice.'

Did nothing ever change? I could see the end of this awful story as clearly as if it were painted on a wall in front of my eyes. *Why* were the Gods so cruel?

'Finish it, Agamemnon,' I said.

'One day I was with my wife and the baby when Klytemnestra happened to remark that Iphigenia was the most beautiful creature in all of Greece – more beautiful, she said, than Helen. Before she was done saying it, I knew Artemis had put the words into her mouth. The Archeress wanted my daughter. Nothing less would satisfy her. But I couldn't do that, Odysseus. We expose babes at birth, but ritual human sacrifice has not been practised in Greece since the New Religion drove out the Old. So I prayed to the Goddess and begged her to understand why I couldn't do as she wanted. And as time went by and she did nothing, I thought she had understood. Now I see that she was only biding her time. She demands what I cannot give her, the life she let begin and insists upon ending while it is still virgin. The story of my daughter is come full circle. But I *cannot* permit human sacrifice!'

I hardened my heart. My son was lost to me: why should he keep his daughter? He had two others. His ambition had separated me from all *I* held dear – why shouldn't *he* suffer as well? If lesser men were compelled to obey the Gods, so too should the High King, who was everyone's representative before the Gods. He had promised, then withheld the promise for sixteen years only because it affected him personally. If the most beautiful thing born that year in his kingdom had been the child of any other man, he would have made the offering with a clear conscience. So I looked into his face with deliberate intention, my chest filled with the ache of exile, and succumbed to the urging of some daimon which had taken up residence within me the day that my house oracle had pronounced my fate.

'You have committed a terrible sin, Agamemnon,' I said. 'If

Iphigenia is the price Artemis demands, then you must pay it. Offer up your daughter! If you do not, your kingdom will collapse in ruins and your enterprise against Troy will turn you into the laughingstock of all time.'

How he hated being a laughingstock! Not the dearest member of his family could mean as much to Agamemnon as his kingship, his pride. I watched the conflict march across his face, the despair and grief, the vision of his own miserable descent into ignominy and ridicule. He turned to Nestor, hoping for support.

'Nestor, what should I do?'

Torn between horror and pity, the old man wrung his hands together and wept. 'Terrible, Agamemnon, terrible! But the Gods *must* be obeyed. If Almighty Zeus instructs you to give the Archeress what she demands, then you have no choice. I am very sorry, but I must agree with Odysseus.'

Weeping desolately, our High King appealed to each of the others; one by one, white-faced and grave, they sided with me.

I alone kept an eye on Kalchas, wondering whether he had made a few discreet enquiries into Agamemnon's past. Who could forget the hatred and vindictiveness in his face the day the storm had begun? A subtle man. And a Trojan.

After that, it was a matter of simple logistics. Agamemnon, reconciled, convinced – thanks to me – that he had no other alternative than to sacrifice his daughter, explained how difficult it would be to get the girl away from her mother.

'Klytemnestra would never permit that Iphigenia be brought to Aulis as a victim for the priest's knife,' he said, looking old and sick. 'As Queen, she would go to the people, and the people would uphold her in this.'

'There are ways,' I said.

'Then describe them.'

'Send me to Klytemnestra, Agamemnon. I'll tell her that, thanks to the storms, Achilles has become very restless and talks of taking himself and his Myrmidons back to Iolkos. I'll tell her that you had the bright idea of offering him Iphigenia as his wife provided he remains at Aulis. Klytemnestra won't question this. She told me that it was her ambition to marry Iphigenia to Achilles.'

'But it's a slur on Achilles,' Agamemnon said doubtfully. 'He would never consent. I've seen enough of him to know that he goes straight. After all, he's the son of Peleus.'

Exasperated, I cast my eyes skyward. 'Sire, *he will never know*! Surely you don't intend to tell the whole world about this business? Each of us here today will gladly take an oath of secrecy. Human sacrifice wouldn't win any hearts among our troops – they'd start to wonder who might be next. But if no rumour of it leaks out, then no harm is done, and Artemis is appeased. *Achilles will never know!*'

'Very well, do it,' he said.

As we left I took Menelaos to one side. 'Menelaos, do you want Helen back?' I asked.

A wave of pain flooded into his face. 'How can you ask?'

'Then help me, or the fleet will never sail.'

'Anything, Odysseus!'

'Agamemnon will send a messenger to Klytemnestra ahead of me. The man will warn her to take no notice of my story and instruct her to refuse me custody of the girl. You have to intercept him.'

His mouth set into a thin, hard line. 'I swear, Odysseus, that you'll be the only one who speaks to Klytemnestra.'

I was satisfied. For Helen he would do it.

It was easily done. Klytemnestra was delighted with the match she thought Agamemnon had arranged for this beloved youngest child, and it suited her to wed the girl to a man about to embark for a foreign war. She adored Iphigenia; marriage to Achilles would enable her to keep the girl with her at Mykenai until Achilles returned from Troy. So the Lion Palace rang with laughter and rejoicing while Klytemnestra packed boxes of finery with her own hands, spent time with her daughter to initiate her into women's mysteries and marriage. She was still beside the litter talking to Iphigenia when it passed through the Lion Gate, her nubile yet unwed elder child Chrysothemis weeping in frustration and envy. Whereas Elektra, the oldest one of all, a thin, dour and unattractive replica of her father, stood on the ramparts with her baby brother, Orestes, clasped tenderly in her arms. There was no love lost between her and her mother, I had noticed that.

At the foot of the path Klytemnestra reached inside the curtains to kiss Iphigenia's wide white brow. I shuddered. The High Queen was a woman given to passionate loves and hates; what would she do when she learned the truth, as eventually she must? If once she brought herself to hate Agamemnon, he would have good reason to fear her vengeance.

I hurried as fast as the bearers could carry the litter, anxious to reach Aulis. Whenever we stopped to rest or to camp Iphigenia chattered away to me artlessly – how much she had admired Achilles when she stole secret glances at him in the Lion Palace, how ardently she had fallen in love, how wonderful it was that she would marry him, for it was the desire of her heart.

I had steeled myself to feel no pity for her, but at times that proved difficult; her eyes were so innocent, so happy. But Odysseus is a man stronger than any others in that part of a man which gives him endurance, victory in adversity.

After night had fallen I brought the litter with its curtains drawn into the imperial camp and bundled Iphigenia straight inside a little tent near her father's. I left her with him, Menelaos hanging on doggedly for fear the sight of her would break down Agamemnon's resolve. Deeming it wiser not to draw attention to her advent, I posted no guards around her tent. Menelaos would have to make sure she stayed there.

CHAPTER ELEVEN

NARRATED BY
ACHILLES

Each day in the rain and cold I exercised my men, warming them with hard work. Other commanders might let their troops grow slack, but the Myrmidons knew me better than that. They revelled in the conditions under which they lived, liked the rigid discipline and enjoyed a sense of superiority over other soldiers, knowing themselves more professional.

I never bothered to go to imperial headquarters, deeming it pointless. And when the second moon, a sliver, came into the sky, all of us began to assume that there would be no expedition to Troy. We simply waited for the command to disband.

On the first night the moon waxed full Patrokles went to spend the evening with Ajax, Teukros and Little Ajax. I had been invited, but elected to remain where I was, not in a mood for frivolity when the ignominious end of the grand enterprise loomed. For a while I played my lyre and sang, then lapsed into inertia.

The noise of someone entering my tent made me lift my head to see a woman holding the flap apart, a woman muffled in a wet, steaming cloak. I stared dumbfounded, hardly believing my eyes. Then she stepped inside, pulled the curtain across the entrance, twitched off the hood of her cloak and shook her head to free her hair of a few inquisitive drops of rain.

'Achilles!' she cried, eyes shining like clear, brownish amber.

'I saw you at Mykenai when I peeped through the door behind Father's throne. Oh, I am so happy!'

By this time I was on my feet, still gaping.

She was not more than fifteen or sixteen, that I saw before she took off her cloak to show me skin like milky marble faintly veined and two plump breasts. Her mouth was softly pink and tenderly curved, her hair the colour of the heart of a fire. So alive she made the air around her brittle, she had laughter in her face and a hidden strength beneath her extreme youth.

'My mother didn't need to persuade me,' she hurried on when I said nothing. 'I couldn't wait until tomorrow to tell you how happy I am! Iphigenia will marry you gladly!'

I jumped. *Iphigenia?* The only Iphigenia I knew of was the daughter of Agamemnon and Klytemnestra! But what was she talking about? Whom could she have mistaken for me? I continued to stare at her like some shambling idiot, bereft of words.

My silence, the amazement in my face, finally altered her expression from glowing pleasure to uncertain anxiety.

'What are you doing in Aulis?' I managed to ask.

At which moment Patrokles walked in, saw, and propped. 'A visitor, Achilles?' His eyes twinkled. 'I'll go.'

I crossed the space between us quickly to take him by the arm. 'Patrokles, she says she is Iphigenia!' I whispered. 'She must be Agamemnon's daughter! And from what she says, she thinks I sent to her mother at Mykenai and asked to marry her!'

His amusement fled. 'Ye Gods! Is it a plot to discredit you? Or a test of your loyalty?'

'I don't know.'

'Shall we take her back to her father?'

Calmer now, I considered it. 'No. Obviously she stole out to see me, no one knows she's here. The best thing I can do is detain her while you try to get close enough to Agamemnon to learn what's afoot. Be as quick as you can.'

He disappeared.

'Sit, lady,' I said to my visitor, and sank into a chair. 'Would you like some water? A cake?'

The next thing she landed in my lap, wound her arms about my neck and pillowed her head on my shoulder with a soft sigh. Half inclined to tip her onto the floor, I looked down on her rioting curls and changed my mind. She was a child, and she was in love with me. To her I was immensely older, which was a novel sensation. It was half a year since I had seen Deidamia and this girl was arousing quite different emotions in me. My lazy, self-satisfied wife was seven years older than I, and she had done all the wooing. To a thirteen-year-old lad, just awakening to the sexual functions of his body, that had been marvellous. Now I found myself wondering what I would feel for Deidamia when I returned from Troy a battle-hardened man. It was very nice to hold Iphigenia, inhale not perfume but the sweet and natural smell of youth.

Smiling and content, she lifted her head to look at me, then laid it back against my shoulder. I felt her lips caressing my throat, and the breast flattened against my chest burned like a hot poker. *Patrokles, Patrokles, hurry back!* Then she said words I couldn't hear; I put my hand in her thick flame hair and pulled her head up until I could see her enchanting face.

'What is it?' I asked.

She blushed. 'I only asked if you were going to kiss me.'

I winced. 'No. Look at my mouth, Iphigenia. It wasn't made for kisses. The sensation for kissing is in the lips.'

'Then let me kiss you all over.'

A statement which ought to have made me push her away, but I could not. Instead I let her lips, soft as swan's down, roam around my face, press against my lowered eyelids, nestle into the side of my neck, where the nerves set a man's heart to hammering. Longing to fold her into me and crush her against me until she gasped for breath, I had to fight myself to free her, look down into her eyes sternly.

'Enough, Iphigenia. Sit still.' I held her so until at last Patrokles returned.

He remained in the doorway, his derisive eyes quizzing me. I took my arms from about her and lifted them in the air, torn between laughter and annoyance. It was not like Patrokles to mock me. Then I touched her cheek, pushed her off my lap into the chair. The teasing look had faded from his face; he looked grim and very angry. Nor would he speak until he was sure she couldn't hear.

'They've hatched a pretty plot, Achilles.'

'I never thought otherwise. What plot?'

'I was lucky. Agamemnon and Kalchas were alone in his tent, talking. I managed to lie unobserved in its lee and overhear most of what they said.' He drew a breath, trembled. 'Achilles, they've used your name to lure this child from her mother! They told Klytemnestra that you had asked to marry Iphigenia before the sailing in order to get the girl to Aulis. Tomorrow she's to be sacrificed to Artemis to expiate some old wrong Agamemnon did the Goddess.'

Anger is something every man experiences, though some men more than others. I had never thought of myself as an angry man, but now I shook with it, an anger so great it wiped out sense, ethics, principles, decency. The Gods on Olympos must have quailed. My mouth peeled back from my teeth, I shook as if the Spell had come upon me, and I would have gone out then and there into the rain to cut Agamemnon and the priest down with my axe had Patrokles not grasped my wrists with a strength I did not know he possessed.

'Achilles, *think*!' he whispered. '*Think!* What good will killing them do? Her blood is needed to allow the fleet to sail! From what passed between Agamemnon and Kalchas, it was plain to me that our High King has been cowed and badgered into this!'

I clenched my fists so hard that I broke his hold. 'Do you expect me to stand aside and applaud, then? They've used my name to perpetuate a crime forbidden by the New Religion! The thing is barbaric! It fouls the very air we breathe! And they used *my* name!' I shook him until his teeth rattled. 'Look at her,

Patrokles! Can you stand by and watch her sacrificed like a lamb?'

'No, you mistake me!' he said urgently. 'All I meant was that we should approach this with cool heads, not in blind rage! Achilles, think! *Think!*'

I tried to. I fought to. The daimon of madness was boiling within me so violently that conquering it almost killed me. Grey in its wake, I found logic returning. Trick them! There had to be a way to trick them! I took his hands in mine.

'Patrokles, would you do anything I asked of you?'

'Anything, Achilles.'

'Then go and find Automedon and Alkimos. We can trust them in any enterprise, they're Myrmidons. Tell Alkimos he has to find a young deer, then paint its antlers gold. He *must* have the beast by morning! Take Automedon into your full confidence. Both of you must be hidden behind the altar tomorrow before the sacrifice is scheduled to begin. You'll have the deer with you on a golden chain. Kalchas uses a great deal of smoke in his rituals. When Iphigenia is lying on the altar and the smoke billows – the priest wouldn't dare cut her throat in full view of her father – snatch the girl away and leave the deer in her place. Kalchas will know, of course, but Kalchas likes living. He won't say a thing beyond exclaiming at the miracle.'

'Yes, it might work … But how do Automedon and I manage to get her away?'

'There's a little shelter behind the altar where they keep the victim. Hide her in there until after everyone leaves. Then bring her to my tent. I'll send her back to Klytemnestra with a message explaining the plot. Can you see to all this?'

'Yes, Achilles. What of you?'

'I haven't attended one of Kalchas's auguries in many days, but tomorrow I'll stroll up to headquarters just in time for the ceremony. For now, I'll send her back to her tent. How she got here unobserved I'll never know, but it's just as important that she's returned unobserved. I'll take her myself.'

'Perhaps she was seen coming here,' Patrokles said.

'No. They'd never permit her to spend enough time with me to deflower her. Artemis likes virgins.'

He frowned. 'Achilles, wouldn't it be better to send her back to her mother right now?'

'I can't, Patrokles. That would mean an open break with Agamemnon. If all goes well tomorrow at the sacrifice, we will have sailed before Klytemnestra knows.'

'Then you believe that the death of Iphigenia is necessary to lift the weather?' he asked, his tone peculiar.

'No, I think the weather will lift of its own accord within the next day or two. Patrokles, I dare not risk an open break with Agamemnon, surely you can see that? *I want to go to Troy!*'

'I see it.' He shrugged. 'Well, I ought to go. Poor Alkimos will die of fright when he learns he has to find a young deer! I'll stay with Automedon for the rest of the night. Unless I send word that our plan's gone wrong, you may take it that we're behind the altar at noon.'

'Good.'

He slipped out into the rain.

Iphigenia had been watching us round-eyed. 'Who was that?' she asked, dying of curiosity.

'My cousin Patrokles. There's trouble with the men.'

'Oh.' She thought for a moment, then said, 'He looks very like you, except that his eyes are blue and he's smaller.'

'And has lips.'

She chuckled. 'That reduces him to an ordinary man. I love your mouth the way it is, Achilles.'

I hauled her to her feet. 'Now I must get you back to your tent before someone discovers you're not in it.'

'Not yet,' she cajoled, stroking my arm.

'Yes, Iphigenia.'

'We marry tomorrow. Why not let me stay the night?'

'Because you're the daughter of the High King of Mykenai, and the daughter of the High King of Mykenai must be a virgin on her wedding day. The priestesses will confirm it beforehand,

and afterwards I must display the bridal sheet to prove I'm your husband in every way,' I said firmly.

She pouted. 'I don't want to go!'

'Want or not, go you will, Iphigenia.' I put my hands one on either side of her face. 'Before I take you home, I require a promise of you.'

'Anything,' she said, bright and brilliant.

'Don't mention this visit to your father or to anyone else. If you do, your virginity will be suspect.'

She smiled. 'Only one more sleep, then! I can bear that. Take me back, Achilles.'

No word came from Patrokles that our plans had gone wrong. Well before noon I put on my dress armour, the suit my father had given me from the Minos hoard, and made my way to the altar beneath the plane tree. Things looked quite normal; I breathed a sigh of relief. Patrokles and Automedon were in place.

Oh, the looks on the Kings' faces when they saw me! Odysseus took Agamemnon's arm in a hard grasp immediately, Nestor shrank between Diomedes and Menelaos, while Idomeneus, the only other present, looked startled and uneasy. They were all in on it, then. Nodding a casual greeting to them, I ranged myself off to one side as if the impulse to attend today had been pure chance. Came the sound of footsteps in the sodden grass behind us; Odysseus shrugged, realising there was no time for them to persuade me to leave. Not that I saw his mind work. Being Odysseus, his very openness and normality were evidence of his subtlety. The most dangerous man in the world. Red-haired and left-handed. Omens of evil.

As if mildly curious, I turned round to see Iphigenia approaching the altar slowly and proudly, chin up, an occasional quiver of her lips betraying her inward terror. When she saw me she flinched as if I had struck her; I gazed down through the windows of her eyes to see her last hope destroy itself. Her shock became anger, a sour and corroding emotion having nothing to do with the kind of anger I had felt when Patrokles told me of the plot. She hated me, she despised me, she stared at me as my mother had. While I stood looking stolidly at the altar, longing for the moment when I could explain.

Odysseus had been joined by Diomedes. One on either side of him, their hands beneath his armpits, they held Agamemnon upright. His face was wrung out, ghastly. Kalchas pushed Iphigenia onwards with a finger in the small of her back. She wore no chains. I could imagine how she scorned them – she was daughter of Agamemnon and Klytemnestra, whose pride was unassailable.

At the foot of the altar she turned to look at us, eyes bright with contempt, then she ascended the few steps and lifted herself easily onto the table, lay with her hands clasped beneath her breasts, her profile etched against the grey, heaving sea. No rain had fallen that morning; her marble bed was dry.

Kalchas threw various powders on the flames in three tripods ranged about the altar; smoke billowed green and bilious yellow, giving off a stench of sulphur and decay. Brandishing a long, jewelled knife, Kalchas flittered back and forth like some huge, obscene bat. As his arm lifted and the knife glinted, I remained rooted where I was, horrified yet spellbound. The blade flashed downwards; smoke rolled across the priest, blotted him out. Someone screamed, a shrill, gurgling shriek of despair that died away into a rattle. We stood like statues. Then a gust of wind roared down and swept the smoke away. Iphigenia lay still on the altar, her blood coursing along a channel in the stone to where a great gold cup sat between Kalchas's hands, catching it.

Agamemnon vomited. Even Odysseus gagged. But I could look nowhere except at Iphigenia, dying away into ashes, my mouth gaping open on a single howl of torment. Madness flooded my veins. My sword was in my hand as I sprang; if it had not been Odysseus and Diomedes who held Agamemnon I would have beheaded him as he hung between them with the sick dripping off his pampered beard. They dropped him like a stone to take hold of me, struggling desperately to wrench my sword off me while I flung them about like dolls. Idomeneus and Menelaos leaped to help them; even old Nestor waded into the fray. The five of them bore me to the ground, where I lay with my face not a handspan from Agamemnon's, cursing him until my voice rose to a scream. Suddenly my strength drained away and I began to weep. Then they prised my fingers from my sword and lifted both of us to our feet.

'You used my name to do this vile thing, Agamemnon,' I said through my tears, the anger gone, the hatred remaining. 'You allowed your Last Born to be sacrificed to feed your pride. From this day forward you are less to me than the meanest slave. You are no better than I. Yet I am worse. If I had not yielded to my ambition, I could have prevented this. But this much I tell you, King of Kings! I'm going to send a message to Klytemnestra to tell her what's happened here today. I'll spare no one – not you, not the others here, and least of all myself. Our honour is stained beyond cleansing. We are accursed.'

'I tried to stop it,' he protested listlessly. 'I sent a message to Klytemnestra to warn her, but the man was murdered. I did try, I did try … For sixteen years I've tried to avert this day. Blame it on the Gods. They tricked us all.'

I spat at his feet. 'Don't blame the Gods for your own failings, High King! The weakness lies in us. *We* are mortal.'

Somehow I reached my tent; the first thing I saw was the chair in which I had held her. Patrokles sat in another, weeping. When he heard me he took a sword from where it lay on the rug at his feet and knelt before me, the sword extended.

'What is this?' I asked, not knowing how to take more anguish.

The tip of the weapon went to his throat, he offered me its hilt. 'Kill me! I failed you, Achilles. I took away your honour.'

'I failed myself, Patrokles. *I* took away my honour.'

'Kill me!' he implored.

I took the sword and flung it away. 'No.'

'I deserve to die!'

'We all deserve to die, but that won't be our fate,' I said, fingers busy with the buckles on my cuirass.

He began to help me; habits are ineradicable, even in pain.

'I'm to blame, Patrokles. My pride and my ambition! How could I leave her fate hanging on such thin, flimsy strands? I was learning to love her, I would have married her gladly. No shame in it to divorce Deidamia – she was a shrewd plot between my father and Lykomedes to keep me out of trouble. You told me to send Iphigenia straight back to her mother, and that was sound advice. I said no because I couldn't bear to imperil my position in the army. I listened to pride and ambition, and I fell.'

The armour was off. Patrokles began to stow it away in its chest. Always acting as my servant.

'What happened then?' I asked him as he poured wine for us.

'It looked good,' he said, coming to sit opposite me. 'We got the deer.' His eyes darkened, gathered tears. 'But I decided not to share the glory with Automedon. I wanted all your praise for myself alone. So I went with the deer and hid behind the altar on my own. Then the creature grew agitated, began to bleat. I had forgotten to drug it! Had Automedon been with me, we could have muzzled it. But on my own – impossible. Kalchas found me. He's a warrior, Achilles! One moment I was staring up at him, the next he had taken hold of the chalice and struck me with it. When I came to I was bound hand and foot, a cloth in my mouth. That is why I beg you to kill me. Had I taken Automedon, all would have gone as planned.'

'To kill you, Patrokles, would mean I'd have to kill myself. Too easy. Only as living men can we eke out our punishment. As dead men we feel nothing, shades knowing neither joy nor pain. No fitting retribution,' I said, the wine sour on my tongue.

He swallowed, nodded. 'Yes, I understand. While I live I must remember my jealousy. While you live you must remember your ambition. A worse fate than death by far.'

But Patrokles did not have to remember the look in her eyes, the contempt. What must have passed through her mind between the time they told her the truth and the moment Kalchas's knife found her throat? How must she have thought of me, who had acted like her well beloved, then heartlessly abandoned her? Her shade would haunt me for the rest of my life. Short and glorious, then! Let my life be short and glorious.

'When do we go back to Iolkos?' Patrokles asked.

'*Iolkos?* No! We sail for Troy.'

'After this?'

'Troy is a part of my punishment. And Troy means I will not have to face my father, for I will die there. What would he think of me if he knew? Let the Gods spare him that.'

CHAPTER TWELVE

NARRATED BY
AGAMEMNON

I had my daughter buried at dead of night in a deep grave, unmarked, under a pile of rocks by the grey sea. Nor could I dower her fittingly in death, save to dress her richly and put all her little hoard of girlish jewels on her.

Achilles had promised to send a message to my wife blaming all of us; I could try to avert that by getting to her first. Yet I couldn't find the words or the man. What man could I trust who wasn't sailing with me? And what words could soften the blow I dealt Klytemnestra – what words could lessen her loss? No matter what disagreements had flared between us, my wife had always considered me a great man, one worthy to be her husband. Yet she was a Lakedaimonian, and the influence of Mother Kubaba was still very much alive there. When she learned of Iphigenia's death, she would try to bring back the Old Religion, rule in my stead as High Queen in fact – and in power.

At which moment I thought of a man in my train whom I could spare: my cousin Aigisthos.

The history of our House – the House of Pelops – is horrible. My father, Atreus, and Aigisthos's father, Thyestes, were brothers who vied for the throne of Mykenai after Eurysthesus died; Herakles should have inherited, but he was murdered. Many crimes were committed for the sake of the Lion Throne of Mykenai. My father did the unspeakable: murdered his nephews, stewed them, and served them up to Thyestes as a dish fit for a king. Even knowing this, the people chose Atreus as High King, banished Thyestes. Who fathered Aigisthos on a

Pelopid woman and then tried to foist the child off on Atreus as *his* son after Atreus married the woman. That was not the end of it. Thyestes connived at my father's murder and returned to the throne as High King until I was grown enough to wrest it off him, banish him.

But I had always liked my cousin Aigisthos, who was far younger than I, a handsome and charming fellow I got on with better than I did with my own brother, Menelaos. However, my wife neither liked nor trusted Aigisthos because he was the son of Thyestes and had a legitimate claim to the throne she was determined none but Orestes would inherit.

I sent for him as soon as I had worked out how much to tell him. His standing depended absolutely upon my good favour, which meant it behooved him to please me. So I sent Aigisthos to Klytemnestra, well primed and loaded with gifts. Iphigenia was dead, yes, but not at my command. Odysseus had planned and executed it. She'd believe *that*.

'I won't be away from Greece long,' I said to Aigisthos before he left, 'but it's vital that Klytemnestra doesn't go to the people and revive the Old Religion. You'll be my watchdog.'

'Artemis has always been your enemy,' he said, kneeling to kiss my hand. 'Don't worry, Agamemnon. I'll see that Klytemnestra behaves herself.' He cleared his throat. 'Of course, I was hoping for spoils from Troy. I'm a poor man.'

'You'll have your share of the spoils,' I said. 'Now go.'

The morning after the sacrifice I woke from a wine-soaked sleep to find the day clear and calm. The clouds and wind had fled during the night; only the water dripping off the tent eaves spoke of the moons of storm we had endured. I forced myself to offer Artemis thanks for her co-operation, but never again would I petition the Archeress for help. My poor little daughter was gone, not even a grave stele to keep her from anonymity. I couldn't look at the altar.

Phoinix was in my tent flap agog to commence embarkation; I decided on the morrow if the weather held.

'It will hold,' the old man said confidently. 'The seas between Aulis and Troy will stay as placid as milk in a bowl.'

'In which case,' I said, suddenly remembering how Achilles had criticised my supply plans, 'we'll offer to Poseidon and take a chance. Cram the ships, Phoinix. Cram them to the gunwales with food. I'll ransack the countryside for it.'

He looked startled, then grinned. 'I will, sire, I will!'

Achilles haunted me. His curses rang in my memory, his contempt seared my marrow. Why he blamed himself I couldn't begin to understand; he was no more capable of defying the Gods than I was. Yet I felt a grudging admiration for him. He had had the courage to flog his guilt in front of his superiors. I wished that Odysseus and Diomedes had not been so concerned for my safety. I wished that Achilles had lopped my head off, ended it there and then.

They pushed my flagship off its slips the next morning as dawn was beginning to suffuse the pale sky with rose. My hands planted firmly on the rail, I stood in the prow, feeling it dip and tremble in the quiet water. The start at last! Then I made my way down to the poop, where the ship's sides curled up and over into a cowl and the figurehead of Amphitryon watched forward. I turned my back on the oarsmen, glad that mine was a decked ship, that the rowers sat atop the deck and thereby left enough room below for my baggage, my servants, the war chest and all the impedimenta a High King needed. My horses were penned up along with a dozen others right beside the spot where I stood, and the sea rushed smoothly not far below the deck. We were very laden.

In my rear they slipped into the water, big red-and-black ships like centipedes with bristling oars for legs, crawling over the surface of Poseidon's unfaltering, eternal deeps. Twelve hundred of them altogether when the tally was in; eighty thousand fighting men and twenty thousand helpers of all kinds. Some of the extra ships contained nothing but horses and oarsmen; we are a chariot people, as are the Trojans. I still believed that the campaign would be a short one, but I also

171

understood that we would see no fabled Trojan horses before Troy fell.

Fascinated, I watched the scene, hardly able to credit that mine was the hand at the helm of this mighty force, that the High King of Mykenai was destined to be the High King of the Greek Empire. But not a tenth of the ships had gone down into the sea before my crew had rowed me out into the middle of the Euboian Strait and the beach was tiny in the distance. I knew a momentary panic, wondering how such a vast fleet could manage to hold itself together through the open leagues ahead.

We rounded the tip of Euboia in blazing sun, passed between it and Andros isle, and as Mount Ocha faded at the stern we struck the breezes which always blow around the open Aegaean. Oars were fettered gratefully to stanchions, men swarmed around the mast; the scarlet leather sail of the imperial flagship blossomed under the pressure of a southwest wind, warm and tender.

I strolled back along the deck between the rowing benches and mounted the short steps to the foredeck, where my special cabin was built. In our wake many vessels plied steadily through the swell breaking in tiny waves about their beaked prows. It seemed as if we were staying together; Telephos was standing right forward, turning his head occasionally to shout instructions to the two men who leaned on the rudder oars, steering us straight. He smiled at me contentedly.

'Excellent, sire! If the weather holds we'll keep up our pace in this wind, it's perfect. There shouldn't be any need to put in at Chios or Lesbos. We'll make Tenedos in good time.'

I was satisfied. Telephos was the best navigator in all of Greece, the one man who could guide us to Troy without our running the risk of beaching on some strand far from our destination. He was the only man to whom I would have entrusted the fates of those twelve hundred ships. Helen, I thought, your freedom is short-lived! You'll be back in Amyklai before you know it, and it will give me enormous pleasure to issue the command to cut off your lovely head with the sacred double axe.

The days passed happily enough. We sighted Chios but pressed on. There was no need to revictual, and the weather was so good that neither Telephos nor I cared to stretch our luck by dallying ashore. The coast of Asia Minor was scarcely out of sight now and Telephos knew the landmarks well, for he had passed up and down that coast hundreds of times during his career. He pointed out the huge isle of Lesbos to me gleefully, sure enough of his course to sail west of it, out of sight of land. The Trojans would not know we were coming.

We came to harbour on the southwest side of Tenedos, an isle very close to the Trojan mainland, on the eleventh day after sailing from Aulis. There was no room to beach so many ships; the best we could do was to let them ride at anchor as close inshore as possible, and hope that the clement weather persisted for a few more days. Tenedos was a fertile place, but boasted only a small population due to its proximity to a city held the largest in the world. As we came in the Tenedians clustered along the shore, their helpless gesticulations betraying their awe.

I clapped Telephos on the shoulder. 'Well done, pilot! You've earned a prince's share of the spoils.'

Swollen with his triumph, he laughed, then clattered down the steps to the midships, where he was soon surrounded by the hundred and thirty men who had sailed with me.

By nightfall the last of the fleet was nearby; all the top leaders came to join me at my temporary headquarters in Tenedos town. I had already done the most important job, which was to round up every living human soul on the island. No one could be let reach the mainland to inform King Priam what lay on the far side of Tenedos. The Gods, I thought, were united behind Greece.

The following morning I set off on foot for the top of the hills which crowned the centre of the isle, some of the Kings with me for the exercise, glad to be on solid ground. We stood with our cloaks flapping behind us in the wind, looking down across the blue, tranquil water to the Trojan mainland a few leagues away.

We couldn't miss Troy the city; my first sight of it made my stomach sink. I had thought of it, of course, in the only terms I knew: Mykenai atop the Lion Mountain; the mighty trading seaport of Iolkos; Korinthos commanding both sides of the isthmus; fabulous Athens. But they paled to insignificance. Troy not only towered, it spread as well, like some kind of gigantic stepped ziggurat too far away to discern details.

'What now?' I asked Odysseus.

He seemed lost in thought, his grey eyes fixed. But at my question he came back into himself, grinned. 'My advice is to sail across tonight under cover of darkness, marshal the army at dawn and strike Priam unaware, before he can close his gates. By tomorrow night, sire, you'll own Troy.'

Nestor squawked, Diomedes and Philoktetes looked horrified. I contented myself with a smile, while Palamedes smirked.

Nestor spoke, saving me the trouble. 'Odysseus, Odysseus, have you *no* idea of right or wrong at all?' he demanded. 'There are laws governing everything, including the conduct of war, and I for one will have no part in a venture wherein the formalities haven't been observed! *Honour*, Odysseus! Where is honour in your plan? Our names would stink out Olympos! We cannot disregard the law!' He turned to me. 'Don't listen to him, sire! The laws of warfare are unequivocal. We *must* obey them!'

'Calm down, Nestor, I know the law as well as you do.' I took Odysseus by the shoulders and shook him gently. 'Surely you didn't expect me to listen to such impious advice?'

For answer, he laughed, then said, 'No, Agamemnon, no! But you did ask me what now. I felt obliged to give you my choicest morsel of wisdom. If it falls on deaf ears, why should I repine? I'm not the High King of Mykenai. I'm merely your loyal subject Odysseus from rocky Ithaka, where a man must sometimes forget things like honour in order to survive. I've told you how to do the job in one day, and what I said is the only way that could be done. For I warn you – if Priam is given the chance to close his gates, you'll howl outside his walls for the whole ten years Kalchas prophesied.'

'Walls can be scaled, gates can be battered down,' I said.

'Can they?' He laughed again and seemed to forget us, his eyes turned inward.

His mind was a wondrous entity; it could lock upon the truth instantly. If in my heart I knew his advice was right, I also knew that if I were to take it, no one would follow me. It meant sinning against Zeus and the New Religion. What always fascinated me was how he managed to escape retribution for these impious ideas. Though it was said that Pallas Athene loved him more than any other man, and interceded with her almighty Father on his behalf at all times. She loved him, it was said, for the quality of his mind.

'Someone will have to journey to Troy bearing the symbols of war for Priam and demand the return of Helen,' I said.

They all looked eager, but I already knew which men I wanted.

'Menelaos, you're Helen's husband. You must go, of course. Odysseus, you and Palamedes will go too.'

'Why not me?' asked Nestor, annoyed.

'Because I need one of my chief advisers here,' I said, hoping it sounded convincing. Let him think I was deliberately shielding him from stress and he would fly out at me fiercely. He did eye me suspiciously, but I think the long sea journey must have taken its toll, for he didn't argue any further.

Odysseus came out of his reverie. 'Sire, if I'm to go on this mission, then I ask one favour. Let there be no suggestion that we're already here, hiding behind Tenedos. Let us give old Priam the impression that we're still at home in Greece preparing for war. All we're obliged to do under the law is formally notify him of a state of war before we attack. We don't have to do more. Also, Menelaos ought to demand suitable compensation for the mental anguish he's suffered since the abduction of his wife. He should demand that Priam reopen the Hellespont to our merchants and abolish the trade embargoes.'

I nodded. 'Good points.'

We made our way back down the slope towards the town, the more energetic striding ahead of me, Odysseus and Philoktetes in the lead, talking and guffawing like a pair of lads. Both were excellent men, but Philoktetes was the better warrior. Herakles himself had given Philoktetes his bow and arrows while he lay dying, though Philoktetes had been a boy at the time.

They leaped over tussocks of grass, the clear air a tonic; Odysseus jumped high above a clump of plants and clicked his heels together to demonstrate his agility. Philoktetes emulated him, landing light and lithe. A moment later he gave a short, sharp cry of alarm, his face contorting as he sank to one knee, his other leg extended. Wondering if he had broken it, we all ran to where he hunched panting, holding the extended leg between his hands. Odysseus was unsheathing his knife.

'What is it?' Nestor asked.

'I stepped on a serpent!' Philoktetes gasped.

I went numb with fear. Lethal serpents were rare in Greece, a type of creature very different from the house and altar snakes we loved and honoured so much because they hunted rats and mice.

Odysseus cut the two punctures deeply with his knife, then bent his head and fastened his lips over the gashes, spitting out blood and venom after each audible suck. Then he beckoned Diomedes.

'Here, Argive, lift him and carry him to Machaon. Try not to jar him, that will drive the poison closer to his vital parts. My friend,' he said to Philoktetes, 'lie very still, and be of good cheer. Machaon isn't the son of Asklepios for nothing. He will know what to do.'

Diomedes went on ahead of us, carrying his heavy load as

comfortably as if Philoktetes had been a child, in a smooth run I had seen him keep up in full armour for a long time.

Of course we went to Machaon's surgery immediately. He had been given a good house to share with his much shyer brother, Podalieros; men ail, even before the war begins. Philoktetes lay on a couch, eyes closed, breathing stertorously.

'Who treated the bite?' Machaon asked.

'I did,' said Odysseus.

'Well done, Ithakan. Had you not acted so expeditiously, he would have died on the spot. Even now he might die. The poison must be very deadly. He's had four convulsions and I can feel his heart fibrillate beneath my hand.'

'How long before we know the outcome?' I asked.

Like every physician loath to predict a fatal prognosis, he shook his head. 'I have no idea, sire. Did anyone catch the serpent, or at least see it?'

We shook our heads.

'Then I do not know,' said Machaon, sighing.

The delegation set off for Troy the next day in a big ship with its decks disarrayed to indicate that it had just made the long voyage from Greece alone; the rest of us settled down to await its return. We kept very quiet, made sure that the smoke from our fires didn't drift above the hills to betray our presence to any possible watchers on the mainland. The Tenedians gave us no trouble, still stunned by the size of the fleet which had descended upon them out of the blue.

I saw little of the younger leaders. They had elected Achilles as their chief and looked to him for their example rather than to me. Since the day Iphigenia died he had not come near me. More than once I had seen him, his height and carriage quite unmistakable, but he had pretended not to notice me and gone on his way. Though I could not help but see his methods with his Myrmidons, for he wasted no time and would not let them be idle, as all the other troops were. Every day he drilled and exercised them; those seven thousand soldiers were the fittest, most capable-looking men I had ever beheld. I had been a little surprised to learn that he had brought no more than seven thousand Myrmidons to Aulis, but I could see now that Peleus and his son had preferred quality to quantity. Not one of them was over twenty years of age and all of them were soldiers by profession rather than volunteers more used to pushing a plough or treading grapes. None, gossip had informed me, were married. Very wise. Only youths without wife or babes leap into battle careless of their fate.

Seven days after it had departed, the delegation returned. Its ship sailed in after dark and my three ambassadors came to my house at once. Their faces told me they had had no success, but I waited until Nestor arrived before I let them say a word. No need to summon Idomeneus.

'They refused to give her back, Agamemnon!' my brother said, smiting the table with his fist.

'Calm down, Menelaos! I never thought they would give her back. What actually happened? Did you see Helen?'

'No, they kept her hidden. We were escorted to the Citadel – they knew me from my previous visit, even in Sigios. Priam was sitting on his throne and asked me what I wanted this time. I said, Helen, and he laughed at me! If that wretched son of his had been there. I would have killed him on the spot!' He sat down, clutching his head between his hands.

'And been killed yourself. Go on.'

'Priam said Helen came of her own free will, that she did not wish to return to Greece, that she regarded Paris as her husband, and that she preferred to have the property she had taken with her in Troy, where she could use it to make sure that she never became a financial burden to her new country. He actually insinuated that I had usurped the throne of Lakedaimon, can you credit that? He said that after her brothers Kastor and Polydeukes died, *she* should have ruled in her own right! *She* was the daughter of Tyndareus! *I* am only Mykenai's puppet!'

'Well, well,' said Nestor, chuckling. 'It sounds to me as if

Helen was plotting rebellion even if she had elected to remain with you in Amyklai, Menelaos.'

When my brother rounded on the old man fiercely, I struck the floor with my staff. 'Go on, Menelaos!'

'So I handed Priam the red tablet with the symbol of Ares on it and he stared at it as if he had never seen anything like it. His hand shook so much that he dropped it on the floor. It broke. Everyone jumped. Then Hektor picked it up and took it away.'

'All of which must have occurred some days ago. Why didn't you return at once?' I asked.

He looked hangdog, didn't answer, and I knew why as well as Nestor did. He had hoped to see Helen.

'You haven't told them how that first audience finished,' Palamedes prompted.

'I will, if I'm let!' Menelaos snapped. 'Priam's eldest son, Deiphobos, publicly begged his father to murder us. Then Antenor stepped forward and offered to lodge us. He invoked Hospitable Zeus and forbade any Trojan to lift a hand against us.'

'Interesting, coming from a Dardanian.' I patted Menelaos soothingly. 'Be of good cheer, brother! You'll have your chance to be revenged soon enough. Now go and sleep.'

Only when Nestor and I were alone with Odysseus and Palamedes did I discover what I really wanted to know. Menelaos was the only one who had ever been to Troy, but during the year of our girding for war he had never managed to volunteer any useful information. How high were the walls? Very high. How many men could Priam call to arms? A lot. How firm were his ties to the rest of Asia Minor? Quite firm. It had been almost as bad as trying to prise information out of Kalchas, though my brother couldn't offer the priest's smooth excuse – that Apollo had tied his tongue.

'We must move quickly, sire,' said Palamedes quietly.

'Why?'

'Troy is a curious place, dominated by wise men and fools in equal number. Both can be dangerous. Priam is a mixture of wise man *and* fool. Among his counsellors I gained the most respect for Antenor and a youth named Polydamas. The son Menelaos just mentioned, Deiphobos, is a hotheaded pig. However, he isn't the Heir. He seems to hold no position of importance other than that he's one of the imperial sons – Priam's by his Queen, Hekabe.'

'As eldest he ought to be the Heir, surely.'

'Priam has been a regular old goat in his day. He boasts the incredible number of fifty sons – by his Queen, his other wives, and many concubines. Of daughters I understand the tally is over a hundred – he throws more girls than boys, he told me. I asked why he hadn't exposed some of the girls. He giggled and said that the beautiful ones made good wives for his allies, while the ugly ones wove enough cloth to keep the palace looking gorgeous.'

'Tell me about the palace.'

'It's huge, sire. As big, I'd say, as the old House of Minos at Knossos. Each of Priam's married children has a separate suite of rooms, and they live in luxury. There are other palaces within the Citadel. Antenor has one. So does the Heir.'

'Who is the Heir? I remember Menelaos mentioned the name of Hektor, but naturally I assumed he's the eldest.'

'Hektor is a younger son by Queen Hekabe. He was there when we first arrived, but left almost at once on some urgent mission to Phrygia. I might add that he begged to be relieved of the duty, but Priam insisted he go. As he leads their army, at the moment it lacks its commander-in-chief. Which leads me to assume that Hektor is a wiser man than his father. He's young – no more than twenty-five, I'd guess. A very big man. About the size of Achilles, in fact.'

I turned then to Odysseus, who was stroking his face slowly. 'And what of you, Odysseus?'

'On the subject of Hektor, I'd add that the soldiers and the common people adore him.'

'I see. So you didn't confine your activities to the palace.'

'No, Palamedes did that. I prowled the city. A very useful and instructive exercise. Troy, sire, is a nation within walls. *Two* sets of walls. Those around the Citadel are imposing enough – higher than the walls around Mykenai or Tiryns. But the outer set which surrounds the entire city is mammoth. Troy *is* a city in the true meaning of that word, Agamemnon. It's built entirely within the outer set of walls, not scattered outside the walls as our cities are. The people don't need to flee inside when an enemy threatens because they already live inside. There are many narrow streets and countless, towering houses they call apartment buildings, each of which accommodates several dozen families.'

'Antenor told me,' Palamedes interrupted, 'that at the last census one hundred and seventy thousand citizens declared their presence. I would judge from that fact that Priam could raise an army of forty thousand good men without looking any further than the city itself – fifty thousand if he used older men as well.'

Thinking of my own eighty thousand troops, I smiled. 'Not enough to keep us out,' I said.

'More than enough,' Odysseus said. 'The city measures some leagues in circumference, though it's more oblong than round. The outer ramparts are fantastic. I measured one stone from my fist knuckles to my elbow, then counted the rows. The walls are thirty cubits high and at least twenty cubits thick at their base. They're so old that no one remembers when they were built, or why. Legend has it that they're cursed and must disappear from sight for ever, thanks to Priam's father, Laomedon. But I doubt they'll disappear from sight thanks to our assaulting them. They slope gently and the stones have been polished. No secure grip for ladder or grapple.'

Conscious of a niggling depression, I cleared my throat. 'Is there no weakness, Odysseus? No lesser wall? Or the gates?'

'Yes, there is a weakness – though I wouldn't count on it, sire. A section of the original walls collapsed on the western side during what I would judge was the same earthquake that finished Crete. Aiakos repaired the breach, which the Trojans now call the Western Curtain. It's about five hundred paces in length, and rough hewn. Plenty of ledges and crannies for grapples. There are only three gates: one close by the Western Curtain, called the Skaian; one on the south side, called the Dardanian; and one on the northeast, called the Idan. The only other entrances are easily guarded drains and conduits which permit the passage of no more than one man at a time. The gates themselves are massive. Twenty cubits tall, arched over by the pathway which runs right around the top of the outer walls, enabling rapid transfer of troops from one section to another. The gates are built of logs reinforced with bronze plates and spikes. No ram would so much as make them shudder. Unless those gates are open, Agamemnon, you'll need a miracle to enter Troy.'

Well, Odysseus was always pessimistic. 'I can't see their holding out against a force as large as ours, I just can't.'

Palamedes studied the contents of his wine cup and said not one word; Nestor was of like mind. Odysseus continued.

'Agamemnon,' he said earnestly, 'If the gates of Troy are closed, they have more than enough men to hold you off. You must attempt to scale at one place only, the Western Curtain. But it's only five hundred paces long. Forty thousand men would smother it like flies a lump of carrion. Believe me, they can keep you out for years! Everything hinges on whether they really believed that we're still at home in Greece. But let them sail a fishing boat to this side of Tenedos and we're undone. I think you have to plan for a long campaign.' His eyes twinkled. 'You could, of course, starve them out.'

Nestor gasped in outrage. 'Odysseus, Odysseus! There you go again! We'd be cursed to instant madness!'

He wriggled his red brows, unrepentant as ever. 'I know, Nestor. But as far as I can see, all the rules of war seem to favour the enemy. Which is a great pity. Starvation makes sense.'

Suddenly tired, I rose to my feet. 'Woe the race of men when your like has command, Odysseus. Go to bed. In the morning I'll call a general council. The following day we'll sail at dawn.'

As they went out, Odysseus turned. 'How is Philoktetes?'

'Machaon says there is no hope for him.'

'I'm sorry to hear that. What's to be done with him?'

'What can be done? He'll have to stay here. It would be the height of folly to take him into a battle camp.'

'I agree he can't come with us, sire, but nor can we leave him here. Once we turn our backs on these Tenedians they'll slit his windpipe. Send him to Lesbos. The Lesbians are more cultured people, they'll not harm a sick man.'

'He'd never survive the voyage,' Nestor protested.

'It's still the least of the various evils.'

'You're right, Odysseus,' I said. 'Lesbos it is.'

'My thanks. He's a man worth saving if at all possible.' Odysseus looked suddenly brisk. 'I'll tell him now.'

'He wouldn't understand you. He's been in a coma for three days,' I said

CHAPTER THIRTEEN

NARRATED BY
ACHILLES

Kalchas made another prophecy, one which caused Agamemnon to change his mind about being the first of the Kings to set foot on Trojan soil; the first of the Kings to do that, said the priest, would die in the initial battle. I glanced at Patrokles and shrugged. If the Gods had chosen me as the doomed man, why should I worry? There was glory in it.

We had our sailing and landing orders, we knew when we would sweep onto the shore and beach our men. Patrokles and I stood on the foredeck of my flagship watching the vessels ahead of us, far fewer than those behind us, for we of Iolkos were among the first. Agamemnon's flagship led the way with his huge Mykenaian convoy on his left and the ships of one of my father's subject Kings, Iolaos of Phylake, on his right. I came next, after me Ajax and all the rest.

Before we pushed off Agamemnon made it clear that he didn't expect to be greeted by hostile men bearing arms; he expected to invest the city without organised opposition.

But the Gods were not with us that day. The moment the seventh ship in Agamemnon's line rounded the tip of Tenedos, great billows of smoke arose on the headland flanking Sigios. They had learned that we lurked nearby and they were ready for us.

Our orders were to take Sigios, then press on immediately to the city. When my own ship sailed out into the strait I could see the Trojan troops lining up along the beach.

Even the winds were against us. We had to furl our sails and break out the oars, which meant half of our army would be too weary to fight well. To add to our woes, the current issuing from the mouth of the Hellespont fanned out into the open sea, and it too was against us. It took the whole morning to row the short distance to the mainland.

I smiled sourly when I noticed that the order of precedence had changed; Iolaos of Phylake forged ahead of Agamemnon now, with the men of Phylake in their forty ships close behind him and the High King's mighty fleet out on his left. Did Iolaos curse his fate, or welcome it? I wondered. He had been elected the first King ashore, he was the one Kalchas said must die.

Honour dictated that I should ask a bigger effort of my oarsmen, yet prudence urged that I ensure my Myrmidons retained enough breath to do battle.

'You can't catch Iolaos,' Patrokles said, reading my mind. 'What will be, will be.'

This wasn't my first military engagement, for I had fought alongside my father since I came down from Pelion and the years with Chiron; but all those campaigns were as nothing compared to what awaited us on the beach at Sigios. The Trojans were lining up in thousands upon thousands, more and more of them, and the few ships which had sat on the pebbles yesterday were now inland, beyond the village.

When I touched Patrokles on the arm I felt it shaking, looked down at my own limbs: firm.

'Patrokles, go to the stern and call across to Automedon in the next ship. Tell him to have his steersmen close up the gap between us, and tell him to pass the message on, not only to our ships, but to everyone else's. When we beach we'll not be doing much more than floating in the water, so the beaks won't break down hulls. Tell Automedon to get his men across my deck onto the beach, and everybody else the same. Otherwise we'll never manage to get enough troops ashore to avert a massacre.'

He sped through the waist to the afterdeck, cupped his hands about his mouth and shouted to the vigilant Automedon, whose armour sparkled in the sun as he shouted back. Then I saw him obey, saw his ship closing upon ours until it ran with its beaked bow just clear of our beam. The other ships in view were doing the same; we had turned into a floating bridge. Below me my men were up from their oars and arming, our impetus sufficient to run us aground. There were only ten ships ahead of me now, and the first of them belonged to Iolaos.

It plunged its beak into the shingle and came to a halt, shuddering; for a moment Iolaos stood in its bow hesitating, then he shrieked the Phylakian war cry and sped down into the waist. He was over the side with his men after him, swarming as they took up the battle song. Frightfully outnumbered, they did some havoc nonetheless. Then a massive warrior in a suit of gold cut Iolaos down and hacked him to ribbons with an axe.

Others were beaching now. Ships to my left were sliding in, their men jumping from the rails down into the mêlée, not willing to wait for ladders. I strapped on my helmet and clipped its golden plume out of the way, wriggled inside my gold-trimmed bronze cuirass to straighten it, and picked up my axe in both hands. It was a lovely thing, one of the pieces of plunder Minos had picked up during a foreign campaign, bigger and heavier by far than any Cretan axe. My sword brushed my leg, but Old Pelion lay put away, no use in close fighting. This was axe work, and my arms could swing that double-bladed beauty back and forth the whole day without flagging. Only Ajax and myself chose an axe for hand-to-hand combat; an axe big enough to be more useful than a sword was too cumbersome for an ordinary man. Little wonder then that I hungered to come at the gold-suited giant who had killed Iolaos.

Too intent upon the beach, too engrossed in taking everything into account, I lost whatever passed through my mind during those last few moments. When a shudder told me that we were aground, another followed hard upon it, almost causing me to lose my balance. A glance behind me revealed that Automedon had married his ship to mine and that his men were already pouring across my deck. Like some pampered

Cretan woman's monkey I leaped onto the prow and hung there looking down on the heads of such a mixture of men I could hardly tell friend from foe. But it was necessary that I be seen by all the men who surged behind, those on Alkimos's vessel coming across Automedon's deck, more and more of them as my ship still endured the weakening spasms of collisions occurring further and further away.

Then I brandished my axe high above my head, roared out the war cry of the Myrmidons in a brazen voice, and sprang from the prow down onto the seething mass of heads below me. Luck was with me; a Trojan head shattered beneath the impact of my heels. I fell on top of him still holding the axe fast in my hands, my shield somewhere on the deck above, too much of a hindrance in a struggle like this. In an instant I was upright, howling the battle call at the top of my lungs until the Myrmidons took it up and the air resonated with the chilling sound of Myrmidons out to kill. The Trojans wore purple plumes atop their helms, another piece of good luck; purple was forbidden to any Greek save the four High Kings – and Kalchas.

Eyes glared at me, a dozen swords menaced, but I reared up and brought the axe down with such force that I cleaved a man in two from skull to groin. It stopped them. Good counsel from my father, who had taught it to every Myrmidon: that absolute ferocity of aggression in hand to hand combat would make men back away instinctively. I used the axe again, this time in a circle like a spoke on a wheel, and those who were still foolish enough to try to get at me felt its blade slice their bellies through their armour, which was bronze. No leather for a Trojan! But then, they had the bronze monopoly. How rich Troy must be.

Patrokles was behind me with his shield to protect my back and Myrmidons were dropping countless in our rear from ships to shore. The old team was in action. I advanced, the axe breaking the ranks in front of me like a priest's wand, cutting down anyone wearing a purple plume. This was nothing like the battle of a true test of strength; there was neither time nor room to single out a prince or a king, no space separating the opposing forces. This was just a pack of warriors of all degree, breast to breast. What seemed like years ago I had vowed to keep a tally of those I slew, but I soon became too excited to count, in love with the sudden give of soft flesh through hard bronze as the axe bit.

Nothing existed for me save blood and faces, terror and fury, gallant men who tried to parry the axe with their swords and died for it, cowards who met their fates in gibbering dread, worse than cowards who turned their backs and tried to flee. I felt myself invincible, I *knew* none on that field would bring me down. And I took pleasure in the sight of faces split wide in bloody yawns; the lust to kill soaked into my very marrow. A kind of madness, reaping a harvest of chests and bellies and heads, the axe dripping blood, blood running down the handle into the rough rope fibres wound around its base so that my hands wouldn't slip. I forgot everything. All I wanted was to see purple plumes dyed red. If someone had put a Trojan helmet on my head and turned me loose on my own men I would have slaughtered just the same. Right and wrong did not exist, only the lust to kill. This was the meaning of all my years under the sun, this was what I had been left a mortal man to become: a perfect killing machine.

We ground the soil of Sigios to powder under the trample of our boots, it drifted far above our heads and rose to the vault of the sky. Though in later battles I behaved with more logic and had a thought for my men, in that one their welfare never entered what passed for my mind. I didn't care who was winning or losing as long as *I* was winning. If Agamemnon himself had fought next to me, I wouldn't have known. Not even Patrokles penetrated my furore, though he was the sole reason why I survived that first fight, for he kept the Trojans off my back.

Suddenly someone swung a shield across my path. I struck with all my might to come at the face behind it, but like a bolt from a bow he stepped aside and his sword came within a hair of my right arm. I gasped as if flung into a pool of icy water, then shook in exultation when he lowered his shield to see me better. A prince at last! Clad all in gold. The axe he had used to cut Iolaos down had vanished, replaced by a longsword. Snarling my pleasure, I faced him eagerly. A very big man, he had the look of one used to excelling in battle, and he was the first man who dared to challenge me. We circled warily, my axe dragging on the ground by its thong until he gave me an opening. When I leaped and swung he flicked aside, but I was fast too; I dodged the sweep of his sword as easily as he had evaded my axe. Understanding that we had each found a worthy foe, we settled down to the duel steadily and patiently. Bronze rang on bronze-backed gold, always a parry, neither of us able to wound the other, each of us conscious that the soldiers, Trojan and Greek, had moved back to give us room.

Whenever I missed my mark he laughed, though in four places his golden shield gaped to show the bronze, the innermost layers of tin. I had to fight my rising rage as hard as I fought him – how dared he laugh! Duels were sacred work, not to be desecrated by ridicule, and it infuriated me that he couldn't seem to feel that sanctity. I made two mighty lunges one after the other and missed him. Then he spoke.

'What's your name, Clumsy?' he asked, laughing.

'Achilles,' I said between my teeth.

That made him laugh harder. 'Never heard of you, Clumsy! I'm Kyknos, son of Poseidon of the Deeps.'

'All dead men stink alike, son of Poseidon, be they fathered by Gods or men!' I cried.

Which only made him laugh.

The same kind of rage swelled up in me that I had endured when I saw Iphigenia lying dead on the altar, and I forgot all the rules of combat Chiron and my father had taught me. With a shriek I sprang on him, in under the point of his blade, my axe raised. He leaped backwards, stumbling; his sword fell, and I broke it into a hundred fragments. Round came his wasp-

189

waisted, man-sized shield to cover his back as he turned and ran, pushing through the Trojan troops in savage desperation, calling for a spear. Someone thrust the weapon into his hand, but I was too close on his tail for him to use it. He went on retreating.

I plunged into the closing ranks of Trojans after him. Not one man among them aimed a blow at me, whether because they were too frightened or because they respected the time-honoured tenets of duel, I never discovered. The throng dwindled until the battle lay behind us, until a looming cliff brought Kyknos the son of Poseidon to a halt. The spear describing lazy circles, he turned to face me. I stopped too, waiting for him to cast, but he preferred to use the spear as a lance than as a javelin. Wise, since I had both axe and sword. When he flicked the head forward, I jumped to one side. Time and time again it darted at my chest, but I was young and as easy on my feet as a much lighter man. I saw my chance, went in and broke the spear in two. All he had now was his dagger. Not finished yet, he groped for it.

Never had I wanted anyone dead as much as I wanted this buffoon dead – yet not cleanly dead, felled by axe or sword. I dropped the axe and pulled the heavy baldric holding my sword over my head. My dagger followed. The amusement left his face at last. He finally gave me the respect I had vowed to wrest from him. But he could *still* speak words!

'What was your name, Clumsy? Achilles?'

The pain consumed me; I was unable to answer. He was not close enough to the God to understand that a duel between those of the Royal Kindred was as silent as it was holy.

I jumped at him and sent him sprawling before he had his dagger out; he scrambled to his feet and backed away until his heels collided with the buttresses of the cliff. Over he went, flung out against the sloping rock behind him. Perfect. I took his chin in one hand and used the other as a hammer, smashed his face to pulp and broke every bone beneath it without caring what damage I did to myself. His helmet had come undone; I grasped its long, dangling straps and drew them tight under his jaw, twined them about his neck and put my knee in his belly, dragging on them until his maimed face was black and his eyes bulged to glaring balls of red-streaked horror.

Not until he must have been dead for some time did I let the straps go; I looked at something more an object than a man. For a moment I felt sick at the realisation that I had a lust for the kill as deep as that, but I crushed the weakness and lifted Kyknos athwart my shoulders, slinging his shield across my own back to protect it as I made the return journey through the Trojan ranks. I wanted my Myrmidons and the rest of the Greeks to see that I had lost neither him nor the fight.

A small detachment led by Patrokles met me on the edge of the battle; we got back to our own lines unscathed. But I paused to drop Kyknos at the feet of his own men, his swollen tongue puffed between his ribboned lips, his eyes still goggling.

'My name,' I howled, 'is Achilles!'

The Trojans fled; the man they had deemed an Immortal was proven just another man like them.

There followed the ritual at the end of a duel to the death between members of the Royal Kindred; I stripped him of his armour as my prize and sent his carcase to the Sigios refuse pit, where it would be eaten by the town dogs. But not before I cut off his head and stuck it on a spear, an odd apparition with its ghastly face and beautiful, unmarked golden braids of hair. I gave it to Patrokles, who embedded it in the shingle like a banner.

The whole Trojan force suddenly broke. Since they knew where to flee, they outdistanced us easily, their retreat fairly well disciplined. The field and Sigios were ours.

Agamemnon called a halt to the pursuit, an order I was loath to obey until Odysseus caught my arm as I loped past him and swung me roughly around. He was strong! Much stronger than he looked.

'Leave it be, Achilles,' he said. 'The gates will be shut – save your strength and your men in case the Trojans try again tomorrow. We have a mess to sort out before darkness.'

Seeing the good sense in his words, I turned with him to trudge back to the beach, Patrokles by my side as always, the Myrmidons falling in behind us singing the victory paean. We ignored the houses: if there were women inside them we wanted none of them. At the edge of the pebbles we stood aghast. Men were sprawled everywhere. Screams, cries, groans, babbling pleas for help came from all sides. Some of the bodies moved, others lay still, their shades fled into the dreary wastes of the Dark Kingdom, the realm of Hades.

Odysseus and Agamemnon stood apart as men swarmed over the ships, prying them loose where beaks had stove into sides or sterns, while the beach was tidied up, our men were transferred onto the ships, and the outer ranks of vessels moved into the stream. When I glanced up at the sun I found it sinking, about a third of the day remaining. My bones felt leaden with weariness, my arm felt too heavy to lift, and the axe dragged on the ground from its thong. I could think of nothing else to do than join Agamemnon, who stared at me with jaw dropped. Obviously he had not avoided battle, for his cuirass was buckled, his face grimed with gore and filth. And now I saw him with the leisure to look, Odysseus presented an odd sight. His breastplate was split open to display his chest, yet his skin was unmarked.

'Did you sit down and bathe in blood, Achilles?' the High King asked. 'Are you hurt?'

I shook my head dumbly; the reaction against the storm of emotions I had experienced was beginning, and what I had learned about myself threatened to summon the Daughters of Kore permanently into my mind. Could I live with such a burden and not go mad? Then I thought of Iphigenia, and understood that to live on as a sane man was a part of my punishment.

'So it was you with the axe!' Agamemnon was saying. 'I thought it must be Ajax. But you've earned our thanks. When you brought back the body of the man who killed Iolaos, the Trojans lost heart.'

'I doubt I was responsible, sire,' I managed to say. 'The Trojans had had enough, and we kept spewing men ashore without end. The man Kyknos was a personal thing. He mocked my honour.'

Odysseus took my arm again, but this time gently. 'Your ship lies yonder, Achilles. Get aboard before it sails.'

'Where to?' I asked blankly.

'I don't know, except that we can't stay here. Let Troy cope with the dead bodies. Telephos says there's a good beach inside a lagoon around the corner on the Hellespont shore. We intend to have a look.'

In the end most of the Kings sailed aboard Agamemnon's ship, north along the coast until we reached the mouth of the Hellespont; the first Greek ships to enter those waters in a generation surged serenely on. Only a league or two further the hills dabbling their flanks in the sea gave way to a beach longer and wider by far than the one at Sigios, more than a league in length. At either end of it a river flowed into the water, their sandbars forming an almost landlocked lagoon. The sole entrance to the salt lake was a narrow passage in the middle; within, the sea was dead calm. The farther bank of each river was crowned by a headland, and on top of the one beside the bigger, dirtier river was a fortress, deserted now, its garrison undoubtedly fled to Troy. No one emerged from it to see Agamemnon's flagship sail in, and every neat little toll-collecting warship was still beached.

As we lined up along the rail, Agamemnon turned to Nestor. 'Will this do?' he asked.

'It looks quite splendid to my untrained eye, but ask Phoinix.'

'It is a good place, sire,' I offered diffidently. 'If they try to raid us here they'll find their task a hard one. The rivers make it impossible for them to outflank us, though whoever lies against each river will be most vulerable.'

'Then who will volunteer to draw his ships up on the rivers?' the High King asked, then added, a trifle shamefaced, 'Mine will have to be in the centre of the beach – ease of access, you know.'

'I'll take the bigger river,' I said quickly, 'and fence my camp off with a stockade in case we're attacked. A defence within a defence.'

The High King's brow darkened. 'That sounds as if you think we're going to be here for a long time, son of Peleus.'

I looked him in the eye. 'We are, sire. Accept it.'

But he wouldn't. He started giving orders as to who would beach whose ships where, emphasising impermanence.

The flagship remained in the middle of the lagoon as one by one the ships were slowly rowed in, though not a third of them had been beached before night fell. My own vessels were still riding the open Hellespont, as were those belonging to Ajax, Little Ajax, Odysseus and Diomedes. We would be last of all. Luckily the weather was holding well, the Hellespont was unruffled.

As the sun died into the sea at my back I took my first cool look at the place, and was satisfied. With a good stout defence wall behind the rows of beached ships, our camp would be almost as invulnerable as Troy. Which rose in the east like a mountain, closer here than at Sigios. We were going to need that good stout defence wall; Agamemnon was wrong. Troy wouldn't fall in a day, any more than it had been built in a day.

Once all the ships were in and properly beached, the chocks hammered under their hulls and their masts stepped down – there were four rows of them – we buried King Iolaos of Phylake. His body was fetched from his flagship and set on a high bier atop a grassy knoll while one by one the men of Greece's nations marched past as the priests chanted and the Kings poured the libations. As slayer of his slayer it was my duty to give his funeral oration; I told the silent host how calmly he had accepted his fate, how gallantly he had fought before he died, and the identity of his slayer, a son of Poseidon. Then I suggested that his courage be marked by something more enduring than a eulogy, and asked Agamemnon if he might be renamed Protesilaos, which meant 'the first of the people'.

Solemn consent was accorded; from that moment on his people of Phylake called him Protesilaos. The priests fitted the death mask of hammered gold over his sleeping face and twitched his shroud away to reveal him clad in all the fire of a robe woven from gold. Then we laid him on a barge and rowed him across the biggest river, to where the masons had worked day and night, hollowing his tomb out of the headland. The death car was rolled inside, the tomb was closed and the masons began to tip earth across the stone-filled doorway; in a season or two no eye, even the most discerning, would be able to see whereabouts King Protesilaos was interred.

He had fulfilled the prophecy and made his people proud.

CHAPTER FOURTEEN

NARRATED BY
ODYSSEUS

Beaching over eleven hundred ships took all my time and energy in the few days after that first battle on Trojan soil. The tally had diminished a little, for some of the poorest among Helen's suitors had not been able to afford ships as well built as, for instance, Agamemnon's. Several dozen vessels had gone down, holed during the frantic rush to get sufficient men onto Sigios beach, but we had not lost any of the supply ships or those holding horses for our chariots.

To my surprise, the Trojans didn't venture anywhere near our mushrooming camp, a fact which Agamemnon interpreted as a sure sign resistance was finished. Thus, with the entire fleet safe ashore so the hulls wouldn't swell and crack by sucking up too much water, our High King held a council. Flushed by his success at Sigios, there was no stopping him as he made much of what I thought would soon prove to be very little. I let him run on, wondering who else would question his confident opinions. As was his due, he had his say amid silence, but no sooner had he handed the Staff to Nestor (Kalchas was not in attendance, why I didn't know) than Achilles was on his feet demanding it.

Yes, of course it would be Achilles. I didn't trouble to conceal my smile. The Lion King had bitten off a large mouthful in the lad from Iolkos, and from the frown gathering on his brow I fancied he was suffering acute pangs of indigestion. Did any enterprise so brave and bold ever get off to a worse start than ours? Tempests and human sacrifice, jealousy and greed, no love lost between some who might end in needing each other.

And *what* had possessed Agamemnon to send his cousin Aigisthos to Mykenai to mount guard over Klytemnestra? An action I judged as foolhardy as Menelaos's wandering off to Crete with Paris in his house. Aigisthos had a legitimate claim to the throne! Perhaps the problem was that the sons of Atreus had forgotten what Atreus had done to the sons of Thyestes. Stewed them and dished them up to their father at a banquet. The much younger Aigisthos had escaped the fate of his elder brothers. Well, it wasn't my problem. Whereas the widening rift between Agamemnon and Achilles most definitely was.

Had Achilles been a simple fighting machine like his cousin Ajax the rift would not have opened. But Achilles was a thinker who also excelled in battle. The smile slipped from my mouth when I realised that if I had been born with this young man's size and circumstances, yet retained my own mind, I might have conquered the world. Mine was the stronger life strand; it seemed likely that I would be there watching when they covered the lipless face of Achilles with a lipless mask of gold, but there was a glory about him that was never mine. I felt a sensation akin to loss, understanding that Achilles owned some key to the meaning of life always dangling just out of my reach. Was it a good thing to be so detached, so cool? Oh, just once to burn, as Diomedes yearned just once to freeze!

'I doubt, sire,' said the son of Peleus levelly, 'that if the Trojans don't venture outside to fight, we can take Troy. My long sight is better than most men's, and I've been studying those walls you seem to think overrated. I can't agree. I feel we underrate them. The only way we can crush Troy is to lure the Trojans out onto the plain and defeat them in open battle. And that's not easy. We'd have to outflank them as well, prevent their retiring back inside the city to fight another day. Don't you think it's wise to talk bearing that in mind? Can't we devise some sort of trick to lure the Trojans out?'

I laughed. 'Achilles, if you sat within walls as thick and high as Troy's, would you march outside to do battle? Their best chance was the beach of Sigios while we were landing. They couldn't defeat us even then. If I were Priam, I'd keep the army on top of the walls and let it thumb its noses at us.'

He was not at all dashed. 'It was no more than a faint hope, Odysseus. But I can't see how we can storm those walls or batter down those gates. Can you?'

I pulled a face. 'Oh, I'm silent! I've already spoken on the subject. When there are ears prepared to listen, I'll do so again. Not before.'

'*My* ears are prepared to listen,' he said quickly.

'Your ears aren't prominent enough, Achilles.'

Not even this little joke pleased Agamemnon's ears. He leaned forward. 'Troy *cannot* withstand us!' he cried.

'Then, sire,' Achilles persisted, 'if there's no sign of a Trojan army on the plain tomorrow, may we drive to the foot of the walls to inspect them at close quarters?'

'Of course,' said the High King stiffly.

When the meeting ended without resolving to do anything more significant than drive out to see the walls, I jerked my head at Diomedes. Shortly afterwards he joined me in my tent. After the wine was poured and the servants dismissed he allowed his curiosity to show; Diomedes was learning not to burn.

'What is it?' he asked eagerly.

'Does it have to be anything? I enjoy your company.'

'I'm not questioning our *friendship*. I'm questioning the look on your face when you signalled me. What's afoot, Odysseus?'

'Ah! You're growing too accustomed to my little habits.'

'My thinking apparatus may be war-battered, but it can still tell the difference between the smell of a jonquil and a corpse.'

'Call this a private council, then, Diomedes. Of all of us you know war best. Of all of us you should know best how to take a fortress city. You conquered Thebes and built a shrine out of the skulls of your enemies – by all the Gods, what passion it must have taken to do that!'

'Troy isn't Thebes,' he answered soberly. 'Thebes is Greek, a part of our united nations. Here is war with Asia Minor. Why won't Agamemnon see that? There are only two powers of any consequence on the Aegaean – Greece and the Asia Minor federation, which *includes* Troy. Babylon and Nineveh aren't greatly worried by what happens around the Aegaean, and Egypt is so far away that Rameses cares not at all.' He stopped, looked embarrassed. 'But who am I to lecture you?'

'Don't hold yourself too light. It was an admirable summation. I wish a few more at today's council were half as logical.'

He drank deeply to wash the flush of pleasure away. 'I took Thebes, yes, but only after a pitched battle outside its walls. I entered Thebes over the bodies of its men. Achilles was very likely thinking of that when he spoke of luring the Trojans outside first. But Troy? A handful of women and children can keep us baying at the gates for ever.'

'Starve them out,' I said.

That made him laugh. 'Odysseus, you're incurable! You know full well that the laws of Hospitable Zeus forbid that. Could you honestly face the Furies if you starved a city into submission?'

'The Daughters of Kore hold no fears for me. I looked them in the eye years ago.'

Was this further evidence of my impiety? he was clearly asking himself. But he did not ask *me*. Instead, he asked, 'Then tell me what conclusion you've reached?'

'One, thus far. That this campaign will be very long – a matter of years. I'll therefore make my arrangements with that fact in mind. My house oracle said I'd be away for twenty years.'

'How can you believe so implicitly in a humble house oracle when you can advocate starvation?'

'The house oracle,' I said patiently, 'belongs to the Mother. To Earth. She's very close to us in all things. She thrusts us into this world and calls us back to her breast when our course is run. Yet war lies in the province of men. It ought to be a man's own decision as to how to pursue war. Every wretched law governing it seems to me to protect the other side. One day a man is going to want to win a war so badly that he'll break those laws, and after him everything will be different. Starve one city into submission and you start a landslide of hunger. I want to be the first such man! No, Diomedes, I am *not* impious! Just impatient of restrictions. Doubtless the world will sing of Achilles until Kronos remarries the Mother and the day of men comes to an end. But is it hubris in me to want the world to sing of Odysseus? I don't have the advantages Achilles has – I'm not physically huge or the son of a High King – all I have to work with is what I am – clever, cunning, subtle. Not bad instruments.'

Diomedes stretched. 'No, indeed. How will you plan for this long campaign?'

'I'll commence tomorrow after we return from our inspection of Troy's walls. I intend to select my own little army from out the ranks of this too large one.'

'Your own army?'

'Yes, my very own. Not the usual kind of army, nor the usual kind of troops. I'm going to recruit the worst of our daredevils, trouble makers and malcontents.'

He gaped, thunderstruck. 'Surely you're joking! Trouble makers? Malcontents? Daredevils? What kind of troops are those?'

'Diomedes, let's put aside for the moment the question of whether my house oracle is right in saying twenty years, or Kalchas is right in saying ten. Whichever is a long time.' I put my wine cup down and sat up straight. 'In a short campaign a good officer can keep his trouble makers busy, his daredevils so closely watched that they can't harm the rest of his men, and his malcontents separated from those they might influence. But on a long campaign there's bound to be strife. We won't be fighting battles every day – or even every moon – throughout the course of ten or twenty years. There'll be moons on end of idleness, particularly during winter. And during these lulls tongues will work such mischief that the mutters of discontent will reach the proportions of a howl.'

Diomedes looked amused. 'What about the cowards?'

'Oh, I have to leave the officers sufficient unsatisfactory men to dig the cesspits!'

That provoked a laugh. 'All right, then, you have acquired your own little army. What will you do with it?'

'Keep it very busy all the time. Give its members something to work on that their dubious talents will relish. The kind of men I mean aren't craven. They're cantankerous. Trouble makers live to stir up trouble. Daredevils aren't happy unless they're endangering other lives as well as their own. And malcontents would complain to Zeus about the quality of the nectar and ambrosia in Olympos. Tomorrow I'll go to every commanding officer and ask for his three worst men, excluding cowards. Naturally he'll be delighted to be rid of them. When I've finished recruiting them, I'll put them to work.'

Though he knew I was deliberately teasing him, Diomedes could not resist rising to the bait. '*What* work?' he demanded.

I continued to tease him. 'On the fringes of the beach not far from where my ships are drawn up there is a natural hollow. It's out of sight of everyone, yet close enough to the camp to be put on this side of the wall Agamemnon is going to have to erect to shield our ships and men from Trojan raids. It's quite a deep hollow, big enough to contain enough houses to board three hundred men in extreme comfort. My army will live in that hollow. There in complete isolation I'll train them for their work. Once they're recruited, they'll have no contact whatsoever with their old units or the main army.'

'*What* work?'

'I'm going to create a spy colony.'

An answer he hadn't expected. He stared, confused. 'A spy colony? What sort of thing is that? What can spies do? What use will they be?'

'A great deal of use,' I said, warming to my theme. 'Consider, Diomedes! Even ten years are a long time in any man's life –

perhaps as little as a seventh or an eighth, but perhaps as much as a third or a half. Among my three hundred men there'll be some fit to walk the floors of a palace, and that's what they will do. Within this next year I'll scatter some of them inside Troy's very Citadel. Others who also love to live a lie I'll scatter through every middle and lower stratum in the city, from slaves to traders and merchants. I want to know every move Priam makes.'

'By the Thunderer!' said Diomedes slowly. Then he looked sceptical. 'They'll be detected at once.'

'Why? They won't go into Troy green, you know. What you don't seem to have grasped is that my three hundred men will have superior intelligence – all good trouble makers, daredevils and malcontents are bright fellows. A dull man isn't a danger in the ranks. I've been inside Troy already, and while I was there I memorised the Trojan version of Greek – accent, grammar, vocabulary. I'm very good at languages.'

'I know,' said Diomedes, relaxing into a genuine grin.

'I also discovered a great deal I didn't transmit to our dear friend Agamemnon. Before *one* of my spies sets foot inside Troy he'll know everything he needs to know. Some of them – those who don't have an ear for languages – I'll instruct to say that they're slaves escaped from our camp. Having no need to conceal their essential Greekness, they'll be particularly valuable. Others who have half an ear for languages will pose as Lykians or Karians. And that,' I said gleefully, putting my hands behind my head, 'is just the beginning!'

Diomedes drew a breath. 'I thank all the Gods you're on our side, Odysseus. I'd hate to have you for an enemy.'

All Troy was up on top of the walls to see the High King of Mykenai lead his Royal Kindred past. I noticed the mounting flush in Agamemnon's cheeks as he absorbed the jeers and rude noises carried to us by that incessant Trojan wind, and I was profoundly glad he hadn't brought the army with him.

My neck ached from constantly craning it upwards, but

when we came to the Western Curtain I scanned it very carefully, not really having seen it from the outside during my visit to Troy. Only here was it possible to assault the ramparts. Though even Agamemnon had abandoned the idea by the time we left it behind. Too short in length. Forty thousand defenders would be tipping boiling oil down on our heads, heated rocks, coals, even excrement.

When he ordered us back to camp Agamemnon had a very long face.

He called no council; the days meandered off one by one without action or decision. And I left him alone to stew, for I had better things to do with my time than argue with him. I began to gather in the men I wanted for my spy colony.

The commanding officers gave me no opposition; they were only too glad to see the end of the worst of their problems. Masons and carpenters were hard at work in the hollow, erecting thirty stout stone houses and a larger building which would be used for dining, recreation and instruction. As my recruits came in they were put to work too; from the moment they were chosen, they were kept in isolation by a guard of Ithakan soldiers posted all around the rim of the hollow. As far as the commanding officers knew, I was simply constructing a jail wherein I intended to keep all the offenders.

By autumn everything was ready. I herded my recruits into the main hall of the large building, there to address them. Three hundred pairs of eyes followed me as I made my way to the dais: wary or curious, mistrustful or apprehensive. They had been confined in the hollow for long enough now to have made the ghastly discovery that they had been deprived of victims, that they were all of like kind.

I sat on a king's chair, carved with claw feet, Diomedes on my right. When silence fell, I put my hands on the chair arms and extended one foot in the pose of a king.

'You're wondering why I had you brought here, what's going to happen to you. Until now it's been conjecture. After this you'll know, because I'm about to tell you. First of all, each of you has certain traits of character which render you odious to any commanding officer. None of you in this room is a good soldier, whether because you endanger other lives, or because you give all men a bellyache with your perpetual mischief or whining. I want no misapprehension in your minds as to why you've been singled out. You've been singled out because you're utterly unloved.'

I stopped and waited, ignoring the stunned faces, the anger, the indignation. Several of the faces were carefully blank, and these I took special note of; they were the fellows with superior ability and intelligence.

Everything had been arranged. My Ithakan guard was stationed all around the building; its commander, Hakios, was absolutely to be trusted. His orders were to kill any man who came out of the door before I did. Those who decided that my terms were unacceptable could not be allowed to return to the general ranks of the army. They would have to die.

'Have you realised the magnitude of the insult?' I asked. 'I insist that you do! The very qualities which decent men abhor are the qualities I'll turn to best advantage. There will be rewards for serving me – you'll live in quarters fitted out for princes, you'll do no manual work, and the first women the High King apportions from the spoils will go to you. Between your tours of duty you'll have adequate periods of rest. In fact, you'll comprise an elite body under my sole command. You will no longer answer to your respective Kings, or to the High King of Mykenai. You will answer only to me, Odysseus of Ithaka.'

I went on to tell them that the work I required of them was very dangerous and unusual, then concluded this segment of my address by saying, 'One day your kind will be famous. Wars will be won or lost on the sort of work you're going to do. Each of you is worth a thousand foot soldiers to me, so you should understand that it is a great thing to be chosen. Now, before I elaborate any further, I'm going to allow you to discuss the matter among yourselves.'

Silence persisted for a short while; they were sufficiently surprised to find it difficult to converse. Then as the talk began I sat scanning their faces closely; there were about a dozen of them making up their minds to have nothing to do with my proposal. One of them got up and left, a few more followed, and Hakios loomed beyond the opened door. No commotion came from outside. Eight others left. And Hakios continued to obey instructions. If they never returned to their companies, it would be assumed they were with me. If they were not with me, it would be assumed they had returned to their companies. Only Hakios and his men would know; they were Ithakans and they knew their King.

Two men in particular interested me. One was a cousin to Diomedes, and the worst thorn in the side of a commanding officer I had encountered during my recruitment. His name was Thersites. Besides his ability, something else attracted me to Thersites, for it was rumoured that he had been got on the aunt of Diomedes by Sisyphos. The same tale was told of me, that Sisyphos and not Laertes fathered me. This slur upon my birth never caused me a moment's anguish; the blood of a brilliant wolfshead probably stood a man in better stead than the blood of a king like Laertes.

The other man was very well known to me, and he was the only one among the three hundred who knew exactly why he was there. This was my own cousin Sinon, who had come with me in my train. A wonderfully useful man who was looking forward to his new profession.

Both Thersites and Sinon sat without moving, their dark eyes riveted upon my face, now and again breaking their scrutiny of me to turn their heads and assess the calibre of the men they had been lumped with.

Suddenly Thersites cleared his throat. 'Go ahead, sire, tell us the rest,' he said.

I told them the rest. 'So you see why I regard you as the most valuable men in the army,' I said towards the end of it. 'Whether your role is to transmit information to me or to concentrate upon making trouble for those who administer Troy, you will matter in the scheme of things. A safe system of communication will be set up, liaisons and meeting places arranged between those of you in more or less permanent residence within Troy, and those of you who will pay only fleeting visits to Troy. Though the work is very dangerous, you'll be fully equipped to deal with the risks by the time you're asked to start work.' I grinned. 'Besides which, it's work you'll find really interesting.' I rose to my feet. 'Think on it until I return to you.'

Diomedes and I retired to an anteroom, there to sit talking and drinking wine while the sound of voices rose and fell on the other side of the curtain.

'I presume,' said Diomedes, 'that you and I will also enter Troy from time to time?'

'Oh, yes. In order to control men like these, it's necessary to demonstrate that we're willing to take even bigger risks than we'll ask of them. We're Kings, our faces are recognisable.'

'Helen,' he said.

'Exactly.'

'When do we start to make our visits?'

'Tonight,' I said placidly. 'I found a good conduit in the northwest section of the walls big enough to admit one man at a time. Its opening on the inside of the walls is more concealed than most, and isn't guarded. We'll dress as poor men, explore the streets, talk to the people, and escape tomorrow night the same way we got in. Don't worry, we'll be safe enough.'

He laughed. 'I don't doubt it, Odysseus.'

'Time to join the others,' I said.

Thersites had been elected spokesman for the group; he was on his feet waiting for us.

'Speak, cousin of King Diomedes,' I commanded.

'Sire, we're with you. Of those remaining when you left the room, only two decided against your offer.'

'They don't matter,' I said.

His eyes mocked me; Thersites knew their fate. 'The life

you've outlined for us,' he went on, 'is a much better one than kicking our heels inside a siege camp. We are your men.'

'I require an oath of each of you to that effect.'

'We will swear,' he said stolidly, knowing that the oath would be too awful even for him to break.

After the last man had sworn, I informed them that they would live in units of ten men, one of whom would be their officer, to be chosen by me after I got to know them better. However, I knew two men well enough right there and then: I appointed Thersites and Sinon the co-leaders of the spy colony.

That night we entered Troy with relative ease. I went first, Diomedes following close behind; the conduit just took the width of his shoulders. Once inside we slipped into a cosy alley and slept until morning, when we emerged to mingle with the crowds. In the big marketplace inside the Skaian Gate we bought honey cakes and barley bread and two cups of sheep's milk, and listened. The people were unconcerned about the Greeks occupying the Hellespont beach; the general mood was cheerful. They regarded their towering bastions with loving eyes, and laughed at the idea of the Greek behemoth sitting impotent scant leagues away. One and all seemed to think that Agamemnon would give up, sail away. Food and money were plentiful, the Dardanian and Idan Gates were still open, and traffic proceeded through them as usual. Only the complicated system of lookouts and guards atop the walls themselves demonstrated that the city was ready to close the Dardanian and Idan Gates the moment danger threatened.

The city, we learned, was endowed with many wells of sweet water, and contained a large number of granaries and warehouses in which nonperishable food was stored.

No one contemplated a pitched battle outside; what soldiers we saw lolled or wenched, had left their arms and armour at home. Agamemnon and his grand army were openly laughed at.

ODYSSEUS

*

Diomedes and I started work in the spy colony the moment we returned to the camp, and we laboured. There were those who showed great aptitude and enthusiasm, but there were others who flagged, who walked about with long faces. I had a quiet word with Thersites and Sinon, who agreed that the misfits should vanish. Of the three hundred original recruits I ended up keeping two hundred and fifty-four, and thought myself lucky.

CHAPTER FIFTEEN

NARRATED BY
DIOMEDES

A remarkable man, Odysseus. Even to watch him dealing with a slave was an education. At the end of a single moon he had those two hundred and fifty-four men exactly where he wanted them, though they were not yet ready for action. I spent almost as much time with him as I did with my men of Argos, but what I learned from him enabled me to control and direct my troops better in only half the time it used to take. There were no more signs of discontent in my contingent when I was away, no more quarrels among the officers; I used Odysseus's methods to good effect. Of course I overheard a few jests, caught the sly looks which passed between my Argive officer barons whenever they saw me with Odysseus; even the other Kings were beginning to question the nature of our friendship. I wasn't upset at all. If there had been truth in what they thought, I would not have minded, nor – to give everyone his due – was there malice of disapproval in it. All men were at liberty to assuage their sexual itches with whichever sex they preferred. Usually women, but a long foreign campaign meant women were less available. Foreign women could never take the place of wives and sweethearts, the women of one's own land. Better under such circumstances to seek the softer side of love with a friend who fought alongside you in battle, held the enemy off with his sword while you picked up your own.

When autumn was full blown Odysseus told me to go and pay my respects to Agamemnon. I went, curious as to what was in the wind; Odysseus had been doing a lot of huddling with old Nestor of late, but hadn't told me what was discussed during their huddles.

For five moons we had not seen a sign of a Trojan army, and the mood within our camp was gloomy. Food hadn't turned out to be a difficult problem, as the coast well to the north of the Troad and the far shore of the Hellespont provided excellent forage. The tribes living thereabouts took one look at our scavenging parties and made themselves scarce. Which could not alter the fact that we were so far from home that we couldn't contemplate returning on furlough. No orders had come from the High King to disband, or attack, or do *anything*.

When I came into Agamemnon's tent I found Odysseus already there, looking casual.

'I might have known you'd not be far away when Odysseus turned up,' Agamemnon commented.

I smiled, but did not speak.

'What do you want, Odysseus?'

'A council, sire. There's much overdue for discussion.'

'I agree entirely! For instance: what's going on down in a certain hollow, and why can I never find you or Diomedes after dark? I intended calling a council last night.'

Odysseus extricated himself from imperial disfavour with all his usual grace. A smile began it; the smile which could win over implacable enemies, the smile which could charm a far colder man than Agamemnon.

'Sire, I'll tell all – but in council.'

'Very well. Stay here until the others come. If I let you go, you mightn't come back.'

Menelaos came in first, hangdog as ever. Nodding to us shyly, he hunched himself on a seat in the darkest, furthest corner of the room. Poor, downtrodden Menelaos. Perhaps he was beginning to realise that Helen was a very secondary component in the schemes of his more masterful brother, or perhaps he was beginning to despair of ever getting her back again. The thought of her stirred memories almost nine years old; what a little baggage she had turned out to be! Purely concerned with her own satisfaction, indifferent to what a man wanted. *So* beautiful! And *so* selfish. Oh, the dance she must have led Menelaos! I could never hate him; he was too small a man, more to be pitied than despised. And he loved her as I could never love any woman.

Achilles strolled in with Patrokles, Phoinix trailing them the way Odysseus's hound Argos trailed him whenever he was in Ithaka. As faithful as he was vigilant. They made their obeisances, Achilles stiffly and with obvious reluctance. He was an odd one. Odysseus, I had noticed, didn't really care for him. My own emotions about him, however, were sufficiently indifferent for me to make a private resolution to warn him to be nicer to Agamemnon. Even if the lad did lead the Myrmidons, he ought not to make his dislike so manifest. To find oneself abandoned out on a wing in battle is easily done – and very hard to pin down to anything more than routine bad generalship. When I saw the expression in Patrokles's eyes I had to smile – now *there* was a tender friendship! At least on one side. Achilles took him for granted. He also burned far more for battle than bodily pleasure.

Machaon came in alone and sat down quietly. He and his brother, Podalieros, were the finest medical men in Greece, worth more to our army than a cavalry wing. Podalieros was a recluse, preferring his surgery to councils of war, but Machaon was a restless and energetic man who had the gift of command and could fight like ten Myrmidons. Idomeneus drifted gracefully through the door with Meriones in tow, using the importance of his Cretan crown and his position as co-commander to bow to Agamemnon rather than bend the knee. Agamemnon's eyes flashed at the slight; I wondered if he thought that Crete was getting too big for its boots, but the High King's face didn't say. Idomeneus was a fop, but strongly built and a fine leader of men. Meriones, his cousin and heir, was possibly the better man of the two – I never minded

211

feasting or fighting with him. Both of them had the same openhanded Cretan air.

Nestor trod briskly to his special seat, nodding in passing to Agamemnon, who took no offence at all. He had dandled all of us on his knee when we were babes. If he had a fault, it was that he tended to reminisce excessively about 'the old days', and regarded the present generation of Kings as cissies. However, one couldn't help but love him. Odysseus adored him, I thought. With him he brought his eldest son.

Ajax arrived with his boon companions, his half-brother Teukros and his cousin from Lokris, Little Ajax the son of Oileus. They sat mumchance by the far wall, looking uncomfortable. I longed for the day when I would see Ajax on a battlefield (he had not been near me at Sigios), see with my own eyes those bulging arms wield his famous axe.

Menestheus followed closely on their heels, a good High King of Attika, but with more sense than to set himself up as another Theseus. He was not a tenth the man Theseus had been – but then, nor was anyone else. Palamedes was the last. He sat between me and Odysseus. It was impolitic for me to dare to like him when Odysseus hated him. Why, I didn't know, though I gathered that Palamedes had injured him in some way when he and Agamemnon went to Ithaka to fetch him to the war. Odysseus was patient enough to bide his time, but he would have his revenge, of that I was certain. Not a hot and bloody revenge. Odysseus ate cold. The priest Kalchas was not present, a curious omission.

Agamemnon began stiffly. 'This is the first proper council I've called since we landed at Troy. As you're all aware of the situation, I see no point in belabouring it. Odysseus will put the case to you, not I. Though I am your suzerain, you gave me your troops gladly, and I respect your right to withdraw that support if you think fit, the Oath of the Quartered Horse notwithstanding. Patrokles, keep the Staff, but give it to Odysseus.'

He stood in the middle of the floor (Agamemnon had

succumbed to the increasing cold and built himself a stone house, even if its presence suggested permanence), red mane flowing back from his fine face in a mass of waves, his great grey eyes stripping us to the marrow, to our true stature: Kings, but men for all that. We Greeks have always honoured foreknowledge, and Odysseus had it in full measure.

'Patrokles, pour the wine' was all he said to begin, then waited while the young man went the rounds of everyone. 'It is five moons since we landed. Nothing has happened during that time outside the confines of a hollow near my ships.'

This statement was followed by a brisk explanation that he had taken it upon himself to imprison the army's worst soldiers in a place where they could do no harm. I knew why he would not divulge the real purpose of that hollow: he didn't trust Kalchas or some of the tongues, even if bound by oath.

'Though we've held no official council,' he continued in his smooth and pleasant voice, 'it hasn't been difficult to ascertain the main sentiments among you. For instance, no one wants to besiege Troy. I respect your views, for the same reasons Machaon might offer – that siege brings plague and other disease in its wake – that in conquering by such means, we too might perish. So I don't intend to discuss siege.'

He paused to quiz us with his eyes. 'Diomedes and I have made many nocturnal visits to the interior of Troy, where we've learned that if we're still here next spring, the situation will change radically. Priam has sent to all his allies along the coast of Asia Minor, and they've all promised him armies. By the time the snow is off the mountains, Priam will have two hundred thousand troops at his disposal. And we will be ejected.'

Achilles interrupted. 'You paint a black picture, Odysseus. Is that what we were called from our homes to endure – total ignominy at the hands of an enemy we've encountered only once? What you're saying is that we've embarked upon a fruitless crusade, enormously costly and without prospect of being paid for by enemy spoils. Where's the plunder you promised us, Agamemnon? What has happened to your ten days' war? What has become of your easy victory? No matter which way we turn, defeat stares at us. And in this cause some of us here today connived at human sacrifice. There are worse defeats than to go down in battle. To be forced to evacuate this beach and return home is the worst defeat of all.'

Odysseus chuckled. 'Are the rest of you as cast down as Achilles? I'm sorry for you, then. Yet I can't deny that the son of Peleus speaks the truth. Added to which, if we're here through the winter, supplies are going to be hard to get. At the moment we can take what we need from Bithynia, but the winters hereabouts, they say, are cold and snowy.'

Achilles leaped to his feet, snarling at Agamemnon. 'This is what I told you at Aulis, long before we sailed! You paid no attention to the problems of feeding a huge army! Choice? Do we have a choice as to whether we stay here or go home? I don't think so. Our only alternative is to take advantage of the early winter winds and sail to Greece, never to return. You are a fool, King Agamemnon! A conceited fool!'

Agamemnon sat very still, but held onto his temper.

'Achilles is right,' growled Idomeneus. 'It was very badly planned.' He drew in a breath, glaring at his co-commander. 'I ask you, Odysseus: can we or can't we storm the Trojan walls?'

'There's no way to storm them, Idomeneus.'

Feeling was rising, sparked by Achilles and fuelled by the fact that Agamemnon chose to say nothing. They were all ready to fly at him, and he knew it. He sat biting his lips, his body tense with the effort of restraining his own anger.

'Why couldn't you have admitted that you weren't capable of planning an expedition as big as this?' Achilles demanded. 'Were you less than you are – and were you not what you are by the grace of the Gods! – I would strike you down. You led us to Troy with no thought in your head beyond your own glory! You used the Oath to get your grand army together, then proceeded to ignore the wishes and needs of your brother – how much have you really considered Menelaos? Can you say in all honesty that you do this for the sake of your brother? Of course you can't! You never even pretended that! From the very beginning your aim has been to enrich yourself from the sack of Troy, and carve an empire for yourself in Asia Minor! We'd all grow fat on it, I admit, but none so fat as you!'

Menelaos cried out, tears streaming down his cheeks, his grief betraying a terrible disillusionment. While he sobbed like a child in pain, Achilles took him by the shoulder and rubbed it. The atmosphere was stormpacked; one more word and they would all be at Agamemnon's throat. Feeling my sword arm begin to tingle, I looked at Odysseus, standing motionless with the Staff in his hand while Agamemnon locked his hands together in his lap and looked down at them.

In the end it was Nestor who stepped into the breach. He turned on Achilles savagely. 'Young man, your lack of respect deserves a flogging! What gives you the right to criticise our High King when men like myself do not? Odysseus levelled no charges – how dare *you* presume to do so? Hold your tongue!'

Achilles took this without a murmur. He bent the knee to Agamemnon in apology, and sat down. By nature he was not a hothead, but there had been bad blood between him and Agamemnon ever since Iphigenia had died at Aulis. Understandable. His name had been used to lure the girl away from Klytemnestra, but Agamemnon hadn't asked for his consent. Achilles couldn't seem to forgive any of us, least of all Agamemnon, for our parts in it.

'Odysseus,' said Nestor, 'it's clear that you don't have the seniority to manage this collection of noble autocrats, so give me the Staff and let me speak.' He glared at us. 'This meeting is a disgrace! In my young days no one would have dared to say the things I've heard this morning! For instance, when *I* was a youth and Herakles was all over the land, things were different.'

We sat back and resigned ourselves to one of Nestor's famous homilies, though when I thought about it afterwards, I was sure the old man started to ramble deliberately; in being forced to listen, we calmed down.

'Now take Herakles,' Nestor went on. 'Unjustly bound to a king not fit to wear the sacred purple of office, set a series of tasks coldbloodedly chosen to bring him death or humiliation, Herakles didn't even protest. His word was holy to him. He had nobility of mind as well as might of arm. God-got he might have been, but he was a *man*! A better man than you can ever hope to be, young Achilles. And you, young Ajax. The King is the King. Herakles never forgot that – not when mired to the knees in ordure, not when slipping on the brink of despair and madness. His very manliness put him above Eurystheus, the man he served. *That* was what all other men admired in him, honoured in him. He knew what was owed to the Gods and he knew what was owed to the King. To each he rendered scrupulously at all times. Though it did my heart good to treat him like a brother, he never took encouragement from my friendliness – I the Heir of Neleus, he accounted little better than a freak. It was his consciousness of his position as a slave, his deference and his patience won him undying love and the status of a Hero. Ai, ai! The world will never see his like again.'

Good! He was done, he'd give the Staff back to Odysseus and the council could proceed. But he wasn't done; instead, he embarked upon a new homily.

'Theseus!' he cried. 'Take Theseus as another example! It was madness overtook him, not lack of nobility or forgetfulness of what is owed to the King. High King himself, I never knew him as any other than a *man*. Or take your father, Diomedes. He was the mightiest warrior of his day, was Tydeus, and he died before the very walls you took a generation later, Diomedes, his life unmarred by dishonour. If I had known what sort of men call themselves Kings and Heirs to Kings here on this beach at Troy, I would never have left sandy Pylos, never sailed the wine-dark sea. Patrokles, pour more wine. I wish to go on speaking, but my throat is parched.'

Patrokles got up slowly, the most put out of all of us; it

visibly hurt him to hear Achilles dressed down. The old King of Pylos guzzled an unwatered draught without blinking, licking his lips and sat down on a vacant chair near Agamemnon's.

'Odysseus, I intend to steal your thunder. I mean no offence to you in doing so, it is just that apparently it needs an ancient to keep insolent young men in their place,' he said.

Odysseus grinned. 'Go ahead, sire! You'll put the case as well as I could, if not better.'

Which was when I began to smell something fishy. The two of them had been huddling together for days – was this cooked up ahead of time?

'I doubt that,' Nestor said, bright blue eyes twinkling. 'For one so young, you have a remarkable head on your shoulders. I shall sit here, forget personalities and stick to facts. We *must* approach this business without emotion, understand it without confusion or mistake. What is done is done, that's first and foremost. What's in the past must be kept there, not dragged up to fuel grudges.'

He leaned forward in his chair. 'Consider this: we have an army over one hundred thousand strong, combatant and non-combatant, sitting about three leagues from the walls of Troy. Among the noncombatants are cooks, slaves, sailors, armourers, grooms, carpenters, masons and engineers. It seems to me that if the expedition was as badly planned as Prince Achilles tries to make out, then we'd have no skilled tradesmen. Very well. That needs no discussion. We have also to consider the time factor. Our worthy priest Kalchas said ten years, and I for one am inclined to believe him. We aren't here to defeat one city! We're here to defeat many nations. Nations stretching from Troy to Kilikia. A task of that magnitude can't be done in a wink. Even could we throw down Troy's walls, it couldn't be done. Are we pirates? Are we brigands? Are we raiders? If we are, then we would assault one city, go home again with the spoils. But I say we're not pirates. We can't stop with Troy! We have to go on and defeat Dardania, Mysia, Lydia, Karia, Lykia and Kilikia.'

DIOMEDES

Achilles was caught; he was watching Nestor as if he had never seen him before. So, I noted, was Agamemnon watching.

'What would happen,' said Nestor almost musingly, 'if we were to split our army down the middle? One half left to sit before Troy and the other half a free agent. The force at Troy would contain Troy, large enough to be at least of equal strength to any army Priam might send against it. The second force would roam up and down the coast of Asia Minor, attacking, pillaging and burning every settlement between Andramyttios and far Kilikia. It would decimate and ravage, take slaves, loot cities, lay waste the land, never appear where expected. Thus it would accomplish two things – keep both halves of our army amply supplied with food and other necessities – perhaps even luxuries – and keep Troy's allies in Asia Minor in such perpetual fear that they'll never manage to send Priam aid of any kind. At no point along the coast are there sufficient concentrations of people to resist a large and well-led army. But I very much doubt that any of the Asia Minor Kings will have the foresight to abandon their own lands in order to congregate at Troy.'

Of course the pair of them had cooked this up beforehand! Everything just rolled off Nestor's tongue like syrup off a cake. Odysseus was sitting smiling in absolute content and approval and Nestor was in his element.

'The half of the army left before Troy would prevent the Trojans from making an assault on our camp or our ships,' Nestor continued. 'It would also steadily whittle down morale inside the city. What we have to do is turn the walls from a protection to a prison within the minds of the inhabitants. Without going into details, there are ways we can influence Trojan thinking, from the Citadel to the meanest hovel. Take my word for it, there are. Craft is essential, but with Odysseus, we have craft.'

He sighed, wriggled, demanded more wine; but this time when Patrokles made the rounds he did so with increased respect for the aged King of Pylos.

'If we decide to persist in this war,' said Nestor, 'there are a host of rewards ripe for the plucking. Troy is wealthy beyond our dreams. The spoils will enrich all of our nations, and ourselves too. Achilles was right about that. I would remind you that Agamemnon always saw the advantage of crushing the Asia Minor allies. If we do crush them we'll be free to colonise, resettle our people in greater plenty than they currently enjoy cramped up in Greece. And,' he went on, his voice dropping in tone but increasing in power, 'most importantly of all, the Hellespont and the Euxine Sea will be *ours*. We can colonise in the Euxine as well. We'll have all the tin and copper we need to make bronze. We'll have Skythian gold. Emeralds. Sapphires. Rubies. Silver. Wool. Emmer wheat. Barley. Electrum. Other metals. Other foods. Other commodities. An exciting prospect, don't you agree?'

We stirred, began to smile at each other, while Agamemnon visibly revived.

'The walls of Troy must be left severely alone,' the old man went on firmly. 'The half of the army left here must serve a purely irritative function – keep the Trojans unsettled and content itself with minor skirmishes. We have an excellent camp site here, I see no need to move to another location. Odysseus, what are the two rivers called?'

Odysseus answered crisply. 'The bigger stream with the yellow water is Skamander. It's polluted from Trojan effluent, which is why there's a ban on bathing or drinking. The smaller stream with untainted water is Simois.'

'Thank you. Our first task, then, is to build a defensive wall from Skamander clear across to Simois about half a league in from the lagoon. It will have to be at least fifteen cubits high. Outside it we'll put a palisade of spiked stakes and dig a trench fifteen cubits deep, more sharpened stakes in its bottom. This will keep the half of the army left before Troy busy right through the coming winter – and keep the men warm, labouring.'

Suddenly he stopped, waved at Odysseus. 'I've had enough. Odysseus, continue.'

Of course they'd hatched it huddled together! Odysseus continued as if he'd been speaking all along. 'No troops ought to be permanently inactive, so the two halves of the army will take turns of duty – six moons before Troy, six moons attacking up and down the coast. This will keep everyone fresh. I cannot emphasise too strongly,' he said, 'that we must create and maintain the impression that we intend to remain on this side of the Aegaean forever if necessary! Be they Trojans or Lykians, I want the people of the Asia Minor states to despair, to wither, to become more stripped of hope with every passing year. The mobile half of our army will bleed Priam and his allies to death. Their gold will end up in *our* coffers. I estimate that it will take two years for the message to sink in, but sink in it will. It must.'

'I take it, then,' said Achilles, his tone and manner very polite, 'that the free-agent half of the army won't live here?'

'No, it will have its own headquarters,' said Odysseus, well pleased at the politeness. 'Further south, perhaps where Dardania abuts onto Mysia. There's a port in those parts called Assos. I haven't seen it, but Telephos says it's adequate for the purpose. The spoils from the coast will be taken there, as will all the food and other items. Between Assos and our beach here a feeder line will operate continually, sailing close to the coast for safety in all weathers. Phoinix is the only true sailor among the high nobility, so I suggest that he take charge of the feeder line. I know he vowed to Peleus that he'd stay with Achilles, but he can do that in this role.'

He stopped for a moment to let his grey eyes look into each pair watching him. 'I would end by reminding everyone here that Kalchas said the war will last ten years. I think it can't be concluded in less. And that's what all of you have to think about. Ten years away from home. Ten years during which our children will grow up. Ten years during which our wives will have to rule. Home is too far away and our task here too demanding to allow us to visit Greece. Ten years is a very long time.' He bowed to Agamemnon. 'Sire, the plan that Nestor and I have outlined is only valid with your approval. If you dislike it, then Nestor and I will say no more. We are, as always, your servants.'

Ten years away from home. Ten years of exile. Was the conquest of Asia Minor worth that price? I for one didn't know. Though I think that if it hadn't been for Odysseus I would have elected to sail home on the morrow; but because he had obviously made up his mind to remain, I never did voice my heart's desire.

Agamemnon sighed deeply. 'So be it. Ten years. I think the price is worth it. We have much to gain. However, I shall put the decision to the vote. You must want it as much as I.'

He got to his feet and stood before us. 'I would remind you that almost all of you here are either Kings or the Heirs of Kings. We in Greece have founded our concept of kingship on the favour of the sky Gods. We threw off the yoke of matriarchy when we replaced the Old Religion with the New. But while men rule they must look to the sky Gods for support, for men have no proof of fertility, no intimate association with children or the things of Mother Earth. We answer to our people differently than we did under the Old Religion. Then, we were the sacrificial victims, the hapless creatures the Queen offered up to appease the Mother when the harvest failed, or the war was lost, or some terrible plague descended. The New Religion has freed men from that fate, it has elevated us to proper sovereignty. We answer for our people directly. Therefore I am in favour of this mighty enterprise. It will be the salvation of our people, it will spread our customs and traditions everywhere. If I return home now, I am humbled before the people and must admit defeat. How then can I resist if the people, sharing my humiliation, decide to return to the Old Religion, sacrifice me and elevate my wife?'

He sat down on his chair and put his white, shapely hands on his purple-draped knees. 'I will see the vote. If any man wishes to withdraw and sail back to Greece, let him show his hand.'

No one moved his arm. The room was quiet.

'So be it. We stay. Odysseus, Nestor, do you have any further suggestions?'

'No, sire,' said Odysseus.

'No, sire,' said Nestor.

'Idomeneus?'

'I'm well content, Agamemnon.'

'Then we had best get down to details. Patrokles, since you've been appointed our cupbearer, go and summon food.'

'How will you divide the army, sire?' Asked Meriones.

'As I suggested, a rotation of contingents. However, I do add one proviso to that. I think the Second Army ought to have a hard core of permanent men, men who will remain with it throughout the course of the war. Some of you in this room are young men of great promise. It would chafe you to sit before Troy. I must remain at Troy all year, as must Idomeneus, Odysseus, Nestor, Diomedes, Menestheus and Palamedes. Achilles, the two Ajaxes, Teukros and Meriones, you're young. To you I entrust the Second Army. The high command goes to Achilles. Achilles, you'll answer either to me or to Odysseus. All the decisions on active service or within Assos will be yours, no matter how senior the men might be who'll come from Troy to do their six moons' duty. Is that clear? Do you want the high command?'

Achilles sprang to his feet, trembling; I could hardly bear the brightness of his eyes, yellow and strong as Helios Sun. 'I swear by all the Gods that you will never have cause to regret your confidence in my leadership, sire.'

'Then take the high command from me, son of Peleus, and choose your lieutenants,' said Agamemnon.

I looked at Odysseus and shook my head; up flew one red brow and the grey eyes twinkled. Wait until I got him alone! Huddled hatching, indeed.

CHAPTER SIXTEEN

NARRATED BY
HELEN

Under the shadow of Troy Agamemnon raised a city stone by stone; every day when I stood on my balcony I looked out over the walls and down to the Greeks sitting by the Hellespont shore. They toiled like ants in the distance, rolling boulders and piling the trunks of mighty trees into a wall which stretched from sparkling Simois to cloudy Skamander. Houses proliferated behind the beach itself, tall barracks to accommodate soldiers over the winter, grain bins to store emmer wheat and barley away from rats and weather.

Since the Greek fleet arrived my life had grown a great deal harder, though it never was what I had imagined before I reached Troy. Why is it that we do not see the future clearly on the loom of time, even when it is depicted there, manifest? I should have known. I ought to have known. But Paris was my all; I could get no further than Paris, Paris, Paris.

In Amyklai I had been the Queen. It was *my* blood legitimised Menelaos on the throne. The people of Lakedaimon looked to me, Tyndareus's daughter, for their wellbeing and their contacts with the Gods. I was important. When I rode in my royal car through the streets of Amyklai its populace abased themselves before me. I was worshipped. I was adored. I was Queen Helen, the only one of Leda's divine quadruplets left at home. And, looking back, I realised how full was my life there – the hunts, the sports, the festivals, the Court, the diversions of all kinds. I used to tell myself that time hung heavily on my hands in Amyklai, but now I knew that in those days I had no concept of what boredom actually entails.

223

HELEN

I learned all about boredom after I arrived in Troy. Here I am no queen. Here I am unimportant in the scheme of *everything*. I am the wife of a minor imperial son. I am a detested foreigner. I am constrained by rules and regulations I have neither the power nor the authority to set aside. And there is nothing to do, nowhere to go! I can't snap my fingers and order a car, go into the countryside or watch the men playing games or drilling at being soldiers. I can't escape from the Citadel. When I tried to venture down into the city everyone from Hekabe to Antenor protested that I was fast, immoral, capricious enough to want to go slumming. Didn't I understand that the moment the men around some low tavern saw my exposed breasts I would be raped? But when I volunteered to cover them, Priam still said no.

My own apartments (Priam had been generous in that respect – Paris and I occupied a large and beautiful set of rooms) and the chambers in which the noblewomen of the Citadel gathered were suddenly the limits of my world. While Paris, my wonderful Paris, I have discovered, is a typical man. He wants – and gets! – his own way. Which doesn't include keeping his wife company. I am there for love, and love is a short business once the lovers have no new things to learn about each other.

After the Greeks came my life, boring though I had already deemed it, worsened. People looked at me as if I was the precursor of disaster and blamed me for Agamemnon's advent. Fools! At first I tried to convince the Trojan nobility that Agamemnon went to war for no woman, even his sister-in-law twice over: that Agamemnon had talked of war with Troy as far back as the night the priests quartered the white horse and I was given to Menelaos. No one would listen to me. No one *wanted* to listen to me. *I* was the reason the Greeks were there on the beach along the Hellespont shore. *I* was the reason the Greek city grew behind the mighty wall they erected from sparkling Simois to cloudy Skamander. Everything was *my* fault!

224

Priam was very worried, poor old man. He perched himself on the edge of his gold and ivory chair instead of sinking back into it the way he used to. He plucked strands from his beard, he sent man after man to the western watchtower to report back to him on Greek progress. Since the day I had walked into his Throne Room he had run the full gamut of emotions, from glee at having tweaked Agamemnon's nose to sheer bewilderment. While the Greeks gave no indication that they planned to stay he chuckled; while the promise of aid came from his allies he looked happy. But when the Greek defence wall began to rise his face fell and his shoulders sagged.

I was quite fond of him, though he lacked the strength and dedication of a Greek king. A man had to be very strong to hold onto what was his in Greece – or have a brother strong enough for both. Whereas Priam's ancestors had ruled Troy for aeons. His people loved him as Greek peoples could not love their Kings, yet he held his duties more lightly, being secure in the tenure of his throne. The word of the Gods was not so precious to him.

Old Antenor the royal brother-in-law never ceased to carp at me; I hated him more than Priam did, and that was saying something. Whenever Antenor turned his rheumy eyes upon me I could see them burn with enmity. Then his mouth would open and he would start, on and on and on. Why did I refuse to cover my breasts? Why did I beat my servant girl? Why did I have no womanly skills like weaving and embroidery? Why was I permitted to stay and hear the men's councils? Why was I so open with my opinions when women had none? There was always something to criticise, Antenor made sure of it.

When the wall behind the Hellespont beach was finished, Priam's patience with him came to an end.

'Be silent, you old simpleton!' he hissed. 'Agamemnon did not come here to get Helen back. Why would he and his subject Kings spend so much money just to retrieve a woman who left Greece of her own free will? It's Troy and Asia Minor Agamemnon wants, not Helen. He wants Greek colonies in our lands – he wants to stuff his coffers full from our vaults – he wants to pour his ships through the Hellespont into the Euxine. My son's wife is an excuse, nothing more. To return her would play into Agamemnon's hands, so I'll hear no more from you about Helen! Is that quite clear, Antenor?'

Antenor dropped his eyes and made a flourish out of his bow.

The Asia Minor states began to send their ambassadors to Troy; the next assembly I attended was swollen with their ranks. I couldn't keep all the names straight in my head, names like Paphlagonia, Kilikia, Phrygia. Some of their representatives meant more to Priam than others, though none was treated lightly. But of all of them Priam greeted the delegate from Lykia most fervently. He was the co-ruler of Lykia with his first cousin, and his name was Glaukos. His first cousin's name was Sarpedon. Paris, who had been commanded to attend, informed me in a whisper that Glaukos and Sarpedon were twinnishly inseparable, and lovers into the bargain. A foolish thing in Kings. They had neither wives nor Heirs.

'Rest assured, King Glaukos, that when we've driven the Greeks from our shores, Lykia will get a large share of the spoils,' said Priam, tears in his eyes.

Glaukos, a relatively young man (and very handsome), smiled. 'Lykia isn't here for a share of the spoils, Uncle Priam. King Sarpedon and I want only one thing – to crush the Greeks and send them squealing back to their own side of the Aegaean. Our trade is vital to us because we occupy the southern corner of this coast. Trade goes through us to our northern neighbours, as well as south to Rhodos, Cypros, Syria and Egypt. Lykia is the linchpin. We believe we must band together out of necessity, not out of greed. Rest assured, you'll have our troops and other aid in the spring. Twenty thousand men, all fully equipped and provisioned.'

The tears were falling; Priam wept an old man's easy grief. 'My heartfelt thanks to you and Sarpedon, dearest nephew.'

The others came forward, some as generous as Lykia, others haggling for money or privileges. Priam promised each what he wanted, and so the toll of men and aid grew. At the end of it I wondered how Agamemnon would ever manage to hold his ground. Two hundred thousand men would Priam marshal on the plain when the crocuses burst through the melting snow in the spring of next year. Unless my erstwhile brother-in-law had either reinforcements or tricks up his purple sleeve, he would be defeated. Why then did I continue to worry? Because I knew my people. Give a Greek enough rope and he'll hang everyone else in sight. Never himself. I knew Agamemnon's advisers of old, and I had lived in Troy long enough to understand that King Priam possessed no advisers to equal Nestor, Palamedes and Odysseus.

Oh, those meetings were boring! I attended them only because the rest of my life was even more boring. No one was permitted to sit except the King, and certainly not a woman. My feet hurt. So while a Paphlagonian clad in what looked like soft embroidered skins prated on in a dialect I couldn't comprehend, my eyes wandered idly over the throng until they lit upon a man at the back who had apparently only just come in. Oh, nice! *Very* nice!

He pushed his way through the crowd easily, taller than any other man present save Hektor, who stood, as usual, beside the throne. The newcomer had all the haughtiness of a king – and one who held himself in high regard into the bargain. I was reminded irresistibly of Diomedes; he had the same graceful walk and hard, warrior air about him. Dark-haired and black-eyed, he was dressed richly; the cloak tossed carelessly back over his shoulders was lined with the most beautiful fur I had ever seen, long and fluffy and tawny-spotted. At the foot of the throne dais he bowed very slightly and stiffly, as a king does to one he has difficulty in admitting is his senior in rank.

'Aineas!' Priam said, a curious undertone in his voice. 'I have looked for you these many days.'

'You perceive me, sire,' said the man called Aineas.

227

'Have you seen the Greeks for yourself?'

'Not yet, sire. I came in through the *Dardanian* Gate.'

His emphasis on the name of the gate was meaningful; I now remembered where I had heard his name. Aineas was Dardania's Heir. His father, King Anchises, ruled the southern part of this land from a town called Lyrnessos. Priam always sneered when he spoke of Dardania, Anchises or Aineas; I gathered that in Troy all three were considered upstarts, though Paris had told me that King Anchises was Priam's first cousin, that Dardanos had founded both the royal house in Troy and the royal house in Lyrnessos.

'I suggest, then, that you go outside onto the balcony and look towards the Hellespont,' said Priam, oozing sarcasm.

'As you wish.'

Aineas disappeared for a very few moments, came back shrugging. 'They look as if they mean to stay, don't they?'

'A perspicacious conclusion.'

Aineas ignored this sally. 'Why did you summon me?' he asked.

'Surely it's obvious? Once Agamemnon has his teeth firmly fixed in Troy, Dardania and Lyrnessos will be next. I want your troops to help crush the Greeks in the spring.'

'Greece has no quarrel with Dardania.'

'Greece doesn't need excuses these days. Greece is after lands, bronze and gold.'

'Well, sire, looking at the formidable array of allies here today, I can't see that you'll have need of the men of Dardania to help crush the Greeks. When your need is genuine, I'll bring an army. But not in the spring.'

'My need is genuine next spring!'

'I doubt that.'

Priam struck the floor with his ivory sceptre; the emerald in its head gave out blue sparks. 'I want your men!'

'I can't pledge anything without my father the King's explicit permission, sire, and I have not got it.'

Beyond speech, Priam turned his head away.

As soon as we were alone, consumed with curiosity, I quizzed Paris about that strange argument.

'What lies between your father and Prince Aineas?'

Paris tugged my hair lazily. 'Rivalry.'

'Rivalry? But one rules Dardania, the other Troy!'

'Yes, but there's an oracle which says that Aineas will rule Troy one day. My father fears the word of the God. Aineas knows the oracle too, so he always expects to be treated like the Heir. But when you consider that my father has fifty sons, Aineas's attitude is quite ridiculous. My theory is that the oracle refers to another Aineas some time in the future.'

'He seems a man,' I said thoughtfully. 'Very attractive.'

Liquid eyes gleamed at me. 'Never forget whose wife you are, Helen. Stay away from Aineas.'

The feeling between me and Paris was waning. How could that have happened, when I had fallen in love with him at first glance? Yet it had, I suppose because I soon discovered that despite his passion for me, Paris couldn't resist the urge to philander. Nor, in the summer, his urge to frolic in the vicinity of Mount Ida. In that one summer between my arrival in Troy and the advent of the Greeks, Paris disappeared for six full moons. When he finally returned, he didn't even apologise! Nor could he be brought to see how I suffered in his absence.

Some of the Court women did everything they could think of to make my existence prickly and unbearable. Queen Hekabe loathed me; she considered me her beloved Paris's ruination. Hektor's wife, Andromache, loathed me because I had usurped her title of Most Beautiful – and because she was terrified Hektor might succumb to my charms. As if I could have bothered! Hektor was a prig and a nuisance, so up and down and rigid that I soon deemed him the most boring man in a court of boring men.

It was the young priestess Kassandra who terrified me. She would sweep around the halls and corridors with her black hair streaming wildly, her eyes stark with madness, her white face ravaged. Every time she saw me she would launch into a shrill diatribe of abusive nonsense, words and ideas so tangled that no one could see their logic. I was a daimon. I was a horse. I was the agent of misrule. I was in league with Dardania. I was in league with Agamemnon. I was the downfall of Troy. And so on, and so forth. She upset me, which Hekabe and Andromache soon discovered. That led them to encourage Kassandra to lie in wait for me; they hoped, of course, that I would confine myself to my room. But Helen is made of stronger stuff than that. Instead of retreating, I got into the annoying habit of joining Hekabe, Andromache and the other high noblewomen in their recreation chamber, there to irritate them by stroking my breasts (they really are gorgeous) under their scandalised eyes (not one of them could have bared her own collection of loose beans in the bottom of a bag). When that palled I would slap the servants, spill milk on their boring tapestries and lengths of cloth, engage in monologues about rape, fire and plunder. One memorable morning I enraged Andromache so much that she flew at me with teeth and nails, only to discover that Helen had wrestled as a girl, and was more than a match for a carefully nurtured lady. I tripped her up and walloped her on the eye, which swelled, closed and blackened for almost a moon. Then I went round coyly whispering that Hektor had done it.

Paris was always being nagged to discipline me; his mother in particular badgered him constantly. But whenever he sought to remonstrate with me or beg me to be nicer, I laughed at him and gave him a litany of the offences the other women committed against me. All of which meant that I saw less and less of Paris.

In early winter the first disquiet gripped the Trojan Court. It was rumoured that the Greeks were gone from the beach, that they were raiding up and down the Asia Minor coast to strike at cities and towns far apart. Yet when heavily armed detachments were sent to investigate the beach, they found the

Greeks very much present, ready to issue out and skirmish. Even so, word of the raiding became positive as winter drew on; one by one Priam's allies sent word that they could no longer honour their promises of armies in the spring. Their own lands were threatened. Tarses in Kilikia went up in flames, its people dead or sold into slavery; the fields and pastures for fifty leagues around were burned, the grain taken and loaded on board Greek ships, the stock slaughtered and smoked for Greek bellies in Kilikian smokehouses, the shrines stripped of their treasures, King Eetion's palace looted. Mysia suffered next. Lesbos sent aid to Mysia, and in its turn was attacked. Thermi was razed to the ground, the Lesbians licked their wounds and wondered whether it might be more politic to remember the Greek half of their ancestry, and declare for Agamemnon. Then when Priene and Miletos in Karia succumbed, the panic increased. Even Sarpedon and Glaukos, the double Kings, were forced to stay at home in Lykia.

We received news of each fresh strike in a most novel way. The message was brought by a Greek herald who stood outside the Skaian Gate and shouted his news for Priam to the captain of the western watchtower. He would detail the city sacked, the number of dead citizens, the number of women and children sold into slavery, the value of the spoils, the dippers of grain. And he always ended his message with the same words:

'Tell Priam, King of Troy, that Achilles the son of Peleus sends me!'

Trojans grew to dread the mention of that name, Achilles. In the spring Priam had to endure the presence of the Greek camp in silence, for no allied forces arrived to swell his ranks, nor money to buy mercenaries from the Hittites, Assyria or Babylonia. Trojan money had to be carefully conserved; it was the Greeks who now collected the Hellespont tolls.

A certain greyness entered both Trojan hearts and Trojan rooms. And, as I was the only Greek in the Citadel, everyone from Priam to Hekabe asked me who was this Achilles. I told them as much as I could remember, but when I explained that

231

he was hardly more than a lad – though of splendid stock – they doubted me.

As time went on fear of Achilles grew greater; the mere mention of his name turned Priam pale. Only Hektor displayed no evidence of fright. He burned to meet Achilles. His eyes would light up, his hand seek his dagger each time the Greek herald came to the Skaian Gate. Indeed, to meet Achilles became such an obsession with him that he took to offering at every altar, praying for the chance to slay Achilles. When he sought me out to quiz me, he refused to believe my answers.

As autumn of the second year arrived, Hektor lost patience and begged his father to let him lead the whole Trojan army out.

Priam stared as if his Heir had gone mad. 'No, Hektor.'

'Sire, our investigations have revealed that the Greeks left on the beach number less than half of the total Greek strength! We could beat them! And when we do, Achilles's army will have to return to Troy! Then we'll beat him!'

'Or be beaten ourselves.'

'Sire, we outnumber them!' Hektor cried.

'I don't believe that.'

Hands clenched, Hektor kept finding new reasons to convince the terrified old man that he was right. 'Then, sire, give me leave to go to Aineas in Lyrnessos – with the Dardanians added to our reserves, we *would* outnumber Agamemnon!'

'Aineas doesn't wish to involve himself in our dilemmas.'

'Aineas would listen to me, Father.'

Priam drew himself up, outraged. 'Authorise my son, the Heir himself, to *beg* from the Dardanians? Are you out of your mind, Hektor? I'd rather be dead than bow and scrape to Aineas!'

At which moment I chanced to see Aineas. He had only just entered the Throne Room, but he had heard enough of the exchange at the dais. His mouth was drawn down; his eyes went from Hektor to Priam, the thoughts behind them veiled. Before anyone important noticed him – *I* was not important – he turned and left.

'Sire,' said Hektor desperately, 'you can't expect us to remain within our walls for ever! The Greeks are intent upon reducing our allies to ashes! Our wealth is dwindling because our income is gone and provisioning ourselves is costing more and more. If you won't let me lead the whole army out, then at least let me lead out raiding parties to catch the Greeks unaware, harry their hunting parties and make them stop these insolent expeditions to our walls to insult us!'

Priam wavered. He dropped his chin into his hand and thought for a long time. After which he sighed and said, 'Very well. Get you to drilling the men. If you can convince me that this isn't a foolhardy scheme, you may do as you ask.'

Hektor's face shone. 'We won't disappoint you, sire.'

'I hope not,' said Priam wearily.

Someone in the Throne Room began to laugh. I looked around, surprised; I had thought Paris away again. But there he stood, laughing helplessly. Hektor's expression darkened; he stepped down from the dais and pushed his way through the crowd.

'What's so amusing, Paris?'

My husband sobered a little, threw an arm around Hektor's shoulders. 'You, Hektor, you! Fussing about mere skirmishing when you have such a lovely wife at home. How can you prefer war to women?'

'Because,' said Hektor deliberately, 'I'm a man, Paris, not a pretty boy.'

I stood turned to stone. My husband was not only a fool, he was also a coward. Oh, the humiliation! Feeling all the contemptuous looks around me, I walked out.

Two beautiful fools, Paris and I. I had given up my throne, my freedom and my children – why did I miss them so little? – to live in prison with a beautiful fool who was also a coward. Why *did* I miss them so little? The answer was easy. They belonged to Menelaos, and somewhere in my mind I now had to lump Menelaos, my children and Paris into the same unpalatable parcel. Was there ever a fate worse for a woman than to know that not one person in her life is worthy of her?

Needing fresh air, I went to the courtyard below my own apartments, and there paced up and down until my pain abated. Then, turning quickly, I ran full tilt into a man coming the other way. We put out our hands instinctively; he held me at arm's length for a moment looking curiously into my face, the last traces of his own anger dying out of his dark eyes.

'You must be Helen,' he said.

'And you're Aineas.'

'Yes.'

'You don't come to Troy often,' I said, very much enjoying looking at him.

'Can you think of one reason why I should?'

No point in dissimulating. I smiled. 'No.'

'I like the smile, but you're angry,' he said. 'Why?'

'That's my own business.'

'Quarrelled with Paris, have you?'

'Not at all,' I answered, shaking my head. 'To quarrel with Paris is as difficult as taking hold of quicksilver.'

'True.'

Whereupon he caressed my left breast. 'An interesting fashion, to bare them. But they inflame a man, Helen.'

My lashes fell, my mouth turned up at its corners. 'That's nice to know,' I said, low voiced. Expecting a kiss, I leaned towards him with my eyes still shut. But when, feeling nothing, I opened them, I found he had gone.

Boredom a thing of the past, I went to the next assembly intent upon seducing Aineas. Who was not present. When I asked Hektor very casually what had become of his cousin from Dardania, he said that Aineas had packed his horses in the night and gone home.

CHAPTER SEVENTEEN

NARRATED BY
PATROKLES

The states of Asia Minor nursed their wounds, sullenly crouching back against the vast mountains which belonged to the Hittites. They were frightened to move to Troy and frightened to band together in any one place because they had no idea whereabouts we Greeks would strike next. Actually we defeated them before we so much as sailed on our first campaign; all the advantages lay with us, cruising down the coast just too far out to be spied from land, mobile beyond any move they could make, for there were no easy roads between the various foci of settlement in that land of river valleys between rugged ranges. The Asia Minor nations communicated by sea, and we ruled the sea.

During the first year we intercepted many ships bearing arms and food for Troy, but these convoys ceased after they realised that we Greeks benefited, not Troy. We were too many for them; none of the cities dotted up and down that very long coast could hope to marshal resistance strong enough to defeat us in battle, nor were their city walls able to keep us out. Thus we sacked ten cities in two years, far down past Rhodos to Tarses in Kilikia, as close to Troy as Mysia and Lesbos.

When we ranged the seas Phoinix always gave charge of the feeder line between Assos and Troy to his second-in-command, and sailed with us in command of two hundred empty ships to accommodate the spoils. Their bellies rode low in the water when we shook our sails free of the smoke of a burning city, our troop vessels creaking with extra plunder. Achilles was ruthless. Few were left behind to breed future resistance. Those

235

we could not carry into slavery or sell to Egypt and Babylon were slain – old crones and withered men, those no one had any use for. His was a hated name along that shoreline, and I could not find it in my heart to condemn them for hating Achilles.

As we entered our third year Assos stirred and came to life sluggishly; the snow was melting, the trees in bud. We knew no quarrels or differences, for we had long forgotten any loyalties save those we owed to Achilles and the Second Army.

Sixty-five thousand men were quartered at Assos: a core of twenty thousand veterans who never left for Troy, thirty thousand more who stayed with us for the duration of the campaign season, and fifteen thousand tradesmen and artificers of all kinds, some of whom remained in Assos year round. One of the permanent leaders always garrisoned Assos in case of attack from Dardania while the fleet was away; even Ajax took his turn at this, though Achilles always sailed. As I would not be parted from Achilles, I always sailed too. He was a fierce commander, one who never gave quarter or listened to pleas for surrender. Once he donned armour he was as cold as the North Wind, implacable. The object of our existence, he would say to us, was to ensure Greek supremacy and leave no opposition against the day the Greek nations would begin to send their surplus citizens to colonise Asia Minor.

When we sailed into Assos harbour after a late winter campaign in Lykia (Achilles seemed to have some sort of pact with the Gods of the sea, for we sailed as safely in winter as in summer), Ajax was waiting on the beach to greet us, waving gaily to signal that he hadn't been threatened in our absence, and was spoiling to go back to war. Spring had come in full measure, the grass ankle high; early flowers dotted the meadows, the camp horses leaped and frolicked in their pastures, the air was soft and heady as undiluted wine. Filling our chests with the scent of home, we scrambled to jump down onto the shingle.

We split up then to meet later, Ajax going off with Little Ajax and Teukros, his great arms about them, while Meriones stalked ahead in Cretan superiority. I strolled with Achilles, delighted to be back in Assos. The women had been busy in our absence; pale green shoots in their garden beds promised herbs and vegetables for the cooking pots, garlands of flowers for our heads. A pretty place, Assos, not at all like the dour war camp Agamemnon had built at Troy. The barracks were scattered randomly through groves of trees and the streets wandered the way streets did in an ordinary town. Of course we were secure. A wall, palisade and ditch twenty cubits high surrounded us, fully guarded even through the coldest moons of winter. Not that our closest enemy, Dardania, seemed interested in us, rumour had it that its King, Anchises, was always at logger-heads with Priam.

There were women everywhere through the camp, some bulging in late pregnancy, and over the winter a landslide of babies had arrived. The sight of them and their mothers pleased me, for they soothed away the ache of war, the emptiness of killing. There were none of mine among those babies, nor any from Achilles. I find women interesting creatures, despite the fact that I am not attracted to them. All of ours were captives of our swords, yet once the initial shock and disorientation had worn off, they seemed able to forget whatever past lives they had known, whatever men they had loved then; they settled down to love again, to have new families and espouse Greek ways. Well, they are not warriors. They are the prizes of warriors. I daresay feminine realities are taught to them by their mothers while they're still little girls. Women are nest makers, so the nest is of first importance. Of course there were always a few who couldn't forget, who wept and mourned; they didn't last at Assos, were sent to toil in the greasy, muddy fields where the Euphrates almost marries the Tigris, there, I imagine, to die still grieving.

The hall was the biggest room in our house, serving both as a sitting room and as a council chamber. Achilles and I entered together, our shoulders combined just clearing the frame on either side of the doorway. Noting that always gave me a pang of pleasure, as if it spoke in some way of who and what we had become. Leaders, masters.

I took off my own armour, whereas Achilles let the women strip his gear from him, standing like a tower with half a dozen women tugging at straps and knots, clucking when they saw the long black ribbon of a half-healed wound on his thigh. I could never bring myself to permit slaves to disarm me; I had seen their faces when we chose them from the spoils as part of our share. But Achilles worried not one bit. He let them remove his sword and dagger without seeming to realise that one of them could turn with the weapon in her hand and slay him as he stood defenceless. I looked them over dubiously, but had to admit that the danger of such an occurrence was very slight. From youngest to oldest, they were all in love with him. Our baths were already filled with warm water, fresh kilts and blouses laid out.

Afterwards, when the wine was poured and the remains of our meal cleared away, Achilles dismissed the women and lay back with a sigh. Both of us were tired, yet it was no use trying to sleep; broad daylight poured through the windows, we were still likely to be invaded by friends.

Achilles had been very quiet all day – not unusual, save that today's silence hinted at withdrawal. I disliked these moods in him. It was as if he went somewhere I couldn't follow, into a world his alone, leaving me to cry fruitlessly at its gates. So I leaned across to touch him on the arm, more strength in my fingers than I had intended.

'Achilles, you've hardly touched the wine.'

'I've no appetite for it.'

'Are you off colour?'

The question surprised him. 'No. Is it a sign of illness in me when I refuse the wine?'

'No. More your mood, I think.'

He sighed deeply, gazed about the hall. 'I love this room more than any other room I've ever known. It belongs to *me*.

Because not one thing in it wasn't won with my sword. It tells me that I'm *Achilles*, not the son of Peleus.'

'Yes, it's a beautiful room,' I said.

He frowned. 'Beauty is an indulgence of the senses, I despise it as an infirmity. No, I love this room because it's my trophy.'

'A splendid trophy,' I floundered.

He ignored this banality, went somewhere else again; I tried again to bring him back.

'Even after so many years, you say things I don't begin to understand. Surely you love beauty in *some* guises? To live deeming it an infirmity is no life, Achilles.'

He grunted. 'It matters little to me how I live or how long I live, provided that I've ensured my fame. Men must never forget me when I'm in my grave.' His mood swung anew. 'Do you think I've gone about the getting of fame the wrong way?'

'That lies between you and the Gods,' I answered. 'You haven't sinned against them – you haven't slain fertile women or children too young to bear arms. It's no sin to give them over into bondage. Nor have you starved a place out. If your hand's been heavy, it's never been criminally so. I'm softer, is all.'

A smile dawned. 'You underestimate yourself, Patrokles. Put a sword in your hand and you're as hard as any of us.'

'Battle is different. I can kill without mercy in battle. But sometimes my dreams are dark and heavy.'

'As are mine. Iphigenia cursed me before she died.'

Not able to sustain the talk, he drifted away; I fell to watching him, as there was nothing I liked better to do. Many of his qualities were beyond my comprehension, yet if any man knew Achilles, that man was I. He possessed the ability to make people love him, be they his Myrmidons or his captive women – or me, for that matter. But the cause didn't lie in his physical attractiveness; it was a facet of his spirit, a vastness other men always seemed to lack.

Since we had sailed from Aulis three years ago he had become extremely self-contained; I sometimes wondered if his wife would even recognise him when they met again. Of course his troubles were rooted in the death of Iphigenia, and that I shared as well as understood. But not where his thoughts led, nor the deepest layers of his mind.

A sudden breath of cold wind stirred the drapes at either side of the window. I shivered. Achilles still lay on his side, his head propped on one hand, but his expression had changed. I spoke his name sharply. He did not answer.

Suddenly alarmed, I sprang from my couch to drop down on the edge of his. I put my hand on his bare shoulder, but he didn't seem to know it. My heart singing, I looked down at the skin beneath my palm and bent my head until my lips rested against it; tears leaped under my lids so swiftly that one fell upon his arm. Appalled, I snatched my mouth away as he shuddered and turned his head to look at me, something in his eyes only half formed – as if in this moment he saw the real Patrokles for the first time.

He opened that poor lipless gash to speak, but whatever he might have said was never said. His eyes went to the open door and he said, 'Mother.'

Horrified, I saw that he drooled, that his left hand was jerking, that the left side of his face twitched. Then he fell from couch to floor and stiffened, his spine arched, his eyes so blind and white that I thought he was going to die. Down on the floor I collapsed to hold him, to wait for the blackened face to fade to a mottled grey, for the jerking to stop, for him to live. When it was over I wiped the saliva from his jaw, cradled him more easily and stroked his sweat-matted hair.

'What was it, Achilles?'

He gazed at me cloudily, recognition dawning slowly. Then he sighed like an exhausted child. 'Mother came bearing her Spell. I think I've been feeling her coming all day.'

The Spell! Was *this* the Spell? It looked to me like an epileptic seizure, though the people I had known who suffered them always wasted away in mind until imbecility negated them; soon after, they died. Whatever afflicted Achilles had not

attacked his mind, nor had the Spell become more frequent. I
thought this was the first Spell since that one in Skyros.

'Why did she come, Achilles?'

'To remind me that I will die.'

'You can't say that! How do you know?' I helped him to his
feet, put him on his couch and sat down beside him. 'I saw you
in this Spell, Achilles, and what it looked like to me was an
epilepsy.'

'Perhaps it is an epilepsy. If so, then my mother sends it to
remind me of my mortality. And she's right. I must die before
Troy falls. The Spell is a taste of death, existence as a shade,
uncaring and unfeeling.' His mouth drew in. 'Long and
ignominious or short and glorious. There is no choice, which is
what she will not see. Her visitations as the Spell can change
nothing. My choice was made in Skyros.'

I turned away and rested my head on my arm.

'Don't weep for me, Patrokles. I've chosen the fate I want.'

I dashed my hand across my eyes. 'I don't weep for you. I
weep for myself.'

Though I wasn't looking at him, I felt him change.

'We share the same blood,' he said then. 'Just before the Spell
descended, I saw something in you I've never seen before.'

'My love for you,' I said, throat constricted.

'Yes. I'm sorry. I must have hurt you many times, not
understanding. But why are you weeping?'

'When love isn't returned, we weep.'

He got up from the couch and held out both hands to me. 'I
return your love, Patrokles,' he said. 'I always have.'

'But you're not a man for men, and that's the love I want.'

'Perhaps that would be so if I'd chosen a long and ignominious life. As it is, and for what it's worth, I'm not averse to love
with you. We're in exile together, and it seems very sweet to
me to share that exile in the flesh as well as in the spirit,' said
Achilles.

So it was that he and I became lovers, though I didn't find
the ecstasy I had dreamed of. Do we ever? Achilles burned for

many things, but the satisfaction of his body was never one of them. No matter. I had more of him than any woman, and found a kind of contentment at least. Love isn't truly the body. Love is freedom to roam the heart and mind of the beloved.

It was five years before we visited Troy and Agamemnon. I went with Achilles, of course; he also took Ajax and Meriones. I was aware that this visit was long overdue, but I thought that even then he wouldn't have gone were it not that he needed to confer with Odysseus. The Asia Minor states had grown wary, devised stratagems to anticipate our attacks.

The long, bristling beach between Simois and Skamander was nothing like the place we had left over four years earlier. Its ramshackle, makeshift air had vanished; permanence and purpose were self-evident. The fortifications were businesslike and well designed. There were two entrances to the camp, one at Skamander and one at Simois, where stone bridges had been thrown across the trench and big gates yawned in the wall.

Ajax and Meriones disembarked at the Simois end of the beach while Achilles and I came in up Skamander, to find that barracks had been built to house the Myrmidons on their return. We walked along the main road which traversed the camp, seeking Agamemnon's new house, which, we had been informed, was very grand.

Men nursed wounds as they sat in the sun, others whistled cheerfully as they oiled leather armour or polished bronze, some of them engaged in stripping purple plumes from Trojan helmets so that they could wear them into battle themselves. A busy, happy place telling us that the troops left at Troy were far from idle.

Odysseus was emerging from Agamemnon's house just as we arrived. When he saw us he leaned his spear against the portico and opened his arms, grinning. There were two or three fresh scars on his sturdy body – had he got them in open combat or during one of those night excursions? He is the only devious man I have ever met who isn't afraid to risk life and limb in a good fight. Perhaps that was the red man in him, or perhaps he was convinced he led a charmed life, thanks to Pallas Athene.

'About time!' he exclaimed, embracing us. And, to Achilles, 'The conquering hero!'

'Hardly apt. The coastal cities have learned to anticipate my coming.'

'We can talk about that later.' He turned to accompany us inside. 'I must thank you for your consideration, Achilles. You send us generous spoils and some very fine women.'

'We're not greedy in Assos. But it looks as if you've been busy here too. Much fighting?'

'Enough to keep everybody fit. Hektor leads a nasty attack.'

Achilles looked suddenly alert. 'Hektor?'

'Priam's heir and the leader of the Trojans.'

Agamemnon was graciously pleased to welcome us to his half of our army, though he offered us no incentives to stay and spend the morning with him. Nor would Achilles have liked it if he had; ever since Hektor's name was mentioned he was itching to find out more, and knew Agamemnon wasn't the right person to ask.

None of them had really changed or aged, give or take a new battle scar or two. If anything, Nestor looked younger than of yore. He was in his element, I suppose, occupied and constantly stimulated. Idomeneus had become less indolent, which was good for his figure. Only Menelaos seemed not to have benefited from life in a campaign camp; he still missed Helen, poor man.

We stayed as the guests of Odysseus and Diomedes, who had also become lovers. Part expedience, part sheer liking for each other. Women were a complication when men led our kind of life, and Odysseus I think never noticed any woman other than Penelope, though his stories revealed that he was not above seducing some Trojan woman to obtain information. Achilles and I were told about the existence of the spy colony, an amazing tale in itself. Word of it had never got out.

'And that's astonishing,' said Achilles. 'Ye Gods, if they only knew! But I didn't, nor anyone else I mix with.'

'Not even Agamemnon knows,' said Odysseus.

'Because of Kalchas?' I asked.

'Shrewd guess, Patrokles. I don't trust the man.'

'Well, neither he nor Agamemnon will know of it from us,' said Achilles.

For the duration of the moon we remained at Troy, Achilles thought of one thing only – meeting Hektor.

'Best forget it, lad,' said Nestor at the end of a dinner Agamemnon gave in our honour. 'You might dally here all summer and not see Hektor. His sorties are random. They can't be predicted despite Odysseus's uncanny knowledge of what goes on in Troy. And at the moment we don't plan any sorties ourselves.'

'Sorties?' asked Achilles, looking alarmed. 'Are you going to take the city in my absence?'

'No, no!' cried Nestor. 'We're in no position to assault Troy, even if the Western Curtain came down in ruins tomorrow. You have the better part of our army in Assos, and well you know it. Go back there! Don't wait here hoping for Hektor.'

'There's no hope of Troy's falling in your absence, Prince Achilles,' said a soft voice behind us: the priest Kalchas.

'What do you mean?' asked Achilles, obviously discomposed by those crossed and rosy eyes.

'Troy cannot fall in your absence. The oracles say so.' He moved away, his purple robe shimmering with gold and gems. Odysseus was right to keep some of his activities secret. Our High King esteemed the man greatly; his residence (right next door) was sumptuous, and he had his pick of all the women we sent up from Assos. Diomedes told me that on one such occasion Idomeneus was so enraged when Kalchas snatched the woman he fancied that he took his case to the council and forced Agamemnon to take her off Kalchas, give her to his co-commander.

Thus Achilles left Troy a disappointed man. So too, it turned out, did Ajax. Both of them had wandered all over the windy Trojan plain hoping to tempt Hektor out, but there had been no sign of him, or of Trojan attack troops.

The years ground on inexorably, always the same. The Asia Minor nations toppled slowly into ashes while the slave markets of the world overflowed with Lykians, Karians, Kilikians and a dozen other nationalities. Nebuchadrezzar took all we cared to send to Babylon, while Tiglath-Pileser of Assyria forgot his Trojan–Hittite ties sufficiently to take thousands more. No land, I discovered, ever seemed to have enough slaves, and it had been a long time since any war had provided the fount Achilles did.

Apart from our raids, life was not always peaceful. There were times when the mother of Achilles plagued him with her wretched Spell day after day; then she would make off for some other place and leave him undisturbed for moons on end. But I had learned how to make the Spell periods easier for him; he had grown to depend upon me for *all* his needs. And is there anything more comforting than knowing that one's beloved is a dependant?

A ship came once from Iolkos bearing messages from Peleus, Lykomedes and Deidamia. Thanks to the steady flow of bronze and goods across the Aegaean from our spoils, things at home were prospering greatly. While Asia Minor bled to death, Greece was waxing fat. The first colonists were being assembled at Athens and Korinthos, Peleus said.

For Achilles the most important item of news concerned his son, Neoptolemos. Rapidly attaining manhood already! Where did the years go? Deidamia told him that the boy was almost as tall as his father, and displayed the same aptitude for combat and arms. Though he was wilder, had a roving disposition and a thousand female conquests. Not to mention a quick temper and a tendency to drink too much unwatered wine. Soon, said Deidamia, he would be sixteen.

'I'll instruct Deidamia and Lykomedes to send the boy to my

father,' Achilles said after the messenger had been dismissed. 'He needs a man's hand on his neck.' His face twisted. 'Oh, Patrokles, what sons Iphigenia and I would have had!'

Yes, that continued to eat at him – even more, I thought, than his mother and her Spell did.

It took us nine years to kill Asia Minor. By the end of the ninth summer there was nothing left to be done. The shiploads of Greek colonists were arriving in places like Kolophon and Appasas, everyone eager to begin a new life in a new place. Some would farm, some would trade, some would probably wander eastwards and northwards. Of no moment to us who formed the nucleus of the Second Army in Assos. Our task was over, save for an autumn attack on Lyrnessos, hub of the kingdom of Dardania.

CHAPTER EIGHTEEN

NARRATED BY

ACHILLES

Dardania lay closer to us at Assos than any other nation of Asia Minor, but I had deliberately left it alone through all the nine years of our campaign to reduce coastal Asia Minor to ruins. One reason for this lay in the fact that it was an inland territory sharing a boundary with Troy, while another reason was more subtle: I wanted to lull the Dardanians into a false sense of security, into believing that their distance from the sea rendered them inviolable. Besides which, Dardania didn't trust Troy. While I left them in peace, old King Anchises and his son Aineas kept aloof from Troy.

Now all that was about to change. The invasion of Dardania was about to begin. Instead of the usual long voyage, I prepared my troops for an arduous trek; if Aineas expected any attack at all, he would assume that we would sail around the corner of the peninsula and beach on the coast opposite Lesbos isle. From there to Lyrnessos was a mere fifteen-league march. Whereas I intended to march straight inland from Assos itself, almost a hundred leagues of wilderness spanning the slopes of Mount Ida, down into the fertile valley where Lyrnessos lay.

Odysseus had given me trained scouts to spy out our line of march; they reported that it was heavily forested, that few farms lay in our way, and that the season was too late for the shepherds to be at large. Furs and strong boots came out of storage, for Ida was already white with snow halfway down its flanks, and it was possible that we would encounter a blizzard. I estimated that we'd march about four leagues a day; twenty days ought to see us within sight of our goal. On the fifteenth of these twenty days old Phoinix my admiral was under orders to sail his fleet into the deserted harbour at Andramyttios, the nearest port on the coast. No fear that he would meet opposition. I had burned Andramyttios level with the ground earlier in the year – for the second time.

We moved out silently and the days on the march passed without incident. No shepherds tarried in the snowy hills to fly to Lyrnessos bearing news of our coming. The tranquil landscape belonged to us alone, and our journey was easier than expected. Consequently we came within scouting distance of the city on the sixteenth day. I ordered a halt and forbade the lighting of fires until I could ascertain whether or not we had been detected.

It was my habit to do this final investigation myself, so I set off on foot alone, ignoring the protests of Patrokles, who sometimes reminded me of a clucky old hen. Why is it that love breeds possessiveness and drastically waters down freedom?

Not more than three leagues on I climbed a hill and saw Lynessos below me, sprawling over a fair area of land, with good strong walls and a high citadel. I studied it for some time, combining what I saw with what Odysseus's agents had told me. No, it wouldn't be an easy assault; on the other hand, it wouldn't be half as difficult as Smyrna or Hypoplakian Thebes.

Yielding to temptation, I descended the slope a little way, enjoying the fact that this was the lee side of the hill and quite free of snow, the ground still surprisingly warm. A mistake, Achilles! Even as I told myself this, I nearly stepped on him. He rolled aside lithely and pulled himself to his feet in a single supple movement, ran until he was out of spear-cast, then paused to survey me. I was vividly put in mind of Diomedes; this man had the same deadly, feline look about him, and from his clothing and his bearing I could tell that he was a high nobleman. Having listened to and memorised the catalogue of all the Trojan and Allied leaders which Odysseus had made for us and circulated through messengers, I decided that he was Aineas.

'I am Aineas, and unarmed!' he called.

'Too bad, Dardanian! I am Achilles, and armed!'

Unimpressed, he raised his brows. 'There are definitely times in the life of a careful man when discretion is the better part of valour! I'll meet you in Lyrnessos!'

Knowing myself swifter of foot than others, I started after him at an easy pace, intending to wear him down. But he was very speedy, and he knew the lie of the land; I did not. So he led me into thorny thickets and left me floundering, over ground riddled with craters from foxes and rabbits, and finally to a wide river ford, where he streaked across on the hidden stones with light familiarity while I had to stop on each rock and look for the next. So I lost him, and stood cursing my own stupidity. Lyrnessos had a day's warning of our impending attack.

As soon as dawn came I marched, my mood sour. Thirty thousand men poured into the Vale of Lyrnessos, lapping about the city walls like syrup. A shower of darts and spears met them, but the men took the missiles on their shields as they had been taught, and sustained no casualties. It struck me that there was not much force behind the barrage, and I wondered if the Dardanians were a race of weaklings. Yet Aineas hadn't looked like the leader of a degenerate people.

The ladders went up. Leading the Myrmidons, I attained the little pathway atop the walls without having encountered one stone or pitcher of boiling oil. When a small band of defenders appeared I hacked them down with my axe, not needing to call for reinforcements. All along the line we were winning with truly ridiculous ease, and soon found out why. Our opponents were old men and little boys.

Aineas, I discovered, had returned to the city on the previous day and immediately called his soldiers to arms. But not with the intention of fighting me. He decamped to Troy with his army.

ACHILLES

'It seems the Dardanians have an Odysseus in their midst,' I said to Patrokles and Ajax. 'What a fox! Priam will have an extra twenty thousand men led by an Odysseus. Let us hope the old man's prejudices blind him to what Aineas is.'

CHAPTER NINETEEN

NARRATED BY
BRISE

Lyrnessos died, folding up its wings and spreading its plumage across the desolation with a shriek that was all the cries of the women put into one mouth. We had given Aineas into the care of his immortal mother, Aphrodite, glad he had been granted the opportunity to save our army. All the citizens had agreed it was the only thing to do, so that at least some part of Dardania would live on to strike a blow at the Greeks.

Ancient suits of armour had been lifted from chests by gnarled hands which shook with the effort; boys donned their toy suits with white faces, toy suits never designed to take the bite of bronze blades. Of course they died. Venerable beards soaked up Dardanian blood, the war cries of small soldiers turned into the terrified sobbing of little boys. My father had even taken my dagger from me, tears in his eyes as he explained that he couldn't leave me with the means to escape drudgery; it was needed, along with every other woman's dagger.

I stood at my window watching impotently as Lyrnessos died, praying to Artemis the merciful daughter of Leto that she would send one of her darts winging quickly to my heart, still its clamour before some Greek took me and sent me to the slave markets of Hattusas or Nineveh. Our pitiful defence was bludgeoned into the ground until only the citadel walls separated me from a seething mass of warriors all in bronze, taller and fairer than Dardanians; from that moment I envisioned the Daughters of Kore as tall and fair. The only

251

consolation I had was that Aineas and the army were safe. So too was our dear old King, Anchises, who had been so beautiful as a young man that the Goddess Aphrodite had loved him enough to bear him Aineas. Who, good son that he is, refused to leave his father behind. Nor did he abandon Kreusa, his wife, and their little son, Askanios.

Though I couldn't tear myself away from the window, I could hear the sounds of preparation for battle in the rooms behind me – old feet pattering, reedy voices whispering urgently. My father was among them. Only the priests remained to pray at the altars, and even among them my uncle Chryses, the high priest of Apollo, elected to cast aside his holy mantle and don armour. He would fight, he said, to protect Asian Apollo, who was not the same God as Greek Apollo.

They brought the rams to bear on the citadel gate. The palace shuddered deep in its bowels, and through the din beating on my ears I thought I heard the Earth Shaker bellow, a sound of mourning. For his heart was with them, not with us, Poseidon. We were to be offered up as victims for Troy's pride and defiance. He could do no more than send us his sympathy, while he lent his strength to the Greek rams. The wood crumpled to splinters, the hinges sagged and the door gave way with a roar. Spears and swords at the ready, the Greeks poured into the courtyard, no pity in them for our pathetic opposition, only anger that Aineas had outwitted them.

The man at their head was a giant in bronze armour trimmed with gold. Wielding a massive axe, he brushed the old men aside as if they were gnats, cleaving their flesh contemptuously. Then he plunged into the Great Hall, his men after him; I closed my eyes on the rest of the slaughter outside, praying now to chaste Artemis to put the idea into their heads to kill me. Far better death than rape and enslavement. Red mists swam before my lids, the light of day forced itself relentlessly in, my ears would not be deaf to choked cries and babbling pleas for mercy. Life is precious to the old. They understand how hard won it is. But I did not hear the voice of my father, and felt that he would have died as proudly as he had lived.

When came the clank of heavy, deliberate feet I opened my eyes and swung round to face the doorway at the other end of the narrow room. A man loomed there, dwarfing the aperture, his axe hanging by his side, his face under the gold-plumed bronze helm stained with grime. His mouth was so cruel that the Gods who made him had neglected to give him lips; I understood that a lipless man would not feel pity or kindness. For a moment he stared at me as if I had issued out of the earth, then he stepped into the room with his head tilted like a pricking dog's. Drawing myself up, I resolved that he would hear no cry or whine from me, no matter what he did to me. He would not conclude from me that Dardanians lacked courage.

The length of the room disappeared in what I fancied was one stride; he grabbed one of my wrists, then the other, and lifted me by my arms until I dangled with my toes just clear of the floor.

'Butcher! Butcher of old men and little boys! Animal!' I panted, kicking out at him.

My wrists were suddenly crushed together so hard that the bones crunched. I longed to scream in agony, but I would not – I *would* not! His yellow eyes like a lion's showed his rage; I had wounded him where his self-esteem was still sensitive. He didn't like being called a butcher of old men and little boys.

'Curb your tongue, girl! In the slave markets they flog defiance out of you with a barbed lash.'

'Disfigurement would be a gift!'

'But in your case, a pity,' he said, putting me down and releasing my wrists. He transferred his grip to my hair and dragged me by it towards the door while I kicked and struck at his metal form until my feet and fists felt broken.

'Let me walk!' I cried. 'Allow me the dignity of walking! I will not go to rape and slavery cringing and snivelling like a servant woman!'

He stopped quite still, turned to stare down into my face with confusion on his own. 'You have her courage,' he said slowly. 'You're not like her, yet you have a look of her ... Is that what you deem your fate, rape and slavery?'

'What other fate is there for a captive woman?'

Grinning – which did make him look more like other men because grinning thins the lips out – he let my hair go. I put my hand to my head, wondering if he had torn my scalp, then I walked ahead of him. His hand shot out, fingers fastening about my bruised wrist in a hold I had no hope of breaking.

'Dignity notwithstanding, my girl, I am no fool. You'll not escape from me through sheer carelessness.'

'As your leader let Aineas escape on the hill?' I gibed.

His face didn't change. 'Exactly,' he said impassively.

He led me through rooms I hardly recognised, their walls spattered with blood, their furnishings already heaped for the plunder wagons. As we entered the Great Hall his feet spurned a pile of corpses, tossed one on top of the other without respect for their years or standing. I stopped, seeking anything in that anonymous collection which might let me identify my father. My captor halfheartedly tried to pull me away, but I resisted.

'My father might be here! Let me see!' I begged.

'Which one is he?' he asked indifferently.

'If I knew that, I wouldn't have to ask to look!'

Though he wouldn't help me, he let me tug him wherever I willed as I plucked at garments or shoes. At last I saw my father's foot, unmistakable in its garnet-studded sandal – like most of the old men he had kept his armour, not his fighting boots. But I couldn't free him. Too many bodies.

'Ajax!' my captor called. 'Come and help the lady!'

Weakened by the terror of the day, I waited as another giant strolled over, a bigger man than my captor.

'Can't you help her yourself?' the newcomer asked.

'And let her go? Ajax, Ajax! This one has spirit, I can't trust her.'

'Taken a fancy to her, little cousin? Well, it's high time you took a fancy to someone other than Patrokles.'

Ajax put me aside as if I had been a feather, then, still holding his axe, he tossed the bodies about until my father lay uncovered, until I could see his dead eyes staring up at me, his beard buried in a gash which almost severed him across the chest. It was an axe wound.

'This is the ancient who faced me like a fighting cock,' the one called Ajax said admiringly. 'Fiery old fellow!'

'Like father, like daughter,' the one holding me said. He jerked at my arm. 'Come, girl. I haven't the time to indulge your grief.'

I got up clumsily, tearing my hair into disorder as I saluted him, my father. Better by far to go knowing him dead than have to wonder if he had survived, hope the most foolish hope of all. Ajax moved away, saying he would muster any left alive, though he doubted there were.

We halted at the doorway into the courtyard so my captor could strip a belt from a body lying on the steps. He fastened the leather tightly about my wrist, then secured its other end to his own arm, forcing me to walk closely beside him. Two steps higher up, I watched his bent head as he completed the small task with a thoroughness I fancied typical of him.

'You didn't kill my father,' I said.

'Yes, I did,' he answered. 'I'm the leader your Aineas outwitted. That means I'm responsible for every death.'

'What's your name?' I asked.

'Achilles,' he said shortly, tested his handiwork and hauled me after him into the courtyard. I had to run to keep up with him. Achilles. I should have known. Aineas had said it last, though I had been hearing it for years.

We left Lyrnessos through its main gate, open as Greeks wandered in and out, looting and wenching, some with torches in their hands, some with wineskins. The man Achilles made no effort to reprimand them. He ignored them.

At the top of the road I turned to look down into the Vale of

BRISE

Lyrnessos. 'You have burned my home. There I dwelled for twenty years, there I expected to dwell until a marriage was arranged for me. But I never expected this.'

He shrugged. 'The fortunes of war, girl.'

I pointed to the tiny figures of plundering soldiers. 'Can't you prevent their acting like beasts? Is there any need for it? I heard the women screaming – *I saw!*'

His eyelids drooped cynically. 'What do you know of exiled Greeks or their feelings? You hate us, and I understand that. But you don't hate us as those men hate Troy and Troy's allies! Priam has cost them ten years of exile. They delight in making him pay. Nor could I stop them if I tried. And frankly, girl, I don't feel like trying to stop them.'

'I've listened to the stories for years, but I didn't know what war is,' I whispered.

'Now you do,' he said.

His camp was three leagues distant; when we reached it he found a baggage officer.

'Polides, this is my own prize. Take the belt and harness her to an anvil until you can forge better chains. Don't let her free for one moment, even if she pleads privacy to relieve herself. Once you have her chained, put her where she has everything she needs, including a chamber pot, good food and a good bed. Start for the ships at Andramyttios tomorrow and give her to the lord Phoinix. Tell him I don't trust her, that she isn't to be freed.' He took my chin and pinched it lightly. 'Goodbye, girl.'

Polides found light chains for my ankles, padded the cuffs well, and took me to the coast on the back of an ass. There I was given to Phoinix, an upright old nobleman with the blue, crinkled gaze and rolling gait of a sailor. When he saw my fetters he clicked his tongue, though he made no attempt to remove them after he ensconced me on board the flagship. He bade me sit with gentle courtesy, but I insisted upon standing.

'I'm so sorry for the chains,' he said, grief in his eyes. But not grief for me, I understood. 'Poor Achilles!'

It annoyed me that the old man thought light of me. 'This

256

Achilles has a better idea of my mettle than you do, sir! Only let me within reach of a dagger and I'll fight my way out of this living death, or die in the attempt!'

His sadness vanished in a chuckle. 'Ai, ai! What a fierce warrior you are! Don't hope for it, girl. What Achilles binds fast, Phoinix won't free.'

'Is his word such sacred law?'

'It is. He's Prince of the Myrmidons.'

'Prince of the ants? How appropriate.'

For answer he chuckled again, pushed a chair forward. I looked at it with loathing, but my back ached from the donkey ride and my legs were trembling, for I had refused to eat or drink since my captivity. Phoinix pressed me into the chair with a hard hand and unstoppered a golden wine flagon.

'Drink, girl. If you want to maintain your defiance, you'll need sustenance. Don't be silly.'

Sensible advice. I took it, to find that my blood was thin and the wine went straight to my head. I could fight no longer. I propped my head on my hand and went to sleep in the chair, waking a long time later to find I had been put down on the bed. Shackled to a beam.

The next day I was taken on deck, my chains fastened to the rail so I could stand in the weak, wintry sun and watch the busy comings and goings on the beach. But when four ships hove into view over the horizon, I noticed a huge scurry and flutter pass through the toiling men, particularly among their supervisors. Suddenly Phoinix was there releasing me from the rail, hustling me not to my previous prison but to a shelter on the afterdeck which stank of horses. He took me inside and locked me to a bar.

'What is it?' I asked, curious.

'Agamemnon, King of Kings,' said Phoinix.

'Why put me here? Aren't I good enough to meet the King of Kings?'

He sighed. 'Have you no mirror in your Dardanian home,

girl? One look at you and Agamemnon would have you in spite of Achilles.'

'I could scream,' I said thoughtfully.

He stared at me as if I had gone mad. 'If you did you'd regret it, I promise you! What good would changing masters do? Believe me, you'd end in preferring Achilles.'

Something in his tone convinced me, so when I heard voices outside the stable door I crouched down behind a manger listening to the pure, liquid cadences of proper Greek – and to the power and authority one of the voices owned.

'Isn't Achilles back yet?' it asked imperiously.

'No, sire, but he ought to arrive before nightfall. He had to supervise the sack. A rich haul. The wagons have been laden.'

'Excellent! I'll wait in his cabin.'

'Better to wait in the tent on the beach, sire. You know Achilles. Comfort isn't important.'

'As you wish, Phoinix.'

Their voices faded; I crawled from my hiding place. The sound of that cold, proud voice had frightened me. Achilles was a monster too, but better the monster you know, as my nurse used to say when I was little.

No one came near me during the afternoon. At first I sat on the bed I presumed belonged to Achilles and inspected the contents of the bare and featureless cabin curiously. A few spears were propped against a stanchion, no attempt had been made to paint the plain plank walls, and the dimensions of the room were tiny. It contained only two striking items, one an exquisite white fur rug on the bed, the other a massive four-handled pouring cup of gold, its sides worked to show the Sky Father on his throne, each handle surmounted by a horse in full gallop.

At which moment my grief opened and swallowed me, perhaps because for the first time since my capture I had no urgent or dangerous situation to push it away. As I sat here my father would be sprawled on the Lyrnessos refuse heap, food for the perpetually hungry town dogs; that was the traditional fate for high noblemen killed in battle. Tears poured down my face; I threw myself on the white fur rug and wept. Nor could I stop. The white fur became slick under my cheek and still I wept, keening and snuffling.

I didn't hear the door open, so when a hand rested on my shoulder my heart ran about the inside of my chest like a trapped animal. All my grand ideas of defiance fled; I thought only that the High King Agamemnon had found me, and cringed away.

'I belong to Achilles, I belong to Achilles!' I wailed.

'I'm aware of that. Who did you think came in?'

Carefully wiping the relief from my face before I lifted it, I dabbed at the tears with the palm of my hand. 'The High King of Greece.'

'Agamemnon?'

I nodded.

'Where is he?'

'In the tent on the beach.'

Achilles went to a chest by the far wall, opened it, rummaged inside it and threw me a square of fine cloth. 'Here, blow your nose and mop your face. You'll make yourself sick.'

I did as I was told. He came back to my side and gazed at the rug ruefully.

'I hope it dries unmarked. It was a gift from my mother.' He looked me over critically. 'Was it beyond Phoinix's resources to find you a bath and a clean dress?'

'He offered. I refused.'

'But you won't refuse me. When the servants bring you a tub and fresh raiment, you'll use them. Otherwise I'll order it done by force – and not by women. Is that understood?'

'Yes.'

'Good.' His hand was on the latch when he paused. 'What's your name, girl?'

'Brise.'

259

He grinned appreciatively. 'Brise. "She who prevails". Are you sure you didn't make that one up?'

'My father's name was Brises. He was first cousin to King Anchises and Dardania's Chancellor. His brother, Chryses, was high priest of Apollo. We are of the Royal Kindred.'

During the evening a Myrmidon officer came to me, un-bolted my chains from the beam and led me by them to the side of the ship. A rope ladder was suspended from the rail; silently he indicated that I was to descend, doing me the courtesy of going first so he wouldn't look up my skirts. The ship was high on the pebbles, which rolled about and hurt my feet.

A huge leather tent squatted on the shore, though I couldn't remember seeing it when I had arrived on my donkey. The Myrmidon ushered me in through a flap in the back, into a room crammed with about a hundred women of Lyrnessos, none of whom I recognised. I alone had the distinction of chains. Many pairs of eyes fastened on me in hangdog curiosity as I searched the throng for a familiar face. There, in the corner! A head of glorious golden hair no one could mistake. My guard still kept hold of my fetters, but when I moved towards the corner he let me do as I wanted.

My cousin Chryse's hands were across her face; when I touched her she jumped in panic, her arms falling. She looked at me in dawning wonder, then flung herself at me, weeping.

'What are you doing here?' I asked, at a loss. 'You're the daughter of the high priest of Apollo, therefore inviolate.'

Her answer was a howl. I shook her.

'Oh, stop crying, do!' I snapped.

Since I had been bullying her from the days of our shared childhood, she obeyed me. Then she said, 'They took me all the same, Brise.'

'That is a sacrilege!'

'They say not. My father put on armour and fought. Priests don't fight. So they classified him as a warrior and took me.'

'*Took* you? Have you been raped already?' I gasped.

'No, no! According to the women who dressed me, only the ordinary women are thrown to the soldiers. Those in this room have been saved for some special purpose.' She looked down, saw my hobbles. 'Oh, Brise! They've chained you!'

'At least I bear visible evidence of my status. No one could mistake me for a camp follower, wearing these.'

'Brise!' she choked, a familiar expression on her face; I always managed to shock poor, tame little Chryse. Then she asked, 'Uncle Brises?'

'Dead, like all the rest.'

'Why aren't you mourning him?'

'I am mourning him!' I snarled. 'However, I've been in the hands of the Greeks for long enough to have learned that a captive woman needs her wits about her.'

She looked out of her depth. 'Why are we here?'

I turned to my Myrmidon. 'You! Why are we here?'

Though he grinned at my tone, he answered respectfully enough. 'The High King of Mykenai is the guest of the Second Army. They're dividing the spoils. The women in this room are to be apportioned among the Kings.'

We waited for what seemed an aeon. Too tired to talk, Chryse and I sat upon the ground. From time to time a guard would enter and remove a small group of women according to coloured tags on their wrists; they were all very handsome girls. No crones, no strumpets, no horse faces, no skeletons. Yet neither Chryse nor I wore tags. The numbers dwindled, we were ignored; finally we were the only two left in the room.

A guard entered and flung veils over our faces before we were led into the next room. Through a thin mesh over my eyes I saw a huge blaze of light from what seemed a thousand lamps, a canopy of cloth overhead, and all around a sea of men. They sat on benches at tables, with wine cups at their elbows and servants hurrying back and forth. Chryse and I were shepherded to stand before a long dais on which stood the high table.

Perhaps twenty men sat on one side of it only, facing the

diners. On a high-backed chair in the middle was a man who looked as I had always fancied Father Zeus might. He had a frowning, noble head; his elaborately curled grey-black hair cascaded over his shimmering garments and a great beard bound with threads of gold fell down his chest, gems sparkling from hidden pins. A pair of dark eyes surveyed us broodingly as one white, aristocratic hand toyed with his moustache. Imperial Agamemnon, High King of Mykenai and Greece, King of Kings. Anchises looked not one-tenth as royal.

I tore my gaze away from him to scan the others as they lounged at their ease in their chairs. Achilles sat on Agamemnon's left, though he was hard to recognise. I had seen him in armour, grimed and hard. Now he was in a company of kings. His hairless bare chest gleamed below a massive collar of gold and gems across his shoulders, his arms glittered with bracelets and his fingers with rings. He was clean-shaven and his bright gold hair was loosely combed back from his forehead, gold pendants in his ears. His yellow eyes were clear and rested, their unusual colour striking under his strongly marked brows and lashes, and he had painted them in Cretan fashion. I blinked, then looked away, confused. Upset.

Next to him was a man of truly noble aspect, tall in his chair, with red hair massed in curls around his broad, high forehead, his skin white and delicate. Under surprisingly dark brows his beautiful eyes shone grey and piercing, the most fascinating eyes I had ever seen. When my gaze dropped to his bare chest I saw in pity how scarred he was; his face seemed to be the only part of him had escaped.

On Agamemnon's right was another red-haired man, a shambling fellow who kept his gaze on the table top. As he raised his cup to his lips I noticed that his hand shook. His neighbour was a most kingly old man, tall and erect, with a silvery white beard and wide blue eyes. Though he was dressed very simply in a white linen robe, his fingers were smothered in rings from knuckles to tips. The giant Ajax was next to him; I had to blink again, hardly able to associate him with the man who had uncovered my father's body.

But my eyes grew tired of their different faces, all so deceptively noble. The guard drew Chryse forward, twitching away her veil. My stomach fluttered. She was so beautiful in her foreign clothes, Greek stuff given to her from some Greek chest, clothes bearing no resemblance to the long, straight gowns Lyrnessian women wore between neck and ankles. In Lyrnessos we hid ourselves from all save our husbands; Greek women evidently dressed like whores. Scarlet with shame, Chryse covered her bare breasts with her hands until the guard struck them down so that the table of silent men could see how tiny her waist was in the tight girdle, and how perfect her breasts were. Agamemnon ceased to look like Father Zeus, became Pan instead. He turned to Achilles.

'By the Mother, she's exquisite!'

Achilles smiled. 'We're pleased you like her, sire. She's yours – a mark of the Second Army's esteem. Her name's Chryse.'

'Come here, Chryse.' The elegant white hand gestured; she dared not disobey. 'Come, look at me! There's no need to be afraid, girl, I won't hurt you.' White teeth flashing, he smiled at her, then stroked her arm without seeming to notice that she flinched. 'Take her to my ship at once.'

She was led away. It was my turn. The guard threw off my veil to display me in my immodest garb. I stood as tall as I could, my hands by my sides, my face expressionless. The shame was theirs, not mine. Staring down the lust in the High King's eyes, I forced him to glance away. Achilles said nothing. I moved my legs a little to make my manacles clink. Agamemnon raised his brows.

'Chains? Who ordered that?'

'I did, sire. I don't trust her.'

'Oh?' There was a world of meaning in that single word. 'And whose property is she?'

'Mine. I captured her myself,' said Achilles.

'You should have offered me my choice of the two girls,' said Agamemnon, displeased.

'I've told you, sire, I captured her myself, which makes her mine. Besides which, I don't trust her. Our Greek world will survive without me, but not without you. I have ample proof that this girl's dangerous.'

'Hmph!' said the High King, not really mollified. Then he sighed. 'I've never seen hair halfway between red and gold, nor eyes so blue.' He sighed again. 'More beautiful than Helen.'

The nervous man on the High King's right, he with the red hair, brought his fist down on the table so hard that the wine cups leaped. 'Helen has no peer!' he cried.

'Yes, brother, we're aware of that,' said Agamemnon patiently. 'Calm yourself.'

Achilles nodded to his Myrmidon officer. 'Take her away.'

I waited in a chair in his cabin, lids drooping, though I dared not allow myself to sleep. No woman is more defenceless than a sleeping one.

A long time later Achilles came. When the latch lifted I was dozing despite my resolution, and jumped in fright, gripping my hands together. The moment of reckoning had arrived. But Achilles didn't seem consumed with want; he ignored me to go to the chest and open it. Then he ripped off the collar, the rings, the bracelets, the jewelled belt. Not his kilt.

'I can never be rid of that rubbish soon enough,' he said, staring at me.

I stared back, at a loss. How *did* a rape begin?

The door opened and another man entered, very like Achilles in colouring and features but smaller in size, and with a more tender face. His lips were lovely. Blue, not yellow, his eyes surveyed me with an apprehensive gleam.

'Patrokles, this is Brise.'

'Agamemnon was right. She is more beautiful than Helen.' The glance he gave Achilles was fraught with meaning and filled with pain. 'I'll leave you. I only wanted to see if you needed anything.'

'Wait outside, I won't be long,' said Achilles absently.

Already on the way to the door, Patrokles propped, gave Achilles a look no one could have mistaken. Absolute joy and absolute possession.

'He's my lover,' said Achilles when he had gone.

'That I gathered.'

He lowered himself onto one side of the narrow bed with a sigh of weariness, and indicated my chair. 'Sit again.'

I sat regarding him steadily for some time while he stared at me with what seemed detachment; he didn't, I was beginning to suspect, desire me in the least. Why then had he claimed me?

'I had thought you women of Lyrnessos very sheltered,' he said at last, 'but you appear to know the ways of the world.'

'Some ways. Those which are universal. What we don't understand are fashions like these.' I touched my bare breasts. 'Rape must be rife in Greece.'

'No more than anywhere else. A thing tends to lose its novelty when it is – universal.'

'What do you intend to do with me, Prince Achilles?'

'I have no idea.'

'My nature isn't easy.'

'I know.' His smile was wry. 'In fact, your question was a telling one. I really don't know what to do with you.' He shot me a yellow look. 'Do you play the lyre? Can you sing?'

'Very well.'

He got to his feet. 'Then I'll keep you to play and sing to me,' he said, and barked, 'Sit down on the floor!'

I sat. He flipped the heavy skirt up around my thighs, then left the room. When he came back he was carrying a hammer and a chisel. The next moment I was free of my chains.

'You've spoiled the floor,' I said, pointing to the deep scores where the chisel had bitten too hard.

'This is no more than a shelter on a foredeck,' he said, climbing off his knees and hauling me to my feet. His hands were firm and dry. 'Go to sleep,' he said, and left me.

But before I crawled into the bed I offered up a prayer of thanks to Artemis. The virgin Goddess had heard me; the man who had taken me for his prize was not a man for women. I was safe. Why then was a part of my sadness not on behalf of my beloved father?

In the morning they ran the flagship down into the water, sailors and warriors hurrying about the deck and rowing benches, filling the air with laughter and choice curses. It was plain that they were delighted to be leaving blackened, denuded Andramyttios. Perhaps they could hear the shades of thousands of innocents reproaching them.

Patrokles the tender man threaded his way gracefully through the crowded midships and climbed the few steps to the foredeck, where I stood watching.

'Are you well this morning, lady?'

'Thank you, yes.'

I turned away, but he stayed by my side, apparently content with my chilly company.

'You'll get used to things in time,' he said.

I just looked at him. 'A more stupid remark is hard to think of,' I said. 'Could you get used to it if you were forced to live in the household of the man who was responsible for the death of your father and the destruction of your home?'

'Probably not,' he answered, flushing. 'But this is war, and you're a woman.'

'War,' I answered bitterly, 'is a man's activity. Women are its victims, just as they're the victims of men.'

'War,' he countered, amused, 'was equally prevalent when women ruled under the thumb of the Mother. High Queens were as avaricious and ambitious as any High King. War isn't an aspect of sex. It's an intrinsic part of the race.'

As that was inarguable, I changed the subject. 'Why do you, a man of sensitivity and perception, love a man as hard and cruel as Achilles?' I asked.

His blue eyes stared at me in amazement. 'But Achilles isn't hard or cruel!' he said blankly.

'That I don't believe.'

'Achilles isn't what he seems,' said his faithful hound.

'Then what is he?'

He shook his head. 'That, Brise, you'll have to discover for yourself.'

'Is he married?' Why did women always have to ask that?

'Yes. To the only daughter of King Lykomedes of Skyros. He has a son, Neoptolemos, sixteen years old. And, as the only son of Peleus, he's Heir to the High Kingdom of Thessalia.'

'None of which alters my opinion of him.'

To my surprise, Patrokles picked up my hand and kissed it. Then he went away.

I stood in the stern as long as there was a smudge of land on the horizon. The sea was under me, I could never go back. No escaping my fate now. I was to be a woman musician, I who had expected to marry a king. Should already have been married to a king, save that the Greeks had arrived and those men who in other days would have come to negotiate for my hand were suddenly too busy to think of marriage alliances.

The water hissed under the hull, broken into white foam by the slap of the oars, a steady, soothing sound which filled my head so subtly that long moments had passed before I realised that I had made up my mind what to do. The rail wasn't difficult; I clambered onto it and prepared to jump.

Someone jerked me roughly down. Patrokles.

'Let me do it! Forget you've seen me!' I cried.

'Never again,' he said, white-faced.

'Patrokles, I'm not important, I mean nothing to anyone! Let me do it! Let me!'

'No, never again. Your fate matters to him. Never again.'

Mysteries. Who? What? *Never again?*

*

It took a full seven days to reach Assos. Once we rounded the corner of the peninsula opposite Lesbos, the oars proved useless; the winds blew fitfully, pushing us to within sight of the beach, then blowing us away again. Most of the time I sat alone in a curtained off alcove on the afterdeck, and whenever I emerged Patrokles would drop whatever he was doing to hurry to my side. I saw no sign of Achilles, and finally I learned that he was on board the ship of someone called Automedon.

We managed to beach on the morning of the eighth day. I wrapped my cloak about me to shut out the bitter wind and watched the operations with fascination, never having seen anything like them before. Ours was the second ship mounted on its chocks; Agamemnon's preceded it. As soon as the ladder was down I was let descend to the shingle. When Achilles passed within a few cubits of me I put up my chin and prepared for war, but he didn't notice me.

Then the housekeeper arrived, a stout and cheery old woman named Laodike, and led me to the house of Achilles.

'You're rarely privileged, little dove,' she crooned. 'You're to have your own chamber within the master's house – which is more than I do, let alone the others.'

'Doesn't he have hundreds of women?'

'Yes, but they don't live with him.'

'He lives with Patrokles,' I said, striding out.

'Patrokles?' Laodike grinned. 'He used to, until they became lovers. Then, a couple of moons later, Achilles made him build his own house.'

'Why? That doesn't make sense.'

'Oh, it does if you know the master! He likes to own himself.'

Hmmm. Well, perhaps I don't know Achilles either, but I was learning fast. He liked to own himself, did he? The pieces of the puzzle were there to be picked up, just as they had been when I was a child. The real problem was putting them together.

Which kept me occupied all through that long winter, a prisoner of the cold. Achilles was always out and about, quite often dined elsewhere – sometimes slept elsewhere too, I supposed with Patrokles, who, poor man, seemed more agonised by his love than happy in it. The other women were prepared to hate me because I lived in the master's house and they didn't, but I am able to deal with women, so we were soon on good terms; they fed me all the gossip about Achilles.

He had periods of illness culminating in some kind of spell (they had heard him refer to this spell); he could be strangely withdrawn; his mother was a Goddess, a sea creature named Thetis who could change her physical form as quickly as the sun went in and out of clouds – cuttlefish, whale, minnow, crab, starfish, sea urchin, shark; his father's grandfather was Zeus himself; he had been taught by a Kentaur, a most fabulous being who had the head, arms and torso of a man, though the rest of him was a horse; the giant Ajax was his first cousin, and a great friend; he lived for battle, not for love. No, they didn't think him a man for men, despite his cousin Patrokles. But no, he was not a man for women either.

Occasionally he would summon me to play and sing, which I did with gratitude; my life palled. And he would sit, brooding in his chair, listening with only half his mind, while the other half went somewhere unrelated to the music or to me. No flicker of desire, ever. No indication as to why he kept me. Nor did I manage to find out what lay behind the things Patrokles had said when I tried to jump into the sea. *Never again!* Who? What had happened to kill desire in Achilles?

To my sorrow I found that Lyrnessos and my father were gradually fading from first place in my thoughts. I was becoming more and more caught up in what was going on in Assos than in what had happened to Dardania. Three times Achilles dined alone in his house, and on those three occasions he commanded that I should wait on him, that no other woman was to be present. Silly Laodike would primp me and perfume me, convinced that I was to be his at last, but he said nothing, did nothing.

In late winter we moved from Assos to Troy. Phoinix went

back and forth countless times, gradually all the warehouses, granaries and barracks were emptied, and finally the army itself sailed north.

Troy. Even in Lyrnessos Troy ruled, for Troy was the centre of our world. Not to the taste of King Anchises or Aineas, yet a truth for all that. Now for the first time I laid eyes on Troy. The restless wind swept its plain clear of snow; its towers and pinnacles, ice-festooned, glittered in the sun. It was like a palace on Olympos – remote, chill, beautiful. Aineas lived inside it with his father, his wife and his son.

The move to Troy burdened me in some way I didn't begin to understand; I became prone to fits of depression and bouts of weeping, unreasonable ill temper.

This was the tenth year of the war, and the oracles all spoke of an end at last. Was this why I moped? Knowing that when it was over Achilles would take me with him to Iolkos? Or fearing that he intended to sell me as a fine musician? I seemed not to please him in any other way.

In earliest spring the raiding parties began to come out of the city; with all the Greeks in one enormous camp, provender had to be found to eke out what was stored in vast quantities. Hektor lurked in wait for foraging expeditions, while Greeks like Achilles and Ajax lurked in wait for Hektor. By this time I knew how desperately Achilles wanted to meet Hektor in combat; the desire to kill the Trojan Heir all but consumed him, the other women said. All day and half the night the house rang to the sound of masculine voices. I came to know the other leaders by name.

Then spring filled the air with drenching, heady scents, the ground was starred with tiny white flowers, and the waters of the Hellespont grew bluer. Small skirmishes occurred almost every day; Achilles was even hungrier for Hektor. His bad luck continued to dog him, however. He never did manage to encounter the elusive Heir. Nor did Ajax.

Though Laodike deemed me too nobly born for menial work, I

would set to with a will whenever she disappeared. Working was better than picking at some unnecessary scrap of embroidery with a dull and uninspired needle.

One of the most intriguing stories about Achilles concerned how he had finally taken Patrokles as his lover after so many years of friendship having nothing to do with the pleasures of the body. According to Laodike, the transformation had taken place during one of Thetis's spells. At such times, she said, our master was peculiarly susceptible to the wishes and desires of others, and Patrokles had seen his chance. I thought that too trite an explanation, simply because I had seen nothing in Patrokles to indicate such unscrupulousness. But the ways of the Goddess of Love are passing strange: who could have predicted that I too would suffer the Spell? Perhaps the truth was that Achilles armoured himself so effectively he had no vulnerable chinks under any other circumstances.

It happened one day when I sneaked off to do the work I liked best, polish the armour in the special room where it was kept. And was caught. Achilles came in. His pace was slower than usual, nor did he see me, though I stood in plain view with a rag in one hand and my excuses ready. His face was tired and drawn, there was blood sprayed up his right arm. Not his own! I relaxed. The helmet came off, was dropped on the floor; he put both hands to his head as if it pained him. Frightened, I began to tremble as he fumbled with the ties on his cuirass, managed to shed it and the rest of his paraphernalia. Where was Patrokles?

Clad in the quilted shift he wore beneath all that metal, he stumbled towards a seat, blank face turned to me. But instead of sinking into the chair he collapsed to the floor, began to shake and twitch, drool copiously, mumble. Then his eyes rolled back; he went stiff, all four limbs extended, and started to jerk. The drool became great drops of foam, his face went black.

I could do nothing while he moved so violently, but after that ceased I knelt beside him.

'Achilles! Achilles!'

He didn't hear me; he lay grey-faced on the floor, arms moving aimlessly. When his hands encountered my side he groped until he managed to transfer them to my head, rocked it back and forth gently.

'Mother, leave me alone!'

His voice was so slurred and altered I hardly knew it; I began to weep, terrified for him.

'Achilles, it's Brise! Brise!'

'Why do you torment me?' he asked, but not of me. 'Why do you think I need reminding that I go to my death? I have sorrows enough without you – can't you be content with Iphigenia? Leave me alone, leave me alone!'

After that he lapsed into a stupor. I fled from the room to find Laodike.

'Is the master's bath ready?' I asked, breathless.

She mistook my state of distress for anticipation, began to tee-hee and pinch me. 'About time too, silly girl! Yes, it's ready. You can bathe him, I'm busy. Tee-hee!'

I bathed him, though he didn't know me from Laodike. Which freed me to look at him, and so taught me what I had refused to admit: how beautiful he was, and how much I wanted him. The room was steamy, my Dardanian robe clung to me because I sweated, and I scorned my own foolishness. Brise had joined the ranks. Like all his other women, Brise was in love with him. In love with a man who was neither a man for men nor a man for women. A man who lived for one thing only, mortal combat.

I dipped a cloth in cold water and wrung it out, stepped onto the stool by the bath to sponge his face. Some semblance of awareness entered his eyes. He lifted his hand and put it on my shoulder.

'Laodike?' he asked.

'Yes, lord. Come, your bed is here. Take my hand.'

His fingers tightened; I knew without needing to look that he had recognised my voice. Slipping from his hold, I picked up a jar of oil from the table. When I glanced quickly at his face he was smiling at me, the smile which almost gave him a proper mouth and was unexpectedly gentle.

'Thank you,' he said.

'It was nothing,' I answered, hardly able to hear what I was saying above the beating of my heart.

'How long have you been here?'

I couldn't lie to him. 'From the beginning.'

'You saw me, then.'

'Yes.'

'So we have no secrets.'

'We share the secret,' I said.

And then I was in his arms, how I do not know. Save that he didn't kiss me; afterwards he told me that, lacking lips, kisses gave him scant pleasure. But oh, the body did. His and mine both. There was not a fibre of me those hands couldn't make sing like a lyre; I hung inarticulate, feeling the blinding intensity that was Achilles. And I who had hungered vainly for so many moons, not knowing I hungered, knew at last the power of the Goddess. We were neither divided nor consumed; for a sliver of time I felt the Goddess move in him and in me.

He loved me, he said afterwards. He had loved me from the beginning. For though I wasn't like her, he had seen Iphigenia in me. Then he told me that terrible story, content now, I fancied, for the first time since she had died. And I wondered how I would ever have the courage to face Patrokles, who out of the purity of love had tried to work the cure, but failed. All the pieces were together.

CHAPTER TWENTY

NARRATED BY
AINEAS

I brought a thousand chariots and fifteen thousand infantry with me to Troy. Priam swallowed his dislike and made much of me, took my poor, demented old father into his embrace and gave Kreusa, my wife (who was his own daughter by Hekabe), a warm welcome; when he saw our son, Askanios, he beamed and compared him to Hektor. Which pleased me a great deal more than if he had likened my boy to Paris, whom he resembled greatly.

My troops were billeted around the city and I and my family were dowered with our own little palace inside the Citadel. I smiled sourly when no one was looking; it hadn't been a mistake to withhold my aid for so long. Priam was so desperate to be rid of the Greek leech sucking the lifeblood out of Troy that he was prepared to pretend Dardania was a gift from the Gods.

The city had changed. Its streets were greyer and less well kept than of yore; the atmosphere of unlimited wealth and power was missing. So too, I noted, were some of the golden nails in the Citadel doors. Delighted to see me, Antenor told me that a great deal of Troy's gold had gone to buy mercenaries from the Hittites and Assyria, but that no mercenaries had come. Nor had the gold been returned.

All through the winter between the ninth and tenth year of that conflict, messages arrived from our allies down the coast, promising what aid they could muster. This time we were inclined to believe that they would come, the rulers of Karia, Lydia, Lykia and the rest. The coast was razed from end to end,

Greek settlers were pouring in, there was nothing left at home to stay and try to protect. The last hope Asia Minor had was to unite with Troy and fight the Greeks there. Victory would enable it to return home and throw the interlopers out.

We heard from everyone, even some we had abandoned all hope of. King Glaukos came with word from his co-ruler, King Sarpedon, to inform Priam that they were acting as marshallers of the forces remaining; twenty thousand troops scraped together from among those once populous states from Mysia to far Kilikia. Priam wept when Glaukos told him the full story.

Penthesileia the Amazon Queen promised ten thousand horse cavalry; Memnon, Priam's blood relation who sat at the foot of Hattusilis, King of the Hittites, was coming with five thousand Hittite foot and five hundred chariots. Forty thousand Trojan soldiers were already ours; if everyone came who said he was, then we would outnumber the Greeks comfortably by the summer.

The first to arrive were Sarpedon and Glaukos. Their army was well equipped, but as I cast my eyes over its ranks it was easy to see how deeply Achilles had struck at the coast. Sarpedon had been obliged to include raw youths and greying men feeling their years, rough peasants and shepherd lads from the mountains who knew nothing of soldiering. But they were enthusiastic, and Sarpedon was no fool. He would mould them.

Hektor and I sat over wine in his palace, discussing it.

'Your fifteen thousand foot, twenty thousand coastal troops, five thousand Hittites, ten thousand Amazon horse warriors, and forty thousand Trojan foot – plus ten thousand war cars all up – Aineas, we can do it!' Hektor said.

'One hundred thousand ... How many Greeks do you estimate are left to face us?' I asked.

'That would be difficult to estimate, except for some of the slaves who've escaped from the Greek camp over the years,' said Hektor. 'One in particular I've come to love – a man named Demetrios. An Egyptian by birth. Through him and

275

others I've learned that Agamemnon is down to fifty thousand men. And all he has is a thousand war cars.'

I frowned. 'Fifty thousand? That seems impossible.'

'Not really. They numbered only eighty when they came. Demetrios told me that ten thousand Greeks have grown too old to bear arms – and that Agamemnon has never once called for more men to join him from Greece – they've sent everyone to the coast to colonise it instead. Five thousand troops died in an epidemic two years ago. Ten thousand members of the Second Army have either died or been incapacitated, and five thousand sailed back to Greece out of sheer homesickness. Thus my estimate. Not a man more than fifty thousand, Aineas.'

'Then we ought to make mincemeat out of them,' I said.

'I agree,' said Hektor eagerly. 'You'll back me in assembly when I ask Father to lead our army out?'

'But we haven't got the Hittites or the Amazons yet!'

'We don't need them.'

'You ought to weigh their experience against our inexperience, Hektor. The Greeks are battle hardened, we're not. And their troops understand how well they're led.'

'I admit the inexperience, but I can't agree about their leadership. We have our fair share of famous warriors – you, for instance. And there's Sarpedon, a son of Zeus! His troops adore him.' Hektor coughed, embarrassed. 'Then there's Hektor.'

'It's not the same,' I said. 'What do Dardanians think of Hektor, or Trojans of Aineas? And who outside of Lykia knows the name of Sarpedon, son of Zeus or not? Think of the Greek names! Agamemnon, Idomeneus, Nestor, Achilles, Ajax, Teukros, Diomedes, Odysseus, Meriones – and more, and more! Why, even their chief surgeon, Machaon, fights brilliantly. And every Greek soldier knows every name. He could probably tell you what a particular leader likes to eat, or his favourite colour. No, Hektor, the Greeks are one nation fighting under a King of Kings, Agamemnon. Whereas we're factions, petty rivalries and jealousies.'

Hektor looked at me for a long moment, then sighed. 'You're right, of course. But once battle is joined, our polyglot army will think only of driving the Greeks out of Asia Minor. They fight for gain. We fight for our lives.'

I laughed. 'Hektor, you're an incurable idealist! When a man has his spear at your throat, do you stop to rationalise that he fights for gain? They fight for life as much as we do.'

Not caring to comment on that, he refilled the wine cups.

'So you intend to ask to lead the army out?'

'Yes,' said Hektor. 'Today. To think that I look at our walls and see them as barriers, my home as my prison!'

'It sometimes happens that the things we love the most are the very things which destroy us,' I said.

He smiled, though he was not amused. 'What a strange fellow you are, Aineas! Do you believe in nothing? Love nothing?'

'I believe in myself and I love myself,' said I, me, myself.

Priam wavered, commonsense warring with his overwhelming desire to drive the Greeks out. But in the end he listened to Antenor, not to Hektor.

'Don't do it, sire!' Antenor begged. 'It would be the death of all our hopes to meet the Greeks prematurely. Wait for Memnon of the Hittites and for the Amazon Queen! If Agamemnon didn't have Achilles and the Myrmidons it might be different, but he does have them, and I fear them greatly. From the day of his birth a Myrmidon lives only for the fight. His very body is fashioned from bronze, his heart is stone, his spirit as dogged as the ant he's named for! Without the Amazon warriors to deal with the Myrmidons, your van will be cut to pieces. Wait, sire!'

Priam decided to wait. On the surface Hektor seemed to accept his father's verdict philosophically, but I knew the Heir better. It was Achilles he most yearned to meet, yet his father's fear of that selfsame man defeated him.

Achilles ... I remembered encountering him outside Lyrnessos, and wondered which was the better man, Achilles or Hektor. They were about the same size, they were equally martial. But somehow I seemed to feel in my bones that Hektor was doomed. Virtue is overrated in my opinion; Hektor was *so* virtuous. Now I, I burned for other things.

When I left the Throne Room it was in a mood of disquiet. Because of that hoary old prophecy which said I would rule Troy one day, Priam had alienated himself from me and my people. For all his civility since my arrival, the veiled sneer was still there. Only my troops made me welcome. But how could I possibly outlive fifty sons? Unless Troy lost the war, in which case it was feasible that Agamemnon would choose to put *me* on the throne. A nice dilemma for one whose blood was the same as Priam's.

I walked into the great courtyard and paced up and down, hating Priam, wanting Troy. Then I became aware that someone was watching me from the shadows. The back of my neck grew icy cold. Priam hated me. Would he sin by murdering a close relative?

Deciding he would, I drew my dagger and crept behind the flower-decked altar to Zeus of the Courtyard. When I was no more than an arm's length away from the watcher I jumped, clapping my hand across his mouth, my blade at his throat. But the lips pressing softly against my palm were not a man's, nor was the bare breast below my dagger. I let her go.

'Did you take me for an assassin?' she asked, panting.

'It's stupid to hide, Helen.'

I found a lantern on the altar step and lit it from the eternal fire, then held it up and looked long upon her. Eight years had passed since last I saw her. Incredible! She must be thirty-two years old. But lamps are kind; later, in better light, I was able to see the mild ravages of age in the faint lines about her eyes, the slight subsidence of those breasts.

Gods, she was beautiful! Helen, Helen of Troy and Amyklai. Helen the Leech. All the grace of Artemis the Huntress flowed in her pose, all the delicacy of features and wanton attraction of Aphrodite shone in her face. Helen, Helen, Helen ... Only now as I looked at her did I fully realise how many nights her image had torn my dreams asunder, how many times in my sleep she had unlaced her gem-studded girdle and let her skirts fall about her ivory feet. In Helen was Aphrodite born to mortal form, in Helen I recognised the shape and countenance of the Goddess mother I had never seen, only heard about in the ravings of my father, who had been driven mad by his amorous encounter with the Goddess of Love.

Helen was all the senses incarnate, a Pandora who smiled and kept her secrets, enslaved and enslaving, she was earth and love, wetness and air, fire mixed with an ice fit to crack a man's veins open. She dangled all the fascinations of death and mystery, she taunted.

Her polished nails gleaming like the inside of a shell, she put her hand on my arm. 'You've been in Troy for four moons, yet this is the first time I've seen you, Aineas.'

Revolted and maddened, I dashed her hand away. 'Why should I seek you out? What good will it do me with Priam if I'm seen dancing attendance on the Great Harlot?'

She listened to this unmoved, eyes lowered. The black lashes lifted then, her green eyes looked up at me gravely. 'I agree with all of that,' she said, settling herself on a seat, shaking out her frills and ruffles with little chiming noises. 'In the eyes of a man,' she said composedly, 'a woman is a chattel. A piece of solid property he owns. He may abuse her as he sees fit without fear of reprisal. Women are passive creatures. We have no voice of authority because we are not deemed capable of logical thought. We bear men, though that is forgotten.'

I yawned. 'Self-pity doesn't suit you,' I said.

'I like you,' she said, smiling, 'because you're so turned in upon your own ambitions. And because you're like me.'

'Like you?'

'Oh, yes. I'm Aphrodite's bauble. You're her son.'

She came into my embrace with eagerness and dizzying

caresses; I lifted her into my arms and walked with her through the silent corridors to my own private room. No one saw us. I suppose my mother ensured that, the vixen.

Even when the depths of her passion shook me to the core of my being, there was a part of her which didn't even know that she was possessed, some corner of herself withdrawn and secretive. I met her in an agony of pleasure, but while she drained me of all my spirit she kept her own locked fast in some hiding place, and I had no hope of ever finding the key.

CHAPTER TWENTY-ONE

NARRATED BY
AGAMEMNON

B attle orders had long been issued to the army, but Priam remained within his walls. Even the Trojan raiding parties ceased to plague us; my troops fretted from uncertainty and inaction. Having nothing to discuss, I called no council until Odysseus appeared.

'Sire, would you call a council for noon today?' he asked.

'Why? There's nothing to say.'

'Don't you want to know how to lure Priam out?'

'What are you up to, Odysseus?'

Came a brilliant, laughing look. 'Sire! How can you ask me to reveal my secrets now? As well might you ask for immortality!'

'Very well, then. A council at noon.'

'Another favour, sire?'

'What?' I asked warily. He was using that irresistible grin he saved to get what he wanted. I weakened; I could do nothing else when Odysseus smiled like that. One had to love him.

'Not a general council. Only certain men.'

'It's your council, ask whom you like. Give me their names.'

'Nestor, Idomeneus, Menelaos, Diomedes and Achilles.'

'Not Kalchas?'

'Least of all Kalchas.'

'I wish I knew why you mislike the man so much, Odysseus. If he was a traitor we'd know it by now, surely. Yet you insist upon excluding him from every significant council. As the Gods bear the man witness, he's had innumerable opportunities to give our secrets to the Trojans, but he never has.'

'Some of our secrets, Agamemnon, he knows as little about as you do. I believe that he waits for the one secret worth his betraying where his heart belongs.'

I chewed my lip, huffed. 'All right then, no Kalchas.'

'Nor can you mention it to him. More than that, I want the doors and windows sealed with boards once we're assembled, and guards posted outside so thickly they touch each other.'

'Odysseus! Isn't that going too far?'

He grinned wickedly. 'I'd hate to make Kalchas look like a fool, sire, so we have to finish this business in the tenth year.'

The handful of men Odysseus had asked for came expecting a full council, and were curious when they understood they were all.

'Why not Meriones?' asked Idomeneus a little peevishly.

'And why not Ajax?' asked Achilles truculently.

I cleared my throat; they settled down. 'Odysseus asked me to call you together,' I said. 'Just the five of you, him and I. The noises you can hear are guards boarding up this room. Which will tell you more emphatically than I could how secret our business is. I require your individual oaths on this: whatever is said here can't be repeated outside these walls, even in sleep.'

One by one they knelt and took the oath.

When Odysseus began, his voice was soft; a trick of his. He would commence so quietly one had to strain to hear him, and as he outlined his ideas his voice would rise, until at the end it resonated among the rafters like beating drums.

'Before I begin to talk about the real reason for this very small council,' he said almost inaudibly, 'it's necessary to tell some of you what others among you already know. Namely, the actual function of that jail of mine in the hollow.'

I listened in growing anger and amazement as Odysseus told the rest of us what Nestor and Diomedes had always known. Why did it not occur to any of us to investigate activities in that hollow? Perhaps because, I admitted in the midst of my outrage, it had suited us not to enquire; Odysseus had removed some of our worst problems, which had never returned to plague us. Not, I learned now, due to weary prison sentences. They were his spies.

'Well,' I said at the end of it, tight lipped, 'at least now we know how you can predict what Troy is going to do next so uncannily! But why the secrecy? I am King of Kings, Odysseus! I was entitled to know from the very beginning!'

'Not,' said Odysseus, 'while you favoured Kalchas.'

'I still favour Kalchas.'

'But not the way you did, I suspect.'

'Perhaps. Perhaps. Go on, Odysseus. What have your spies to do with this meeting?'

'They haven't been as idle as our army,' he said. 'You've all heard the rumours as to why Priam has made no move to come outside his walls. The commonest one is that his reinforcements haven't come up to expectations – that he lacks our numbers. That isn't true. At this moment he has seventy-five thousand men, a figure not including almost ten thousand chariots. When Penthesileia of the Amazons and Memnon of the Hittites arrive, he'll outnumber us drastically. Added to which, he's under the misapprehension that we'll be lucky to field forty thousand men. You may take it all of this is accurate. I have people in the confidence of Priam and Hektor.'

He took a little turn about the room, sparsely populated and therefore free of obstacles. 'Before I go any further, I must talk about the King of Troy. Priam is an old, old man, and prone to the doubts, vacillations, fears and prejudices of the very old. In short, he's no Nestor. Never think he is. He rules Troy with a far more autocratic hand than any Greek king owns – he's literally king of all he surveys. Not even his son and Heir would dare to *tell* him what to do. Agamemnon calls councils. Priam calls assemblies. Agamemnon listens to what we have to say and heeds us. Priam listens to himself and whoever echoes what he's thinking.'

He stopped to face us. 'This is the man we must outwit, this is the man we must bend to our will without his ever suspecting it. Hektor weeps as he walks the battlements, counting his own men and seeing us sitting on the Hellespont shore like fruit ripe for the plucking. Aineas chafes and burns. Antenor alone does nothing, because Priam is doing as Antenor wishes – Priam too does nothing.'

Another march around the chairs; every head followed him. 'So why exactly is Priam unwilling to commit himself when he has more than a good chance of driving us out of the Troad right now? Does he truly wait for Memnon and Penthesileia?'

Nestor nodded. 'Undoubtedly,' he said. 'That's what a very old man ought to do.'

Odysseus drew a breath; his voice was swelling. 'But we cannot allow him to wait! He *must* be lured from the city before he can afford to lose men by the countless thousands. My sources of information are much better than Priam's, and I can tell you that both Penthesileia and Memnon will arrive before winter closes the passes from the interior. The Amazons are horsed, so they count as cavalry. With them, Troy will field over twenty thousand cavalry. In less than two moons she'll be here, with Memnon hard on her heels.'

I swallowed. 'Odysseus – I hadn't realised – couldn't you have told me earlier?'

'My information is just now complete, Agamemnon.'

'I see. Go on.'

'Does Priam hold off purely from prudence, or is there more to it?' Odysseus asked of no one. 'The answer isn't prudence. He'd give Hektor permission to come out at this moment were it not for Achilles and the Myrmidons. He fears Achilles and the Myrmidons more than the rest of our troops put together with all our other leaders. Part of his fear is rooted in certain oracles about Achilles – that he personally holds destruction for the flower of Troy. Part of it stems from the general feeling within the Trojan ranks that the Myrmidons are unbeatable – that Zeus conjured them up out of an army of ants to dower Peleus with the best soldiers in the world. Well, we all know what ordinary men are – superstitious and gullible. But both parts combined mean Priam wants a scapegoat to pit against Achilles and the Myrmidons.'

'Penthesileia or Memnon?' asked Achilles, face grim.

'Penthesileia. There are mysteries surrounding her and her horse warriors and they bring women's magic with them. You see, Priam can't let Hektor face Achilles. Even if a Trojan victory was guaranteed by Apollo, Priam wouldn't let Hektor face the man his oracles say holds destruction for the flower of Troy.'

There was no joy in Achilles's face, but he said no word.

'Achilles has rare gifts,' Odysseus commented drily. 'He can lead an army like Ares himself. And he leads the Myrmidons.'

Nestor sighed. 'Too true!'

'No need to despair yet, Nestor!' Odysseus answered cheerily. 'I still possess all *my* faculties.'

Diomedes – of course he was in on it already, whatever it was – sat grinning. Achilles watched me and I watched him, while Odysseus watched both of us. Then he brought the butt of the Staff down on the floor with a ring that made us jump, and when he spoke, his voice boomed like thunder.

'There must be a quarrel!'

We gaped.

'The Trojans aren't strangers to the spy system,' Odysseus went on in more normal tones. 'In fact, Trojan spies in our camp have served me almost as well as my spies inside Troy. I know every single one of them, and feed them selected morsels to take back to Polydamas, who recruited them – an interesting man, this Polydamas, though not appreciated as he ought to be. For which we must thank the Gods who side with us. Needless to say, his spies take back only what I let them take back, such as the paltry number of soldiers we have. But for the past moons I've been encouraging them to send one certain snippet of gossip to Polydamas.'

'Gossip?' asked Achilles, frowning.

'Yes, gossip. People love to believe gossip.'

'What gossip?' I asked.

'That there is no love lost between you, Agamemnon, and you, Achilles.'

I think I stopped breathing for longer than I should, for I had to suck in air audibly. 'No love lost between Achilles and me,' I said slowly.

'That's correct,' said Odysseus, looking pleased with himself. 'Ordinary soldiers gossip about their betters, you know. And it's common knowledge among them that there have been differences between the pair of you from time to time. Of late I've been fanning the rumour that feeling between you is deteriorating very rapidly.'

Achilles got to his feet, white-faced. 'I don't like this gossip, Ithakan!' he said angrily.

'I didn't think you would, Achilles. But sit down, do!' Odysseus looked pensive. 'It happened at the end of autumn, when the spoils from Lyrnessos were divided at Andramyttios.' He sighed. 'How sad it is to watch great men topple over a woman!'

I clutched the arms of my chair to stay in it and looked at Achilles in mortified comradeship; his eyes were quite black.

'Of course it's inevitable that such a degree of ill feeling should come to a head,' Odysseus continued chattily. 'No one will be in the least surprised when the two of you quarrel.'

'Over what?' I demanded. '*Over what?*'

'Patience, Agamemnon, patience! First I must dwell a little more fully on events at Andramyttios. A special prize was given to you as a mark of respect by the Second Army. The girl Chryse, whose father was high priest of Sminthian Apollo in Lyrnessos. He donned armour, picked up a sword, and was killed in the fighting. But now Kalchas is saying that the omens are very inauspicious if the girl isn't returned to the custody of Apollo's priests in Troy. Apparently we're in danger of the God's wrath if Chryse isn't returned.'

'That is true, Odysseus,' I said, shrugging. 'However, as I told Kalchas, I fail to see what more Apollo can do to us – he's completely on the Trojan side. Chryse pleases me, so I have no intention of giving her up.'

Odysseus clicked his tongue. 'Tch! I've noticed, however, that opposition annoys Kalchas, so I'm sure he's going to renew his exhortations that the girl be sent to Troy. And to help him out, I think we'd better have an outbreak of plague in our camp. I have a herb which makes a man very ill for about eight days, after which he recovers completely. Very impressive! Once the plague breaks out, Kalchas is bound to increase his demands that you give up Chryse, sire. And, faced with the full force of the God's anger in the form of disease, Agamemnon, you *will* acquiesce.'

'Where is this going?' asked Menelaos, exasperated.

'You'll see very shortly, I promise.' Odysseus focused his attention upon me. 'However, sire, you're no petty princeling to have your legal prize so arbitrarily removed. You are the King of Kings. Therefore you will have to be compensated. You might argue that, as the Second Army gifted you with the girl, the Second Army must replace her. Now from the same spoils a second girl was allotted – rather highhandedly – to Achilles. Her name is Brise. All the Kings plus two hundred senior officers saw how much our King of Kings would have liked her for himself – more than he wanted Chryse, as a matter of fact. Gossip travels, Agamemnon. By now the whole army knows that you preferred Brise to Chryse. However, it's also widely known that Achilles has developed a very deep regard for Brise, and would be loath to part with her. Patrokles, you see, goes round with a woefully long face.'

'Odysseus, you're treading a very thin line,' I said before Achilles could speak.

He ignored me, swept on. 'You and Achilles are going to quarrel over a woman, Agamemnon. I've always found that disputes over women are accepted without question by all and sundry – after all, let us admit that such disputes are extremely common, and have caused the deaths of many men. If one might presume, my dear Menelaos, one could include Helen in the catalogue.'

'Do not presume!' my brother growled.

Odysseus blinked. Oh, he was a reprobate! Once launched, no one could restrain him. 'I myself,' he said, thoroughly enjoying himself, 'will undertake to set a few omens beneath our worthy priest Kalchas's nose, and I myself will manufacture the plague. I promise you, the sickness will fool Podalieros and Machaon! Terror will stalk our camp within a day of the outbreak. When you're informed of its seriousness, Agamemnon, you'll go at once to Kalchas and ask him what has vexed which God. He'll like that. But he'll like your request for a public augury even more. In front of the army's senior ranks he'll demand that you send Chryse to Troy. Your position, sire, will be quite untenable. You'll have to acquiesce. However, I'm sure no one will blame you if you take offence when Achilles laughs at you. During a public augury? Intolerable!'

By this we were beyond speech, though I doubt Odysseus would have paused had Zeus thrown a thunderbolt at his feet.

'Naturally you'll be furious, Agamemnon. You'll turn on Achilles and demand that he give you Brise. Then you'll appeal to the assembled officers – your prize has been removed from you, therefore Achilles must yield his prize to you. Achilles will refuse, but his position will be just as untenable as yours was when Kalchas asked for Chryse. He'll have to give you Brise, and he'll do so then and there. But, having handed her over, he'll remind you that neither he nor his father swore the Oath of the Quartered Horse. In front of the assembly he'll announce that he is withdrawing himself and the Myrmidons from the war.' Odysseus roared with laughter, shook his fists at the ceiling. 'I have a special nook reserved for a certain furtive Trojan I know. Within the day all Troy will be aware of the quarrel.'

We sat like men struck to stone by Medusa's glare. What storms of emotion he had unleashed in the others I could only guess at; my own storms were hideous enough. Out of the corner of my eye I saw Achilles move, and swung my attention to him, agog to know his reaction. Odysseus could unearth more secret skeletons out of secret graves and rattle them than any other man I've ever known. But by the Mother, he was brilliant!

Achilles wasn't angered, which amazed me. His eyes held nothing but admiration.

'What kind of man are you, Odysseus, to dream up such strife? It's a wicked scheme – staggering! However, you must admit that it's hardly flattering to Agamemnon and me. It's our two carcases must bear the ridicule and contempt if we do as you want. And I tell you now that if I die for it, I will not give Brise up.'

Nestor coughed softly. 'You won't be giving anything up, Achilles. Both young women will be handed into my custody, and with me they'll remain until things work out as Odysseus plans. I'll lodge them secretly, no one will know whereabouts they are. Including Kalchas.'

Achilles was still unsure. 'A fair offer, Nestor, and one I trust. But surely you can see why I mislike the scheme. What if we do succeed in duping Priam? Without the Myrmidons to hold the van intact we'll suffer losses we just can't afford. I'm not exaggerating. It's our function in battle to hold the van intact. I can't like a plan which endangers so many lives.' His eyes brooded. 'And what of Hektor? I've vowed to kill him, but what if he should die while I'm out of the battle? And how long am I expected to be out of the battle?'

Odysseus answered. 'Yes, we'll lose men we wouldn't if the Myrmidons were there. But Greeks aren't inferior warriors. I've no doubt we'll do well enough. For the moment I won't answer your big question – how long will you be out of the battle? I'd rather speak about getting Priam outside his walls first. I ask you: what if this war drags on for years more? What if our men grow old without seeing their homes again? Or what if Priam comes out when Penthesileia and Memnon arrive? Myrmidons or no, we'll be hacked to pieces.' He smiled. 'As for Hektor, he'll live to face you, Achilles. I know it in my bones.'

Nestor spoke. 'Once the Trojans come out from behind their walls they're committed,' he said. 'They can't withdraw for good. If they suffer heavy casualties, Priam will receive information that our casualties are even heavier. Once we lure them out, the dam will break. They won't rest until they've driven us from Troy, or until the last one of them is dead.'

Achilles stretched his arms wide, the great muscles moving under his skin. 'I doubt if I have the strength of character to refrain from fighting while everyone else does, Odysseus. For ten whole years I've waited to be in at the kill. And there are other considerations too. What will the army say of a man who can desert them in their time of need because of a woman – and what will my own Myrmidons think of me?'

'No one will speak of you kindly, Achilles, so much is sure,' said Odysseus soberly. 'To do what I ask will take a very special kind of courage, my friend. More courage than it would take to storm the Western Curtain tomorrow. Don't mistake me, any of you! Achilles hasn't coloured the thing a scrap darker than it is in reality. Many will revile you, Achilles. Many will revile you, Agamemnon. Some will curse. Some will spit.'

Smiling wryly, Achilles looked at me not unsympathetically. Odysseus had managed to draw us closer together than I had deemed possible after the events at Aulis. My daughter! My poor little daughter! I sat still and cold, tasting the unpalatable role I must fill. If Achilles would look an intemperate fool, what sort of fool would I look? Was fool the right word? Idiot, more like.

Then Achilles slapped his thigh sharply. 'It's a heavy thing you charge us with, Odysseus, but if Agamemnon can humble himself to take his share of the load, how can I refuse?'

'What is your decision, sire?' asked Idomeneus, his tone announcing that *he* would never consent to it.

I shook my head, propped my chin on my hand and

thought, while the rest of them watched me. Achilles broke in on my reverie, speaking to Odysseus again.

'Answer my big question, Odysseus. How long?'

'It will take two or three days to draw the Trojans out.'

'Which is no answer. How long must I remain out of things?'

'First let us wait for the High King's decision. Sire, what is it to be?'

I let my hand drop. 'I'll do it on one condition. That each of you in this room takes a solemn oath to see it through to the absolute end, no matter what the end might be. Odysseus is the only one who can guide us through this maze – such scheming was never meant for the High Kings of Mykenai. It is the lot of the Kings of the Out Islands. Do you all agree to swear?'

They agreed.

With no priest present, we swore on the heads of our male children, on their ability to procreate and on the extinguishing of our lines. Heavier than the quartered horse.

'So, Odysseus,' said Achilles, 'finish it.'

'Leave Kalchas to me. I'll ensure he does what's expected and never knows it was expected. He'll believe in himself as completely as the poor shepherd lad plucked out of the crowd to play Dionysos at the Maenad revels. Achilles, once you've handed Brise over and spoken your piece, you'll take your Myrmidon officers and return to your compound immediately. Handy that you insisted on building a stockade within our camp! Your isolation will be easily noted. You'll forbid the Myrmidons to leave the stockade, nor can you leave it yourself. Henceforth you'll be visited, but never visit. Everyone will assume that those who visit you go to plead with you. At all times and to every member of your inner circle of friends you must seem an extremely angry man – a man who is bitterly hurt and utterly disillusioned – a man who thinks himself grossly wronged – a man who would rather die than patch up his relations with Agamemnon. Even Patrokles must see you like this. Is that understood?'

Achilles nodded gravely; now that the matter was decided

and the oath sworn, he seemed resigned. 'Are you going to answer me yet?' he asked then. 'How long?'

'Not until the very last moment,' said Odysseus. 'Hektor must be absolutely convinced that he can't lose, and his father must feel the same way. Play out the rope, Achilles, play it out until they have to choke on it! The Myrmidons will return to action before you do yourself.' He drew a breath. 'No one can predict what will happen in battle, even I, but some things are fairly certain. For instance, that without you and the Myrmidons, we'll be driven inside our own camp. That Hektor will break through our defence wall and get in among our ships. I can help events a little by using some of my spies among our troops. They can, for instance, start a panic leading to retreat. It's up to you to decide exactly when the time is right to intervene, but don't return to the battle yourself. Let Patrokles lead the Myrmidons out. That way, it will seem that you're obdurate. They know the oracles, Achilles. They know that we can't beat them if you don't fight with us. So play out the rope! Don't return to the field yourself until the very last moment.'

And after that there seemed no more to say. Idomeneus got up, rolling his eyes at me wildly; no one understood quite as well as he how hard it would be for Mykenai to let himself be so reviled. Nestor bestowed his bland smile on us – he knew it all long before this morning's work, of course. So did Diomedes, grinning broadly at the prospect of other men's acting the fool.

Only Menelaos spoke. 'May I offer a little advice?'

'Certainly!' said Odysseus heartily. 'Advise, do!'

'Kalchas. Let him in on the secret. If he knows, then you halve your difficulties.'

Odysseus pounded his fist into the palm of his other hand. 'No, no, no! The man is a Trojan! Put your trust in no man born to an enemy woman in an enemy country when you are fighting on his own soil and likely to win.'

'You're right, Odysseus,' said Achilles.

I made no comment, but I wondered. For years I had

championed Kalchas, but something inside me had turned this morning, quite what I didn't know. He had been at the root of things which had done much harm. It had been he who had forced me to sacrifice my own daughter and thereby create the breach with Achilles. Well, if he was in truth not to be trusted, it would be evident on the day when I quarrelled with Achilles. For all its careful blankness his face would betray his inner pleasure – if indeed he felt any. After so many years, I *knew* him.

'Agamemnon,' came the plaintive voice of Menelaos from the door, 'we're boarded in! Would you kindly give the order to let us out?'

CHAPTER TWENTY-TWO

NARRATED BY
ACHILLES

D reading having to face those I loved and keep my counsel from them, I returned to the Myrmidon stockade with a dragging step. Patrokles and Phoinix were sitting on either side of a table in the sun, playing knuckle bones amid much laughter.

'What happened? Anything important?' asked Patrokles, and got up to throw his arm about my shoulders. Something he was more prone to do since Brise had entered my life, and that was a pity. It couldn't help his cause to lay public claim to me, and it irritated me into the bargain. As if he was trying to put a burden of guilt on me – I am your first cousin as well as your lover, and you can't just drop me because of a new plaything.

I shrugged him off. 'Nothing happened. Agamemnon wanted to know if we were having difficulty in curbing our men.'

Phoinix looked surprised. 'Surely he could have seen that for himself if he'd bothered to tour the camp?'

'You know our imperial overlord. He hasn't called a council in a moon, and he hates to think his grip on us is slackening.'

'But why only you, Achilles? I pour the wine and see to everyone's comfort at a council,' said Patrokles, looking wounded.

'It was a very small group.'

'Was Kalchas there?' asked Phoinix.

'Kalchas is out of favour at the moment.'

'Over the girl Chryse? He'd have done better to have kept his mouth shut on that subject,' said Patrokles.

'Perhaps he thinks that if he pushes hard enough, he'll get his own way in the end,' I said casually.

Patrokles blinked. 'Do you honestly think so? I don't.'

'Can neither of you find anything more significant to do than play at knuckle bones?' I asked, to change the subject.

'What more pleasurable thing could one do on a beautiful day which won't see the Trojans come out?' asked Phoinix. He looked at me shrewdly. 'You've been gone all morning. A long time for a trivial meeting.'

'Odysseus was in fine form.'

'Come and sit down,' said Patrokles, stroking my arm.

'Not now. Is Brise inside?'

I had never seen Patrokles in a rage, but suddenly it was flaring in his eyes; his mouth shook, he bit it. 'Where else would she be?' he snapped, turned his back and sat down at the table. 'Let's play,' he said to Phoinix, who rolled his eyes.

I called her name as I stepped inside, and she came flying through an inner door to land in my arms.

'Did you miss me?' I asked fatuously.

'It seemed like days!'

'Half a year, more like.' I sighed, thinking of what had gone on in that boarded-up council chamber.

'No doubt you've already drunk more than your share of wine, but would you like more?'

I looked down at her, surprised. 'Come to think of it, we drank no wine.'

Laughter brimmed in her vivid blue eyes. 'Absorbing.'

'Boring, I'd say.'

'Poor thing! Did Agamemnon feed you?'

'No. Be a good child and find me something to eat.'

She busied herself about the task of waiting on me, chattering like a hedge bird while I sat and watched her, thinking how lovely her smile, how graceful her walk, how swanlike the turn of her neck. War carries a perpetual threat of death, but she seemed oblivious to any impending doom; I never spoke to her of battle.

'Did you see Patrokles outside in the sun?'

'Yes.'

'But you preferred me to him,' she said with satisfaction, proving that the rivalry was not merely one sided. She handed me hot bread and a dish of olive oil to dip it in. 'Here, fresh from the oven.'

'Did you bake it?' I asked.

'You know perfectly well I cannot bake, Achilles.'

'True. You have no womanly skills.'

'Tell me that tonight when the curtain is drawn across our doorway and I'm in your bed,' she said, unruffled.

'All right, I concede you one womanly skill.'

The moment I said it, she plumped herself down in my lap, took my free hand and slipped it inside the loose gown she wore, covering her left breast.

'I love you so much, Achilles.'

'And I you.' I put my hand in her hair and lifted her face so she had to look at me. 'Brise, will you make me a promise?'

Her wide eyes betrayed no anxiety. 'Anything you ask.'

'What if I should dismiss you, command that you go to some other man?'

Her mouth trembled. 'If you so commanded, I would go.'

'What would you think of me?'

'No less than I think of you now. You would have sufficient reason. Or else it would mean that you had tired of me.'

'I'll never tire of you. Never in all the time left to me. Some things can't change.'

Her colour returned in a flood. 'So I believe too.' She laughed breathlessly. 'Ask me to do something easy, like dying for you.'

'Before bed time?'

'Well, tomorrow, then.'

'I still require a promise of you, Brise.'

'What?'

I twisted a lock of her amazing hair between my fingers. 'That if there should come a time when I seem a fool, or stupid, or coldhearted, you'll continue to believe in me.'

'I'll always believe in you.' She pressed my hand a little harder against her breast. 'I'm not stupid either, Achilles. Something troubles you.'

'If it does, I can't tell you.'

Whereupon she left the subject alone, and never tried to bring it up again.

It was beyond any of us how Odysseus went about the tasks he had set himself; we knew his hand was there, yet we could see no sign of it. Somehow the whole army was buzzing with the news that the bad blood between me and Agamemnon was coming to a head, that Kalchas was being aggravatingly persistent about the affair of Chryse, and that Agamemnon's temper was fraying.

Three days after the council meeting these interesting topics of conversation were forgotten. Disaster struck. At first the officers tried to hush it up, but soon the men who fell ill were too many to hide. The dread word flew from tongue to tongue: plague, plague, plague. Within the space of one day four thousand men succumbed, then four thousand more the next day – there seemed no end to them. I went to see some of my own men who were among the stricken, and the sight of them had me praying to Leto and Artemis that Odysseus knew what he was doing. They were feverish, delirious, covered in a weeping rash, whimpering under the onslaught of headache. I talked to Machaon and Podalieros, who both assured me it was definitely a form of plague.

Not many moments later I encountered Odysseus himself. He was grinning from ear to ear.

'You have to admit, Achilles, that I've created something of a landmark when I can fool the sons of Asklepios!'

'I hope you haven't overstepped yourself,' I said dourly.

'Rest you, there'll be no permanent casualties. They'll all rise from their sickbeds well men.'

I shook my head, exasperated at his self-congratulatory glee. 'About the moment Agamemnon obeys Kalchas and yields up

Chryse, I suppose. A magnificent, miraculous recovery at the hands of the God. Only this time it will be the god out of the machine.'

'Don't say it too loudly,' he said, drifting away to minister to the sick with his own hands, and thereby earn an undeserved reputation for bravery.

When Agamemnon went to Kalchas and asked for a public augury, the army sighed with relief. There was no doubt in any mind that the priest would insist upon the return of Chryse; hearts began to lighten at the prospect of an end to the epidemic.

A public augury involved the personal attendance of every officer in the army senior to those who commanded mere squadrons. They gathered in the space set aside for assemblies, perhaps a thousand of them ranged behind the Kings, all facing the altar; most of them, of course, were related to the Kings, some closely.

Only Agamemnon was seated. As I passed in front of his throne I made no attempt to bend the knee to him, and scowled fiercely. It was noticed; every face grew rigid with concern. Patrokles even went so far as to put a warning hand on my arm, but I threw it off angrily. Then I found my place, listened to Kalchas say that the plague wouldn't lessen until Apollo was given his due, the girl Chryse. Agamemnon must send her to Troy.

Neither he nor I needed to do much acting; we twisted in the web woven by Odysseus and hated it. I laughed and jeered at Agamemnon, he retaliated by ordering me to give him Brise. Shoving the frantic Patrokles aside, I left the assembly ground to make my way to the Myrmidon stockade. After one look at my face Brise said nothing, though her eyes filled with tears. Back we went in silence. Then in front of all that great company I put her hand into Agamemnon's. Nestor volunteered to care for both girls and ship them to their fates. As

Brise walked away with him she turned her head to look at me one last time.

When I told Agamemnon that I was withdrawing myself and my troops from his army I sounded as if I meant every word. Neither Patrokles nor Phoinix doubted my sincerity for an instant. I stalked off to the Myrmidon stockade, leaving them to follow.

The house was full of echoes, empty without Brise. Avoiding Patrokles, I slunk about it all day, alone in my shame and sorrow. At the supper hour Patrokles came to dine with me, but there was no conversation; he refused to speak to me.

In the end I spoke to him. 'Cousin, can't you understand?'

Eyes filmed with tears, he looked at me. 'No, Achilles, I can't. Ever since that girl came into your life, you've become someone I don't know. Today you answered for all of us in something you had no right to decide on our behalf. You withdrew our services without consulting us. Only our High King could do that, and Peleus never would. You're not a worthy son.'

Oh, that hurt. 'If you won't understand, will you forgive?'

'Only if you go to Agamemnon and retract what you said.'

I drew back. '*Retract?* Are you insane? Agamemnon offered me a mortal insult!'

'An insult you brought on yourself, Achilles! If you hadn't laughed and derided him, he would never have singled you out! Be fair! You act as if your heart is broken at being parted from Brise – did it never occur to you that perhaps Agamemnon's heart is broken at being parted from Chryse?'

'That pig-headed tyrant has no heart!'

'Achilles, *why* are you so obdurate?'

'I'm not obdurate.'

He struck his hands together. 'Oh, I don't believe this! It's her influence! How she must have worked on you!'

'I can see why you'd think that, but it isn't so. Forgive me, Patrokles, please.'

'I can't forgive you,' he said, and turned his back on me. The

ACHILLES

idol Achilles had toppled from his pedestal at last. And how
right Odysseus was. Men believed in trouble made by women.

Odysseus slipped in the next evening very quietly. I was so glad
to see a friendly face that I greeted him almost feverishly.

'Ostracised by your own?' he asked.

'Yes. Even Patrokles has wiped his hands of me.'

'Well, that's maybe to be expected, eh? But take heart. In a
few more days you'll be back in the field, vindicated.'

'Vindicated. An interesting word. Yet something has occurred to me, Odysseus, that ought to have occurred to me at
the council. It didn't. If it had, I could never have agreed to
your scheme.'

'Oh?' He looked as if he knew what I was about to say.

'What will become of us all? We naturally presumed that
after the scheme succeeded – if it does! – we'd be free to tell of
it. Now I see that we can never tell. Neither the officers nor the
soldiers would condone such an expediency. A coldblooded
means to an end. All they'd see are the faces of the men who
must die to fulfil it. I'm right, aren't I?'

He rubbed his nose ruefully. 'I wondered which one of you
would see it first. My money was on you – I win again.'

'Can you ever lose? But have I made the correct conclusion,
or have you worked out a solution that will make everyone
happy?'

'There's no such solution, Achilles. You've finally seen what
should have been screaming at you in the council chamber. A
little less passion inside that rib cage of yours and you would
have seen it then. There can never be a revelation of the plot. It
must remain our secret to the tomb, each of us bound by the
oath Agamemnon was moved to suggest – thus saving me the
trouble, not to mention some questions I would have found it
difficult to answer,' he said soberly.

I closed my eyes. 'So to the tomb and beyond Achilles will
seem a selfish braggart, so puffed up with his own importance

that he allowed countless men to perish to feed his wounded pride.'

'Yes.'

'I ought to cut your throat, you twisted conniver! You've saddled me with a load of shame and dishonour that will forever cast a shadow on my name. When in future ages men speak about Achilles, they'll say that he sacrificed everything for the sake of his wounded pride. I hope you go to Tartaros!'

'No doubt I will,' he said, unworried, unimpressed. 'You're not the first man to curse me, nor will you be the last. But we will all feel the repercussions of that council, Achilles. Men may never know what really went on, but the hand of Odysseus is bound to be suspected somewhere. And what of Agamemnon? If you seem to be the victim of overweening pride, what will he seem? You at least were wronged. He did the wronging.'

Suddenly I realised how foolish this conversation was, how little even men as brilliant as Odysseus had to do with the plans of the Gods. I said, 'Well, it's a form of justice. We deserve to lose our stainless reputations. In order to get this ill-starred venture started, we consented to be parties to human sacrifice. It's for that we pay. And because of it I'm willing to continue this idiocy. My greatest ambition is forever denied me.'

'What ambition is that?'

'To live in the hearts of men as the perfect warrior. It's Hektor who'll do that.'

'You can't say for sure, Achilles, though your great-grandsons might. Posterity judges differently.'

I looked at him curiously. 'Don't you hunger to be remembered by many generations of men, Odysseus?'

He laughed heartily. 'No! I don't care what posterity says about Odysseus! Or even whether posterity knows his name. When I'm dead I'll be rolling the same boulder up some hill in Tartaros, or leaping for the water flagon forever out of my reach.'

'With me alongside you. For all our talk, it's too late.'

'And there you have the right of it at last, Achilles.'

We lapsed into silence, the curtain drawn against intruders who wouldn't come to commiserate with their hubristic leader. The wine jar stood upon the table. I poured our cups full to the brim and we drank reflectively, neither of us willing to part with his private thoughts. No doubt Odysseus experienced the prettier reverie, since he didn't expect rewards from posterity. Though he seemed to believe in nothing beyond eternal punishment, I thought it marvellous that he could contemplate his fate with his confidence unimpaired.

'Why did you come to see me?' I asked.

'To apprise you of a strange occurrence before someone else does,' he answered.

'A strange occurrence?'

'This morning some soldiers went along the banks of Simois to fish. When the sun rose they saw something rolling in the water. The body of a man. They ran to fetch the officer of the watch, who brought the body in. Kalchas. He died, they think, not long after nightfall.'

I shivered. 'How did he die?'

'An excruciating head injury. An officer of Ajax's happened to notice him walking along the clifftop on the far bank of Simois as the sun was setting. The officer swears it was Kalchas – he's the only man in our camp who wears long, flapping vestments. He must have stumbled and fallen headlong.'

I stared at him as he sat looking soulful, the light of the godly shining out of his beautiful grey eyes. Could it be? *Was it?* With a shudder of sheer terror I found myself wondering if he was weighed down with a fresh sin on the long list of sins he was already whispered to carry. Add murder of a high priest to sacrilege, profanity, blasphemy, aetheism and ritual murder and you had a list which outdid Sisyphos and Daidalos combined. Godless Odysseus who was yet beloved of the Gods. Mortal paradox, knave and King rolled in one.

He read my thoughts and smiled blandly. 'Achilles, Achilles!

How could you think such a thing, even of me?' A chuckle erupted. 'If you want my opinion, I think Agamemnon did it.'

CHAPTER TWENTY-THREE

NARRATED BY
HEKTOR

No news of Penthesileia came; the Amazon Queen lingered in her far off wilderness while Troy hung in agony, a city's fate depending on the whim of a woman. I cursed her and I cursed the Gods for permitting a woman to remain on any throne after the death of the Old Religion. The absolute rule of Mother Kubaba was gone, yet Queen Penthesileia reigned undisturbed. Demetrios, my invaluable escaped Greek slave, informed me that she hadn't even begun to summon in the women of her countless tribes; she would not come before winter closed the passes.

All the omens spoke of war's finishing in this tenth year, yet my father still dithered, humbling himself and Troy to wait on this woman. I gnashed my teeth at the injustice of it, I railed at him in the assemblies. But his mind was made up and he refused to budge. Time and time again I assured him that I stood in no personal danger from Achilles, that our crack troops could hold the Myrmidons at bay, that we could win without Memnon or Penthesileia. Even when I told Father what Demetrios had reported about Amazonian tardiness he remained adamant, saying that if Penthesileia didn't come before the winter, then he was content to wait until the eleventh year.

Now that the whole Greek army was on the beach we had taken to walking the battlements again, looking at the various standards fluttering atop the Greek houses. On the flank of Skamander at a place where an internal wall split off some of the barracks there waved a banner I hadn't seen before, a white

ant on a black background holding a red lightning bolt in its
jaws. Achilles the Aiakid, his Myrmidon standard. The face of
Medusa could not have thrown more fear into Trojan hearts.

Obliged to listen to petty business when my loins burned for
battle, I attended every assembly. Someone had to be there to
protest that the army was stale and overtrained, someone had
to be there to watch the King turn his notoriously deaf ear, to
watch Antenor, the enemy of all positive action, smile.

I sensed nothing different about the day which changed our
lives, went morosely to the assembly. The Court stood about
chatting desultorily, ignoring the throne dais, at the foot of
which a plaintiff was outlining his case – really earth-shaking
litigation to do with the drains emptying Troy's storm waters
and excrement into unclean Skamander. His new apartment
block had been refused access to the drains, and he, the owner-
landlord, was very angry.

'I've better things to do than stand here contesting the right
of a pack of mindless bureaucrats to thwart honest taxpayers!'
he shouted at Antenor, who, as Chancellor, was defending the
city drainage authorities.

'You failed to apply to the correct person!' Antenor snapped.

'What *are* we, Egyptians?' asked the landlord, waving his
arms about. 'I spoke to my usual man, who said yes! Then,
before I could make the connection, a squad of enforcers
arrived to forbid it! A man would fare better in Nineveh or
Karchemish! Somewhere – *anywhere!* – that the bureaucrats
haven't managed to paralyse with their stupid regulations! I tell
you, Troy is almost as inert as Egypt! I'm going to emigrate!'

Antenor's mouth was already open to wade into the fray in
defence of his beloved bureaucrats when a man burst into the
hall.

I didn't recognise him, but Polydamas did.

'What is it?' Polydamas asked him.

The man groaned with the agony of breathing, licked his
lips, tried to speak and ended in pointing wildly at my father,
who was leaning forward, sewers forgotten. Polydamas helped

the fellow to the dais and sat him on its bottom step, signalling for water. Even the irate landlord sensed something more important than effluent in the offing, and moved away a little – though not far enough to prevent his hearing whatever was going to be said.

Water and a few moments' rest enabled the man to speak. 'My lord King, great news!'

Father looked sceptical. 'What?' he asked.

'Sire, at dawn I was in the Greek camp attending an augury called by Agamemnon to divine the cause of a plague which has killed ten thousand men!'

Ten thousand men dead of disease in the Greek camp! I almost ran to stand beside the throne. *Ten thousand men!* If my father couldn't understand the significance of that, then he was blind to all reason, and Troy must fall. Ten thousand less Greeks, ten thousand more Trojans. Oh, Father, let me lead our army out! I was about to say it when I realised that the man wasn't done yet, that he hadn't told all his news; I held my peace.

'There was a terrible quarrel between Agamemnon and Achilles, sire. The army is split. Achilles withdrew himself, his Myrmidons and the rest of Thessalia from the war. Sire, Achilles will not fight for Agamemnon! The day is ours!'

I clutched at the throne-back for support, the landlord whooped, my father sat white-faced, Polydamas was staring at his man in disbelief, Antenor was leaning limply against a pillar, and the rest of those in the room seemed turned to stone.

A loud, bleating laugh rang out. 'How are the mighty fallen!' my brother Deiphobos brayed. 'How are the mighty fallen!'

'Silence!' my father snapped, then looked down at the man. 'Why? What caused this quarrel?'

'Sire, it was over a woman,' the man said, more collected now. 'Kalchas had demanded that the woman Chryse, given to the High King out of the spoils of Lyrnessos, be sent to Troy. The Lord Apollo was so outraged at her capture that he arranged the plague and wouldn't lift it until Agamemnon gave up his prize. Agamemnon had to obey. Achilles laughed at him. Jeered at him. So Agamemnon ordered Achilles to hand over his own prize out of Lyrnessos, the woman Brise, as compensation. After Achilles gave her to the High King, he withdrew himself and all the men under his banners from the war.'

Deiphobos found this even funnier. 'A woman! An army split in two over a woman!'

'Not quite down the middle!' said Antenor sharply. 'Those who have withdrawn can't number more than fifteen thousand. And if a woman can split an army, never forget that it was a woman brought that selfsame army here in the first place!'

My father rapped his sceptre on the floor. 'Antenor, hold your tongue! Deiphobos, you're drunk!' He returned his attention to the messenger. 'Are you sure of your tidings, my man?'

'Oh, yes. I was there, sire. I heard and saw everything.'

A great sigh went up; the atmosphere lightened in an instant. Where before gloom and apathy reigned, now smiles broke out. Hands clasped hands, a murmur of delight swelled. Only I mourned. It seemed we were fated never to meet on the field, Achilles and me.

Paris strutted up to the throne. 'Dear Father, when I was in Greece I heard that the mother of Achilles – a Goddess – dipped all her sons in the waters of the River Styx to make them immortal. But as she held Achilles by the right heel something startled her – she forgot to change her grip to his left heel. That's why Achilles is a mortal man. But fancy his right heel being a woman! Brise. I remember her. Stunning.'

The King glared. 'I've said that's enough! When I rebuke one son, Paris, the rebuke extends to all of you! This isn't a matter for jest. It's of paramount importance.'

Paris looked crestfallen. I watched him and pitied him. During the last two years he had aged; the coarseness of the forties was creeping inexorably into his skin, blighting its youthful bloom. Whereas once he had fascinated Helen, he bored her now. The whole Court knew it. And knew that she was in the midst of an affair with Aineas. Well, she'd get little satisfaction there. Aineas loved Aineas best.

But it was never possible to read her. After Father's sharp words to Paris she did no more than shake Paris's hand off and move a small distance away. Not a flicker of emotion showed in eyes or face. Then I realised she was not *quite* enigmatic; a touch of smugness had settled about her lips. Why? She knew them, those Greek Kings. *So why?*

I knelt before the throne. 'Father,' I said strongly, 'if we are ever fated to drive the Greeks from our shores, the time is now. If it was genuinely Achilles and the Myrmidons held you back when I asked before, then the reason for your reluctance has vanished. They are besides ten thousand men less from plague. Not even with Penthesileia and Memnon would we stand the chance we do right at this moment. Sire, give me the battle orders!'

Antenor stepped forward. Oh, Antenor! Always Antenor!

'Before you commit us, King Priam, grant me one favour, I beg. Let me send one of my own men to the Greek camp to verify what this man of Polydamas's says.'

Polydamas nodded vigorously. 'A good idea, sire,' he said. 'We ought to confirm it.'

'Then, Hektor,' King Priam said to me, 'you'll have to wait a little longer for my answer. Antenor, find your man and send him at once. I'll call another assembly tonight.'

While we waited I took Andromache up onto the ramparts at the top of the great northwestern tower which looked directly at the Greek beach. The minute speck of banner still fluttered above the Myrmidon compound, but in the tiny progress of men about the camp, it was significant that there was no traffic between the Myrmidon compound and its neighbours. Unable to think about eating, we watched all afternoon; that visible proof of disunity within the Greek camp was all the sustenance we needed.

At nightfall we returned to the Citadel, more hopeful now that Antenor's man would confirm the story. He came before we had time to grow restless, and in a few rapid sentences repeated what Polydamas's man had told us. There had been a terrible quarrel, Agamemnon and Achilles could not be reconciled.

Helen stood by the far wall well away from Paris, openly beckoning to Aineas, her smiling mask secure in the knowledge that for the time being all rumours about herself and the Dardanian were eclipsed by news of the quarrel. When Aineas came up to her she put her hand on his arm, her long eyes slanting up at him in naked invitation. But I was right about him. He ignored her. Poor Helen. If it came to a choice between her charms and those of Troy, I knew what Aineas would decide. An admirable man, yes, but one who held himself just a little too high.

She did not, however, seem disconcerted by his abrupt departure. I fell again to wondering what she thought of her countrymen. She knew Agamemnon very well indeed. For a moment I debated as to whether I should question her, but Andromache was with me, and Andromache loathed Helen. What little I might get from her, I decided, would not be worth the verbal drubbing I'd get from Andromache if she learned about it.

'Hektor!'

I went to the throne and knelt before my father.

'Receive the battle command of our armies, my son. Send out the heralds to order mobilisation for battle at dawn two days hence. Tell the Skaian gatekeeper to oil the boulder in its tracks and hitch up the oxen. For ten years we've been incarcerated, but now we go forth to drive the Greeks from Troy!'

As I kissed his hand the room erupted into deafening cheers, though I did not smile. Achilles wouldn't be on the field, and what kind of victory was that?

*

The two days passed with the swiftness of a cloud shadow on a mountainside, my time filled by interviews with men and orders to armourers, engineers, charioteers and infantry officers, among many others. Until everything was in train I couldn't think of rest, which meant I didn't see Andromache until the night before we were to do battle.

'What I fear is upon us,' she said harshly when I came into our room.

'Andromache, you know better than to say that.'

She brushed at her tears impatiently. 'It's still tomorrow?'

'At dawn.'

'Couldn't you find a little time for me?'

'I'm finding time now.'

'One sleep, then you'll be gone.' Her fingers plucked at my blouse restlessly. 'I can't like it, Hektor. Something's very wrong.'

'Wrong?' I forced up her chin. 'What's wrong with fighting the Greeks at last?'

'Everything. It's just too convenient.' She held up her right hand, clenched into a fist save for the little and forefingers, stuck up in the sign to ward off evil. Then she said, shivering, 'Kassandra's been at it day and night since Polydamas's man came with the news of the quarrel.'

I laughed. 'Oh, Kassandra! In the name of Apollo, wife, what ails you? My sister Kassandra is mad. No one listens to her croaks of doom.'

'She may be mad,' Andromache said, determined to be heard, 'but haven't you ever noticed how uncannily accurate her predictions are? I tell you, Hektor, she's been raving without let that the Greeks have laid a trap for us – she insists Odysseus has put them up to it, that they're simply luring us out!'

'You're beginning to annoy me,' I said, and actually shook her – a first. 'I'm not here to discuss war or Kassandra. I'm here to be with you, my *wife*.'

Wounded, her dark eyes went to the bed; she shrugged. Then

she turned the covers down and slipped off her robe, went about snuffing lamps, her tall body as firm and lovely as it had been on our wedding night. Motherhood had left her unmarked; her warm skin glowed in the last lonely light. I lay down and held out my arms, and for a while forgot the morrow. After which I dozed, sliding into sleep, my body content, my mind relaxed. But in the final giddy moments before the veil of unconsciousness is drawn tight, I heard Andromache weep.

'What is it now?' I demanded, up on one elbow. 'Are you still thinking about Kassandra?'

'No, I'm thinking of our son. I'm praying that after tomorrow he still knows the joy of a living father.'

How *do* women manage to do that? How do they always seem to be able to find the one thing a man doesn't want or need to hear?

'Stop snivelling and go to sleep!' I barked.

She stroked my brow, sensing that she'd gone too far. 'Well, perhaps that was too pessimistic. Achilles won't be on the field, so you ought to be safe.'

I wrenched myself away, pounded my fist on the pillow. 'Hold your tongue, woman! I don't need to be reminded that the man I itch to fight won't be there to face me!'

She gasped. 'Hektor, are you out of your mind? Does meeting Achilles mean more to you than Troy? – than me? – than our son?'

'Some things are for men's hearts only. Astyanax would understand better.'

'Astyanax is a little boy. Since the day of his birth his eyes and ears have been filled with war. He sees the soldiers drilling, he rides beside his father in a magnificent war car at the head of an army parade – he's completely deluded! But he's never seen the field after a real battle is over, has he?'

'Our son doesn't shirk any part of war!'

'Our son is nine years old! Nor will I allow him to turn into

311

one of these hardheaded, coldblooded warriors Troy has bred out of your generation!'

'You go too far, madam,' I said in tones of ice. 'As well that you won't have any say in Astyanax's future education. The moment I return from the field victorious I'm going to take him off you and give him into the care of men.'

'Do that and I'll kill you myself!' she snarled.

'Try, and you'll find yourself dead!'

Her answer was to burst into loud tears.

I was too angry to touch her or seek any kind of reconciliation, so I spent the rest of the night listening to her frenzied weeping, unable to soften my heart. The mother of my son had indicated that she would rather raise him to be a cissy than a warrior.

In the grey twilight before dawn I rose from the bed to stand beside it and look down on her; she lay with her face to the wall, refused to face me. My armour lay ready. Andromache forgotten as my excitement rose, I clapped my hands. The slaves came, put me into my padded shift, laced on my boots, fitted the greaves over them and buckled them on. I swallowed down the desperate eagerness I always felt before combat as the slaves went on to dress me in the reinforced leather kilt, the cuirass, the arm guards, the forearm braces and the sweat leathers for wrists and brow. My helmet was put into my hand, my baldric looped over my left shoulder to hold my sword on my right hip; finally they slung my huge, wasp-waisted shield over my right shoulder by its sliding cord and settled it along my left side. One servant gave me my club, another assisted me to tuck my helmet beneath my right forearm. I was ready.

'Andromache, I'm going,' I said, my tone unforgiving.

But she lay without moving, her face turned to the wall.

The corridors shuddered, the marble floors echoed hollow to the sounds of bronze and hobnails; I felt the noise of my coming spread before me like a wave. Those not going to the battle came out to cheer me as I walked, men falling into place behind me at each door. Our boots assaulted the flags, sparks flew under the impact of bronze-tipped heels, and in the distance we could hear the drums and horns. Ahead now was the great courtyard, beyond it the Citadel gates.

Helen was waiting in the portico. I stopped, nodding to the others to go on without me.

'Good luck, brother-in-law,' she said.

'How can you wish me luck when I fight your own countrymen?'

'I have no country, Hektor.'

'Home is always home.'

'Hektor, never underestimate a Greek!' She stepped back a little, seeming surprised at her words. 'There, I've given you better advice than you deserve.'

'Greeks are like any other race of men.'

'Are they?' Her green eyes were like jewels. 'I can't agree. I'd rather a Trojan for my enemy than a Greek.'

'It's a straight, open fight. We're going to win it.'

'Maybe. But have you stopped to ask yourself why Agamemnon should create so much fuss over one woman when he has hundreds?'

'The most important thing is that Agamemnon did make a fuss. The why is immaterial.'

'I think the why is everything. Never underestimate Greek cunning. Above all, never underestimate Odysseus.'

'Pah! He's a figment of the imagination!'

'So he'd have you think. Whereas I know him better.'

She turned on her heel and went inside. There was no sign of Paris. Well, he'd be watching, not participating.

Seventy-five thousand infantrymen and ten thousand chariots waited for me, rank on rank along the side streets and smaller squares leading to the Skaian Gate. Within the Skaian Square itself waited the first detachment of cavalry, my own charioteers. Their shouts rang like thunder when I appeared, lifting my club high to salute them. I mounted my car and took time to insert my feet carefully into the wicker stirrups which took the lurch of travel, especially at a gallop. As I did so my eyes swept over those thousands of purple-plumed helmets; the glitter of bronze was blood and rose in the long gold sun, the gate towered above me.

Whips cracked. The oxen harnessed to the great boulder supporting the Skaian Gate bellowed in anguish as they bent their heads to the task. The ditch was already oiled and fatted; the beasts drove their noses almost to the ground. Very slowly the gate opened, squealing and roaring as the stone slid, halting, along the bottom of the ditch; the door itself grew smaller and the expanse of sky and plain between the battlements grew wider. Then the noise which was the opening of the Skaian Gate for the first time in ten years was drowned out by the scream of joy ripping from the throats of thousands of Trojan soldiers.

As the troops began to move down towards the square the wheels of my chariot began to rotate; I was through, I was onto the plain with my charioteers behind me. The wind probed my face, birds flew in the pale vault of the sky, my horses pricked up their ears and stretched out their slender legs in a gallop as my driver, Kebriones, wound the reins about his waist and began to practise the leans and lunges he used to control the team. We were going into battle! This was true freedom!

Half a league from the Skaian Gate I drew up and turned to direct my troops, making the front a straight line with chariots in the first rank; the Royal Guard of ten thousand Trojan foot and a thousand war cars formed the centre of my van. All was done neatly and quickly, without panic or confusion.

When everything was in order, I turned to look at the foreign wall grown across the plain from river to river, cutting off the Greek beach. The causeways at each end of the wall flashed with a million points of fire as the invaders poured out onto the plain. I gave my spear to Kebriones and fitted the helmet on my head, shaking back its plume of scarlet horsehair. My eyes met those of Deiphobos next to me in the line, and one by one I told them off as far as I could see down the one-league front. My cousin Aineas was in command of the left flank, King Sarpedon of the right. I led the van.

The Greeks came closer and closer, the sun on their armour increasing in brightness; I strained to see who would be drawn up opposite me, wondering if it would be Agamemnon himself, or Ajax, or some other among their champions. My heart slowed because it wouldn't be Achilles. Then I looked down our line again and jumped in shock. Paris was there! He stood with his precious bow and quiver at the head of the portion of the Royal Guard which had been allocated to him somewhere back in the mists of time. I wondered what wiles Helen had used to lure him out of the safety of his apartments.

CHAPTER TWENTY-FOUR

NARRATED BY

NESTOR

I said a little prayer to the Cloud Gatherer; though I had fought in more campaigns than any other living man, I had never faced an army like Troy's. Nor had Greece ever spawned an army like Agamemnon's. My eyes lifted to the gauzy, lofty peaks of distant Ida and I wondered if all the Gods had forsaken Olympos to perch atop it and watch the struggle. This was well worthy of their interest: war on a scale never dreamed of before by mere mortals – *or* by the Gods, who fought only intimate little wars among their limited ranks. Nor (if they had collected on Ida to watch) would they be allied; everyone knew that Apollo, Aphrodite, Artemis and that crew were violently for Troy, while Zeus, Poseidon, Here and Pallas Athene were for Greece. It was anybody's guess whereabouts Ares Lord of War stood, for though it had been the Greeks who spread his worship far and wide, his secret girlfriend Aphrodite was all for Troy. Hephaistos, her husband, was (rather naturally) on Greece's side. Handy for us, since he looked after the smelting of metals and so forth; our artificers had some divine guidance.

If any man was happy on that day, the man was I. Only one thing marred my pleasure: the lad beside me in my chariot, who chafed and figeted because he longed to be in his own car, a warrior rather than a driver. I glanced at him sidelong, my son Antilochos. He was a babe, my youngest and most beloved, the child of my twilit years. When I left Pylos he had been twelve years old. I had answered all his messengers begging that he be allowed to come to Troy with firm negatives. So he

had stowed away on a message packet and come anyway, the
scamp. On his arrival he had gone not to me but to Achilles,
and between them they managed to talk me into letting the
boy stay. This was his first battle, but with all my heart I wished
that he was still far away in sandy Pylos compiling grocery lists.

We ranged up opposite the Trojans. The line was a league
from end to end; I noted without surprise that Odysseus was
correct. There were far more of them than there were of us,
even if we'd had all Thessalia. I scanned their ranks looking for
the men who led them and saw Hektor at once in the centre of
their van. My troops of Pylos formed a part of our own van,
together with those of the two Ajaxes and eighteen minor
Kings. Agamemnon, leader of our van, faced Hektor. Our left
flank was under the command of Idomeneus and Menelaos,
our right under the command of Odysseus and Diomedes, that
inappropriate pair of lovers. One so hot, the other so cold.
Together, perfect?

Hektor drove a superb team of jet black horses and stood in
his car like Ares Enyalios himself. As big and as straight as
Achilles. However, I saw no whitebeards among the Trojans;
Priam and his kind had kept to the palace. I was the oldest man
on the field.

The drums rolled, the horns and cymbals clashed out the
challenge, and the battle began across the hundred paces
which still separated us. Spears flew like leaves in the awful
breath of winter, arrows swooped like eagles, chariots wheeled
and turned to dash up and down, infantry made charges and
were repulsed. Agamemnon directed our van with a vigour and
alertness I had not suspected lay in him. Many of us, in fact,
had not had prior opportunity to see how the rest behaved in
combat. Cheering, then, to realise that Agamemnon was
competent enough to fare very well indeed this morning
against Hektor, who had made no attempt to engage our High
King in the duel.

Hektor railed and stormed, flung his cars at us time and time again, but couldn't break through our front line. I led a few sallies during the morning, Antilochos shrieking the Pylian war cry while I saved my breath for the fight. More than one Trojan died under the wheels of my chariot, for Antilochos was a good driver, keeping me out of trouble and knowing when to fall back. No one was going to have the chance to say that Nestor's son endangered his old father just to get into battle himself.

My throat grew dry and dust settled quickly on my armour; I nodded to my son and we withdrew to the rear lines to gulp a few mouthfuls of water and get our breath back. When I glanced up at the sun I was amazed to see it approaching its zenith. We drove back to the front line at once, and with a surge of daring I led my men into the Trojan ranks. We did some quick work while Hektor wasn't looking, then I gave the signal to retreat and we fell back safely into our own line without losing a single man. Hektor had lost upwards of a dozen. Sighing in busy satisfaction, I grinned silently at Antilochos. What we both wanted was the armour of a chieftain, but none had opposed us.

At noon Agamemnon sent a herald into the open to blow a horn of truce. Both armies groaned and laid down their arms; hunger and thirst, fear and weariness became realities for the first time since the battle had begun shortly after sunrise. When I saw that all the leaders were converging on Agamemnon, I told Antilochos to drive me to him too. Odysseus and Diomedes drew up with me as I swung in near the High King. All the rest were already there, slaves hurrying back and forth with watered wine, bread and cakes.

'What now, sire?' I asked.

'The men need a rest. This is the first day of intensive fighting in many moons, so I've sent a herald to Hektor asking him and his leaders to meet us in the middle and treat.'

'Excellent,' said Odysseus. 'With any luck we can waste a goodly amount of time while the men get their breath back and eat.'

Agamemnon grinned. 'As the ploy works both ways, Hektor won't refuse my offer.'

Noncombatants cleared the bodies away from the centre of the strip separating our two armies; tables and stools were set up, and from both sides the leaders drove out to parley. I went with Ajax, Odysseus, Diomedes, Menelaos, Idomeneus and Agamemnon; we stood and watched this first meeting between the High King and Troy's Heir with great interest and much curiosity. Yes, Hektor was a future king. A very dark man. Black hair showed under his helm and fell down his back in a braid, and the eyes looking at us as shrewdly as we at him were black too.

He introduced his colleagues as Aineas of Dardania, Sarpedon of Lykia, Akamas the son of Antenor, Polydamas the son of Agenor, Pandaros the captain of the Royal Guard, and his brothers Paris and Deiphobos.

Menelaos growled in his throat and glowered at Paris, but each man feared his imperial brother too much to create trouble. I thought the Trojans a fine group of men, all warriors except for Paris, who was out of place – pretty, pouting, precious. While Agamemnon made his introductions I watched Hektor keenly to note his reaction as he associated a name with a face. When he came to Odysseus he studied our mastermind intently, a light of puzzlement in his gaze. But I didn't find his dilemma at all amusing; I was too consumed with pity. Men who didn't know Odysseus the Ithakan Fox usually dismissed him when they met him because of his oddly proportioned body and the untidy, almost ignoble figure he could cut when he thought it politic. Look into his eyes, Hektor, look into his eyes! I found myself saying silently – look into his eyes, know what the man really is and fear it! But Hektor's nature found Ajax, next to Odysseus in our line, far more interesting and attractive. Thus he missed the significance of Odysseus.

Hektor took in the mighty thews of our second greatest warrior with astonishment; for the first time in his life, we thought, he had to look up into another man's face.

'We haven't talked in ten years, son of Priam,' Agamemnon said. 'It's high time we did.'

'What do you wish to discuss?'

'Helen.'

'That subject is closed.'

'Far from closed! Do you deny that Paris, son of Priam and your own full brother, did abduct the wife of my full brother, Menelaos the King of Lakedaimon, and did bring her to Troy as an affront to the entire nation of Greece?'

'I do deny it.'

'The lady asked to come,' Paris added.

'Naturally you do not admit that you used force.'

'Naturally, since we had no need to use force.' Hektor blew down his nostrils like a bull. 'What do you propose in this very formal language, High King?'

'That you return Helen and all her goods to her rightful husband, that you repay us for our time and trouble by reopening the Hellespont to Greek merchants, and that you do not oppose the settling of our Greek people in Asia Minor.'

'Your terms are impossible.'

'Why? All we ask is the right to peaceful coexistence. I would not fight if I could attain my ends peacefully, Hektor.'

'To accede to your demands would ruin Troy, Agamemnon.'

'War will ruin Troy faster. You defend, Hektor – never a profitable position. For ten years *we* have enjoyed Troy's profits – and the profits of Asia Minor.'

The parleying went on, pointless words tossed to and fro while the soldiers lay on their backs in the trampled grasses and closed their eyes against the sun's glare.

'Very well, then, will you agree to this, Prince Hektor?' Agamemnon asked some time later. 'Here among us are the two parties concerned in the beginning of it all. Menelaos and Paris. Let them duel in the open between our two armies, the winner to dictate the terms of a peace settlement.'

If Paris didn't look a brilliant duellist, Menelaos looked even less brilliant. It took Hektor no more than an instant to decide that Paris was an easy winner. 'Agreed,' he said. 'My brother Paris to duel with your brother Menelaos, the winner to dictate the terms of a treaty.'

I peered at Odysseus, who sat beside me.

'For the sake of Agamemnon's reputation in years to come, Nestor, let's hope it's a Trojan who has to break up the duel,' he whispered to me.

We withdrew to our lines and left the hundred paces of vacant ground to the two men, Menelaos testing his shield and spear, Paris preening himself complacently. They circled each other slowly, Menelaos making lunges with his spear, Paris ducking. Someone in the ranks behind me called out a jeering remark which made a thousand Trojan throats rumble, but Paris ignored the insult and dodged on daintily. I had never given Menelaos much credit for anything, but Agamemnon obviously knew what he was about in proposing this duel. I had deemed Paris an easy winner, but I was wrong. Though Menelaos would never have the dash and instinct which make a leader of men, he had learned the art of the duel as conscientiously as he learned everything. He lacked spirit, not courage, which meant he showed to very good advantage in single combat. When he hurled his spear it plucked Paris's shield away; faced with a drawn sword, Paris chose to run rather than draw his own. He took to his heels with Menelaos hard after him.

Everyone could see who was going to win now; the Trojans were very silent, our men were cheering lustily. My eyes remained on Hektor, who had judged wrongly and was a man of high principle. If Menelaos killed Paris, he would have to treat. Ah! Without any signal from Hektor, Pandaros the captain of the Royal Guard quickly nocked an arrow. I shouted to Menelaos, who stopped and sprang to one side. Amid a howl of outrage from the host at my back, Menelaos stood with the arrow quivering in his flank. A howl of grief from the Trojan side greeted the fact that it was a Trojan broke the truce. Hektor was branded dishonourable.

The armies flung themselves into the fight with a fury that had been absent during the morning; one side was in defence of tainted honour, the other was out to avenge an insult, and both sides hacked and hewed in screaming frenzy. Men fell thickly; the hundred paces which had separated the lines dwindled until there was only a solid mass of bodies and the dust underfoot rose in clouds, blinding and choking us. The guilty man, Hektor, was everywhere at once, ranging up and down the centre in his car, his spear darting viciously. None of us could get close enough to him to try a lucky cast, while men died in fear beneath the hooves of his three black horses. How he forced his team through the frightful crush of men I couldn't understand on that first day of pitched battle, though later on it grew so commonplace that I did it myself and thought nothing of it. I saw Aineas looming with a pack of Dardanians in his wake, and wondered in the midst of the mêlée how he had managed to come in from his wing. My spear abandoned in favour of my sword, I rallied my men and drove into the thick of it, laying about me from my car, hacking without choice at sweat-grimed faces, keeping Aineas in sight as I shrieked the call for reinforcements.

Agamemnon sent more men, Ajax in their lead. Aineas saw him coming and called off his dogs, but not before I had the privilege of seeing that veritable tower of a man lay about him, his arm a tireless sickle cutting down the enemy chaff. He hadn't got his axe, having chosen on this first day of battle to use his sword, two-and-a-half cubits of double-bladed death. Though he used it like an axe, it seemed to me, swinging it around his head with a scream of fierce joy. He carried his enormous, wasp-waisted shield better than any other man alive; it never wavered as he held it just clear of the ground, its weight of bronze and tin covering him from head to toe. At his back came six mighty captains of Salamis, and beneath the shelter of the shield itself Teukros hid with his bow, unencumbered, nocking an arrow and letting it fly, taking another from his quiver in a series of movements so fluid they seemed continuous, flawlessly rhythmic. I saw Greek men too far away from him in the press to spot his bulk grin at each other and take heart just because they heard Ajax's famous cry to Ares and the House of Aiakos: 'Ai! Ai! Woe! Woe!' he shrieked, punning on the meaning of his own name, throwing his derision in a thousand Trojan faces.

Surrounded for the moment by my own men, I raised my hand to him as he rolled towards me; Antilochos stood staring in awe, the reins of our team slack.

'They've gone, old one,' growled Ajax.

'Even Aineas wouldn't stop to face you,' I said.

'Zeus turn them into shades! Why won't they stand and make a fight of it? But I'll catch Aineas yet.'

'Where's Hektor?'

'I've been searching for him all afternoon. The man's a will o' the wisp, and I always lag behind. But I'll wear him down. Sooner or later we'll meet.'

Shrill cries of warning sounded; we drew into formation as Aineas returned, bearing Hektor and a part of the Royal Guard. I looked at Ajax.

'Here's your chance, son of Telamon.'

'I thank Ares for it.' He shook his armoured shoulders to settle the weight of his cuirass and prodded Teukros gently with the toe of one vast boot. 'Up, brother. This one is mine and mine alone. Guard Nestor and keep Aineas at bay for me.'

Teukros ducked from beneath the shield, his bright, devoted eyes unworried as he leaped up beside me and Antilochos. No one ever questioned his loyalty, though his mother was Priam's own sister, Hesione.

'Come, laddie,' he said to my son, 'drive us through these carcases and draw up with Aineas. We've work to do with him. King Nestor, will you cover me while I use my bow?'

'Gladly, son of Telamon,' I said.

'Why is Aineas in the van, Father?' Antilochos asked me as we moved off. 'I thought he commanded a wing.'

'So did I,' Teukros answered when I did not.

My own men and some of Ajax's Salaminians came with us to hold Aineas far enough away from Hektor to let Ajax force him into a duel. Yet once the pair engaged the fighting became halfhearted on both sides; we watched Hektor and Ajax far more closely than we watched where our missiles fell.

Ajax never used a chariot in battle, probably because one had never been built capable of supporting his weight plus Teukros and a driver. It was his habit instead to stand on the ground and pretend *he* was a chariot.

Bronze rang on bronze, an arm guard popped under the sudden expansion of muscles and fell to be crushed underfoot. They were evenly matched, Ajax and Hektor. They stood and parried face to face, while all about them the fighting slowly died away. Aineas caught my wandering attention with a shrill whistle.

'This is too good to miss, my white-haired friend! I'd rather watch than fight, wouldn't you? Truce is called by Aineas of Dardania!'

'I agree to a truce until such time as the duel ends. Then if it's Ajax who falls, I'll defend his body and his armour with my life! But if it's Hektor who falls, I'll help Ajax steal his body and his armour from you! Truce is agreed by Nestor of Pylos!'

'So be it!'

In the circle of faces no arm was raised. All around our territory the battle raged unabated while we neither moved nor spoke. My heart glowed as I watched Ajax. No drop in his guard, no exposure of his body from behind that colossal shield. Hektor danced like a living flame about his bulk, cleaving great slices out of the shield. Neither of them seemed to own a sense of time or an awareness of fatigue; moment after moment their arms rose and fell with undiminished power. Twice Hektor almost lost his shield, yet he took Ajax's blade on his own and fought on, keeping shield and sword both despite the best Ajax could do. It was a long, vicious battle. One of them would see an opening and dart in only to be met with a blade, fight on undiscouraged.

I felt a tap on my arm: a herald from Agamemnon.

'The High King requires to know why the fighting's stopped hereabouts, King Nestor.'

'I've agreed to a temporary truce. Look for yourself, my man! Would you fight if that was going on in your section?'

He stared. 'I recognise Prince Ajax, but who opposes him?'

'Go and tell the High King that Ajax and Hektor fight to the death.'

The messenger slipped away, enabling me to fix my attention on the duel again. Both men still hacked and tilted furiously – how long had they been at it now? I didn't need to shade my eyes as I looked up at the dull yellow ball of the dusty sun to find it westering well and truly, almost down to the horizon. By Ares, what stamina!

Agamemnon pulled his car in beside me.

'Can you be spared from the command, sire?'

'Odysseus holds for me. Gods! How long have they been at it, Nestor?'

'For about an eighth part of the afternoon.'

'They'll have to end soon. The sun's setting.'

'Incredible, isn't it?'

'You called a truce?'

'The men weren't willing to fight. Nor was I. How goes it elsewhere?'

'More than holding our own, though we're badly outnumbered. Diomedes has been a titan all day. He killed the trucebreaker Pandaros and got away with the armour under Hektor's very nose. Ah! There's Aineas, I see. No wonder *he* wanted a truce! Diomedes caught him on the shoulder with a spear and thinks he did some damage.'

'So that's why he came in from the wing.'

'The Dardanian is the shrewdest man Priam possesses. But he always looks after himself first, so the stories say.'

325

'How's Menelaos? Did the arrow hit anything vital?'

'No. Machaon bound him up and sent him back to battle.'

'He put up a very nice show.'

'Surprised you, didn't he?'

The horn of darkness wound its long, dismal call above the dust and clamour of the field. Men laid down their arms and sobbed for breath. Shields were dropped and swords clumsily sheathed, but Hektor and Ajax fought on. In the end night defeated them; they could hardly see their weapons in front of them when I got down from my car and parted them.

'It's too dark to see, my lions. I declare a draw, so put away your swords.'

Hektor took off his helmet with a shaking hand. 'I confess I'm not sorry for an end. I'm almost done.'

Ajax gave his shield to Teukros, whose knees buckled under its weight. 'I'm done too.'

'You're a great man, Ajax,' said Hektor, holding out his right arm.

Ajax twined his fingers about the Trojan's wrist, smiling. 'I can say the same of you, Hektor.'

'If they rate Achilles better than you, I can't see why. Here, take my sword!' He thrust it forward impulsively.

Ajax looked down at the blade with unfeigned pleasure, then hefted it in his hand. 'Henceforth I'll always use it in battle. In return, I offer you my baldric. My father said his father said he had it from his father, who was Immortal Zeus himself.' He ducked his head and slipped the treasured relic off; of brilliant purple leather chased with a design in gold, it was a rare specimen.

'I'll wear it in place of my own,' said Hektor, delighted.

I watched the gratification, the mutual liking and respect they had gained for each other under such terrible circumstances. Then the icy wings of a premonition froze my mind: that exchange of property was ill-omened.

*

We camped where we were that night, under the walls of Troy, with Hektor's army between us and the gaping Skaian Gate. The campfires were lit, the cauldrons hung above them on bars; slaves carried round great trays of barley bread and meat, and watered wine flowed. For a while I watched the sight of a myriad torches flickering in and out of the Skaian Gate as Trojan slaves went to and fro ministering to Hektor's army, then I went to eat with Agamemnon and the rest about a fire in the middle of our men. As I stepped into the light their tired faces turned to greet me, and I saw the hollowness which always lies heavy on a man after a hard-fought battle.

'We haven't advanced a finger's breadth,' I said to Odysseus.

'Nor have they,' he said tranquilly, chewing on a strip of boiled pork.

'How many men have we lost?' asked Idomeneus.

'About the same number as Hektor, a few less, perhaps,' said Odysseus. 'Not enough to tip the balance either way.'

'Tomorrow should tell, then,' said Meriones, yawning.

Agamemnon yawned. 'Yes, tomorrow.'

There was little further conversation. Bodies ached and smarted, lids drooped, bellies were full. Time to roll into furs around the fire. I blinked across the flames, looking at the many hundreds of little lights dotted through the plain, each one a source of comfort and safety in the dark night all about us. Smoke plumed towards the stars, the smoke of ten thousand campfires under the walls of Troy. I lay back and watched those stars wax and wane in the manmade fog until they faded away into Sleep, the Bringer of Mind's Darkness.

The second day was not like the first. No truces broke the slaughter, no duels held our attention, no gallant acts of heroism lifted the struggle above the plane of men. The work was grim and sourly tenacious. My bones cried for rest, my eyes were blinded by the tears every man must weep when he sees a son die. Antilochos wept for his brother, then demanded to take his place in the line. So I put another Pylian to drive my car.

Impossible to catch, as deadly as Ares himself, Hektor was in his element, up and down the field, harrying his troops in a brazen voice which gave no quarter and would never stoop to ask for quarter. Ajax had no time to chase him; Hektor brought the full force of the Royal Guard to bear on him and Diomedes, shackling his two most dangerous foes to one spot by sheer weight of numbers. Where Hektor cast his spear a man was sure to die: he was as good as Achilles. If a gap showed in our line he shoved his soldiers into it, then once he had them in he kept feeding more and more of them in, like a tree cutter driving the thin end of the wedge deeper and deeper into a forest giant.

Oh, the grief! The cruelty, the pain! I couldn't see for the tears when another of my sons fell, his bowels torn out on a lance Aineas threw. Not a moment later Antilochos barely escaped losing his head under a sword – not this one! Please, merciful Here, almighty Zeus, spare me Antilochos!

Every so often heralds came to tell me how other parts of the field were going; I gave thanks that at least our leaders were unscathed. Yet perhaps because our men were tired, or because we lacked the fifteen thousand Thessalians Achilles held out of the battle, or for some other more obscure reason, we began to lose ground. Slowly and imperceptibly the venue moved further and further away from the walls of Troy, closer and closer to our own defence wall. I found myself in the very front ranks, my driver sobbing in rage as our team stepped over their tangled traces and began to rear.

Hektor came down upon us; I called frantically for help as his chariot loomed through the crush. Luck was with me. Diomedes and Odysseus had somehow got into the centre of our van, their men next to mine. Diomedes didn't attempt to fight Hektor himself; he concentrated instead on Hektor's driver, not his usual man and definitely not as experienced. He cast his spear and took the fellow straight back on his heels, dead and stretching the reins until the horses, feeling their bits, began to plunge. With some help from Odysseus we got away safely while Hektor spat curses and sawed through his reins with a knife.

I tried to rally my section of the line, but it was hopeless. Fear was in the wind and talk of ill omens was spreading. None of us could delude ourselves any longer – we were in full retreat. Realising it, Hektor threw the rest of his reserve lines forward with a shriek of triumph.

Odysseus saved the day. He leaped into a vacant chariot – where was his? – and turned the Boiotians when they began to bolt, swung them round to face the enemy and then forced them to give ground quietly and in perfect order. Agamemnon followed his example immediately; what had threatened to become a debacle was at least accomplished with a minimum of loss and without the risk of rout. Diomedes charged his Argives into the teeth of the advancing Trojans, and I followed him with Idomeneus, Eurypylos, Ajax and all their men.

We had drawn our flanks up into the van; the army had turned into a tight droplet formation with its slender tail facing Hektor and the bulk of our men behind us, falling back.

Teukros kept to his nook behind his brother's shield, his arrows flying steadily, always accurately. Hektor was hovering; Teukros saw him and grinned as he nocked another arrow. But Hektor was too wily to fall from an arrow he was surely expecting in Ajax's neighbourhood. One after the other, Hektor caught the arrows on his shield, which infuriated Teukros into making a mistake. He stepped out from behind his brother's shield. Hektor was waiting for him. His spears were long gone, but he had found a rock, and flung it in a cast worthy of a spear. It struck Teukros on the right shoulder, and down he went like a bull at a sacrifice. Too beset to notice, Ajax went on fighting. Ah, there! My cry of relief was echoed in a dozen throats when Teukros's head showed above the carnage on the ground and he began to crawl across the dead and wounded to go to earth with Ajax. But now he was just surplus baggage his brother had to lug; the Trojans charged.

I cast my eyes desperately to the rear to see how far we were from our own wall, and gasped; our back lines were already streaming across the causeways.

Odysseus and Agamemnon between them kept our army calm. The retreat was concluded without much loss of life, and we fled behind our wall to the refuge of our stone city. Too dark for Hektor to follow. We left them on the far bank of our ditch and palisade, jeering and yapping at our tails.

CHAPTER TWENTY-FIVE

NARRATED BY
ODYSSEUS

It wasn't a very cheerful gathering that night in Agamemnon's house; we just sat, beginning the wearisome business of getting our strength back in order to endure tomorrow. My head ached, my throat was raw from yelling war cries, my sides were rubbed clean of skin where my cuirass had chafed despite the padded shift underneath. All of us sported minor wounds – grazes, punctures, gashes, cuts – and sleep screamed in us.

'A shocking reverse,' Agamemnon said into the pit of exhausted silence. 'Shocking, Odysseus.'

Diomedes sprang to my defence. 'Just as Odysseus predicted!'

Nestor nodded confirmation. Poor old man. For once he did look his age, and little wonder. He had lost two sons on the field. Voice reedy, he said, 'Don't despair yet, Agamemnon. Our time will come. And be the sweeter for today's reverses.'

'I know, I know!' Agamemnon cried.

'Someone had better go and report to Achilles,' Nestor said in an undertone audible only to those of us in on the plot. 'He's with us, but if he's not kept informed he may move prematurely.'

Agamemnon glared at me balefully. 'Odysseus, it's your idea. *You* see Achilles.'

I plodded off wearily. To send me down the line of houses to its very end was Agamemnon's way of getting back at me. Yet while I walked, at peace and unmolested, strength began to creep into me again. I felt more rested for the little additional exertion than I would have after a full night's sleep. Since any

who saw me would assume after the day's reverses that
Agamemnon was sending me to plead with Achilles, I passed
openly through the Myrmidon gate to find the Myrmidons and
other Thessalians sitting about dolefully, avid to fight, rendered
impotent.

Achilles was in his house warming his hands at a tripod of
fire, looking as worn and nervy as any of us who had fought
for two days. Patrokles sat opposite him, face stony. I suppose
that didn't really surprise me, given the advent of Brise. The
relationship between Diomedes and me was as friendly as it
was sensuous, a kind of expedience both of us found
immensely pleasing. But if either of us fancied a woman, well
and good. No disaster, no sense of betrayal. Patrokles *loved*, and
had thought himself safe, permanently free of rivals. Whereas
Achilles, like all men who burn for things other than the flesh,
had not truly committed himself. Exclusively a man for men,
Patrokles thought himself cruelly wronged. Poor fellow, he
loved.

'What brings you?' Achilles demanded sourly. 'Patrokles,
find food and wine for the King.'

Sighing gratefully, I sat down in a big chair and waited for
Patrokles to depart.

'I hear things went badly,' said Achilles then.

'As expected, don't forget that,' I answered. 'Hektor kept the
Trojans hard at it, and Agamemnon couldn't do the same with
our men. The retreat began at about the same moment as the
grumbling – the omens were all against us, the sky was thick
with eagles flying on the left hand, a gold light bathed the
Trojan Citadel, and so forth. Omen talk is always fatal. So we
fell back until Agamemnon had to pull us inside the fortifications for the night.'

'I hear Ajax met Hektor yesterday.'

'Yes, they duelled for over an eighth part of the afternoon
without a conclusion. You've nothing to worry about there, my
friend. Hektor belongs to you.'

'But men are dying needlessly, Odysseus! Let me come out tomorrow, please!'

'No,' I said harshly. 'Not until the army is in immediate danger of annihilation, or the ships begin to burn because Hektor breaks into our camp. Even then you'll tell Patrokles to lead your troops – you mustn't lead them yourself.' I stared at him sternly. 'Agamemnon has your oath on it, Achilles.'

'Rest assured, Odysseus, that I break no oaths.'

He bowed his head then and lapsed into silence. When Patrokles came back we were sitting thus, Achilles hunched over, I staring dreamily at his head of golden hair. Patrokles directed the servants to put the food and wine on the table, then stood like a pillar of ice. Achilles glanced at him briefly, then at me.

'Tell Agamemnon I refuse to go back on my word,' Achilles said to me in a formal voice. 'Tell him to find someone else to extricate him from this mess. Or else return Brise.'

I slapped my thigh as if exasperated. 'As you wish.'

'Stay and eat, Odysseus. Patrokles, go to bed.'

Not in this house! Patrokles exited through the door.

Perhaps later I would sleep, but as I walked back I found myself so alive that I craved mischief, so I went to the hollow wherein my spy colony was still headquartered. Most of my agents not living inside Troy were sitting over the remains of dinner; Thersites and Sinon greeted me warmly.

'Any news?' I asked, sitting down.

'One item,' said Thersites. 'I was about to find you.'

'Ah! Enlighten me.'

'Just as the battle ended tonight, a new ally arrived – a distant cousin of Priam's named Rhesos.'

'How many troops did he bring?'

Sinon laughed softly. 'None. Rhesos is a loud-mouthed bag of wind, Odysseus. He calls himself an ally, but he's better summed up as a refugee. His own people threw him out.'

'Well, well!' I said, and waited.

333

'Rhesos drives a team of three magnificent white horses which are the subject of a Trojan oracle,' said Thersites. 'They're said to be the immortal children of winged Pegasos, as fleet as Boreas and as wild as Persephone before Hades took her. Once they've drunk from Skamander and eaten Trojan grass, Troy can never fall. A promise, says the Oracle, from Poseidon, who's supposed to be on our side.'

'And, since Poseidon is on our side, have they drunk from Skamander and eaten Trojan grass yet?'

'They've eaten grass, but they wouldn't drink from Skamander.'

I grinned. 'Who can blame them? *I* wouldn't drink either.'

'Priam's sent for a bucket or two upstream,' said Sinon, sharing my grin. 'He's decided to make a public ceremony out of it at dawn tomorrow. In the meantime, the horses go thirsty.'

'Very interesting.' I got up, stretching. 'I'll have to see these fabulous creatures for myself. It would add a certain – er, elegance – to my image if I drove a team of white horses.'

'You could do with a little more elegance,' gibed Sinon.

'A lot more elegance,' Thersites contributed.

'Thank you for that, sirs! Whereabouts might I find this immortal team?'

'That we haven't been able to find out,' said Thersites, frowning. 'All we know is that they're quartered on the plain with the Trojan army.'

Diomedes, Agamemnon and Menelaos were waiting outside my own house; I strolled up to them as if I'd been enjoying a constitutional, and grinned at Diomedes. Knowing that look, his eyes began to sparkle.

'Achilles is all right,' I said to Agamemnon.

'Thank all the Gods for that! I can sleep now.'

The moment he and Menelaos departed I entered my house with Diomedes and clapped for a servant. 'Bring me a light leather suit and two daggers,' I said.

'Then I'd better go and equip myself similarly, I suppose,' said Diomedes.

'Meet me by the Simois causeway.'

'Are we going to get any sleep at all tonight?'

'Later, later!'

Clad in soft dark leather, two daggers in his belt, Diomedes joined me at the Simois causeway. We threaded our way from shadow to shadow silently until we got to the far end of the bridge, where the ditches joined up with the palisade.

'What are we after?' he whispered then.

'I have a fancy to drive a team of immortal white horses.'

'That would certainly improve your image.'

I shot him a suspicious look. 'Have you been talking to Sinon and Thersites?'

'No,' he said innocently. 'Whereabouts is this team?'

'I have no idea. Somewhere out there in the darkness.'

'So we're looking for a flea in a bear's pelt.'

I squeezed his arm. 'Ssssh! Someone's coming.'

Mentally I saluted my protectress, the Owl Lady herself. My beloved Pallas Athene always dropped fortune in my lap. We sank down into the ditch alongside the causeway and waited.

A man flitted out of the gloom, his armour chinking – a very amateur spy, to sneak about in armour. Nor did he have the wit to skirt a patch of moonlight; the rays bathed him momentarily, revealing a small, plump man in costly gear, his helm waving the purple plume of Troy. We let him get within a spit of us before we sprang, Diomedes darting off to my left so we had him between us. My hand was over his mouth, cutting off his squeal; Diomedes pinned his arms behind his back and we bore him down, dumped him roughly in the grass. Eyes starting from their orbits goggled up at us; we could feel him shaking like a soft little jellyfish. Not one of Palamedes's men. An entrepreneur, more like.

'Who are you?' I growled, low but ferocious.

'Dolon,' he managed.

'What are you doing here, Dolon?'

'Prince Hektor asked for volunteers to enter your camp and discover if Agamemnon means to come out tomorrow.'

Stupid Hektor! Why didn't he leave spying to the professionals like Palamedes?

'A man arrived tonight. Rhesos. Where's his camp?' I asked, drawing my finger lovingly along the blade of my dagger.

He swallowed, shuddered. 'I don't know!' he bleated.

Diomedes loomed over him, sliced off an ear and waved it in front of his face while I gagged him with my hand until the horror faded and he understood.

'Speak, snake!' I hissed.

He spoke. At the end of it we broke his neck.

'Look at his jewels, Odysseus!'

'A very rich man, probably from scavenging. A man not worth Hektor's notice. Strip him of his pretty baubles, old friend, hide them and pick them up on the way back. Your share of the spoils, since I must keep the team.'

He tossed a huge emerald in his hand. 'My team is well enough. This alone will buy half a hundred Sun Cattle to stock the plain of Argos.'

We found the camp of Rhesos exactly where Dolon had described, and lay on a nearby hillock to plan our strategy.

'Fool!' Diomedes muttered. 'Why so isolated?'

'Exclusivity, I suspect. How many can you make out?'

'Twelve, though which is Rhesos I can't tell.'

'I count the same. First we kill the men, then we take the team. No sounds.'

We jammed our knives between our teeth and slithered off, he to take the near side of the fire, I to take the far side. In such matters practice is helpful; they died in their sleep, and the horses, vague white shapes in the background, took no fright.

The one named Rhesos was easy to pick out. He too was a jewel collector. Snoozing closest to the fire, he glittered with them.

'Look at this pearl!' breathed Diomedes, holding it up to twin the moon.

'A thousand Sun Cattle,' I said, keeping my voice low. One could never be sure someone wouldn't arrive unexpectedly.

The horses had been muzzled in case they broke their tethers and headed off to Simois to satiate their thirst. Good for us; they wouldn't start whinnying. While I found halters and said hello to my new team, Diomedes collected anything worth taking from the camp and put it on a mule. Then, our route plotted on the way there, we headed back to the Simois causeway, where my Argive friend picked up Dolon's cache.

Agamemnon wasn't pleased at being woken until I told him the story of Rhesos and his horses, whereupon he laughed. 'I can see why you must keep the sons of winged Pegasos, Odysseus, but what about poor Diomedes?'

'I'm content,' said crafty Diomedes, looking noble.

Yes, that was a politic answer. Why tell a man with a war chest to fill that one has, in the course of a small fraction of the night, accumulated a formidable fortune?

The story of the horses of Rhesos was out and about among our troops by the time they broke their fast at dawn; they were delighted, and cheered me as I drove my new team out over the Simois causeway ahead even of Agamemnon, who wanted Troy to see.

Troy saw, and Troy did not think it a joke.

The battle was bloody, vicious. Agamemnon saw his chance and drove a deep wedge through the Trojan line, forcing them to retreat. Our men were all for finishing it, and drove them back until the walls of Troy loomed. But there the Trojans, who still outnumbered us grossly, rallied, and there our luck changed. The Kings began to go down.

First was Agamemnon, in fine fettle that day. As he drove down the line towards us he speared a man who tried to stop him, but didn't see the man who followed and thrust his own spear deeply into Agamemnon's thigh. The head was barbed, the wound bled copiously; our High King was forced to leave the field.

Then it was Diomedes's turn. He managed to strike Hektor's helm with a javelin, dazing him for a moment. Whooping, Diomedes moved in for the kill while I concentrated on Hektor's horses and driver, intending to disable the car. None of us saw the figure lurking safely behind it until he rose with an arrow nocked, his white teeth flashing in a grin as he let the shaft fly. It was a long shot and almost to earth when it found its mark in the Argive's foot. Pinned to the ground, Diomedes stood cursing and shaking his fist while Paris scuttled off. Troy had a Teukros.

'Bend down and pull it out!' I shouted to Diomedes, coming up with a good number of my Ithakans.

He did as he was told while I swung an axe some dead man had no further use for. It wasn't my normal choice of weapon, too clumsy and heavy, but to fend off a ring of enemies it was peerless. Determined I would see Diomedes safely away, I wielded the awful thing savagely until he limped off painfully, too crippled to be of further use.

At which moment I too went down. Someone's lucky spear-cast lodged in the back of my calf a little below the hamstrings. My Ithakans surrounded me until I could pull it out, but the head was barbed and took a great chunk of flesh with it. Losing blood fast, I had to waste time binding the blood vessels closed with a strip from some dead man's shift.

Menelaos and his Spartans came to reinforce us; I managed to fight my way to his side. Ajax appeared, and the two of them stepped aside to let me dodge down behind Menelaos's chariot. A glorious warrior, Ajax! His blood fired, he laid about him with a strength I could never have mustered and forced the Trojans back, his Salaminians, as always, so proud of him that they went with him anywhere. Some Trojan leader responded by pushing more men in until they were jammed against Ajax's axe by sheer weight from behind. Faster than our struggling

soldiers and the mighty Ajax could mow them down, they
sprang up again like the soldiers of the Dragon's teeth.

Thankful to see that Hektor had disappeared, I had made
myself useful by calling for a concentration of strength in the
area. Eurypylos was the closest, and came in from one side:
just in time to collect one of Paris's arrows in his shoulder.
Machaon was coming up too, and met the same fate. Paris.
What a worm. He wasted no arrows on common men; he
simply lurked somewhere safe and comfortable and waited for
a prince at least. In which he differed from Teukros, who shot
at any target.

Somehow I managed to get behind the lines at last, to find
Podalieros tending Agamemnon and Diomedes, who waited
disconsolately as close to the venue as they dared. Horrified,
they took in the sight of me, Machaon and Eurypylos.

'*Why* must you fight, brother?' Podalieros demanded
through his teeth as he lowered Machaon to the ground.

'See to Odysseus first,' gasped Machaon, the stump of an
arrow in his arm bleeding sluggishly.

So I had my wound packed and bound first; Podalieros went
to Eurypylos then, electing to push the arrow through for fear
it would do more damage inside the shoulder if it were pulled
out the same way it had gone in.

'Where's Teukros?' I asked, sinking down beside Diomedes.

'I sent him off the field a while ago,' said Machaon, still
waiting his turn. 'The blow Hektor dealt him yesterday swelled
to the size of the rock Hektor hit him with. I had to tap the
lump and drain some of the fluid off. His arm was quite
paralysed, but he can move it again now.'

'Our ranks are thinning,' I said.

'Too thin,' said Agamemnon grimly. 'The soldiers know it
too. Can't you feel the change?'

'Yes, I can,' I said, getting to my feet and testing my leg. 'I
suggest we move ourselves back to camp before we become

caught up in a panic. The army will break for the beach soon, I think.'

Though it had been I responsible for it, I found the retreat a blow nonetheless. Too few of the Kings were left to hold the men together; of the major leaders only Ajax, Menelaos and Idomeneus were left. One section of our line broke; the rot spread with astonishing speed. Suddenly the whole army turned and fled for the safety of our camp. Hektor shrieked so loudly that I heard him from where I stood atop our wall, then the Trojans were baying in pursuit like starving dogs. Our men were still pouring in across the Simois causeway with the Trojans attacking their rear when Agamemnon, white-faced, issued his orders. The gate was closed before the last – and the most gallant – could get in. I stopped my ears and closed my eyes. Your fault, Odysseus! All your fault.

Too early in the day for a cease to battle. Hektor would try for our wall. Milling about inside the camp, our troops took some time to rally and understand that their job now was to defend the fortifications. Slaves flew about boiling great cauldrons and urns of water to pour down on the heads of those who would attempt to scale the wall; we didn't dare use oil for fear that the wall would end in burning. Stones were already piled along its top, stacked there for just such an emergency years ago.

The thwarted Trojans massed along the trench, leaders rolling up and down in their chariots, urging men to take up their ranks again. Hektor drove in his golden car with his old driver, Kebriones, at the reins. Even after days of bitter conflict he looked erect and confident. As well he should. I propped my chin on my hands as our own men began to fill the spaces around me on top of the wall, and settled down to see how Hektor meant to storm us: whether he was willing to sacrifice many, or whether he had a better scheme in mind than simple brute force.

CHAPTER TWENTY-SIX

NARRATED BY
HEKTOR

I penned them within their own defences like sheep; victory lay curled in the hollow of my hand. I, who had lived behind walls since the day of my birth, knew better than any other man alive how to attack them. No walls save those of Troy itself were invulnerable. This was my moment. I gloried in Agamemnon's defeat, vowing I would make that proud man feel the despair we had endured ever since his thousand ships sailed out from behind Tenedos. Heads lined their pathetic wall as I drove with Polydamas beside me in my car. Kebriones had gone to find water for the horses, good man.

'What do you think?' I asked Polydamas.

'Well, we face no Troy, but they're tricky ramparts, Hektor. The two causeways so widely separated are clever. So are the trench and the palisade. Can you see their mistake?'

'Oh, yes. The gap between the wall and the trench is too wide,' I answered. 'We'll use their causeways, but not to attack their gates. We'll use them to cross the palisade and trench, then swing our men in behind the trench to attack the wall itself. The stone hereabouts isn't easy to quarry, so they had to build in wood except for their watchtowers and buttresses.'

Palamedes nodded. 'Yes, I'd do the same, Hektor. Shall I send back to Troy for combustibles?'

'At once – anything that will burn, even ordinary cooking fat. While you do that, I'll call an assembly of my leaders,' I said.

When Paris – last to arrive, as always – strolled up, I told the group what I intended to do.

341

'Two thirds of the army will come in across the Simois causeway, one third across at Skamader. I'm going to divide the troops into five segments. I'll lead the first, with Polydamas. Paris, you'll take the second. Helenos, you'll take the third, with Deiphobos. We three will come in here at Simois. Aineas, you'll take the fourth section across at Skamander. Sarpedon and Glaukos will also use Skamander.'

Helenos was beaming because I had preferred to put him in charge than Deiphobos, who couldn't make up his mind whether he was angrier at that slight, or at the fact that Paris had been given his own division. Nor was Aineas very happy at being lumped in with Sarpedon and Glaukos as a foreigner.

'As the men reach the inside ends of the causeways they'll turn to walk towards each other, Simois to Skamander, until they fill all of the space along the wall between it and the trench. In the meantime the noncombatants can be dismantling the palisade and turning it into ladders and firewood. Fire is our best tool. Fire will bring their wall down. So our first job will be to start those fires and make it impossible for the defenders to put them out.'

Among the leaders was my cousin Asios, always a thorn in my side because he never wanted to follow orders.

'Hektor,' he said, too loudly, 'do you intend to abandon your cavalry?'

'Yes,' I said without hesitation. 'What use can it be? The last thing we need are horses and chariots in an enclosed space.'

'What about attacking the gates?'

'They're too easily defended, Asios.'

He snorted. 'Rubbish! Here, let me show you!'

Then, before I could countermand him, off he ran, shouting to his squadron to mount their cars. In the lead, he lashed his team onto the Simois causeway. Though it was wide, so too is a team of three horses abreast; the near and the off animal rolled eyes wildly at the spikes protruding out of the ditch on either side until their panic communicated itself to the middle horse. Next moment all three were rearing and plunging, and had thrown Asios's charioteers behind him into confusion as well. While Asios's driver fought to control the team, the gates at the end of the causeway swung open a little. Into the breach stepped two men at the head of a large company. Their standard showed that they were Lapiths; I shuddered. Asios was a dead man. One of the two leaders cast his spear and plugged my braggart cousin through the chest. He pitched out of the chariot in a huge upward leap to land, sprawled out, on the stakes in the ditch. His driver followed quickly; the Lapiths stepped around the chariot and laid into those who had followed. There was nothing we could do to help. Carnage wrought, the Lapiths retired in good order and the Simois gates were closed.

Now I had a mess to clear off the causeway before I could start my men, but in the meantime Aineas, Sarpedon and Glaukos had a long march to the Skamander causeway – which, I reflected with satisfaction, would not be blocked by any defenders. Achilles sat on the other side of the Skamander gates, and Achilles had abrogated his duty to Agamemnon. A silly girl was more important to him than his fellow countrymen were. What a sham.

The men poured across at a run and turned inwards along the base of the wall, greeted by a storm of spears, arrows and stones from the defenders. Their shields over their heads, they suffered little from the missiles as they trotted steadily towards the Skamander causeway, where the foreign troops were beginning to turn inwards too. Noncombatants were already tearing the wooden palisade apart, turning the longer bits into ladders, chopping up anything not wanted into kindling. Oil, pitch and cooking fat were beginning to arrive from Troy when I had the notion of making my men construct frames on which they could put their shields as roof shingles, work under cover.

The fires were lit; I watched smoke begin to plume towards the suddenly frightened faces along the top of the wall. Water cascaded down, but some of my shelters had been adapted to

shield the fires until they caught too well to be extinguished;
I also found the blackness of watered oily smoke a great
advantage.

We tried scaling with the ladders, but that the Greeks were
too wily to permit. Ajax charged up and down the middle
section, where I was, roaring lustily and shoving ladders down
with his foot. Wasteful. I ordered a cease.

'It must be the fires,' I said to Sarpedon, whose troops had
married mine.

Lit first, the fires in our section now burned fiercely. Lykian
bowmen kept the heads on the parapet down below the
breastworks, while other Lykians and my Trojans fed the fires
with oil.

'Let me try for the walls,' said Sarpedon.

Shielded by smoke, the ladders went up between the fires
and stayed there while Sarpedon's bowmen fired volley after
volley at the defenders. Then, magically it seemed, Lykian
helmet plumes waved atop the wall; the struggle was joined.
Vaguely I heard some Greek captain call for reinforcements,
but I didn't expect Ajax and his Salaminians. Within moments
the little victory became a rout; bodies thudded at our feet,
Lykian war cries turned to screams of pain. And Teukros was
there behind his brother's shield, firing his darts not into the
mêlée atop the wall, but down on us.

A choked whimper beside me was followed by the weight of
someone slumping against me; I lowered Glaukos to earth with
an arrow clear through his shoulder, armour and all. Too deep.
I looked up at Sarpedon and shook my head; pink foam was
bubbling from Glaukos's mouth, a sign of imminent death.

They were as close as twins, they had ruled together and
loved each other for years. The death of one surely meant the
death of the other.

Sarpedon roared his anguish briefly, then seized a horse
blanket from around a wounded soldier, muffled it about his
face and shoulders, and stepped straight over one of the fires. A
rope dangled from a grappling hook above, overlooked by the

Greeks in their anxiety to push the Lykians from the parapet. Sarpedon grasped it and heaved with a strength not normally given to a man, so great was his grief for Glaukos. The wood groaned and creaked, the blackened logs began to gape and split; a big section of wall suddenly collapsed around us. Trojans unlucky enough to be under it were crushed, Greeks unlucky enough to be atop it came plummeting with it, and in an instant the whole middle section of my line was a shambles. Through the gap I saw tall stone houses and barracks, the ranks of ships beyond, and the grey Hellespont. Then Sarpedon blocked my view; he threw the blanket away, picked up his sword and shield, and entered the Greek camp howling murder.

The Greeks broke before us as we advanced, more and more of our men pouring through until the Greeks rallied and faced us. Ajax was there encouraging resistance, but in this crush neither of us could hope for duelling room. The line gave not a fraction either way; Idomeneus and Meriones brought their Cretans up, and my brother Alkathoos dropped. I dashed the tears from my eyes and cursed my weakness, though it was more fury than sorrow. I fought the better for it.

Faces came and went – Aineas, Idomeneus, Meriones, Menestheus, Ajax, Sarpedon. There were many Trojans amid the Lykians and Dardanians now; a glance behind revealed that the gap in the wall was much wider than it had been. Only the purple plumes prevented our killing our own, the crush was so great, the ground so hotly contested. Men died as wastefully as bravely; my boot heels kept slipping on human cobbles, and in places the pressure was so enormous that dead men actually stayed upright, mouths open, wounds bubbling. My arms and chest were covered in the blood of other men, I dripped it.

Polydamas materialised alongside me. 'Hektor, you're needed. We're through the breach in great numbers, but the Greeks are strong. Towards Simois as soon as you can, please!'

It took time to disengage without panicking those I was leaving behind, but eventually I was able to slip backwards until I could edge my way along the Greek wall, cheering the men on as I went, reminding them that ultimate victory was ours the moment we burned those thousand ships and gave them no hope of sailing away.

Someone tripped me. He almost parted with his head for it, save that in gauging the blow I saw who sat there, giggling.

'Why don't you watch where you're going?' Paris asked.

I stared at him, thunderstruck. 'Paris, you never cease to amaze me. While men are dying everywhere, you sit safe and sound. With enough leisure to amuse yourself by tripping me up.'

Even that didn't wipe the smile from his face. 'Well, if you think I'm going to beg your forgiveness, Hektor, think again! If it wasn't for me you wouldn't be here, and that's the truth. Who picked off the Greek somebodies one by one with his arrows, eh? Who forced Diomedes to leave the field, eh?'

I yanked him up by his long black curls and set him on his feet. 'Then pick off some more!' I snarled. 'Ajax, maybe – *eh*?'

Giving me a look of loathing, Paris slithered off, leaving me to discover that the part of our line in trouble was being attacked by Ajax and a big company of Salaminians.

The whole front of the battle had changed direction. We fought now among the houses, difficult and perilous work; every building harboured Greeks lying in ambush. But those in the open were falling back steadily towards the beach and the ships. Ajax heard my war cry and answered with his famous 'Ai! Ai! Woe! Woe!' We pushed through the heaving bodies to come at each other, I with my spear at the ready. Then, almost as I was upon him, he bent suddenly and came up holding a boulder in both hands, a chock used to stabilise a beached ship. My spear was useless. I threw it away and drew my sword, counting on my superior speed to get me to him first. He flung the rock with all his might at pointblank range. I felt a tearing pain as it caught me squarely on the chest, then I fell.

Out of a humming darkness into a world of terrible pain; I felt the taste of blood in my mouth and vomited, opened my eyes to see blackish blood on the ground beside me, then lost my senses again. The second time I came around the pain was not as bad; one of our surgeons was kneeling over me. I struggled to sit up, he helping me.

'You have some badly bruised ribs and a few ruptured veins, Prince Hektor, but nothing more serious,' he said.

'The Gods are with us today!' I gasped, leaning on him as he got me the rest of the way to my feet.

The more I moved, the less the agony; I kept on moving. Some of my men had carried me beyond the Simois causeway and put me down near my own chariot. Kebriones was grinning at me.

'We thought you were dead, Hektor.'

'Get me back there,' I said, climbing aboard.

Not to have to walk the whole way was a blessing, but at the back of the press I had to get down. Deeming me dead, my army had begun to falter, but once enough men learned that I was alive and returning to the fight, they rallied. The sight of my face must have been a bitter blow to the Greeks. They broke and fled through the houses until a leader unknown to me managed to halt them under the bow of a lone ship standing, a kind of figurehead in itself, well forward of the first seemingly endless row of ships. We beat the Greeks to their knees, for they refused to retreat any further; only Ajax, Meriones and a few Cretans remained to defy us.

The prow of the lone ship loomed over my head; I saw success within my very grasp as Ajax planted his feet in front of me and raised his sword – *my* sword, given to him as a gift. I lunged and he parried neatly; it was our duel all over again, but this time no eyes had opportunity to watch us, and all around us others fought with equal savagery.

'Whose – ship?' I gasped.

'Belonged – to – Protesilaos,' he panted.

'I – burn – it!'

'See – you – burn – first!'

More Greeks were arriving to defend what was obviously a talisman vessel as a sudden surge of movement carried Ajax and me apart. Some of my own Royal Guard were with me now, and the Greeks opposing us were not of Salaminian quality. We pushed on, taking life after life. Ajax swam into my vision again, but this time he didn't try to turn us back. With a series of mighty heaves he pulled himself up onto the deck of the Protesilaos ship, as quick and lithe as a tumbler. There he picked up a long pole and swung it back and forth in lazy circles, knocking my men clean off the deck the moment they reached it.

When the last Greek opposing me was dead I seized a pair of Trojan shoulders and scrambled up until I could take hold of the Protesilaos prow. From there down to the deck was a single leap. In front of me Ajax stood swaying on his feet, still unconquered. We took stock of each other, each of us feeling in the same instant all the exhaustion of so much fighting. Shaking his huge head slowly, as if to convince himself that I did not exist, he brought his pole around. I raised my sword and met it with the blade, shearing it in two. The sudden loss of balance almost tipped him over; he righted himself, groping for his sword. I scuttled forward, sure he was done, but again he showed me what a great warrior he was. Instead of meeting me he ran to the stern, bunched his muscles and leaped from the Protesilaos ship to the one directly behind it in the middle of the first row.

I abandoned him. Something within me loved that man as he surely loved me. Mutual affection grows, friends or enemies. I knew the Gods did not want us to kill each other; we had exchanged duelling gifts.

I leaned over the rail and looked down on a sea of purple Trojan plumes.

'Give me a torch!'

Someone tossed one upwards. I caught it, walked down to the empty mast amid its shrouds and let the fire lick lovingly about those worn ropes, the cracked dry wood. From the next ship Ajax watched me, arms hanging limply by his sides, tears rolling down his face. The flames kindled; a sheet of fire ran up the mast to the crosstrees, the deck began to weep trickles of smoke from other torches thrown below through the rowing ports. I ran back to the prow, mounted it.

'Victory is ours!' I shouted. 'The ships are aflame!'

My men took up the cry, surging to meet the Greeks as they clustered in front of the ships resting in line behind the lonely Protesilaos talisman.

CHAPTER TWENTY-SEVEN

NARRATED BY
ACHILLES

I spent most of my time standing on the roof of the tallest
Myrmidon barracks, looking from its height across our wall
to the plain. When the army broke and fled, I saw it; when
Sarpedon breached our wall, I saw it; when Hektor's men
poured in among the houses, I saw it. But no more. Listening to
Odysseus outline his plan was one thing. To see the plan's
outcome was unbearable. I plodded back to my house.

Patrokles sat on a bench outside its door, his face wet with
tears. Seeing me, he turned away.

'Go and find Nestor,' I said. 'I saw him bring Machaon in a
while ago. Ask him what news there is from Agamemnon.'

All futile. What the news would be was obvious. But at least
I wouldn't have to look at Patrokles, or hear him beg me to
change my mind. The noise of the conflict raging on the other
side of the stockade fence which shut my Thessalian people off
was a little distant; it was the Simois end of the camp most
beset. I sat on the bench and waited until Patrokles returned.

'What does Nestor say?'

His face was ugly with contempt. 'Our cause is lost. After
ten long years of work and pain, our cause – is – lost! Through
no one's fault save yours! Eurypylos was with Nestor and
Machaon. The fatalities are shocking and Hektor runs amok.
Even Ajax is powerless to curb his advance. The ships must
burn.'

He drew a breath. 'If you hadn't quarrelled with Agamemnon
none of this could have happened! You sacrificed Greece to
feed your passion for an insignificant woman!'

350

'Patrokles, why won't you believe in me?' I asked. 'Why have you turned against me? Is it jealousy over Brise?'

'No. It's disillusionment, Achilles. You're just not the man I thought you were. This isn't about love. It's about pride.'

I didn't say whatever I thought I might because a great shout went up. We both ran to the stockade wall and mounted the steps to see above it. A column of smoke rose into the sky; the Protesilaos ship was burning. All had come to pass. I could move. But how could I tell Patrokles that he, not I, must lead out the men of Thessalia? The Myrmidons?

When we came down Patrokles went on his knees in the dust.

'Achilles, the ships must burn! If you won't, then let *me* lead our troops out! Surely you've seen how much they hate sitting here while the rest of Greece dies! Do you want the throne of Mykenai, is that it? Do you want to return to a land in no fit condition to resist your conquering forces?'

My face felt tight, but I answered levelly. 'I have no designs on Agamemnon's throne.'

'Then let me lead our men out now! Let me take them down to the ships before Hektor burns them!'

I allowed myself to nod stiffly. 'Very well, then, take them. I see your point, Patrokles. Receive the command.'

Even as I said that, I saw how the scheme might be made to work better, and lifted Patrokles to his feet. 'But on one condition. That you wear my armour and make the Trojans think it's Achilles come among them.'

'Put it on yourself and come with us!'

'That I can't do,' I said.

So I took him to the armoury and dressed him in the golden suit my father had given me from the chest of King Minos. It was too big by far, but I did my best to make it fit by overlapping the front and back plates of the cuirass, padding the helmet. The greaves came up his thighs, which would afford him more protection than greaves usually did. And yes, provided no one got too close, he would pass for Achilles.

351

Would Odysseus see that as my breaking the oath? Would Agamemnon? Well, too bad if they did. I would do what I could to shield my oldest friend – my lover – from harm.

The horns had sounded; the Myrmidons and other Thessalians were waiting in so short a space of time that it was obvious they had been ready to leap into the fray. I walked with Patrokles to the assembly area while Automedon ran to harness up my car; though it would be of little use inside the camp, it was necessary that everyone see Achilles arrive to throw the Trojans out. In the gold armour I had rarely worn, everyone would know Achilles.

But how was this? The men cheered me deafeningly, looked at me with the same love they had always shown me. How *was* this, when even Patrokles had turned against me? I shaded my eyes and glanced up at the sun, to find it not so far above the horizon. Good. The deception need not last long. Patrokles would be all right.

Automedon was ready. Patrokles mounted the car.

'Dearest cousin,' I said, my hand on his arm, 'content yourself with driving Hektor from the camp. Whatever you do, do *not* pursue him onto the plain. Is that order clear?'

'Perfectly,' he said, shrugging me off.

Automedon clicked his tongue at the team and moved off to the gate between our stockade and the main body of the camp, while I ascended to the barracks rooftop to watch.

The fighting now raged in front of the first row of ships, with Hektor looking invincible. A situation which changed in an instant when fifteen thousand fresh troops came at the Trojans from the Skamander side, led by a figure wearing golden armour in a golden chariot drawn by three white horses.

'Achilles! Achilles!'

I could hear both sides crying my name, a sensation as odd as it was uncomfortable. But it was enough. The moment the Trojan soldiers glimpsed the figure in the chariot and heard the name, they were transformed from victors into defeated. They ran. My Myrmidons were out for blood and fell on the stragglers tooth and nail, cutting them down without mercy, while 'I' screamed my war cry and urged them on.

Hektor's army poured out across the Simois causeway. Never again, I vowed, would a Trojan set foot inside our camp. Not the most cunning wile Odysseus could think of would persuade me. I found that I was weeping, and knew not for whom – myself, Patrokles, all those dead Greek soldiers. Odysseus had succeeded in luring Hektor out, but the price was ghastly. I could only pray that Hektor had lost at least as many men.

Ai, ai! Patrokles chased the Trojans out onto the plain. When I saw what he was about, I felt my heart sink. Inside the camp the crush had prevented anyone's getting close enough to him to see the deception, but out there on the plain – oh, anything was possible! Hektor would rally, and Aineas was still in the fight. Aineas knew me. Knew *me*, not my armour.

Suddenly it seemed better not to know. I left the roof and sat on the bench outside my house door, waiting for someone to come. The sun was about to set, hostilities would cease. Yes, he would be all right. He would survive. He had to survive.

Footsteps sounded: Nestor's youngest, Antilochos. He was weeping and wringing his hands together – telltale, telltale. I tried to speak and found my tongue clove to the top of my mouth; I had to struggle to produce the question.

'Is Patrokles dead?'

Antilochos sobbed aloud. 'Achilles, his poor naked body lies out there among a host of Trojans – Hektor wears your armour and flaunts it in our faces! The Myrmidons are heartbroken, but they won't let Hektor near the body, though he shouted a vow that Patrokles would feed the dogs of Troy.'

As I got to my feet my knees went; down I went into the dust where Patrokles had knelt to beg. Unreal, unreal. Yet it had to be real. I had known it was going to happen. For a moment I felt the power of my mother in me and heard the lap and swell of the sea. I cried her name once, hating her.

Antilochos pillowed my head in his lap, his warm tears falling on my arm, his fingers chafing the back of my neck.

'He wouldn't understand,' I mumbled. 'He refused to understand. That never occurred to me. He, of all people, to think I would desert my own? They had my oath on it. He died deeming me prouder than Zeus. He died despising me. And now I can never explain. Odysseus, Odysseus!'

Antilochos stopped weeping. 'What has Odysseus got to do with all this, Achilles?'

I remembered then, shook my head and climbed to my feet. Together we walked towards the gate in the stockade wall.

'Did you think I might kill myself?' I asked him.

'Not for very long.'

'Who did it? Hektor?'

'Hektor wears his armour, but there's some doubt as to who actually killed him. When the Trojans turned to face us on the plain, Patrokles got down from his car. Then he tripped.'

'The armour killed him. It was too big.'

'We'll never know that. He was attacked by three men. Hektor dealt the last stroke, but he may already have been dead. Not unblooded. He killed Sarpedon. When Aineas came to help, he was recognised for an impostor. The Trojans were furious at the trick, and rallied well after the news spread. Then Patrokles killed Kebriones, Hektor's driver. Soon after that he got down and tripped. They set on him like jackals before he could get up – he had no chance to defend himself. Hektor stripped away his armour, but before he could get the body the Myrmidons had come up. Ajax and Menelaos are still fighting to keep him safe.'

'I must go and help.'

'Achilles, you can't! The sun's going down. By the time you got there, it would be over.'

'I have to help!'

'Leave it to Ajax and Menelaos.' He put his hand on my arm. 'I must beg your forgiveness.'

'Why?'

'I doubted you. I should have known it was Odysseus.'

I cursed my loose tongue. Even in the midst of the Spell I was bound by my oath. 'You're to speak of it to no one, Antilochos, do you hear?'

'Yes,' he said.

We ascended to the rooftop and looked to where the plain was filled with men. I made Ajax out easily, and saw that he was holding the fresh Thessalian troops firmly in place while Menelaos and another I fancied was Meriones bore a naked body shoulder high on a shield away from the battle. They were bringing Patrokles in. The dogs of Troy wouldn't feast on him.

'Patrokles!' I screamed. 'Patrokles!'

Some of them heard, looked my way and pointed. I shouted his name again and again. The whole host stood silent. Then the horn of darkness wound its long, braying call across the field. Hektor, my golden armour flashing redly in the dying sunset, turned to lead his army back to Troy.

They laid Patrokles on a makeshift bier in the middle of the great assembly space in front of Agamemnon's house. Menelaos and Meriones, covered in gore and filth, were so exhausted that they could hardly stand. Then Ajax stumbled up. When his helm dropped from nerveless fingers he had not the strength to bend and pick it up. So I did that, gave it to Antilochos and took my cousin into my arms, a way of holding him up with honour, for he was done.

The Kings gathered around to form a circle and gaze down on dead Patrokles. His wounds were the thrusts of curs, one beneath his arm where the cuirass had gaped, one in the back and another in the belly, where the spear had plunged so deeply that his bowels were hanging out. I knew this was Hektor's blow, but thought that whoever had got him in the back had killed him.

One of his hands dangled off the edge of the bier. I took it in mine and sank down beside him on the ground.

'Achilles, come away,' said Automedon.

'No, my place is here. Take care of Ajax for me, and send for the women to come and bathe Patrokles, dress him in a shroud. He'll remain here until I kill Hektor. And this I vow: that I will lay the bodies of Hektor and twelve noble Trojan youths at his feet in the tomb. Their blood will pay the Keeper of the River when Patrokles asks to cross.'

Some time later the women came to cleanse Patrokles of his dirt. They washed his tangled hair, closed the wounds with balms and sweet-smelling unguents, tenderly sponged away the reddened tear marks from around his fast-stuck eyes. For that much I could be thankful; his lids were already down when they brought him in.

All through the night marches I remained holding his hand, my only conscious emotion the despair of a man whose last memory of a loved one was filled with hate. Two shades now thirsted for my blood: Iphigenia and Patrokles.

Odysseus came with the rising sun, bearing two cups of watered wine and a plate of barley bread.

'Eat and drink, Achilles.'

'Not until I've fulfilled my vow to Patrokles.'

'He neither knows nor cares what you do. If you've vowed to kill Hektor, you'll need all your strength.'

'I'll last.' I stared about, blinking, only then realising that there were no signs of activity anywhere. 'What's the matter? Why is everyone still asleep?'

'Hektor had a hard day yesterday too. A herald came at dawn from Troy and asked for a day of truce to mourn and bury the dead. Battle won't be resumed until tomorrow.'

'If then!' I snapped. 'Hektor's back inside the city – he will never come out again.'

'You're wrong,' said Odysseus, eyes flashing. 'I'm right. Hektor thinks he has us now, and Priam won't believe that you mean to take the field again. The ruse with Patrokles worked. So Hektor and his army are still on the plain, not inside Troy.'

'Then tomorrow I can kill him.'

'Tomorrow.' He looked down at me curiously. 'Agamemnon has called a council for noon. The troops are too tired to care what sort of relationship you and Agamemnon enjoy, so will you come?'

I closed my fingers over the cold hand. 'Yes.'

Automedon took my place with Patrokles while I went to the council, still clad in my old leather kilt, still in all my dirt. I sat down beside Nestor, glancing at him with a mute question; Antilochos was present. So was Meriones.

'Antilochos guessed from something you said to him yesterday,' the old man whispered. 'Meriones guessed from listening to Idomeneus curse during the battle. We decided the best thing we could do was to admit both of them into our full confidence, and bind them with the same oath.'

'And Ajax? Has he guessed?'

'No.'

Agamemnon was a worried man. 'Our losses have been appalling,' he said gloomily. 'As far as I can ascertain, we've suffered the loss of fifteen thousand dead or wounded since we joined battle with Hektor outside the walls.'

Nestor shook his white head, his glossy beard straying over his hands. 'Appalling is putting it mildly! Oh, if only we had Herakles, Theseus, Peleus and Telamon, Tydeus, Atreus and Kadmos! I tell you, men are not what they used to be. Myrmidons or no, Herakles and Theseus would have carried all before them.' He wiped his eyes with his beringed fingers. Poor old man. He had lost two sons on the field.

For once Odysseus was angry. He jumped to his feet. 'I told you!' he said fiercely. 'I told you in no uncertain terms what we'd have to endure before we could see the first glimmering of success! Nestor, Agamemnon, why are you whining? To our fifteen thousand casualties, Hektor has suffered twenty-one thousand! Stop woolgathering, all of you! None of those legendary Heroes could have done half what Ajax did – what everyone present here did! Yes, the Trojans fought well! Did you expect anything else? But Hektor's the one who holds them together. If Hektor dies, their spirit will die. And where are their reinforcements? Where's Penthesileia? Where's Memnon? Hektor hasn't any fresh troops to put on the field tomorrow, whereas we have nearly fifteen thousand Thessalians, and they include seven thousand Myrmidons. Tomorrow we're going to defeat the Trojans. We may not get inside the city, but we'll reduce its people to the last stages of utter despair. Hektor will be on the field tomorrow, and Achilles will have his chance.' He looked at me complacently. 'My property is on you, Achilles.'

'I'll bet it is!' said Antilochos nastily. 'Maybe I've seen through your scheme because I didn't listen to your proposing it. I heard at second hand, from my father.'

Odysseus was suddenly watchful, lids lowered.

'The foundation of your scheme was that Patrokles should die. Why did you insist so emphatically that Achilles himself must stay out of things even after the Myrmidons were let join the fight? Was it truly to make Priam think that Achilles would never bend? Or was it to insult Hektor with an inferior man in Patrokles? The moment Patrokles assumed the command, he was a dead man. Hektor would have him, nothing surer. And Hektor did have him. Patrokles died. As you always intended he should, Odysseus.'

I came to my feet, my thick skull burst open by Antilochos's words. My hands reached for Odysseus, itching to break his neck. But then they fell. I sat down limply. It hadn't been Odysseus's idea to dress Patrokles in my armour. That was my own idea. And who can say what might have happened had Patrokles taken the field as himself? How could I blame Odysseus? The fault was mine.

'You're both right and wrong, Antilochos,' said Odysseus, pretending I had never moved. 'How could I possibly know Patrokles would die? A man's fate in battle isn't in our hands. It's in the hands of the Gods. Why did he trip? Isn't it possible one of the Trojan God partisans stuck a foot out? I'm just a mortal man, Antilochos. I can't predict the future.'

Agamemnon got up. 'I would remind all of you that you swore an oath to stick to Odysseus's plan. Achilles knew what he was doing when he took it. So did I. So did we all. We weren't coerced, or dazzled, or fooled. We decided to go with Odysseus because we had no better alternative. Nor were we likely to think of a better alternative. Have you forgotten how we railed and chafed at the sight of Hektor sitting safely inside Troy's walls? Have you forgotten that it's Priam who rules Troy, not Hektor? All of this was designed to deal with Priam far more than with Hektor. We knew the price. We elected to pay it. There's no more to say.'

He looked sternly at me. 'Hold yourselves ready for battle at dawn tomorrow. I'll call a public assembly, and in front of our officers I will return Brise to you, Achilles. I will also swear that I had no congress with her. Is that clear?'

How old he looked, how very tired. The hair which had been sparsely sprinkled with white ten years ago now displayed broad silver ribbons amid its darkness, and a pure white streak ran down each side of his beard. My arm about Antilochos, still trembling, I got up wearily and went back to Patrokles.

I sat down in the dust beside the bier and took his stiff hand from Automedon. The afternoon passed like water falling one drop after another into the well of time. My grief was wearing away, but my guilt never would. Grief is natural; guilt is self-inflicted. The future cures grief; but only death can cure guilt. Those were the kinds of things I thought about.

The sun was setting pink and softly liquid across the far Hellespont shore before anyone came to disturb me: Odysseus, his face obscured by shadows, his eyes sunken, his hands slack by his sides. With a great sigh he squatted down in the dust near me, linked his hands across his knees and rested on his heels. For a long time we didn't speak; his hair was flame in the last of the sun, his profile rimmed in amber purity against the dusk. He looked, I thought, godlike.

'What armour will you wear tomorrow, Achilles?'

'My bronze with the gold trim.'

'A good set, but I would dower you with a better.' His head turned, he stared at me gravely. 'How do you feel about me? You wanted to break my neck when that boy spoke in council, but then you changed your mind.'

'I feel as always. That only some future generation will be able to judge what you are, Odysseus. You don't belong to our times.'

He dipped his head, toyed with the dust. 'I cost you a suit of precious armour which Hektor will take great pleasure in wearing, hoping to eclipse you in every way. But I have a golden suit which will fit you. It belonged to Minos. Would you take it?'

I stared at him curiously. 'How did it come to you?'

He was tracing squiggles in the dust; above one he drew a house, above another a horse, above a third a man. 'Grocery lists. Nestor has grocery-list symbols.' He frowned and obliterated what he had drawn with his palm. 'No, symbols are not enough. We need something else – something which can transmit ideas, thoughts owning no shape, the wings inside the mind ... Have you heard the tales men whisper about me? That I'm no true son of Laertes? That I was got on his wife, my mother, by Sisyphos?'

'Yes, I've heard them.'

'They're true, Achilles. And a good thing at that! Were Laertes my sire, Greece would have been the poorer. I don't openly acknowledge my paternity because my barons would have me off the Ithakan throne in a wink if I did. But I digress. I only wanted you to understand that the armour was come by dishonestly. Sisyphos stole it from Deukalion of Crete and gave it to my mother as a token of his love. Will you wear something dishonestly got?'

'Gladly.'

'I'll bring it at dawn, then. One thing more.'

'What?'

'Don't say I gave it you. Tell everyone it's a gift from our Gods – that your mother asked Hephaistos to weld it through

the night in his eternal fires so that you could take the field as
befits the son of a Goddess.'

'If you wish it, that's what I'll say.'

I slept a little, slumped on my knees against the side of the bier,
a restless and haunted sleep. Odysseus woke me just before the
first light and took me to his house, where a great linen-
shrouded bundle rested on a table. I unwrapped it joylessly,
imagining that it would be a good, workmanlike suit – in gold,
admittedly, but nothing like the suit Hektor now wore. My
father and I had always assumed that was the best outfit Minos
owned.

Perhaps it was, but the suit Odysseus gave me was far the
better of the two. I rapped its flawless gold with my knuckles to
find that it gave off a dull, heavy sound completely unlike the
ring of many layers. Curious, I turned the enormously heavy
shield over to discover that it wasn't made like other shields,
many-layered and thick. There seemed to be two layers only,
an outer plating of gold covering a single layer of a dark grey
material which gave off no glitter or reflection in the lamplight.

I had heard of it, but never seen it before save in the head of
my spear, Old Pelion: men called it hardened iron. But I had
not dreamed it existed in quantities sufficient to make a full
suit of armour the size of this one. Every item was made of the
same metal, each plated with gold.

'Daidalos made it three hundred years ago,' said Odysseus.
'He's the only man in history who knew how to harden iron, to
turn it in the crucible with sand so that it takes up some of the
sand and becomes far harder than bronze. He collected lumps
of raw iron until he had enough to cast this suit, then he
hammered the gold over it afterwards. If a spear gashes the
surface, the gold can be smoothed. See? The figures are cast in
the iron, not fashioned in the gold.'

'It belonged to *Minos*?'

'Yes, to that Minos who with his brother Rhadamanthos and

your grandfather Aiakos sits in Hades to judge the dead as they congregate about the shores of Acheron.'

'I can't thank you enough. When my days are over and I stand before those judges, take the suit back, give it to your son.'

Odysseus laughed. 'Telemachos? No, he'll never fill it. Give it to *your* son.'

'They'll want to bury me in it. It's up to you to see that Neoptolemos gets it. Bury me in a robe.'

'If you want, Achilles.'

Automedon helped me dress for war while the house women stood against the wall muttering prayers and charms to ward off evil and infuse the armour with power. Whichever way I moved, I flashed as brightly as Helios.

Agamemnon spoke at the assembly of our army's officers, who stood wooden-faced. Then it was my turn to accept the imperial humble pie, after which Nestor returned Brise to me; there was no sign of Chryse, but I didn't think she had been sent to Troy. At the end we dispersed to eat: a waste of precious time.

Her head up, Brise walked beside me silently. She looked ill and worn, more upset than when she had walked with me out of the burning ruins of Lyrnessos. Inside the Myrmidon stockade we passed Patrokles on his bier; he had been moved there because of the assembly. She flinched, shuddered.

'Come away, Brise.'

'He fought when you would not?'

'Yes. Hektor killed him.'

Seeking a sign of softness, I looked into her face. She smiled a smile of pure love.

'Dearest Achilles, you're so tired! I know how much he meant to you, but you grieve too much.'

'He died despising me. He threw our friendship away.'

'Then he didn't really know you.'

'I can't explain to you either.'

'You don't need to. Whatever you do, Achilles, is right.'

*

We marched out across the causeways and formed up on the plain in the damp new sunlight. The air was soft, the breeze like the caress of teased wool before it is spun. They fronted us, rank on rank on rank, as we must have looked to them. Excitement was a fist rammed down my throat, my knuckles when I chanced to see them were white on Old Pelion's worn dark shaft. I had given Patrokles my armour, but not Old Pelion.

Hektor came thundering in from his right wing in a chariot drawn by three black stallions, swaying a little with the motion of the car, wearing my armour superbly. I noticed that he had added scarlet to the golden plumes of the helmet. He drew up opposite me; we gazed at each other hungrily. The challenge was implicit. Odysseus had won his gamble. Only one of us would leave the field alive, we both knew it.

The silence was peculiar. Neither army emitted a sound, not the snort of a horse nor the rattle of a shield, as we stood waiting for the horns and drums to start. I was finding this new armour very heavy; it would take time to grow used to it, know how best to manoeuvre in it. Hektor would have to wait.

The drums rolled, the horns blared, and the Daughter of Fate tossed her shears into the strip of bare ground between Hektor and me. Even as I shrieked my war cry Automedon was lashing my car forwards, but Hektor swerved aside and was off down his lines before we met. Blocked by a seething mass of infantry, I knew no hope of following, even had I wanted to. My spear rose and fell, dripping the blood of Trojans; I felt nothing beyond the fascination of killing. Not even my vow to Patrokles mattered.

I heard a familiar war cry and saw another chariot forcing its way through the press, Aineas lunging coolly, holding onto his temper as he found himself opposing neatly dodging Myrmidons. I gave my own cry. He heard me and saluted me, jumped down at once for the duel. His first spear-cast I caught on my shield, the vibration jarring me to the marrow, but that magical metal thwarted the lance completely. It fell to earth, its head

363

mangled. Old Pelion flew in a beautiful arc over the heads of the men between us, high and true. Aineas saw the tip coming at his throat, flung up his shield and ducked. My beloved spear passed clean through the hide and metal just above his head, tipped the shield over, and pinned Aineas beneath it. Sword drawn, I pushed through my men, intent upon reaching him before he could wriggle free. His Dardanians backed before our charge and the smile of triumph was already on my face when I experienced a surge, that frustrating, maddening phenomenon which happens occasionally when a huge number of men are jammed tightly together. It was as if suddenly a mighty wave arose in a sea of tiny ripples, sweeping down the line from end to end; men crashed into each other like a row of bricks set falling.

Almost knocked off my feet, borne along like flotsam on that living wave of men, I cried in despair because I had lost Aineas. By the time I struggled free he had gone and I was a hundred paces further down the line. Calling the Myrmidons into proper formation, I worked my way back; when I reached the spot I found Old Pelion still nailing his shield to the ground, undisturbed. I wrenched my spear out and tossed the shield to one of my baggage noncombatants.

Shortly afterwards I banished Automedon and the chariot to the back of the field, giving Old Pelion into his care. This was axe work. Ah, what a weapon in a crush! The Myrmidons kept with me and we were unbeatable. But no matter how frantic the action, I never ceased to look for Hektor. Whom I found just after I killed a man wearing the insignia of a son of Priam's. Not far away, face twisted by the fate of his brother, Hektor watched. Our eyes met; the field seemed not to exist. I read satisfaction in his sombre contemplation as we saw each other's faces for the first time. We drew closer and closer, striking down our foes with one thought in mind: to meet, to be near enough to touch. Then came another surge. Something crushed my side and I almost lost my footing as I was hurled back through the ranks. Men fell and were mashed to pulp, but

I wept because Hektor was lost to me. From grief I passed to anger and a killing frenzy.

The red furore lifted when there were no more than a handful of purple plumes opposing me and the torn, trampled grass was visible between their feet. The Trojans had disappeared; I dealt with stragglers. They backed off in an orderly withdrawal, their leaders mounted once more in their cars, and Agamemnon let them go, content for the moment to re-form his own lines. My chariot appeared from nowhere, and I climbed up beside Automedon.

'Find Agamemnon,' I panted, letting my shield drop to the floor struts with a sigh of relief. A wonderful protection, but almost too heavy.

All the leaders had come in. I pulled up between Diomedes and Idomeneus. Tasting victory, Agamemnon was the King of Kings again. A piece of linen was bound about a cut in his forearm and dripped slow crimson to the earth, but he seemed not to notice.

'They're in full retreat,' Odysseus was saying. 'However, there's no sign that they intend to take refuge inside the city – not yet, at any rate. Hektor thinks there's still a chance to win. We needn't hurry.' He glanced up at Agamemnon with the look that said he had just had a bright idea. 'Sire, what if we do what we did for nine years? What if we split our army into two and try to drive a wedge through the middle of their ranks? About a third of a league from here Skamander takes a big loop inwards to the city walls. Hektor's already heading that way. If we can manoeuvre them so that they're stretched out across the neck of the loop, we could use the Second Army to push half of them at least into the maw of the loop, while the rest of us continue to drive their other half in the direction of Troy. We won't accomplish much with those running for Troy, but we can slaughter those shut up in the arms of Skamander.'

It was a very good plan, and Agamemnon was not slow to realise that. 'Agreed. Achilles and Ajax, take whatever units you prefer from Second Army days and deal with whatever Trojans you can trap inside the Skamander loop.'

I looked very slightly mutinous. 'Only if you make sure that Hektor doesn't escape into the city.'

'Agreed,' said Agamemnon at once.

They fell into the trap like little fishes into a net. We drew up with the Trojans as they came level with the neck of the loop in the river, whereupon Agamemnon charged his infantry straight through their middle ranks, scattering them. They had no hope of continuing an orderly retreat while coping with the huge mass of men he deployed. On the left Ajax and I held our forces back until a good half of the fleeing Trojans realised they had run into a blind end, then we swung across their only avenue of escape. I massed my infantry and led them into the loop, Ajax bellowing off to the right as he did the same. The Trojans panicked, milled about helplessly, fell ever backwards until their hind ranks stood on the brink of the river. The weight of men still retreating before us pushed them inexorably on; like sheep on the edge of a cliff, those in the rear began to tumble into the foul water.

The old God Skamander did half our work for us; while Ajax and I hacked them to shrill pleas for mercy, he drowned them in hundreds. From my chariot I saw the waters running clearer and more strongly than usual; Skamander was in full spate. Those who lost their footing on the bank had no hope of regaining their feet to fight the current, handicapped as they were by armour and panic. But *why* was Skamander in full spate? There had been no rain. Then I found the time to look towards Mount Ida; the sky above it was roiling with thunderheads, and there were opaque curtains of rain lying like cleavers across the foothills beyond Troy, chopping them off.

I gave Old Pelion to Automedon and got down with my axe in my hands, the shield a weight I couldn't bear to carry. I would have to do without one, and there was no Patrokles to follow me. But before I waded into the fray I remembered to call up one of the baggage noncombatants; I owed Patrokles twelve noble Trojan youths for his tomb. Easily gathered in such a debacle. That awful, mindless lust for other men's blood swept over me again, and I could not find enough Trojans to satiate it. At the river bank I didn't pause, waded out instead after the few terrified men I had cornered. The weight of my iron armour anchored me in the increasing thrust of the current; I slew until Skamander ran ever redder.

One Trojan tried to make a duel of it. He called himself Asteropaios; a high nobleman of Troy at least, for he wore gilded bronze. His was very much the advantage, as he stood on the bank while I was waist deep in the river, with nothing save my axe against his handful of spears. But never think Achilles witless! As he readied himself to cast his first missile I took my axe by the end of its handle and flung it at him like a throwing dagger. He loosed his spear, but the sight of that thing whopping through the air spoiled his aim. Over and over the axe turned, flashing in the sun. Then it took him full in the chest, its jaws deep in his flesh. He lived no more than an instant, then pitched forward and dropped like a stone into the water, face down.

Intending to prise the axe free, I waded to him and turned him over. But the head was rooted in him to its handle, the shattered metal of his cuirass tangled around it. So intent was I that I hardly noticed the dull roaring in my ears, or felt the water bucking like a newly broken stallion. Very suddenly the water was up to my armpits and Asteropaios was bobbing as lightly as a sliver of bark. I grasped his arm and forced him close to me in a mock embrace, using my own body to steady him as I worked at the axe. The roar was now a huge thunder, and I had to fight to keep my footing. At last the axe came free; I snaked its thong fast about my wrist, afraid of losing it. The River God was shouting his anger to me; it seemed he preferred that his own people defile him with their wastes than I defile him with their blood.

A wall of water bore down on me like a landslide. Even Ajax

or Herakles could not have withstood it. Ah, there! An over-hanging branch on an elm tree! I leaped for it. My fingers found leaves and struggled those few enormous handspans higher until I had solid wood in my grasp; the branch bent over with me as I fell back into the torrent.

For an instant the wall hovered over me like some watery arm grown by the God, then he flung it down on my head with all the fury he could muster. I sucked in a last great breath of air before the world turned liquid, before I was pushed and pulled in a hundred directions at once by a strength far superior to my own. My chest was almost to bursting, both my hands clung of themselves to the elm branch; I thought in agony of the sun and the sky, and wept within my heart at the bitter irony of being defeated by a river. I had used too much of myself grieving for Patrokles and killing Trojans, and that iron armour was a death.

I prayed to the dryad who lived in the elm tree, but the water rolled over my head unabated; then the dryad or some other sprite heard me, and my head broke the surface. I gulped air gluttonously, shook Skamander from my eyes and looked about me desperately. The bank which had been almost close enough to touch was gone. I seized fresh hold of the elm, but the dryad deserted me. The last of the bank came away and left the old tree's mighty roots bare. My own body in all that iron formed the extra load; the mass of leaves and branches tilted over, and the elm took the plunge into the river with scarcely a sound of anguish above the howling of the flood.

I kept hold of the branch, wondering if Skamander would be strong enough to sweep everything downstream. But the elm remained with its head in the water, a dam which held back the debris moving towards our camp and the Myrmidon stockade. Bodies piled up against its bulk like brown blossoms with crimson throats, purple plumes wreathed around the green of its trees, hands floated white and repulsively useless.

I let go the branch and commenced wading to the edge of the river, which was lower since the bank had collapsed, but not low enough. Time and time again the unrelenting flood sucked my feet away from their precarious grip on the slimy river bottom; time and time again my head went under. But I fought back, struggling ever closer to my goal. I actually managed to get my hands on a clump of grass, only to watch it part from the saturated soil. I went under, floundered upright and despaired. The earth from Skamander's vanished bank trickling dark through my fingers, I raised my arms to the skies and prayed to the Lord of All.

'Father, Father, let me live long enough to kill Hektor!'

He heard me. He answered me. His awesome head bent down suddenly from the illimitable distances of the heavens; for some few moments he loved me sufficiently to forgive me my sin and my pride, perhaps remembering only that I was the grandson of his son, Aiakos. I felt his presence in all my being and thought I saw the fire-shot shadow of his monstrous hand hover dark over the river. Skamander sighed his submission to the Power which rules Gods as well as men. One moment I was going to die, the next I found the water a trickle around my ankles, had to jump aside as the elm collapsed into the mud.

The opposite, higher bank had crumbled; Skamander dissipated his strength in a thin sheet across the plain, a silver benison the thirsty soil drank in one gulp.

I staggered out of the river bed and sat exhausted on the drowned grass. Above me Phoibos's chariot stood at a little past its zenith; we had been fighting for half of its journey across the vault. Wondering where the rest of my army was, I came back to reality in the shame of knowing I had lusted to kill so much that I had completely ignored my men. Would I ever learn? Or was my lust to kill a part of the madness I had surely inherited from my mother?

Shouts sounded. The Myrmidons were marching towards me, and in the distance Ajax was re-forming his forces. Greeks everywhere, but not one Trojan. I climbed aboard my car, grinning at Automedon.

'Take me to Ajax, old friend.'

369

He was standing with a spear in one massive hand, his eyes dreamy. I got down, water still running off me.

'What happened to you?' he asked.

'I had a wrestling match with the God Skamander.'

'Well, you won. He's spent.'

'How many Trojans survived our ambush?'

'Not many,' he said serenely. 'Between the pair of us we've managed to kill fifteen thousand of them. Perhaps as many again got back to Hektor's army. You did good work, Achilles. You have a thirst for the blood of other men even I cannot match.'

'I'd rather your love than my lust.'

'Time to get back to Agamemnon,' he said, not understanding. 'I brought my car today.'

I rode beside him in his – well, cart is a better word than car, for it needed four wheels – while Teukros travelled in my car with Automedon.

'Something tells me that Priam has ordered the Skaian Gate opened,' I said, pointing towards the walls.

Ajax growled. As we drew closer it was too plain that I was right. The Skaian Gate was open and Hektor's army streamed in ahead of Agamemnon, thwarted by the sheer number of Trojans clustered about the entrance. I glanced sideways at Ajax, showing my teeth.

'Hades take them, Hektor is in!' he snarled.

'Hektor belongs to me, Ajax. You had your chance.'

'I know it, little cousin.'

We trundled into the midst of Agamemnon's forces and went to seek him. As usual, standing with Odysseus and Nestor. Frowning.

'They're closing the gate,' I said.

'Hektor packed them in so tightly we had no hope of turning them away – and no chance to attempt an assault ourselves. Most of them made it inside. Two detachments deliberately elected to remain shut out. Diomedes is hammering them into submission,' said Agamemnon.

'What of Hektor himself?'

'Gone inside, I think. No one's seen him.'

'The cur! He knew I wanted him!'

Some others were coming up: Idomeneus, Menelaos, Menestheus and Machaon. Together we watched Diomedes finish off those who had volunteered to stay outside – sensible men, for when they were courting annihilation they surrendered. Liking their courage and their discipline, Diomedes took them prisoner rather than kill them. He came towards us then, jubilant.

'Fifteen thousand of them lost by Skamander,' said Ajax.

'While we lost not a man more than a thousand,' said Odysseus.

A great sigh came from the resting soldiers behind us, and a shriek of such awful agony from the top of the watchtower that we ceased to laugh.

'Look!' Nestor's bony finger pointed, shaking.

Slowly we turned. Hektor stood leaning on the bronze bosses of the gate, his shield propped against it, two spears in his hand. He wore my golden armour with the alien scarlet among the helmet's plume, and the bright purple baldric Ajax had given him shimmered with amethysts. I, who had never seen myself in that suit, saw how well it became any man who wore it – and fitted it. I should have known the moment I stood back to look at Patrokles that I had strapped him into his doom.

Hektor picked up his shield and walked a few paces forward. 'Achilles!' he called. 'I have stayed to meet you!'

My eyes met Ajax's, who nodded. I took my shield and Old Pelion from Automedon, gave him the axe. Hektor was no man to insult with an axe.

My throat tight with a trembling joy, I stepped out of the ranks of the Kings and went to meet him with measured step, like a man going to the sacrifice; I did not raise my spear and nor did he. Three paces from each other we halted, each of us intent on discovering what kind of man the other was, we who had never seen each other closer than a spear-cast. We had to speak before the duel began, and edged so close together that we could have touched. I looked into the steadfast darkness of his eyes and learned that he was much the same kind of man as I. *Except that, Achilles, his spirit is untainted. He is the perfect warrior.*

I loved him far better than I loved myself, better than Patrokles or Brise or my father, for he was myself in another body; he was the harbinger of death, whether he himself dealt me the killing blow, or whether I lingered on a few days more until some other Trojan cut me down. One of us had to die in the duel, the other soon after, for so it had been decided when the strands of our destinies were interwoven.

'These many years, Achilles,' he commenced, then stopped, as if he could not express what he felt in words.

'Hektor son of Priam, I wish we might have called each other friend. But the blood between us cannot be washed away.'

'Better to be killed by an enemy than a friend,' he said. 'How many perished by Skamander?'

'Fifteen thousand. Troy will fall.'

'Only after I am dead. I will not have eyes to see it.'

'Nor I.'

'We were born for war alone. War's outcome does not concern us, and I am pleased it is so.'

'Is your son of an age to avenge you, Hektor?'

'No.'

'Then I have the edge on you. My son will come to Troy to avenge me, whereas Odysseus will see that your son never lives long enough to weep over his lack of years.'

His face twisted. 'Helen warned me to beware of Odysseus. Is he the son of a God?'

'No. He's the son of a villain. I would call him the spirit of Greece.'

'I wish I could warn my father of him.'

'You will not live to do so.'

'I might beat you, Achilles.'

'If you do, Agamemnon will order you cut down.'

He thought for a moment. 'You leave women to grieve for you? A father?'

'I won't die unmourned.'

And in that moment our love burned more fiercely than our hate; I put out my hand quickly, before the wellsprings of ardour could die in me. He took my wrist in his.

'Why did you stay to meet me?' I asked, holding him.

His fingers tightened, pain darkened his face. 'How could I go within? How could I look at my father, knowing it was my rashness and stupidity lost all those thousands of his people? I should have retreated into Troy the day I killed your friend, the one who wore this armour. Polydamas warned me, but I took no notice. I wanted to meet you. That's the true reason why I kept our army on the plain.' He stepped back, relinquishing my arm, his face an enemy's again. 'I've been watching you, Achilles, in that very pretty gold suit, and I've decided it must be solid gold. It weighs you down. The suit I wear is much lighter. So before we clash swords, let's have a race.'

He took to his heels on the last word, leaving me to stand flat footed for a moment before I started after him. Clever, but a mistake, Hektor! Why should I try to catch you? He would have to turn and confront me not far off. A quarter of a league from the Skaian Gate in the direction of our camp – his direction – the Trojan walls flung a huge buttress southwestwards, and there the Greek army cut him off.

My breath was coming easily; perhaps my wrestle with old Skamander had given me a second wind. He turned, I stopped.

'Achilles!' he shouted. 'If I slay you I give you my oath that I will return your body to your men undefiled! Give me your oath that you'll do the same for me!'

'No! I've sworn to give your body to Patrokles!'

There was a rush of wind about my head, dust blew into my eyes. Hektor was already raising his arm, Old Pelion was already leaving my hand. His spear-cast was true, the shaft bouncing off the centre of my shield, whereas Old Pelion fell limply at my own feet. Hektor cast his second missile before I could bend to pick up Old Pelion, but the capricious wind veered again. I never did pick up Old Pelion. Hektor drew his sword from Ajax's purple baldric and charged me. Now the dilemma: keep my shield and be protected from a brilliant adversary, or toss it away to fight unencumbered? The armour I could manage, but the shield was far too heavy. So I flung it from me and faced him with drawn sword. Even charging he was capable of halting; he threw away his shield too.

When we met we discovered the hugeness of the pleasure in a perfect match. I stopped the downward chop of his blade with my own; our arms stood rigid while neither of us yielded; we sprang back in the same instant and circled, each looking for an opening. The swords whistled a deathsong as they carved the air. I gave him a lightning glance up his left arm when he lunged, but in the same passage of arms he took the leather covering my thigh and ripped the flesh underneath. Both blooded, neither of us paused to consider our wounds; we were too eager to finish it. Thrust after thrust the blades flashed, descended, met a parry, went at it again.

Seeking an opening, I shifted ground cautiously. Hektor was a shade smaller than I, therefore my armour must contain a flaw, a place where he wasn't adequately protected. But where? When I nearly reached his chest he moved aside quickly, and as he lifted his arm I noticed that the cuirass gaped away from the side of his neck, where the helmet didn't come down far enough. I stepped back, making him follow me, manoeuvring for a better stance. Then it happened, that irksome weakness in the tendons at the back of my right heel which twisted the foot, made me stumble. But even as I gasped in horror my body was compensating, keeping me upright. And laying me wide open for Hektor's sword.

He saw his chance immediately, was on me with the speed of a striking serpent, his blade raised high to deal me the death blow, his mouth gaping open in a wild scream of joy. His cuirass – *my* cuirass – moved away from the left side of his neck. I lunged at him at the same moment. Somehow my arm withstood the massive power of his arm, his sword descending. It met mine with a clang and flew aside. My blade passed on without deviation to bury itself in the left side of his neck between cuirass and helm.

Taking my sword with him, he fell so fast I had no chance to help lower him to earth. I let the crosspiece go as if it glowed red hot, seeing him at my feet, not dead yet for all it was a mortal wound. His great dark eyes stared up at me, speaking his knowledge, his acceptance. The blade must have severed all the blood vessels in its path and buried itself in bone, but because it still remained embedded he could not die. He moved his hands slowly, jerkily, until they were clamped fast about the wickedly sharp blade. Terrified that he meant to pull it out before I was ready – would I ever be ready? – I dropped to my knees beside him. But he lay without moving now, gasping hard, his knuckles white about the sword, his lacerated hands trickling blood.

'You fought well,' I said.

His lips moved; he rolled his head a little to one side with the effort of trying to speak, and blood spurted viciously. My hands covered in it, I took his face between them. The helm rolled off and his coiled braid of black hair flopped into the dust, its end beginning to unravel.

'The greatest pleasure would have been to fight with you, not against you,' I said, wishing I knew what he wanted to hear me say. Anything. Or almost anything.

His eyes were bright and knowing. A thin rivulet of blood flowed from one corner of his mouth; his time was ebbing rapidly, yet I couldn't bear the thought of his dying.

'Achilles?'

I could hardly hear my name, and bent until my ear almost touched his lips. 'What is it?'

'Give my body ... Back to my father ...'

Almost anything, but not that. 'I can't, Hektor. I vowed you to Patrokles.'

'Give me back ... If I go to Patrokles ... Your own body ... Will feed the dogs of Troy.'

'What must be, will be. I have sworn.'

'Then it is ... Finished.'

He writhed with a strength God given and his hands tightened their hold; with the last of himself he drew forth the blade. His eyes grew instantly dim, the rattle sounded in his throat, pink foam fluffed about his nostrils, and he died.

His head still between my hands, I knelt without moving. The whole world was struck to silence. The battlements far above me were as still as Hektor lying dead, nor came any murmur from Agamemnon's army at my back. How beautiful he was, this my Trojan twin, my better half. And how much I mourned his going – the pain! The grief!

'Why do you love him, Achilles, when he murdered me?'

I jumped to my feet, heart pounding. The voice of Patrokles had spoken within me! Hektor was dead. I had vowed to kill him, and now, instead of exulting, I wept. I wept! While Patrokles lay without the price of the ferry across the River.

My movement dispelled the silence. A hideous shriek of despair spiralled down from the watchtower, Priam protesting the death of his most beloved son. Others took it up; the air became filled with women's wails, men crying on their Gods, the dull thrumming of fists on breasts like funeral drums, and behind me Agamemnon's army cheering, cheering, cheering.

I began to strip the armour from Hektor savagely, tearing out the unwelcome sorrow in my heart, willing the instinct to mourn out of my marrow with a curse for every piece I ripped away. When I had done the Kings came to form a circle about his naked body, Agamemnon staring down at his dead face with a sneer. He lifted the spear he carried and buried it in Hektor's side; all the others followed his lead, dealing the poor defenceless warrior the blows they couldn't while he lived.

Sickened, I turned away – a chance to fan my rage white-hot and so dry my tears. When I swung round again I discovered that only Ajax had refrained from doing Hektor's body insult.

How could men call him a lubber when he alone understood? I pushed Agamemnon and the rest away roughly.

'Hektor belongs to me. Take your weapons and go!'

Suddenly shamed, they backed off, looking like nothing so much as a pack of furtive curs hunted from their stolen meal.

I took the purple baldric from its buckle on the cuirass and drew my dagger. Then I slit the thin parts at the back of his heels and threaded the dyed, encrusted leather through, while Ajax, face stolid, watched the end of his gift. Automedon drove my chariot up; I secured the baldric to the back of it.

'Get down,' I told Automedon. 'I'll drive myself.'

My three white horses were smelling death and plunging, but when I wrapped the reins about my waist they quietened. Back and forth beneath the watchtower I drove the car to an accompaniment of grief from the top of Troy's walls and jubilation from King Agamemnon's army.

Hektor's hair came unbraided and dragged loose across the trodden earth until it was matted and grey; his arms trailed limply backwards on either side of his head. Twelve times in all I whipped my horses between the watchtower and the Skaian Gate, parading the hope of Troy beneath its very walls, proclaiming the inevitability of our victory. Then I drove to the beach.

Patrokles lay still and shrouded on his bier. Three times I drove around the square, then dismounted, cut the baldric free. To pick up Hektor's limp form in my arms was easy, yet somehow to fling it away, to let it lie ungainly at the foot of the bier, was enormously difficult. Yet I did it. Brise darted away, frightened. I sat down in her place, my head between my knees, and began to weep again.

'Achilles, come home,' she said.

Intending to refuse, I looked up. She too had suffered; I could not let her suffer more. So I got up, still weeping, and walked with her to my house. She sat me down in a chair and gave me a cloth to wipe my face, a bowl to wash the blood off my hands, wine to compose me. Somehow she managed to remove that iron armour, then dressed the wound on my thigh.

When she began to pull at my padded shift I stopped her. 'Leave me,' I said.

'Let me bathe you properly.'

'I cannot while Patrokles lies unburied.'

'Patrokles has become your evil spirit,' she said quietly, 'and that is to mock what he was in life.'

With a burning look of reproach I quit the house, walked not to the square where Patrokles lay, but down to the shingle, and there dropped like another stone.

My sleep was a trance of utter peace until into the featureless abyss wherein I dwelled a thready whiteness came, glittering with unearthly light, the blackness of the abyss looming through its tenuous coils. From the distance it moved ever closer inward to the centre of my mind, gathering form and opacity as it came, until it stood before the core of my spirit in its final shape. The steady blue eyes of Patrokles stared into my nakedness. His soft mouth was harsh, just as I remembered it last, and his yellow hair was streaked with red.

'Achilles, Achilles,' he whispered in a voice that was his and yet not his, mournful and chill, 'how can you sleep while I still lie unburied, unable to cross the River? Free me! Let me loose from my clay! How can you sleep while I am unburied?'

I reached my arms out to him to plead for his understanding, trying to tell him why I had let him fight in my place, babbling explanations one after another. I took him into my arms and my fingers closed on nothing; he shrank and dribbled away in the darkness until the last chirrup of his bat voice faded, until the last lingering thread of his luminescence faded into nothing. Nothing! *Nothing!*

I screamed. And woke still screaming, to find a dozen of my Myrmidons pinning me down. Shaking them off impatiently, I stumbled back between the ships, men stirring and asking each other what was that awful noise?, the grey light of dawn showing me the way.

A night wind had blown the shroud onto the ground; the Myrmidons who formed his guard of honour had not dared approach close enough to retrieve it. So when I staggered into the square I saw Patrokles himself. Sleeping. Dreaming. So peaceful, so benign. A facsimile. I had just seen the real Patrokles, and knew from his lips that he would never forgive me. That heart which had given so generously from the days of our shared adolescence was as cold and hard as marble. Why then was the facsimile's face so tender, so gentle? Could such a face belong to the shade haunting my sleep? Did men truly change so much in death?

My foot touched something chilly; I shivered uncontrollably as I looked down on Hektor sprawled just as I had left him the evening before, his legs twisted up as if they were broken, his mouth and his eyes wide open, his emptied white flesh showing the pink mouths of a dozen wounds, the one at his neck gaping like a gill.

I turned away as Myrmidons came from all directions, wakened by the sound of their leader screaming like one demented. They were led by Automedon.

'Achilles, it's time to bury him.'

'More than time.'

We carried Patrokles across the waters of Skamander on a raft, and then walked garbed for war with his corpse on his shield shoulder high in our midst. I stood behind the shield with his head in the palm of my right hand as his chief mourner, the whole army dotting the cliffs and the beach for two leagues around to witness the Myrmidons put him in his tomb.

We bore Patrokles into the corbelled cavern and laid him tenderly on the ivory death car, clad in the armour he had worn to his death, his body covered in locks of our hair, his spears and all his personal belongings on gold tripods about the painted walls. I glanced towards the roof, wondering how long it would be before I too lay there. Not long, so the oracles said.

The priest fitted the mask of gold over his face and tied the strings under his head, arranged his gold gauntleted hands on his thighs, their fingers meeting over the sword. The words were chanted, the libations poured out on the ground. Then one by one the twelve Trojan youths were held over a huge golden cup standing on a tripod at the foot of the death car, and their throats were cut. We sealed up the entrance to the tomb and marched back to the camp, to the assembly ground in front of Agamemnon's house, where funeral games were always held. I brought out the prizes and went through the misery of presenting them to the winners, then, while the rest feasted, I returned to my own house alone.

Hektor lay now in the dust outside my door, removed there after we had taken Patrokles from his bier; the memory of that wraith out of my dreams had urged me to inter him with Patrokles like a mongrel dog at the foot of a hero, but I couldn't do it. I broke my vow to my oldest and dearest friend – *my lover!* – to keep Hektor with me instead. Patrokles had the price of the ferry ride: twelve noble Trojan youths. Enough and more than enough.

I clapped my hands; the serving women came running. 'Heat water, bring the anointing oils, send for the chief embalmer. I want Prince Hektor prepared for burial.'

I carried him to a small storehouse nearby and laid him on a stone slab the right height for the women to minister to him. But *I* straightened his limbs, *I* put my hand on his face to close his eyes. They opened again very slowly, sightless. An awful thing, to watch Hektor's vacant husk. To think of my own.

Brise was sitting waiting for me, hunched in a chair. She glanced at me, but didn't speak for some time. Then she said in a neutral voice, 'I have water ready for your bath, and there's food and wine afterwards. I must light the lamps, it's dusk.'

Oh, if only water had the power to wash away the stains on a spirit! My body was clean again. But my spirit was not.

Brise sat on the couch opposite me while I toyed with the

food, quenched my thirst. I felt as if I had been running like a madman for years.

Then she used the word too. Madman. She said, 'Achilles, why are you behaving like a madman? The world isn't going to cease because Patrokles is dead. There are others still living who love you as much as he did. Automedon. The Myrmidons. I.'

'Go away,' I said wearily.

'When I'm finished. Heal yourself, Achilles, in the only way possible. Stop pandering to Patrokles and give Hektor back to his father. I'm not jealous, I never have been. That you and Patrokles were lovers didn't affect me or my place in your life. But *he* was jealous, and that warped him. You believe he thought you betrayed your ideals. But to Patrokles the real betrayal was your love of me. That's where it started. After that, nothing you did would have been right as far as he was concerned. I'm not condemning him – I'm just speaking the truth. He loved you and he felt you betrayed his love by loving me. And if you could do that, you couldn't be the person he thought you were. It was necessary that he find flaws. He had to feed his own sense of injury.'

'You don't know what you're talking about,' I said.

'Yes, I do. But it isn't Patrokles I want to talk about. I want to talk about Hektor. How can you do this to a man who faced you so bravely and died so well? Give him back to his father! It isn't the real Patrokles who haunts you, it's the Patrokles you've conjured up to drive yourself mad. Forget Patrokles. He was no true friend to you at the last.'

I struck her. Her head snapped back and she fell from the couch to the floor. Horrified, I scooped her up, laid her down to find that she was moving and groaning. I stumbled to a chair, put my head in my hands. Even Brise was a victim of this madness, and madness it was. But how to heal it? How to banish my mother?

Something wrapped itself about my legs, plucked feebly at the hem of my kilt. I lifted my head in terror to see what new visitation had come to plague me and stared confounded at the white head and twisted countenance of an old, old man. Priam. It could be no one else. Priam. As I took my elbows from my knees he seized my hands and began to kiss them, his tears falling on the same skin Hektor's blood had.

'Give him back to me! Give him back! Don't feed him to your dogs! Don't leave him alone and unhallowed! Don't deny him proper mourning! Give him back to me!'

I looked across at Brise, who was sitting upright, her eyes filled with unshed tears.

'Come, sire, sit down,' I said, lifting him and putting him into my chair. 'A king shouldn't have to beg. Sit down.'

Automedon stood in the doorway.

'How did he get here?' I asked, going to him.

'In a mule cart driven by an idiot boy. I mean that literally. A poor creature full of mindless mumbles. The army is still feasting, the guard on the causeway is Myrmidon. The old man said he had business with you. The cart was empty and neither of them was armed, so the guard let them in.'

'Fetch fire, Automedon. Don't breathe a word to anyone of his presence here. Pass that onto the guard, and thank it for me.'

While I waited for the fire – it was cold – I drew up a chair close to his and took his gnarled hands in mine, chafing them. So chilled.

'It took courage to come here, sire.'

'No, none.' His rheumy dark eyes looked into mine. 'Once,' he said, 'I ruled a happy and prosperous kingdom. But then I went wrong. The wrong was in me. In me … You Greeks were sent to punish me for my pride. For my blindness.' His lip trembled, the moistness in his eyes made them glitter. 'No, it took not one scrap of courage to come here. Hektor was the final price.'

'The final price,' I said, unable not to say it, 'will be the fall of Troy.'

'The fall of my dynasty, perhaps, but not the fall of the city. Troy is greater than that, even now.'

'Troy the city will fall.'

'Well, on that we beg to differ, but I hope not on the reason for my coming. Prince Achilles, grant me the body of my son. I will pay a fitting ransom.'

'I require no ransom, King Priam. Take him home,' I said.

He fell on his knees a second time to kiss my hands; my flesh crawled. Nodding to Brise, I disengaged myself. 'Sit down, sire, and break bread with me while I have Hektor readied. Brise, look after our guest.'

As I spoke to Automedon outside I thought of something. 'Ajax's baldric – it belonged to Hektor, whereas the armour didn't. Find it, Automedon, and put it in the cart with him.'

When I returned it was to find Priam recovered, chattering happily to Brise in one of the bewildering mood changes characteristic of the very old, asking her how she liked life with me when she had been born into the House of Dardanos.

'I'm content, sire,' she was saying. 'Achilles is a good man, and not ignoble.' She leaned forwards. 'Sire, why does he think he must die soon?'

'Their fates are linked, his and Hektor's,' said the ancient King. 'It has been seen in the oracles.'

When they saw me they abandoned the subject, of course. We dined then and I discovered I was famished, but I forced myself to a pace equal to Priam's, and drank sparingly of the wine.

Afterwards I conducted him to his mule cart, in which lay the sheeted body of Hektor. Priam didn't look beneath the covering, but climbed up beside the idiot boy and drove off sitting as erect and proud as if he rode in a car of solid gold.

Brise waited for me with her hair unbound, a loose robe folded about her. I went through to our bed as she lingered to blow out the lamps.

'Too tired even to shed your clothes?'

She unclasped my collar and belt, removed the kilt and let all of them lie on the floor where they landed. Exhausted, I put my arms above my head and lay flat on my back as she lifted herself up beside me, leaning over me and fitting her knotted fists into my armpits. I smiled at her, suddenly as light and happy as a small child.

'I haven't the strength even to pull your hair,' I said.

'Then lie still and go to sleep. I'm here.'

'I'm too tired to sleep.'

'Then rest. I'm here.'

'Brise, promise me that you'll not leave me until the end?'

'The end?'

Gone her laughter; her face hung over me, her eyes dimmed because only one lamp still burned, and it at the farthest reaches of the room. With an enormous effort I lifted my arms and took her head between my hands, holding her frail skull the way I had held Hektor's, bringing her face closer.

'I heard what you asked Priam, and I heard his answer. You know what I mean, Brise.'

'I refuse to believe it!' she cried.

'Some things are required of a man on the day of his birth, and these things are told to him. My father would not, but my mother did. Coming to Troy meant I would die here, and now that Hektor's dead, Troy must fall. My death is the purchase price.'

'Achilles, don't leave me!'

'I'd give my all to stay, but it can't be.'

She was quiet for a long while, her eyes dwelling on the tiny flame sputtering in the lamp's shell, her breathing rhythmic and unhurried. Then she said, 'You had ordered Hektor prepared for burial before you saw me this evening.'

'Yes.'

'Couldn't you have told me? Then some things would never have been said.'

'Maybe it was necessary that they be said, Brise. I struck you. A man must never strike woman or child, anyone weaker than he. When men cast out the Old Religion, that was a part of the bargain by which the Gods gave men the right to rule.'

384

She smiled. 'You struck not at me but at your daimon, and, in striking, you drove it out. The rest of your life belongs to you, not to Patrokles, and for that, I rejoice.'

My exhaustion left me; I lifted myself on one elbow to look at her. The tiny lamp would have been kind to any woman, but because she had no fault it gave her the aura of a goddess, it burnished her pale skin to faint gold and enriched the shimmering fire of her hair, touched her eyes with liquid amber. I put my fingers hesitantly to her cheek and traced a line down to her mouth where it was swollen from the impact of my hand. Her throat was hollow in shadow, her breasts drove me to distraction, her small feet were the terminus of my world.

And because at last I admitted the depth of my need for her, I found things in her beyond my dreams. If I had tried in the past consciously to please her, I no longer thought of her at all except as an extension of my own being. I found I wept; her hair was wet under my face, her hands relaxed and fluttered to mine and locked there in aching comfort, her hands in mine above our heads on the shared pillow.

Thus Hektor dwelled once more in the palace of his forefathers, but this time unknowing. Through Odysseus we learned that Priam had passed over his remaining senior sons to choose the very young man, Troilos, as the new Heir. Not even, so some Trojans were saying, arrived at the Age of Consent – a term we didn't know or use, but (said Odysseus) which apparently formed the Trojan concept of maturity.

The decision had met with great opposition; Troilos himself begged the King to give the Heirdom to Aineas. This provoked Priam into a diatribe against the Dardanian that ended when Aineas stalked from the Throne Room. Deiphobos too was angry; so was the young son-priest, Helenos, who reminded Priam of the oracle which said that Troilos would save the city only if he lived to reach the Age of Consent. Priam maintained that Troilos had already reached the Age of Consent, and that confirmed the phrase's ambiguity in Odysseus's mind. Helenos kept begging the King to change his mind, but the King would not. Troilos was anointed the Heir. And we on the beach began to sharpen our swords.

It took the Trojans twelve days in all to mourn Hektor. During that time Penthesileia of the Amazons arrived with ten thousand mounted women warriors. Another reason to sharpen our swords.

Curiosity oiled our whetstones, for these unique creatures lived lives completely dedicated to Artemis the Maid and an Asian Ares. They dwelled in the fastnesses of Skythia at the foot of the crystal mountains which spear the roof of the world, riding their huge horses through the forests, hunting and marauding in the name of the Maid. They existed under the thumb of the Earth Goddess in her first triple entity – Maid, Mother, Crone – and ruled their men as women had in our part of the world before the New Religion replaced the Old. For men had discovered one vital fact: that a man's seed was as necessary for procreation as was the woman who grew the fruit. Until that discovery was made, a man was deemed an expensive luxury.

The Amazon succession lay entirely in the female line; their men were chattels who didn't even go to war. The first fifteen years of a woman's life after she attained her menses were dedicated exclusively to the Maiden Goddess. Then she retired from the army and took a husband, bore children. Only the Queen did not marry, though she stepped down from the throne at about the same time as other women left the service of Artemis the Maid; instead of taking a husband, the Queen went to the Axe as a sacrifice for the people.

What we didn't already know about the Amazons, Odysseus told us; he seemed to have spies everywhere, even at the foot of the crystal mountains in Skythia. Though, of course, what consumed us most was the fact that Amazons *rode* horses. Other peoples did not, even in far Egypt. Horses were too difficult to sit upon. Their hide was slippery, a blanket wouldn't stay in place; the sole part of them of use to men was the mouth, into which a bit could be inserted attached to a head harness and reins. Therefore the world used horses to pull chariots. They couldn't even be used to pull carts, for a yoke strangled them. How then could the Amazons *ride* their beasts into battle?

While the Trojans mourned Hektor we rested, wondering if we would ever see them outside their walls again. Odysseus remained confident that they would come out, but the rest of us were not so sure.

On the thirteenth day I put on the suit of armour Odysseus had given me, to discover that it felt much lighter. We crossed the causeways in the dimness of dawn, endless threads of men trudging across the dew-wet plain, a few chariots in their lead. Agamemnon had decided to make his stand along a front about half a league from the Trojan wall adjacent to the Skaian Gate.

They were waiting for us, not as many as before, but still more numerous than we were. The Skaian Gate was closed already.

The Amazon horde was positioned in the centre of the Trojan van; as I waited for our wings to come into formation I sat on the side rail of my chariot and looked them over. They were mounted on big, shaggy beasts of some breed I didn't know – ugly aquiline heads, shorn manes and tails, hairy hooves. In colour the horses were uniformly bay or brown, save for one white beauty in the middle. That would be Queen Penthesileia. What I could see was how they stayed aboard – clever! Each warrior fitted her hips and buttocks inside a kind of leather frame strapped beneath the horse's belly so that it remained firmly in place.

They wore bronze helmets but otherwise were clad in hardened leather, and covered themselves from waists to feet in tubes of leather bound about from ankles to knees with thongs. On their feet were soft short boots. The weapon of choice was obviously the bow and arrow, though a few were girt with swords.

At which moment the horns and drums of battle sounded. I stood upright again, Old Pelion in my hand, the iron shield riding my left shoulder comfortably. Agamemnon had concentrated all his chariots in the van opposite the Amazons, pitifully few.

The women ploughed in among the war cars like harpies, shrieking and screaming. Arrows zipped from their short bows, flying over our heads as we stood in our chariots and coming to earth in the foot behind us. The constant rain of death shook even my Myrmidons, not used to fighting an adversary who engaged at a distance preventing instantaneous retaliation. I pushed my little segment of war cars closer together and forced the Amazons out, using Old Pelion like a lance, fending off arrows with my shield, shouting to others to do the same. How extraordinary! These strange women wouldn't aim their barbs at our horses!

I glanced at Automedon, his face set dourly as he struggled with the team. His eyes met mine.

'It will be up to the rest of the army to slaughter Trojans today,' I said. 'I'll count the battle well fought if we can hold our own against these women.'

He nodded, swerving the car to avoid a warrior who launched her steed straight at us, thick and powerful forelegs flailing a pair of hooves big enough to dash out a man's brains. I snatched up a spare javelin and flung it, hissing satisfaction as it took her straight off her mount's back to fall under its trampling legs. Then I put Old Pelion down and picked up my axe.

'Keep close to me, I'm getting down.'

'Don't, Achilles! They'll smash you to pulp!'

I laughed at him.

It was much easier on the ground; I passed the word to my Myrmidons.

'Forget the size of the horses. Come in under their feet – they

ACHILLES

won't kill our horses, but we'll kill theirs. A horse down is as good as a rider down.'

The Myrmidons followed my lead without hesitation. Some got maimed and battered beneath Amazon horses, but most stood their ground amid the deluge of arrows, slashing at hairy bellies, skirted legs, straining equine throats. Because they were neat and quick, because my father and I had never discouraged initiative or versatility in any one of them, they got away with it and forced the Amazons into worried retreat. A costly victory. The field was littered with Myrmidon dead. But they had won the moment. Uplifted, they were ready to kill more Amazons, more Amazon horses.

I heaved myself up beside Automedon again and searched for Penthesileia herself. There! In the midst of her women, trying to rally them. I nodded to Automedon.

'Forward, at the Queen.'

I led the charge at her lines in my car, before they were prepared. Arrows met us all the same; Automedon shouldered a shield to protect himself. But I couldn't get close enough to her to harm her. Three times she managed to drive us off, all the while battling to re-form her lines. Automedon was panting and weeping, unable to command my three white stallions the way Patrokles had.

'Give me the reins.'

Their names were Xanthos, Balios and Podargos, and I called to each of them by his name, asking him for his heart. They heard me, though Patrokles was not there to answer for them. Oh, that was good! I could think of him without guilt.

Without need of the whip they went in again, big enough themselves to shoulder the Amazon beasts aside. Shouting my war cry, I gave Automedon the reins and took up Old Pelion. Queen Penthesileia was within range and moving closer, her warriors in worse disorder than they had been before. Poor woman, she didn't have the gift of generalship. Closer, closer … She had to swing her white mare to one side to avoid crashing into my team. Her pale eyes blazed, her side was presented for Old Pelion. But I couldn't throw. I saluted her and ordered a withdrawal.

A riderless Amazon horse – they seemed all mares – was tethered to its own feet, reins beneath one. As Automedon drove past I reached out, hauled the reins from under the mare's hoof and compelled her to follow us.

Once out of the turmoil I jumped down from the car and surveyed the Amazon horse. Would she like a male smell? How could I get myself seated in that leathery frame?

Automedon went pale. 'Achilles, what are you doing?'

'She wasn't afraid to die, she deserves a better death. I'll fight her as an equal – her axe to mine, from the back of a horse.'

'Are you mad? We can't ride horses!'

'Not now, but after seeing how the Amazons manage to, do you think we won't learn?'

I scrambled onto the mare's back by using my chariot wheel as a step; the corners of the frame were stoutly knobbed, which meant I had great trouble edging into it, for it was too small. But once there, I was amazed. Remaining upright and balanced was so easy! The only difficulty was my legs, which hung down unsupported. My mare was shivering, but by luck I seemed to have chosen a placid-natured beast; when I thumped her on the shoulder and yanked the reins to turn her round, she obeyed. I was horsed; the first man in the world to be so.

Automedon handed me my axe, but the man-sized shield was out of the question. One of my Myrmidons ran up, grinning, to hand me a little round Amazon shield.

Myrmidons following with yells of delight, I charged into the midst of the women warriors, aiming for the Queen. In the crush my mount couldn't move much faster than a snail, and had grown used to me besides. Perhaps all that weight cowed her.

When I saw the Queen I sent my war cry winging to her.

Shrieking her own bizarre, ululating call, she wheeled to face me, pushing her white mare through the crowd with her knees – I learned a new trick – as she slung her bow across her back and transferred her right hand to a golden axe. Some sharp order she gave made her warriors fall back to form a half circle, my Myrmidons eagerly making up its other half. The battle must have been going all our way in other parts of the field, for among the Myrmidon observers I saw troops belonging to Diomedes, and the dark, unpleasant face of his cousin Thersites. What was Thersites doing here? He was co-commander of Odysseus's spies.

'You are Achilles?' the Queen called in atrocious Greek.

'I am!'

She trotted closer, her axe lying along her mare's shoulder, her shield steady. Knowing myself green at this new form of the duel, I decided to make her use her tricks first, trusting to my luck to stay out of trouble until I felt more comfortable. She flung her steed sideways and swung like lightning, but I pulled away in time and took the blow on the bullhide shield, wishing I had one of iron and that size. Her blade bit deep, emerging free of the leather as cleanly as a knife paring cheese. She was no general, but she could fight. So could my brown mare, which seemed to know when to turn before I did. Learning, I swung my axe and missed by a fraction. Then I tried her own trick, crashing into her white mare. Her eyes opened wide; she laughed at me above the rim of her shield. Getting the feel of each other, we exchanged blows with ever increasing speed; the axes resonated and struck sparks. I could feel the power in her arm, and admitted her consummate skill. Her axe was much smaller than mine, designed for one-handed use, which made her a very dangerous foe; the best I could do with my own weapon was to grasp its handle much closer to its head than I normally did, using my right hand only. I kept to her right and forced her to crack her muscles, stopping each of her lunges with a power that jarred her to the marrow.

I could long have outlasted her in strength, but I hated to see her pride humbled. Better to end it swiftly and honourably. As she realised her course was run she lifted her eyes to mine and consented silently; then she tried one final, desperate trick. The white horse reared high, twisting as she came down, thudding against my mount with such impetus that she stumbled, hooves slipping. As I held her together with voice and left hand and heels, the axe descended. I raised my own axe to meet it and push it aside, then did not hesitate. Penthesileia's side was bare and took my blade like unfired clay. Not trusting her while she remained upright, I wrenched it out again quickly, but the hand groping for her dagger wasn't strong enough. Scarlet streams gushing over the white mare's hide, she tottered. I slid off my own mare to catch her before she married the earth.

Her weight bore me to the ground, where I knelt with her head and shoulders in my arms, feeling for her pulse. She was not yet dead, but her shade was called. She looked at me out of eyes as blue and pale as sunstruck water.

'I prayed that it would be you,' she said.

'The King should die at the hands of the worthiest foe,' I said, 'and you are King in Skythia.'

'I thank you for ending it too quickly to betray my lack of your strength, and I absolve you of my death in the name of the Archer Maid.'

The death rattle came, but her lips still moved. I bent over to hear.

'When the Queen dies under the Axe, she must breathe her last into the mouth of her slayer, who will rule after her.' A cough; she struggled to continue. 'Take my breath. Take my spirit until you too are a shade and I must ask it back.'

Her mouth was free of blood; with all of her remaining she breathed into me, and so died. The spell broken, I lowered her carefully to earth and stood up. Screaming their grief and despair, her warriors charged me, but the Myrmidons stepped in front of me and gave me the chance to lead my brown mare off the field, find Automedon. That wood and leather frame was a prize worth more than rubies.

Someone spoke.

'What a spectacle you gave the crowd, Achilles. I'm sure few of the men – or the women either, for that matter – have ever seen someone making love to a corpse.'

Automedon and I spun round, hardly crediting our ears. There postured Thersites the spy, smirking. Was this the depth of the army's contempt for me, that a man like Thersites could voice his foul thoughts to my face, deeming himself safe?

'What a shame they charged and you couldn't finish it,' he sneered. 'I was hoping to catch a glimpse of your mightiest weapon.'

Shaking with ice cold anger, I lifted my hand. 'Get away, Thersites! Go and hide behind your cousin Diomedes or your string puller, Odysseus!'

He turned on his heel. 'The truth hurts, doesn't it?'

I struck him once, my arm sparking pain to the roots of my shoulder as my fist found the side of his neck just below his helmet. He dropped like a stone, twisted on the ground serpentlike. Automedon was weeping with rage.

'The dog!' he said, and knelt down. 'You broke his neck, Achilles, he's dead. Good riddance!'

We beat the Amazons to their knees, for their hearts had died with Penthesileia; they fought on only to be killed in this, their first foray into the world of men. When I had the time I searched for the Queen's body, but it was nowhere to be found. As the day died one of my Myrmidons came to me.

'Lord, I saw the Queen's body taken from the field.'

'Where to? By whom?'

'King Diomedes. He arrived with some of his Argives, stripped her body, then tied it by the heels to his car and drove off with it and her armour.'

Diomedes? I could scarcely believe it, but when men began to tidy the field I went to beard him.

'Diomedes, did you take my prize, the Amazon queen?'

'Yes!' he snapped, glaring. 'I threw her in Skamander.'

I spoke civilly. 'Why?'

'Why not? You murdered my cousin Thersites – one of my

393

men saw you strike him down after he'd turned his back on you. You deserve to lose Queen and armour both!'

I clenched my fists. 'You acted hastily, my friend. Find Automedon and ask him what Thersites said.'

I took some of my Myrmidons and went looking for the Queen, not expecting to find her. Skamander was running strong and full and foul again; during the twelve days of mourning for Hektor we had repaired the river's banks to keep our camp dry, and then there had been more rain over Ida.

Darkness had fallen; we kindled torches and wandered up and down the bank looking under bushes and willows. Then someone shouted. I ran towards the sound, straining to see. She was in the stream, bobbing up and down, caught by one long, pale braid of hair upon a branch of that same elm to which I had clung for my life. I drew her out and wrapped her in a blanket, then laid her across her own white mare, which Automedon had found roving the deserted field, crying for her.

When I returned to my house Brise was waiting for me.

'Dear love, Diomedes called and left a parcel for you. He said it came with his sincere apologies, and he would have done the same to Thersites.'

He had sent me Penthesileia's things. So I buried her in the same tomb as Patrokles, lying in the position of the Warrior King, armoured and with a gold mask covering her face, her white mare at her feet so that she would not go riderless in the realms of the Dead.

The morrow brought no sign of the Trojans, nor the day after that. I went to see Agamemnon, wondering what would happen now. Odysseus was with him, as cheerful and confident as ever.

'Never fear, Achilles, they'll come out again. Priam is waiting for Memnon, who's coming with many crack Hittite regiments, purchased from King Hattusilis. However, my agents tell me that the Hittites are still half a moon away, and in the meantime we have a more urgent problem. Sire, would you explain?' asked that crafty man, who understood exactly when it was politic to defer to our High King.

'Certainly,' our High King said loftily. 'Achilles, it's been eight days since we've seen a supply ship from Assos. I suspect a Dardanian attack. Will you take an army and see what's the matter down there? We can't afford to fight Memnon and his Hittites on empty bellies, but nor can we fight him short-handed. Can you rectify matters in Assos and be back here quickly?'

I nodded. 'Yes, sire. I'll take ten thousand men, but not Myrmidons. Have I your permission to recruit elsewhere?'

'Certainly, certainly!' He was in a very good mood.

Affairs at Assos were much as Agamemnon had predicted. The Dardanians had our base besieged; we enjoyed some hard fighting before we broke out of our defence walls and trounced them on open ground. It was a ragged army, motley and polyglot; from somewhere, probably all down the coast, whoever ruled in ruined Lyrnessos now had picked up fifteen thousand men. In all likelihood they had been bound for Troy, but couldn't resist the temptation Assos offered en route. The walls had held them outside and I arrived too quickly for a breach, so they got nothing and never reached Troy either.

Four days saw the end of it; we set sail again on the fifth. But the winds and currents were against us all the way, so it was fully dark on the sixth night before we made the beach at Troy. I walked straight to Agamemnon's house, discovering as I went that the army had seen a major action in my absence.

I met Ajax in the portico and hailed him, anxious to know the details. 'What happened?'

The corners of his mouth drew down. 'Memnon came sooner than expected, with ten thousand Hittite troops. They can fight, Achilles! And we must be tired. Even though we had the advantage in numbers and the Myrmidons were on the field, they drove us behind our wall just on darkness.'

I jerked my head towards the closed doors. 'Is the King of Kings receiving?'

Ajax grinned. 'Cut out the irony, cousin! He isn't feeling very well – he never does after a reverse. But he is receiving.'

'Go and sleep, Ajax. We'll win tomorrow.'

Agamemnon looked very tired. He was still sitting at his dinner table, only Nestor and Odysseus to keep him company. His head was down on his arms, but he lifted it as I came in and sat.

'Finished with Assos?' he asked.

'Yes, sire. The supply ships will arrive tomorrow, but the fifteen thousand men bound for Troy will not.'

'Excellent!' said Odysseus.

Nestor didn't speak – not like him! I looked down the table to him and was stunned. His hair and beard were untended, his eyes red-rimmed. When he realised I was staring at him he moved one hand aimlessly; tears began to roll down his wrinkled cheeks.

'What, Nestor?' I asked gently. Knowing, I suppose.

His breath caught and quivered on a sob. 'Oh, Achilles! Antilochos is dead.'

I put my hand up to shield my eyes. 'When?'

'Today, on the field. All my fault, all my fault … He came to get me out of trouble and Memnon killed him with a spear. I can't even see his face! The spear entered through the occiput and smashed his face to pieces when it erupted out of his mouth. He was so beautiful. So beautiful!'

I ground my teeth. 'Memnon will suffer, Nestor, I swear it. On my vows to River Spercheus I swear it.'

But the old man shook his head. 'Oh, can it matter, Achilles? Antilochos is *dead*. Memnon's corpse can't bring him back to me. I've lost five sons on this evil plain – five out of my seven sons. And Antilochos was the dearest of them all. He's dead at twenty. I'm alive at close to ninety. There is no justice in the decisions of the Gods.'

'We finish it tomorrow?' I asked Agamemnon.

'Yes, tomorrow,' he answered. 'I'm sick to death of Troy! I couldn't *bear* another winter here. From home I hear nothing – my wife never sends a messenger, nor does Aigisthos. I send my messengers, who return to tell me that all is well in Mykenai. But I long for home! I want to see Klytemnestra. My son. My two remaining daughters.' He looked at Odysseus. 'If the autumn fails to see Troy taken, I'm going home.'

'Troy will be taken by the autumn, sire.' He sighed, that cool and iron-hard man, more than a trace of weariness in his grey eyes. 'I'm sick of Troy too. If I have to remain away from Ithaka for twenty years, then let the second ten of them be spent anywhere save in the Troad. I'd rather contend with a combination of sirens, harpies and witches than more boring Trojans.'

I grinned. 'Sirens, harpies and witches combined won't know what hit them when they have to deal with you, Odysseus. But it doesn't matter to me. Troy is the end of my world.'

Knowing the prophecies, Odysseus said nothing, simply looked down into his wine cup.

'Only promise me one thing, Agamemnon,' I said.

His head was on his arms again. 'Anything you like.'

'Bury me in the cliff with Patrokles and Penthesileia, and see Brise marries my son.'

Odysseus stiffened. 'Are you called, Achilles?'

'I don't think so. But it must come soon.' I held out my hand to him. 'Promise me that my son will wear my armour.'

'I have already promised that. He'll get it.'

Nestor wiped his eyes, blew his nose with his sleeve. 'It will all be as you wish, Achilles.' He plucked at his hair with shaky fingers. 'If only the God would call me! I've prayed and prayed, but he doesn't hear. How can I go back to Pylos without all my sons? What will I tell their mothers?'

'You'll go back, Nestor,' I said. 'You still have two sons. When you stand on your bastions and look down to the sandy shore, Troy will fade to a dream. Only remember those of us who fell, and pour us libations.'

*

ACHILLES

I cut Memnon's head off and flung the body at Nestor's feet. We took fresh heart that day; the shortlived Trojan resurgence ended. They retreated slowly across the plain while I, with an alien agony inside me, killed and killed. My arm felt sluggish, though the axe bit as often and as viciously. But as I ploughed through the best King Hattusilis of the Hittites had to offer on the bloodsoaked altar that was Troy, I grew sick at the carnage. At the back of my mind I could hear a voice sighing, I thought my mother's, blurred with tears.

At the end of the day I paid my respects to Nestor and assisted at Antilochos's last rites. We laid the lad alongside his four brothers in the cliff chamber reserved for the House of Neleus, and hunched Memnon at his feet like a dog. But the thought of the funeral games and the feasting was unbearable; I slipped away.

Brise was waiting. When was she not?

I took her face between my hands and said, 'You always wipe away the grief.'

'Sit down and keep me company,' she said.

I sat, but found myself unable to talk to her; an awful coldness was settling about my heart. She went on chattering brightly until she looked at me, then her animation died.

'What is it, Achilles?'

I shook my head dumbly and got up to go outside, standing there with my head lifted to the infinite reaches of the sky.

'What is it, Achilles?'

'Oh, Brise! I am torn open to the very roots of my being! Never until this moment have I felt the wind so keenly, smelled life so strongly in my nostrils, seen the stars so still, so clear!'

She tugged at me urgently. 'Come inside.'

I let her lead me to a chair and sat down while she sank at my feet and put her arms on my knees, staring up into my face.

'Achilles, is it your mother?'

I took her chin in my fingers, smiling down. 'No. My mother has left me for good. I heard her weeping farewell on the field.

I'm called, Brise. The God has called me at last. I've always wondered what it would be like, never dreaming for an instant that it would be this uttermost consciousness of life. I thought it would be all glory and exultation, something that would carry me physically into my last fight. But it's quiet and merciful. I'm at peace. No daimons of vanished years, no fear for the future. Tomorrow it ends. Tomorrow I will cease to be. The God has spoken. He will not leave me again.'

She started to protest, but I stopped her words with my hand.

'A man must go gracefully, Brise. The God wills it, not I. And I am no Herakles, no Prometheus to resist him. I am a mortal man. I have lived thirty-one years and have seen and felt more than most men do who see the leaves turn golden on the trees one hundred times. I don't want to live longer than the walls of Troy. All the great warriors will die here. Ajax. Ajax! Ajax ... It isn't fitting that I should survive. I'll face the shades of Patroklos and Iphigenia across the River with everything gone. Our hatreds and our loves belong to the world of the living – not one thing so strong can exist in the world of the dead. I've done my best. There is no more. I've prayed that my name will continue to be sung through all the generations of men to come. That is all the immortality any man can hope for. The world of the dead gives no joy, but no sorrow either. If I can fight Hektor a million times over on the lips of living men, I will never truly die.'

She wept and wept; her woman's heart couldn't glimpse the intricacy of the warp on the loom of time, so she could not rejoice with me. But there comes a depth of grief when even tears are dried. She lay still and quiet.

'If you die, then I will die,' she said then.

'No, Brise, you must live. Go to my son, Neoptolemos, and marry him. Give him the sons I have not got out of you. Nestor and Agamemnon have pledged to see it done.'

'Even for you I can't promise that. You took me out of one life and gave me another. There can't be a third. I must share your death, Achilles.'

ACHILLES

I lifted her up, smiling at her. 'When you set eyes on my son, you'll think differently. Women are meant to survive. All you owe me is one more night. Then I give you to Neoptolemos.'

CHAPTER TWENTY-EIGHT

NARRATED BY
AUTOMEDON

We went out across the causeways with light hearts to face an army almost crippled out of existence. Achilles was unusually quiet beside me, but I didn't think to question the significance of his mood. He stood like a beacon in his golden armour, the fine gold plumes of the helm flying in the wind and bouncing around his shoulders as we lurched over the uneven terrain. Expecting his habitual comradely smile, I turned sideways to grin at him, but that day he forgot our little ritual. He looked straight ahead, at what I didn't know. A stern and controlled peace had settled upon that stormy face; suddenly I felt as if I drove a stranger. Not once did he speak to me during our drive to the battle place, nor did he give me any kind of smile. Which should have cast me down, yet inexplicably did not. Rather, I felt buoyed up, as if something in him was rubbing off on me.

He fought better than in all his life, seeming bent on concentrating all his massive glory into the space of a single day. Though instead of working himself into his usual killing furore, he took pains to see that the Myrmidons were prospering. He used his sword, not his axe, and used it in complete silence, as the King does when he makes the annual great sacrifice to the God. That thought gave birth to another; all at once I knew what the difference in him was. He had always been the Prince, he had never been the King. That day he was the King. I wondered if he had some premonition that Peleus was dead.

As I manoeuvred the chariot around the field I took an

occasional glance at the sky, misliking the weather. Even at dawn it had been dull and drear, with the promise not of cold but of tempests. Now the vault was a peculiar copper hue, and to the east and south great black thunderheads were gathering, lightning flickering. Over Ida, where we were sure the Gods congregated to watch the fray.

It was a complete rout. The Trojans couldn't hold us, not when every leader of our army seemed possessed by a lesser form of the grandeur which sat upon Achilles like the rays around the head of Helios. It is reflecting off him, I thought; he has become the highest of all kings.

Not long into the day the Trojans broke and fled. I looked for Aineas, wondering why he was making no effort to hold them together. But he must have been suffering an unlucky day, for there was no sign of him anywhere. Later on I learned that he kept to himself and wouldn't send his men where they were needed as reinforcements. We had heard that there was a new Heir, we had heard his name: Troilos. Then I remembered that Achilles had told me Priam insulted Aineas at the time he had made Troilos the new Heir. Well, today Aineas had demonstrated that it was a foolish old King of Troy who insulted a Dardanian prince, also an Heir.

We had seen Troilos on the field before, when Penthesileia fought, and when Memnon fought. He had been fortunate, never coming up against Achilles or Ajax, but that changed today. Achilles pursued him relentlessly, following whichever way he turned, drawing closer and closer. When Troilos realised the inevitable he called for aid, his men hard pressed. I saw him direct the messenger to go to Aineas, who was nearby. I saw the man speak to Aineas, who leaned down from his car with what appeared to be interest. I saw the messenger remove himself. But I didn't see Aineas lift one finger to help. Instead he wheeled his car and took himself – and his men – elsewhere.

Troilos was game enough. He was a full brother to Hektor and might, with a few more years added, have made another Hektor. At his age, he hadn't a chance. While I came closer he raised his spear, the driver holding his vehicle steady for the cast, the only one he would loose before we got too close. I felt Achilles's arm brush mine, and knew he was lifting Old Pelion. That great spear left on a superb throw, winging its way as straight as a shaft from the hand of Apollo. Its iron barb bit deeply into the lad's throat, felling him voiceless, and above the heads of the despairing Trojan troops I saw Aineas watching with a bitter face. We got Troilos's armour and the team as well, and cut what were left of his men to ribbons.

After Troilos died Aineas came to life. He shook off his apathy and threw the remainder of the Trojan army in our teeth, everywhere among the soldiers, but careful never to get within a spear-cast of Achilles. A wily one, the Dardanian. He wanted very desperately to live; I wondered what passions drove the man, for he was no coward.

The sun had gone, the storm was gathering fast. So massive was the latent power we could feel stored in the sky that the troops began to mutter loudly of omens. The clouds dropped lower and lower, the lightning flashed closer, we could hear the thunder above the roar of battle. I had never seen such a sky before, nor felt the Sky Father prickle and ripple up and down my backbone. The light had grown dim, had an eerie sulphurous glow, and the clouds were as black as the beard of Hades, curling like smoke from a huge oil fire, lit to vivid blue by the lightning. I heard the Myrmidons behind us saying that Father Zeus was sending us an omen of complete victory, and from the way they behaved I fancied that the Trojans took it as a complete Greek victory too.

There was a scorching flash of white fire right in front of us. The team reared and I had to cover my eyes for fear of being blinded. When the afterdazzle faded I looked at Achilles.

'Let's dismount,' I said. 'It's safer on the ground.'

For the first time that day his eyes met mine. Dumbfounded, I stared. It was as if the bolts played around his head; his yellow eyes were alight with joy and he laughed at my fears.

'See it, Automedon? See it? My great-grandfather prepares to mourn me! He holds me a fit descendant of his seed!'

I gaped. *'Mourn?* Achilles, what do you mean?'

In answer he gripped both my wrists hard. 'I'm called. Today I die, Automedon. The Myrmidons are yours until you can send for my son. Father Zeus prepares for my death.'

I couldn't believe it. I wouldn't believe it! Like a man caught in a nightmare I whipped the team onward. When my shock evaporated a little I sought for the best thing to do, and as unobtrusively as possible I began to edge the car nearer and nearer to Ajax and Odysseus, whose men fought side by side.

If Achilles noticed what I was doing he dismissed it as quite irrelevant. I looked up at the sky and prayed, begged the Father to take my life and spare his; but the God only roared his derision and set me shaking. The Trojans made a sudden dash for their walls, we followed pellmell to head them off. Ajax was closer now; I kept edging the chariot up until I could get the message to him that Achilles fancied himself called. If any man could avert it, that man was Ajax.

We were within the shadow of the Western Curtain, too near the Skaian Gate to permit of Priam's opening it. Achilles, Ajax and Odysseus penned Aineas against the gate in a last ditch stand. Achilles was determined to have Aineas; I could feel it in his silence even as I prayed that he wouldn't get the chance to come at this most dangerous of all the Trojan leaders left alive.

I heard him give a grunt of content and saw the Dardanian within range, too beset to take a full account of those ranged against him. He was a perfect target. Achilles raised Old Pelion, the muscles in his arm bulging as he gathered power for the cast, his naked armpit covered in fine golden hair. My eyes followed the line of the spear to Aineas in fascination, knowing that life was over for the Dardanian, that the last great threat was no more.

It all seemed to happen in the same instant, though I swear that it wasn't the chariot made Achilles lose his balance. He went over on his right ankle, even though it looked firmly braced in the stirrup, and his right arm flew even higher as he fought to keep his stance. I heard a thud, saw the arrow stuck almost to its bright blue flights in that naked armpit. Old Pelion fell uncast to the ground as Achilles reared up like some titan, then shrieked out Chiron's war cry in a voice brazen with triumph, as if he conquered mortality itself. His arm fell and drove the arrow in to its hilt, deeper than shame or death. I held onto the team with both hands, Xanthos plunging in terror, Balios hanging his head, Podargos beating a tattoo with his hooves. But Patrokles wasn't there to speak for them, to give their grief and horror human words.

All who heard the war cry turned to look; Ajax screamed as if he too had been hit. The blood gushed from that lipless mouth and from both nostrils, cascading over the golden armour in great rivers. Odysseus was right behind Ajax; he gave a shout of rage and futility, his hand outstretched, pointing. Safe near a rock, Paris stood with his bow in his hand, smiling.

It could not have been long that Achilles hung upright, before he toppled over the chariot's rail into Ajax's arms and bore him to the ground with a clang of armour that echoed in our hearts and would not fade away. I was beside Ajax as he knelt with his cousin in his arms, as Ajax took off the helmet and stared dumbly into the scarlet, running face. Achilles saw who held him, but the vision of death was much bigger, much closer. He tried vainly to speak, the words drowned; for a moment the farewell was there in his eyes. Then the pupils dilated, the yellow irises were driven away by featureless, transparent black. Three frightful jerks which taxed Ajax's strength, and it was over. He was dead. Achilles was dead. We looked into the lucent vacant windows of his eyes and saw nothing behind. Ajax put out a huge, clumsy hand to brush the lids down shut, then put the helm on again and strapped it tightly, his tears falling faster and faster, his mouth all awry.

He was dead. Achilles was dead. How could we ever bear it?

Shock must have held both armies immobile; suddenly the

Trojans fell on us like hounds licking the blood of men. They were after the body and the armour. Odysseus leaped to his feet, careless that he wept. The Myrmidons were standing silent, the impossible a reality at their feet. Bending, Odysseus picked up Old Pelion and brandished it in their faces.

'Are you going to let them take him?' he yelled, spitting. 'You saw what a cur's trick it took to kill him! Are you just going to stand there and let them take his body from you? In the name of Achilles himself, stand by him now!'

They shook off their shock and rallied; no Trojan would get near Achilles while one of them lived. Forming in front of us, they took the charge in savage and sullen grief. Odysseus helped the weeping Ajax to his feet, helped him swing the limp and very heavy form into his arms.

'Carry him back beyond the lines, Ajax. I'll make sure they don't break through.'

As if it were an afterthought, he shoved Old Pelion into Ajax's right hand and pushed him on his way. I had always had my reservations about Odysseus, but he was a king. Sword in his hand, he swung round and planted his feet widely on the earth still steaming with Achilles's blood. We took the Trojan charge and beat it off, Aineas howling like a jackal when he saw Ajax trudging away. I looked at Odysseus.

'Ajax is strong, but not strong enough to walk far carrying Achilles. Let me catch him up, put Achilles with me.'

He nodded.

So I turned the team in pursuit of Ajax, who had emerged from the back of our lines and still plodded towards the beach. At which moment, while I was still too far away to help, a chariot flew past me, its driver aiming to head Ajax off: one of Priam's sons was in it, for he wore the purple insignia of the House of Dardanos on his cuirass. Trying to put some heart into my team, I yelled a warning to Ajax. But he didn't seem to hear.

The Trojan Prince saundered down from his perch, sword in hand, smiling. Which indicated that he didn't know Ajax, who never faltered as he walked on. He lifted Achilles higher in his arms and spitted the Trojan on Old Pelion, the afterthought Odysseus had placed in his hand.

'Ajax, lie Achilles in the car,' I said, drawing level.

'I'll carry him home.'

'It's too far, you'll kill yourself.'

'*I'll carry him!*'

'Then at least,' I said desperately, 'let us take the armour off him, put that in the car. It would be more fitting.'

'And I'd feel his body, not its casing. Yes, we can do that.'

The moment Achilles was freed from that awful weight Ajax walked on, cuddling his cousin, kissing his ruined face, talking to him, crooning.

The army was following us slowly, coming across the plain; I kept the chariot just behind Ajax, his great legs toiling as if he could have walked a hundred leagues holding Achilles.

The God had contained his grief long enough. He let it loose upon our heads, and all the vault of the heavens broke into white bolts of fire. The team shivered and stopped, pinned by fear; even Ajax came to a halt, standing while the thunder cracked and rolled overhead and the lightning played a fantastic lacework in the clouds. The rain began to fall at last, huge heavy drops coming stiffly and sparsely, as if the God was too moved to weep easily. The tempo of the rain increased, we floundered in a sea of mud. The army drew level with us, all conflict abandoned before the might of the Thunderer, and together we brought Achilles in across the Skamander causeway, Ajax leading and the King behind him. In the pouring rain we laid him on a bier, while the Father washed his blood away with sky tears.

I went with Odysseus to the house to find Brise. She was by the doorpost, it seemed expecting us.

'Achilles is dead,' said Odysseus.

'Where is he?' she asked, voice steady.

'Before Agamemnon's house.' Odysseus still wept.

Brise stroked his arm and smiled. 'There's no need to grieve, Odysseus. He will be immortal.'

They had rigged up a canopy over the bier to keep off the rain; Brise ducked under its edge and stood looking down at the ruins of that magnificent man, water and blood matting his bright hair, his face drained and still. I wondered if she saw what I did: that the lipless mouth looked right in death, though it never had in life. Owning it, his was the face of the quintessential warrior.

But what she thought, she did not say, then or ever. With perfect tenderness she leaned over and kissed his eyelids, took his hands and folded them on his chest, tucked and patted at the shift until it suited her idea of rightness.

He was dead. Achilles was dead. How could we ever bear it?

We mourned him for seven full days. On the last evening as the sun was setting we laid his body on the golden death car and ferried him across Skamander to the tomb in the cliff. Brise went with us, for no one had the heart to banish her; she walked at the end of the long cortege with her hands folded and her head bent. Ajax was the chief mourner, held the head of Achilles in the palm of one hand as they carried him into the chamber. He was clad in gold, but not in the golden armour. That Agamemnon had taken into custody.

After the priests had said the words, fitted the golden mask over his face and poured out the libations, we filed slowly out of the tomb he shared with Patrokles, Penthesileia and twelve noble Trojan youths. Strangest of all those many strange events and portents was the atmosphere inside the tomb; sweet, pure, ineffable. The blood of the twelve youths in the golden chalice was still liquid, still richly coloured crimson.

I turned back to make sure Brise was following, to find that she knelt by the death car. Though I had no hope of reaching her, I ran into the tomb, Nestor by my side. We couldn't speak as she laid the knife down with the last of her strength and sank upon the ground. Yes, that was proper! How could any of us face the light of a day that knew no Achilles? I half bent to pick up the knife, but Nestor stopped me.

'Come away, Automedon. They want no others here.'

The funeral feast was held the following day, but there were no games. Agamemnon explained.

'I doubt anyone has the heart to compete. But that isn't why. The why lies in the fact that Achilles didn't want to be buried in the armour his mother – a Goddess! – commissioned from Hephaistos Fire. He wanted it awarded as a prize to the best man left alive before Troy. Instead of funeral games.'

I didn't disbelieve him, exactly, but Achilles hadn't mentioned this to me. 'How, sire, can you possibly decide that? By feats of arms? But sometimes they're not indicative of genuine greatness.'

'Precisely,' said the High King. 'For that reason, I'm going to make it a contest of words. Any man who thinks that he's the best man left alive before Troy, step out and tell me why.'

Two contenders only stepped out. Ajax and Odysseus. How odd! They represented the two poles of greatness: the warrior and the – what did one call him, the man who worked through mind?

'Yes, fitting,' said Agamemnon. 'Ajax, you brought his body in. Odysseus, you made it possible to bring the body in. Ajax, speak first and tell me why you think you deserve the armour.'

We all sat on chairs to either side of Agamemnon, I with King Nestor and the rest because I led the Myrmidons now. There were no others present.

Ajax seemed to be as troubled as he was wordless; he stood there, the biggest man I have ever seen, without a thing to say. Nor did he look well; there was something wrong with his right side from face to leg. When he had walked forward he had dragged that leg, nor did the right arm move in a natural way. A little stroke, I thought. He's had a little stroke. Carrying his cousin so far has strained the weakest part of him, his mind. And when finally he did speak, he kept pausing painfully to search for a word.

'Imperial High King, fellow Kings and Princes … I am the first cousin of Achilles. His father, Peleus, and my father, Telamon, were full brothers. Their father, Aiakos, was a son of Zeus. Ours is a great lineage. Ours is a great name. I claim the armour for myself because I bear that name, come from that line. I can't let it be awarded to a man who is the bastard of a common thief.'

The row of twenty men stirred, frowned. What was Ajax doing, to slander Odysseus? Not that Odysseus protested; apparently deaf, he looked at the ground.

'I came to Troy voluntarily, as did Achilles. No oath bound either of us. *I* didn't have to be unmasked when I feigned madness, but Odysseus did. Only two men in this great host fought Hektor in hand to hand combat – Achilles and I. I need no Diomedes to do my dirty work for me. What use would the armour be to Odysseus? His weak left hand couldn't hope to cast Old Pelion. His red head would sink beneath the weight of that helmet. If you doubt my right to my cousin's property, then throw it into the middle of a pack of Trojans, and see which one of the two of us pulls it out!'

He limped to his chair and sat down heavily.

Agamemnon looked embarrassed, but it was plain that most of us agreed with what Ajax said. Puzzled, I studied Odysseus. Why did he lay claim to the armour at all?

He moved forwards and stood loosely with his feet apart, the redness of his hair pronounced in the light. Red-haired and left-handed. No divine blood there, for sure.

'It's true that I tried to get out of coming to Troy,' said Odysseus. '*I* knew how long this war would last. Oath notwithstanding, how many of you would voluntarily have joined this expedition if you'd had any idea how long you'd be away?

'As for Achilles, I'm the sole reason why he came to Troy – I and none other saw through the plot to keep him in Skyros. Ajax was there, but he didn't see. Ask Nestor, he'll confirm it.

'As for ancestry, I ignore Ajax's vile insinuation. I too am a great-grandson of almighty Zeus.

410

'As for physical courage, do any of you doubt mine? I don't have a better body than anyone else to bolster my valour, but I do very well in battle. If you doubt that, count my scars. King Diomedes is my friend and lover, not my minion.'

He paused, as much at ease with words as Ajax was ill at ease. 'I've laid claim to the armour for one reason only – because I want to see it disposed of as Achilles himself wished.

'If I cannot wear it, can Ajax? If it's too large for me, it's certainly too small for him. Give it to me. I deserve it.'

He threw his arms wide as if to say that there was no contest at all, then returned to his chair. Many wavered now, but that couldn't matter. Agamemnon would decide.

The High King looked at Nestor. 'What do you think?'

Nestor sighed. 'That Odysseus deserves the armour.'

'Then so be it. Odysseus, take your prize.'

Ajax screamed. His sword was out, but whatever he intended to do with it was not done. Even as he sprang out of his chair, he pitched full length on the ground and lay there. Nothing we did could rouse him. In the end Agamemnon ordered a stretcher brought, and eight soldiers bore him away. Odysseus put the armour in a hand cart while the Kings dispersed, saddened and dispirited. I went looking for wine to take the sourness out of my mouth. By the time that Odysseus had finished speaking we had known what he intended to do with his prize – give it to Neoptolemos. Maybe in Troy that would have been possible as a direct gift, but armour belonging to a dead man in our part of the world was either buried with him or put up as a prize at his funeral games. A pity. Yes, as things turned out, a great pity.

Night had long fallen when I gave up trying to get drunk. I walked the deserted streets between the tall houses seeking a light, any place which might offer me comfort. And there it was at last, a flame! Burning inside Odysseus's house. The curtain was still drawn back from the doorway, so I staggered in.

He was sitting with Diomedes, sitting watching the dying embers of a fire and brooding. His arm was thrown about the Argive, his fingers slowly caressing the Argive's bare shoulder. An outsider looking at their solidarity, a masterless dog, I knew a fresh surge of loneliness. Achilles was dead. I led the Myrmidons, I who had not been born to that command. Terrifying. I came into the circle of light and sat down wearily.

'Do I intrude?' I asked then, a little tardily.

Odysseus smiled. 'No. Have some wine.'

My stomach turned over. 'No, thank you. I've been trying to get drunk all night without success.'

'So alone, Automedon?' Diomedes asked.

'More alone than I ever wanted to be. How can I take his place? I'm not Achilles!'

'Rest easy,' Odysseus whispered. 'I sent for Neoptolemos ten days ago, when I saw the shadow of death darken his face. If the winds and Gods are kind, Neoptolemos should be here soon.'

The relief was so enormous I almost kissed him. 'Odysseus, for that I thank you with all my heart! The Myrmidons must be led by the blood of Peleus.'

'Don't thank me for doing the sensible thing.'

We sat talking desultorily while the night passed away, each drawing comfort from the others. Once I fancied I heard a commotion in the distance, but when it died down quickly I turned my attention back to what Diomedes was saying. Then came a great shout; this time all three of us heard. Diomedes got up, pantherish, reaching for his sword, while Odysseus sat uncertainly, his head cocked. The noise grew; we went outside and moved in its direction.

It drew us down towards Skamander and finally to its bank, where we kept a pen of consecrated animals for the altars, each one individually chosen, blessed, and marked with a sacred symbol. Some of the other Kings were ahead of us, and a guard had already been posted to keep the merely curious away. Of course we were let through immediately, and joined Agamemnon and Menelaos as they stood by the fence around the pen peering at some object looming in the darkness. We listened to insane laughter, to a gibbering voice rising higher and higher, shouting names up at the stars, shrieking its rage and derision.

'Take that, Odysseus, you spawn of thieves! Die, Menelaos, you crawling sycophant!'

On and on it went while we probed the night fruitlessly. Then someone handed a torch to Agamemnon, who raised it above his head and sent its light out in a widening pool. I gasped in horror. The wine and the empty belly I hadn't wanted to fill revolted; I turned aside and spewed. As far as the light of the torch could reach was blood. Sheep and cattle and goats lay in lakes of it, their eyes glazed and fixed, their limbs lopped off, their throats cut, their hides showing sometimes dozens of wounds. In the background Ajax capered with a bloody sword in his hand. His mouth was open in that chilling laughter when it was not screaming abuse. A terrified little calf dangled from his hand, beating its hooves against his unyielding bulk while he hacked at it. Each time he struck he called the calf Agamemnon, then went into another peal of laughter.

'To see him come to this!' Odysseus whispered.

I managed to control my heaving. 'What is it?' I gasped.

'Madness, Automedon. The outcome of different things. Too many blows to the head over the years – too much grief – perhaps a stroke. But to come to this! I pray he never recovers enough to understand what he's done.'

'We have to stop him!' I said.

'By all means try, Automedon. I don't have any ambition to tackle Ajax in a fit of madness.'

'Nor I,' said Agamemnon.

So all we did was stand and watch.

With the dawn his madness lifted. He came to his senses ankle deep in blood, stared about him like a man in a nightmare – at the dozens of consecrated animals surrounding him, at the blood which covered him from head to foot, at the sword in his hand, at the silent Kings watching from beyond the fence. He still held a goat in his hand, drained of life, hideously mutilated. With a shriek of horror he dropped it, understanding at last what he had done in the night. Then he ran to the fence and leaped it, flying away from the place as if the Furies pursued him already. Teukros broke away from us to follow him; we remained where we were, shaken to our marrow.

Menelaos recovered his powers of speech first. 'Are you going to let him get away with this, brother?' he asked Agamemnon.

'What do you want, Menelaos?'

'His life! He's killed the sacred animals, his life is forfeit! The Gods demand it!'

Odysseus sighed. 'Whom the Gods love best, they first drive mad,' he said. 'Let it alone, Menelaos.'

'He has to die!' Menelaos insisted. 'Execute him, and let no man dig his grave!'

'That is the punishment,' Agamemnon muttered.

Odysseus struck his hands together. 'No, no, no! Leave him be! Isn't it enough for you, Menelaos, that Ajax has doomed himself? His shade is condemned to Tartaros for this night's work! Let him alone! Don't heap more coals on his poor, crazed head!'

Agamemnon turned away from the carnage. 'Odysseus is right. He's mad, brother. Let him atone as best he can.'

Odysseus, Diomedes and I walked down through the streets and the murmuring, shivering men to where Ajax lived with his chief concubine, Tekmessa, and their son, Eurysakes. When Odysseus knocked on the bolted door Tekmessa peered fearfully through the shuttered window, then opened to him, her son at her side.

'Where's Ajax?' asked Diomedes.

She wiped away her tears. 'Gone, sire. I don't know where, except that he said he was going to seek forgiveness of Palladian Athene by bathing in the sea.' She broke down, but managed to go on. 'He gave Eurysakes his shield. He said it was the only one of his arms not tainted by sacrilege, and told us that all the other pieces were to be buried with him. Then he gave us into the care of Teukros. Sire, sire, what is it? What did he do?'

'Nothing he understood, Tekmessa. Stay here, we'll find him.'

He was down by the shore where the tiny waves lapped gently at the fringe of the lagoon and a few rocks dotted the gravelly sand. Teukros was with him, kneeling with his head bent over, stolid Teukros who never spoke much but was always there when Ajax needed him. Even now, at the last.

What he had done spoke mutely for itself: the flat rock a few fingers above the gravel, its surface cracked from some blow of Poseidon's trident, the sword handle wedged to its hilt in the crack, blade upwards. He had shed his armour and bathed in the sea, he had traced an owl in the sand for Athene and an eye for Mother Kubaba. Then he had positioned himself above the sword and fallen on it with all his weight; it had taken him in the centre of his chest and clove the backbone. Two cubits of it protruded beyond his body. He lay with his face in his own blood, his eyes closed, traces of madness still in his features. His huge hands were slack, the fingers gently curved.

Teukros raised his head to look at us bitterly, his eyes as they rested on Odysseus plainly saying that he knew who was to blame. What Odysseus thought I couldn't begin to guess, but he didn't falter.

'What can we do?' he asked.

'Nothing,' said Teukros. 'I'll bury him myself.'

'*Here?*' asked Diomedes, aghast. 'No, he deserves better!'

'You know that's not true. He knew it. So do I. He'll have exactly what the laws of the Gods say he deserves – a suicide's grave. It's all I'm able to do for him. All that's left between us. He must pay in death, as Achilles paid in life. He said that before he died.'

We went away then and left them alone, the brothers who would never again fight with the little one under the shelter of the big one's shield. In eight days they were both gone: Achilles and Ajax, the spirit and the heart of our army.

'Ai! Ai! Woe! Woe!' cried Odysseus, the tears running down his face. 'How strange are the ways of the Gods! Achilles dragged Hektor by the baldric Ajax gave him. Now Ajax falls on the sword Hektor gave him.' He writhed painfully. 'By the Mother, I am sick unto death of Troy! I hate the very smell of Trojan air.'

CHAPTER TWENTY-NINE

NARRATED BY

AGAMEMNON

The days of open fighting had gone; Priam locked the Skaian Gate and looked down on us from his towers. A handful of them remained, only Aineas still alive among their great ones. With his most beloved sons dead, Priam was left with the worthless to console him. It was a time of waiting, while our wounds healed and our spirits slowly revived. A curious thing had happened, a gift from the Gods no one had dreamed of: Achilles and Ajax seemed to have entered into the very substance of every Greek soldier. To the last one they were determined to conquer the walls of Troy. I mentioned the phenomenon to Odysseus, wondering what he thought.

'There's nothing mysterious about it, sire. Achilles and Ajax have been transformed into Heroes, and Heroes never die. So what the men are doing is taking up the burden. Besides which, they want to go home. But not defeated. The only vindication for the events of these last ten years in exile is the fall of Troy. We've paid dearly for this campaign – in our blood, in our greying hair, in our aching hearts, in the faces so long unseen we can hardly remember the beloved lineaments, in the tears and the bitter emptiness. Troy has chewed its way into our bones. We could no more go home without smashing Troy into dust than we could profane the Mysteries of the Mother.'

'Then,' I said, 'I'll seek counsel of Apollo.'

'He's a Trojan far more than a Greek, sire.'

'Even so, his is the oracular mouth. So we'll ask him what we need to enter Troy. He can't deny the representation of a people – any people! – a truthful answer.'

The high priest, Talthybios, looked into the glowing bowels of the sacred fire, and sighed. He was no Kalchas; a Greek, he used fire and water to divine, saving animals for simple sacrificial victims. Nor did he announce his findings at the augury itself. He waited until we were assembled in council.

'What did you see?' I asked then.

'Many things, sire. Some of them I couldn't even begin to understand, but two things were fully revealed.'

'Tell us.'

'We can't take the city with what we have. There are two items dear to the Gods we must possess first. If we acquire them, we'll know the Gods have consented to our entering Troy. If we can't get them, we'll know that Olympos is united against us.'

'What are these two items, Talthybios?'

'First, the bow and arrows of Herakles. The second is a man – Neoptolemos, the son of Achilles.'

'We thank you. You may go.'

I watched their faces. Idomeneus and Meriones sat sternly sad; my poor inadequate brother Menelaos seemed changeless; Nestor was so old we feared for him; Menestheus soldiered on without complaint; Teukros hadn't forgiven any of us; Automedon was still unreconciled to commanding the Myrmidons; and Odysseus – ah, Odysseus! Who really knew what went on behind those luminous, beautiful eyes?

'Well, Odysseus? You know where the bow and arrows of Herakles are. How do you rate our chances?'

He got to his feet slowly. 'In almost ten years, not one single word from Lesbos.'

'I heard he was dead,' said Idomeneus gloomily.

Odysseus laughed. 'Philoktetes, dead? Not if a dozen vipers had poured their poison into him! I believe he's on Lesbos even yet. We certainly have to try, sire. Who should go?'

'Yourself and Diomedes. You were his friends. If he remembers us with kindness, it will be because of you. Take ship for

Lesbos at once, go and ask him for the bow and arrows he inherited from Herakles. Tell him we've kept his share of the spoils, and tell him he's never been forgotten,' I said.

Diomedes stretched. 'A day or two at sea! What a good idea.'

'But there's still the matter of Neoptolemos,' I said. 'It will be well over a moon before he can arrive here – if old Peleus will let him come.'

Odysseus looked back from the doorway. 'Rest easy, sire, it has already been attended to. I sent for Neoptolemos more than half a moon ago. As for Peleus – offer to Father Zeus.'

Within eight days the saffron-coloured sail Odysseus had chosen showed again on the horizon. My heart in my mouth, I stood on the beach beside the vacant slips. Even supposing he still lived, Philoktetes had been in Lesbos for ten years without ever once sending us a message. Nor had our messengers ever found him. Who knew what illness could do to a man's mind? Look at Ajax.

Odysseus stood high in the prow, waving gaily. I let my breath go in a huge sigh of relief. He was a devious man, but he didn't grin like that if he had failed. Menelaos and Idomeneus joined me as I waited, none of us knowing what exactly to expect. His life had been despaired of; and, in the event he had survived, his leg had been despaired of. So I stood imagining a cripple, a withered wreck, not the man who swung himself over the rails and dropped the many cubits to the ground as lightly as a boy. He hadn't changed. He had hardly aged. He sported a neat golden beard and wore nothing save a kilt. Over his shoulder hung a mighty bow and a grimy quiver stuffed with arrows. I knew he was at least forty-five, but his hard, tanned body looked ten years younger, and his powerful legs were perfect. I could only gape.

'Why, Philoktetes, why?' was all I could find to say when we had settled into chairs at my house and had the wine servant at our elbows.

'Simple, Agamemnon, when you know the story.'

'Then tell it!' I commanded, happier than since Achilles and Ajax died. That was the effect Philoktetes had on us; he sent the winds of life and cheer through my musty halls.

'It took a year to recover my wits and the use of my leg,' Philoktetes began. 'Fearing that the local people wouldn't be kind to a Greek, my servants took me high onto a mountain and settled me in a cave. This was far west of Thermi and Antissa, leagues from any village, even farm. My servants were faithful and loyal, so no one knew who I was or where I was. Imagine my surprise when Odysseus told me that Achilles had sacked Lesbos four times during the last ten years! I knew nothing of it!'

'Well, sacks are visited on cities,' Meriones said.

'True enough.'

'But surely you ventured further afield once you recovered!' Menelaos objected.

'No,' Philoktetes answered, 'I didn't. Apollo spoke to me in a dream and told me to stay where I was. Candidly, I found it no hardship. I took to hunting and running, shooting deer and wild pigs, and had my servants barter the meat for wine or figs or olives in the nearest village – I led an idyllic life! No cares, no kingdom, no responsibilities. The years went by, I was happy, and I never suspected the war was still going on. I thought you'd all be back home.'

'Until we climbed your mountain and found you,' Odysseus said.

'Did Apollo say you could go?' Nestor asked.

'Yes. And I'm very glad to be in at the kill.'

A messenger had come to whisper in Odysseus's ear; he got up and accompanied the man outside. When he returned his face was comical with surprise.

'Sire,' he said to me, 'one of my agents reports that Priam is planning another fight. The Trojan army will be on our doorstep well before dawn tomorrow, with orders to attack while we're asleep. Isn't that interesting? A flagrant breach of the laws governing warfare. I'll bet Aineas plotted it.'

'Oh, come, Odysseus!' said Menestheus unexpectedly, blowing a derisive noise with his lips. 'What's all this about breaching the laws governing warfare? You've been doing that for years!'

His mouth twitched. 'Yes, but they haven't,' Odysseus said.

'Whether they have or have not, Menestheus,' I said, 'they are now. Odysseus, you have my permission to use any means you can devise to get us inside the walls of Troy.'

'Starvation,' he said promptly.

'Short of starvation,' I said.

We were drawn up in the shadows long before darkness was due to dissipate, so Aineas found himself too slow. I led the assault myself and we cut them to pieces, showing them that we could do without Achilles and Ajax. Already uneasy because they couldn't be comfortable with Aineas's trickery, the Trojans panicked when we fell on them. All we had to do was follow to pick them off in hundreds.

Philoktetes used Herakles's arrows with devastating effect. He had developed a system whereby men ran to all his victims, plucked out the precious arrows, cleaned them and returned them to the worn old quiver.

Those who escaped fled into the city; the Skaian Gate closed in our faces. The fight had been very short. We stood victorious with dead Trojans littered everywhere not long after the sun had risen; the final flower of Troy had fallen in the dust.

Idomeneus and Meriones drove up, Menelaos close behind, and then the others; they swung their cars into a circle to scan the field and talk over the battle.

'Herakles's arrows certainly own magic when you fire them, Philoktetes,' I said.

He grinned. 'I admit they like such work more than they like plugging deer, Agamemnon. But when my men count up the tally of arrows, they're going to find three missing.' His eyes went to Automedon, who had done well leading the Myrmidons. 'I have some good news for you to pass on to the Myrmidons, Automedon.'

That riveted all of us.

'Good news?' Automedon asked.

'Indeed! I tricked Paris into a duel. One of the soldiers pointed him out to me, so I stalked him until I caught him with no bolt hole in his vicinity. Then I boasted of my prowess as an archer and made nasty fun of his pansified little bow. Since he didn't know me from an Assyrian mercenary, he fell for it and accepted my challenge. I let my first shaft fly wide to whet his appetite. Though I admit he has a good eye. If I hadn't been quick with my shield his first shot would have punctured me neatly in the midriff. Then I took him. The first arrow in his bow hand, the second in his right heel – I thought that suitable payment for Achilles – and the third straight through his right eye. None of them were mortal enough to kill him outright, but more than enough to ensure that he dies sooner or later. I asked the God to guide my hand, make him perish slowly.' Clapping Menelaos on the shoulder, he laughed. 'Menelaos followed him from the field, but wounded and all he was too slippery, much to our old redhead's disgust.'

By this time we were all laughing; I sent heralds to spread the word through the army that the murderer of Achilles was a dead man. We had seen the last of Paris the seducer.

CHAPTER THIRTY

NARRATED BY
HELEN

Most of the time I kept strictly to myself. How Penelope my cousin would have chuckled! Time hung so heavily on my hands that I had actually taken to *weaving*. The pursuit, I now understood, of neglected wives. Paris literally never came near me. Nor did Aineas.

Since the death of Hektor the palace atmosphere had altered for the worse. Hekabe had gone so peculiar in the head that she never ceased to reproach Priam for the fact that she hadn't been his first wife. Bewildered and upset, he would protest that he had made her his principal wife, his *Queen*! Whereupon she would squat down on her hunkers and start howling like an old dog. Absolutely crazy! But at least now I understood where Kassandra got it from.

A desperately unhappy place. Hektor's widow and therefore tumbled far from her old status, Andromache acted like a shade herself. Rumour had it at the time that she and Hektor had quarrelled bitterly just before he left Troy to fight his last fight, and that the falling out had been her fault. He had begged her to look at him, to say farewell, but she had chosen to lie in their bed with her face to the wall. I believed the tale; she had that ghastly look of terrible pain and unending remorse which only a guilty woman who loves greatly can wear. Nor could she summon up any interest in her son, Astyanax, whom she had given over to the men to educate the moment Hektor was in his tomb.

What was left of Priam's world disintegrated when Troilos fell to Achilles. Even the death of Achilles failed to pull him from his slough of despond. I knew the gossip in the Citadel – that Aineas had deliberately refrained from sending Troilos help because Priam had insulted him so during the assembly at which he had appointed Troilos the new Heir. As with Andromache, I believed the tale. Aineas was not a man to insult.

Then Aineas demanded to lead a surprise raid on the Greek camp, and Priam, abject, agreed.

Nothing could stop the wagging tongues, but nothing could be done either. Aineas was all we had left. Though Priam hadn't given in all the way; he appointed that savage boar, Deiphobos, the Heir. An act of defiance which made no impression upon dear Aineas, very sure of himself these days.

I looked long into that dark Dardanian face, for I knew what fires burned beneath his cool exterior; *I* knew the lengths to which his all-consuming ambition would drive him. Like some slow-moving river of lava Aineas ploughed inexorably onwards, engulfing his enemies one by one.

When Aineas demanded permission to raid the Greek camp, he knew what he was asking the King to do: forsake the laws of the Gods. And only I had any idea of the hugeness of Aineas's triumph when Priam said yes. He had managed at last to drag Troy down to his level.

On the day of the raid I shut myself in my rooms, my ears stuffed with wadding to deaden the thunder and the screams. I was weaving a length of fine wool in an intricate design and using many colours; by dint of rigid concentration I managed to forget that there was a battle going on. And hah! to Penelope Web Face, wife of a bandy-legged red man with no honour and few scruples. I was willing to bet that *she* had never woven anything half so fine. Knowing her, she had probably taken to weaving shrouds.

'Sanctimonious, carping cow!' I was saying to myself savagely when the hairs on my arms began to prickle, as if someone from the grave was watching me. Was Penelope Web Face dead? I couldn't be so lucky.

But when I lifted my head it was Paris watching me, hanging onto the door frame, his mouth opening and closing in utter silence. *Paris?* Paris drenched in blood? Paris with two cubits of an arrow poking out of one eye?

When I pulled the wadding out of my ears the noise rushed in on me like Maenads racing down a mountainside intent on the kill. Paris's one good eye blazed at me with the light of madness in it while words I couldn't understand spilled from his mouth.

As I stared my shock faded. I started to laugh, had to drop onto a couch and shriek helplessly. That brought him to his knees! He crawled with his right hand dragging a crimson trail across the white floor behind him, the arrow protruding from his right eye bobbing up and down so ridiculously that I laughed even harder. Reaching my feet, he wrapped his good arm about my legs and bled all over my robe. Revolted, I lashed out with my foot and knocked him sprawling. Then I ran for the door.

I found Helenos and Deiphobos standing together in the great courtyard, both still in their armour. When neither of them noticed my approach I touched Helenos on the arm; not for all the world would I have touched Deiphobos.

'We lost,' said Helenos wearily. 'They were lying in wait for us.' Tears stood in his eyes. 'We broke the law! We are accursed.'

I shrugged. 'What concern is that of mine? I didn't come for news of your stupid battle – anyone could have told you you'd lose. I came to ask your help.'

'Anything, Helen,' said Deiphobos with a leer.

'Paris is in my rooms – dying, I think.'

Helenos flinched. 'Paris, dying? *Paris?*'

I began to walk away. 'I want him removed,' I said.

When they joined me, they bent to lift Paris onto a couch. 'I want him removed, not made comfortable!'

Helenos looked appalled. 'Helen! You can't turn him out!'

'Watch me! What do I owe him except my ruin? He's ignored me for years! For years he's permitted me to become the butt of every spiteful, bitch-faced old sow in Troy! Yet when he needs me at last, he thinks to find me the same moonstruck idiot he took away from Amyklai! Well, I'm not! Let him die somewhere else. Let him die in the arms of whoever is his current love!'

Paris had quietened; the one eye left to him goggled at me in stupefied horror. 'Helen, Helen!' he moaned.

'Don't "Helen" me!'

Helenos stroked his greying curls. 'What happened, Paris?'

'The strangest thing, Helenos! A man challenged me to a duel over a distance only I or Teukros could shoot accurately. A big, gold-bearded wild man. He looked like a bush king from Ida. But I didn't know him, I'd never seen him before! So I took him on – I knew I'd win! But he outshot me. Then he stood and laughed at me, just like Helen!'

I was paying more attention to the arrow than to this pitiful story. Surely I'd seen one like it before? Or heard it described in some song given by the harper at Amyklai? A very long shaft of willow stained crimson with the juice of berries, tipped with white goose feathers spotted in the same crimson dye.

'The man who shot you was Philoktetes,' I said. 'You're honoured above your deserts, Paris. You carry one of Herakles's arrows in your head. He gave his bow and arrows to Philoktetes before he died. I heard Philoktetes had died too, of a serpent's sting, but obviously the rumour was wrong. This is an arrow that once belonged to Herakles.'

Helenos was glaring at me. 'Shut up, you heartless harpy! Must you vent your spleen on a dying man?'

'You know, Helenos,' I said dreamily, 'you're worse than your loon of a sister. At least she doesn't feign sanity. Now will you *please* remove Paris?'

'Helenos?' asked Paris, plucking weakly at his kilt. 'Take me to Ida mountain, to my dear Oinone. She can heal me – she has the gift from Artemis. Take me to Oinone!'

I pushed between them, afire with rage. 'I don't care where you take him! Just get him out of here! Take him to Oinone – hah! Doesn't he understand he's a dead man? Pull out the arrow, Helenos, let him die! It's what he deserves!'

They levered him onto the edge of the couch and sat him up. The stronger of the two, Deiphobos, bent to lift him, but Paris wouldn't help; craven to the last, he wept in an ecstasy of fear. When Deiphobos finally staggered upright, Paris in his arms, Paris gave him all his weight.

Helenos went behind Deiphobos to assist him. As he reached across, his arm accidently brushed the shaft of the arrow. Paris screamed and panicked, flung his hands out wildly, his body heaving and threshing. Deiphobos lost his balance and the three of them fell in a tangled heap to the floor. I heard a choked off, gurgling grunt. Then Helenos picked himself up and tugged Deiphobos to his feet, and I could see what they had not.

Paris lay half on his back and half on his left side, one leg twisted under the other, his mangled hand outflung. Its fingers were curled into claws, his neck and back were rigidly arched. He must have fallen on his face with Deiphobos on top of him, then Helenos in landing on them both had slewed him around again. The arrow was in two pieces now; the spotted flights of the butt and two cubits of the shaft lay beside him, and from his eye there protruded a finger's breadth of splintered willow. A thin trickle of dark blood ran to form a pool on the marble tiles.

I must have cried out, for they both turned to look.

Helenos sighed. 'He's dead, Deiphobos.'

Deiphobos shook his head dully. 'Paris? Paris *dead*?'

They took him away then. All I had to remind me that my husband had ever existed were the marks of his hands on my skirt and the red stains on the pure white floor. I stood for a moment, then walked to the window and looked out of it, unseeing. There I remained until darkness fell, though what I thought about during that day I have never been able to remember.

The eternal and hateful Trojan wind had risen to a rough whine about the towers when someone knocked on the door. A herald was bowing to me.

'Princess, the King summons you to the Throne Room.'

'Thank you. Tell him I'll come as quickly as I can.'

The huge hall was in semidarkness. Only around the dais were there lamps burning fitfully, casting a sheet of soft yellow light about the King as he sat on his chair, and about Deiphobos and Helenos as they stood one to either side of him, glaring at each other over the top of the King's crystal hair.

I came to stand at the foot of the steps. 'Yes, sire?'

Frowning, he leaned forwards, his displeasure overlying all the other pains stamped permanently into his features: the grief, the despair, the utter hopelessness.

'Daughter, you have lost your husband and I have lost yet another son. I have begun to lose count,' he quavered, voice a rustle in the gloom. 'All the good ones have been snatched away. Now these two come to me snarling and snapping and bickering over their brother's still warm body, each demanding the same thing, each determined to have his way.'

'What *is* this about?' I asked, exasperated beyond courtesy. 'Why does a disagreement between this pair concern me?'

'Oh, it definitely concerns you!' the old man said harshly. 'Deiphobos wants to marry you. Helenos wants to marry you. So tell me which one of them you prefer.'

'Neither!' I gasped, outraged.

'One of them it has to be,' said the King, suddenly looking as if he found the situation piquant, novel, invigorating. 'Give me his name, madam! You'll marry him at the end of six moons.'

'Six moons!' Deiphobos cried. 'Why do I have to wait for six moons? I want her now, Father – *now*!'

Priam drew himself up. 'Your brother isn't cold,' he said.

'There's no need to get upset, sire,' I said before Deiphobos could erupt into one of his famous tantrums. 'I've been married twice. I don't wish to marry a third time. I intend to give myself into the service of the Mother and attend her altar for the rest of my days. So there will be no wedding.'

Helenos and Deiphobos broke into a babble of protestations, but Priam's uplifted hand silenced them.

'Be still and listen to me! Deiphobos, you're my eldest imperial son and my designated Heir. At the end of six moons you may marry Helen, but not until then. As for you, Helenos, you belong to the Lord Apollo. You ought to hold him dearer than any woman, even this one.'

Deiphobos whooped. Helenos looked stunned, but even as I watched, stunned myself, Helenos seemed to grow and change, to melt in some parts and harden in others. It was very strange.

He looked at his father steadily then, and said, 'All my life I've watched others satisfy themselves while I go hungry and thirsty, Father. No one asked me whether I wanted to serve the God – I was dedicated to him on the day of my birth. When Hektor died you would have made me Heir, except that Apollo got in the way. And after Troilos died you passed over me *again*! Now, when I ask you for such a little thing, I am denied once more.' He drew himself up proudly. 'Well, there comes a time when even the least of men will rebel. That time is now for me. I'm leaving Troy. I'm going into voluntary exile. Better to become a wandering nobody than have to stay here and watch Deiphobos ruin everything Troy has left. I hate to say it, Father, but you're a fool.'

While Priam assimilated this, I tried again.

'Sire, I entreat you, don't force me to remarry!' I cried. 'Let me consecrate myself to the Goddess!'

But he shook his head. 'You'll marry Deiphobos.'

I couldn't bear to be in the same room with them; I fled like one pursued by the Daughters of Kore. What happened to Helenos I do not know. Nor do I care.

I sent a note to Aineas, entreating him to come to my rooms. He was the only one left who might be moved to help me. Then doubt gnawed as I waited for him, pacing up and down, up and down. Though our affair was long over, I fancied he still had some affection for me. Or did he? Where *was* he? The time slipped away, each moment longer, more dreary, emptier. I listened vainly for his strong, decisive step in the corridor; since Hektor's death the only footfalls which had the ability to inspire confidence in their owner.

'What do you want, Helen?' he asked, having entered the room so quietly I didn't hear him. He drew the curtain carefully.

Laughing and weeping, I flew to embrace him. 'I thought you wouldn't come!' I said, lifting my face for his kiss.

He moved away. 'What do you want?'

I stared at him; when I spoke, my voice faltered. 'Aineas, help me! Paris is dead!'

'I know that.'

'Then you must understand what it means to *me*! Paris is dead! I'm at their mercy! I'm ordered to wed Deiphobos! That slavering hound! Oh, Gods! In Lakedaimon they wouldn't have deemed him fit to touch the hem of my skirt, yet Priam *orders* me to marry him! If you have any regard for me at all, Aineas, I implore you to see Priam and tell him I meant what I said – I have no desire to remarry! None!'

He looked like a man facing an unpalatable chore. 'You ask the impossible, Helen.'

'The impossible?' I asked, stupefied. 'Aineas, nothing is impossible for you! You're the most powerful man in Troy!'

'My advice is to marry Deiphobos and be done with it.'

'But I thought – I thought – I thought that even if you didn't want me for yourself, you'd feel enough for me to fight for me!'

Hand on the curtain, he laughed. 'Helen, I won't help you. Understand that, please. Every day creates a new gap in the ranks of Priam's sons – every day brings me closer to the Trojan throne. I'm on the rise, and I won't jeopardise my position for you. Is that quite clear?'

'Remember what comes to men of such ambition, Aineas.'

He laughed again. 'A throne, Helen! A throne!'

'I'll buy a curse just for you,' I said dreamily. 'I'll spend everything I own on it. And I'll ask that you never sit on any throne – that you never know peace – that you're forced to wander the width of the world – that you end your days amid savages so poor they live in wicker huts.'

I think that frightened him. The curtain swung; he vanished.

After Aineas had gone I took stock of what I was looking forward to: marriage to a man I loathed, whose touch would set me to puking. Then I realised that for the first time in my life I had no resources beyond my own. That if I was to break free from this dreadful place, I would have to do so unaided.

Menelaos wasn't far away, and two of Troy's three gates were always open. But palace women were not used to walking, nor did they have access to sturdy shoes. To succeed in getting from the Dardanian Gate past the Skaian Gate to the Greek beach wasn't possible. Unless, that is, I rode upon an animal! Women rode donkeys; they simply perched on the beast's back with their legs to one side. Yes, I'd do it! I'd steal a donkey and ride to the beach while night still lay upon the city and the plain.

Stealing the donkey didn't prove difficult. Nor did riding on its back. But when I reached the Dardanian Gate – much further from the Citadel than the Skaian – my transport refused to budge. A city beast, it smelled the open air of the countryside and misliked the perfumes floating on the wind – the tang of coming autumn, a whiff of the sea. When I whipped it with a switch it began to bray mournfully, and that was the end of me. The gate guards came to investigate. I was recognised and arrested.

'I want to go to my husband!' I wept. 'Let me go to my husband, please!'

But of course they didn't let me go, though the wretched donkey had now decided that it liked what it smelled. While it kicked up its hind legs and bolted to freedom, I was returned to the palace. But they didn't wake Priam. They woke Deiphobos.

I waited passively while he came from his bed, gazed at him calmly when he appeared. He thanked the gate guards courteously enough and gave them a gift; when they had finished bowing themselves out he threw the curtain to his bedroom wide.

'Do come in,' he said.

I didn't move.

'You wanted to go to your husband. Well, here I am.'

'We're not married, and you already have a wife.'

'Not any more. I divorced her.'

'No marriage for six moons, Priam said.'

'But, my dear, that was before you tried to escape to the Greeks and Menelaos. When Father hears about that, he won't stand in my way. Especially after I inform him I've already consummated the union.'

'You wouldn't dare!' I snarled.

For answer, he grabbed my ear in one hand and my nose in the other, wrestling me into the bedroom. Dizzy with pain, unable to break his hold, I collapsed on the bed. The only violation worse was death. The last thing I thought before I put my mind in the care of the Mother was that one day I would violate Deiphobos in that worst way of all: I would kill him.

CHAPTER THIRTY-ONE

NARRATED BY
DIOMEDES

S hortly after the unsuccessful Trojan raid Agamemnon
called a council, though Neoptolemos hadn't yet arrived.
A general air of optimism pervaded the beach; all that
stopped us were the walls, and perhaps with Odysseus thinking
on that subject, we would even conquer them. We laughed and
joked among ourselves as Agamemnon dallied with Nestor,
amused at something Nestor said to him low-voiced. Then he
lifted his sceptre and rapped its staff on the floor.

'Odysseus, I believe you have news for us.'

'I do, sire. First of all, I believe I've worked out how to breach
the Trojan walls, though I'm not ready to speak about it yet.
But in other areas, interesting news.'

He looked at Menelaos, then walked across to put his hand
on Menelaos's shoulder, rubbing it. 'I've heard a snippet of
Citadel gossip concerning a difference of opinion between
Priam, Helenos and Deiphobos. Over a woman. Helen, to be
precise. Poor thing! After Paris died she asked to be allowed to
dedicate herself to the service of Mother Kubaba, but Deiphobos and Helenos both demanded to marry her. Priam decided
in favour of Deiphobos, who then married her forcibly. It set
the Court on its ears, but Priam refused to nullify the union.
Apparently Helen was caught in the act of escaping to join you,
Menelaos.'

Menelaos said something beneath his breath and bowed his
head into his hands. While I thought of beautiful, imperious
Helen come down to the level of a common house woman.

'The whole business so disgusted Helenos, the priest-son,'

Odysseus continued, 'that he elected to go into voluntary exile. I intercepted him outside the city, hoping that his disillusionment was great enough to permit of his telling me about the Oracles of Troy. When I found him he was at the altar dedicated to Thymbraian Apollo, who, he informed me, had instructed him to tell me whatever I wanted to know. I asked for the Oracles of Troy in their entirety – a wearisome affair. Helenos recited *thousands*! However, I got what I needed.'

'A great piece of luck,' said Agamemnon.

Odysseus lifted his lip. 'Luck, sire,' he said evenly, 'is an overrated commodity. It's not luck leads to success, it's hard work. Luck is what happens in the moment when the dice land. Hard work is what happens when a prize falls into a man's hands because he's worked for it.'

'Yes, yes, yes!' said the High King, rueing his choice of a phrase. 'I apologise, Odysseus! Hard work, always hard work! I know it, I admit it. Now what of the Oracles?'

'As far as we're concerned, only three of the thousands have any relevance. *Luckily* none of them presents an insurmountable obstacle. They go something like this: Troy will fall this year if the Greek leaders possess the shoulder blade of Pelops, if Neoptolemos takes the field, and if Troy should lose the Palladion of Pallas Athene.'

I jumped up excitedly. 'Odysseus, *I* have the shoulder blade of Pelops! King Pittheus gave it to me after Hippolytos died. The old man was fond of me, and it was his most treasured relic. He said he'd rather I had it than Theseus. I brought it to Troy with me for good – er – *luck*.'

Odysseus grinned. 'Isn't that *lucky*?' he asked Agamemnon. 'Of Neoptolemos we have high hopes, so that's taken care of. Which leaves the Palladion of Pallas Athene, who *luckily* is my protectress. My, my!'

'I'm getting annoyed, Odysseus,' said the High King.

'Ah – where was I? The Palladion. Well, we have to have that ancient image. It's revered above anything else in the city, and its loss would hit Priam hard. As far as I know, the image is located somewhere in the Citadel crypt. A closely guarded secret. But I'm sure I can penetrate the secret. The most difficult part of the exercise will be moving it – they say it's very bulky and heavy. Diomedes, will you come with me to Troy?'

'Gladly!'

As there was nothing else of importance to discuss, the council broke up. Menelaos caught Odysseus at the door and took him by the arm.

'Will you see her?' he asked wistfully.

'Yes, probably,' said Odysseus gently.

'Tell her I wish she'd succeeded in reaching me.'

'I will.' But, as we walked back to his house, he added to me: 'I will not! Helen is for the Axe, not for her old spot in Menelaos's bed.'

I began to laugh. 'Care to bet on it?' I asked.

'Will we go up through the conduit?' was my first question when we settled to work out a plan.

'You will, but I can't. I have to be able to gain access to Helen without suspicion. Therefore I can't look like Odysseus.'

He went from the room but was back in a moment, carrying a short, cruel whip divided into four thongs, each tipped with a ragged bronze knob. I stared at him and it, bewildered, until he turned his back on me and began to strip off his blouse.

'Flog me, Diomedes.'

I leaped up, horrified. 'Are you out of your mind? Flog you, of all men? I couldn't!'

His mouth thinned. 'Close your eyes, then, and pretend I'm Deiphobos. I have to be flogged – *properly*.'

I put my arm around his bare shoulders. 'Ask whatever you like of me, but not that. Flog you – a king! – as if you were a rebellious slave?'

Laughing softly, he laid his cheek on my arm. 'Oh, what are a few scars more on my scraggy carcase? I must look like a rebellious slave, Diomedes. What better than to see a bloody back on an escaped Greek slave? Use the whip.'

I shook my head. 'No.'

He grew grim. 'Use it, Diomedes!'

Unwillingly I picked it up; he bent over. I curled the four thongs about my hand, gathered in my courage and brought them down on his skin. Purple welts rose under them; I watched the things swell in fascinated revulsion.

'Put a little bite into it!' he said impatiently. 'You drew no blood!'

I closed my eyes and did as I was told. Ten strokes in all I gave him with that vile implement; each time it fell I drew blood and scarred him for life like any rebellious slave.

Afterwards he kissed me. 'Don't grieve so, Diomedes. What use is a fair skin to me?' He winced. 'It feels good. Does it look good too?'

I nodded wordlessly.

He dropped his kilt and moved about the room, wrapping a piece of filthy linen around his loins, tousling his hair and darkening it with soot from the fire tripod. I swear his eyes flashed in sheer enjoyment. Then he held out a set of manacles. 'Chain me, you Argive tyrant!'

I did as I was told a second time, aware that I hurt from the flogging in ways he never would. To Odysseus, it was no more than a means to an end. As I knelt to snap the bronze cuffs about his ankles, he talked.

'Once I'm within the city I have to get into the Citadel. We'll travel together in Ajax's car – it's strong, stable and quiet – until we reach the grove of trees near the small watchtower at our end of the Western Curtain. From there we'll go separately. I'll bluff my way through the little door in the Skaian Gate, and do the same at the Citadel gates – my story will be that I have to see Polydamas urgently. I find his name works best.'

'But,' I said, straightening, 'you're not really going to see Polydamas.'

'No, I intend to see Helen. I imagine after this forced marriage she'll be glad to help me. She'll certainly know all about the crypt. She may even know whereabouts the Palladion's shrine is.' He clanked around a little, practising.

'While I?'

'You'll wait in the trees until half the night is gone. Then ascend through our conduit and kill the guards in the vicinity of the small watchtower. I'll get the image to the walls somehow. When you hear the nightlark's song with this variation' – he whistled it three times – 'you'll come down and help me get her through the conduit.'

I dropped Odysseus in the trees without being detected, and settled down then to wait. Limping and staggering, he ran like someone demented towards the Skaian Gate, shouting, screeching, grovelling in the dust, the sorriest specimen of man I had ever seen. He always loved to be someone he wasn't, but I think he enjoyed the escaped slave identity most.

When the night was half over I found our conduit and crawled slowly up its twisting, stifling length, making no noise. At its top I rested and got used to the moonlight, ears tuned to pick up the few sounds which drifted along the pathway atop the walls. I was close to the minor watchtower Odysseus had made our rendezvous because it was well removed from other guarded points.

Five guards were on duty, awake and alert, but they were all inside – who organised these people, to permit them to sit in comfort while the bastions were neglected? They'd not last long in a Greek camp!

I wore a soft, dark leather kilt and blouse, had a dagger between my teeth and a short sword in my right hand. Edging up to the window of the guardroom, I coughed loudly.

'See who's outside, Maios,' someone said.

Out came Maios, strolling; a good, unconcealed cough isn't at all alarming, even when heard on top of the most bitterly contested walls in the world. Seeing no one, he tensed – though, being a fool, he didn't call for reinforcements. Obviously telling himself that he was imagining things, he came on with pike at the ready. I let him pass me before I rose up silently, one hand gagging him, the other using the sword. I lowered him gently onto the path and dragged him into a dark corner.

A few moments later another one emerged, sent to look for Maios. I cut his throat without a sound: two down and three to go. Then before those left inside could grow uneasy, I edged up to the window again and hiccoughed drunkenly. Someone inside heaved an exasperated sigh; another lunged out impatiently. I wrapped my arms about him as if very drunk, and when the bronze slid under his left ribs and up to his heart he didn't so much as grunt. Holding him upright, I reeled about in a tipsy dance, mimicking a Trojan voice. Which brought a fourth man out. I tossed the dead one at him with a low laugh, and while he fended the fellow off I stuck a cubit of sword blade through him from one side to the other. I got both of them to the ground with fading chinks, as if they had moved off into the darkness. Then I peered over the windowsill.

Only the tower captain remained, muttering angrily to himself as he sat at a table. Clearly in a quandary, he was staring at a trapdoor in the floor. Expecting someone he thought he should be there to greet? I slipped into the room and leaped on him from behind, stopping his cry with my hand. He died as quickly as the rest and joined them in that dark corner between the path and the tower wall. Then I sat down outside to wait, deeming it better that, if the expected visitor did appear, he should see no one in the guardroom.

Not long afterwards Odysseus whistled his variation on the nightlark's song – how clever he was! Had he not thought to vary the usual trill, a real nightlark was bound to have decided to sing right near the watchtower. As it was, no real nightlark was in the offing; all I had to hope was that no visitor was either, for I couldn't warn Odysseus.

I opened the trapdoor in the guardroom and shinnied down the side of the ladder to find Odysseus waiting at the bottom.

'Wait!' I whispered, and went outside to scout around. But the streets were quiet, lampless and torchless.

'I have her, Diomedes, but she weighs as much as Ajax!' said Odysseus when I returned. 'It's going to be hard work dragging her up a twenty-five-cubit ladder.'

She – the Palladion – was perched precariously across the back of an ass, so we lugged her into the downstairs chamber after sending the beast scampering off. Awestruck, I stared at her in the lamplight. Oh, she was so *old*! A crudely recognisable female form carved out of some dark wood too grimed by the passage of aeons to be beautiful, and beautiful she was not. She had tiny, joined, pointed feet, huge thighs, an obscene vulva, a distended belly, two bulbous breasts, arms clamped against her sides, a round head and a pouting mouth. She was also enormously fat. Taller than me, she was heavy. The pointed feet might have enabled her to spin like a child's top, but she couldn't stand on them; we had to support her.

'Odysseus, will she fit inside the conduit?' I asked.

'Yes. The bulk of her belly is no bigger than your shoulders and she's rounder. So's the conduit.'

Then I had a bright idea. I searched the room for a piece of rope and found it in a box, then looped it under her breasts, tied it, and had enough left over to hold on to. I went up the ladder first dragging her on the rope, while Odysseus put one hand on her huge, globous buttocks and the other inside her vulva, and shoved from underneath.

'Do you think,' I gasped when we reached the guardroom, 'that she'll ever forgive us the liberties we've had to take?'

'Oh, yes,' he said, lying flat on the floor alongside her. 'She's the first Athene, who is Pallas, and I belong to her.'

Getting her down the conduit was actually easier; Odysseus had been right. Her roundness bumped along more easily than I could with my wide shoulders and masculine angles. We kept her roped, which proved a second boon once we were on the plain; we dragged her to the grove of trees and Ajax's four-wheeled car. There, groaning from our final effort, we hoisted her aboard and collapsed. The half moon was westering, which meant we still had sufficient time to get her home.

'You did it, Odysseus!' I crowed.

'I couldn't have without you, old friend. How many guards did you have to kill?'

'Five.' I yawned. 'I'm tired.'

'How do you think *I* feel? At least your back is whole.'

'Don't talk about it! Tell me what happened inside the Citadel instead. Did you see Helen?'

'I duped the gate guards beautifully, so they let me into the city. The sole guard on the Citadel gates was asleep – I just picked up my chains and stepped over him, dainty as you please. I found Helen alone – Deiphobos was off somewhere. She was a little taken aback to find a bloodied, filthy slave prostrating himself at her feet, but then she saw my eyes and recognised me. When I asked to go to the crypt, she was out of her chair in an instant. I think she was expecting Deiphobos. But we escaped, and as soon as we could find a quiet spot she helped me rid myself of my fetters. Then we went to the crypt.' He chuckled. 'I have an idea it proved very handy when she was intriguing with Aineas, because she knew it like the back of her hand. Once we were down there she plagued me with questions – how was Menelaos? – how were you? – how was Agamemnon? She couldn't hear enough.'

'But the Palladion – how did you manage to move her if your only helper was Helen?' I asked.

His shoulders shook with laughter. 'While I said the prayers and asked the Goddess for her consent to the move, Helen vanished. The next thing, she was back with the ass! Then she led me out of the crypt straight into the street below the Citadel wall, where she kissed me – very chastely! – and wished me well.'

'Poor Helen,' I said. 'Deiphobos must have tipped the balance against Troy's interests.'

'You're absolutely right, Diomedes.'

*

Agamemnon erected a magnificent altar in the assembly square and enthroned the Palladion inside a golden niche. After which he summoned as much of the army as he could fit into the area, and told the story of how Odysseus and I had kidnapped her. She was given her own priest, who offered her the finest victims; the smoke was white as snow and lifted so quickly into the sky that we knew she loved her new home. How she must have hated the cold, dank blackness of her Trojan home! Her sacred snake slithered into his house below her altar without a moment's hesitation, then stuck his head out to lap at his saucer of milk and swallow his egg. An imposing and happy ceremony.

Odysseus, the rest of the Kings and I followed Agamemnon to his house when the ritual was over, there to feast. None of us ever refused an invitation to dine with the King of Kings; he had by far the best cooks. Cheeses, olives, breads, fruits, roast meats, fish, honeyed sweetmeats, wine.

The mood was lively, the conversation larded with mirth and jests, the wine excellent; then Menelaos called for the harper to sing. Maudlin by this time, we settled down comfortably to listen. The Greek was never born who loved not the songs, the hymns, the lays of his country; we would rather have heard the bard than bedded down with women.

The harper gave us one of the Lays of Herakles, then waited patiently for the slightly hysterical applause to die down. He was a fine poet and a fine musician; Agamemnon had brought him from Aulis ten years before, but he came originally from the North, and was said to be descended from Orpheus himself, the singer of singers.

Someone asked for the Battle Hymn of Tydeus, someone else for the Lament of Danai, and Nestor wanted the Tale of Medea; but to every request he smilingly shook his head. Then he bent the knee to Agamemnon.

'Sire, if it pleases you, I've composed a song about events much closer to us than the deeds of dead Heroes. May I sing my own composition to you?'

Agamemnon inclined that imperial, whitening head. 'Sing, Alphides of Salmydessos.'

He passed his fingers tenderly across the stiff strings to draw out his beloved lyre in slow melodic pain; the song was sad and yet glorious, a song of Troy and Agamemnon's army before its walls. He cast us rapt for a very long time, for such a titan of a poem isn't sung in two or three moments. We sat with our chins on our hands, and not an eye was open or a cheek dry. He ended with the death of Achilles. The rest was too sorrowful. Even now we found it hard to think of Ajax.

> 'All gold in death, he who was always gold in life,
> His beautiful mask wafting thin and unfluttered,
> His breath gone forever, his shade dissolved away.
> Heavy his clasped hands sheathed in golden gloves,
> All his mortality melted, his glory become mere metal,
> Peerless Achilles, his brazen voice struck to silence.
> O divine Muse, lift my heart, let me give him life!
> Through my words let him be clothed in living gold,
> Let his footsteps ring hollow with fear and dread,
> Let him stride across the plain before sullen Troy!
> Let me show him shake back his long golden plumes,
> Remember him gleaming like the splendid sun above,
> Running tireless through the dewed grasses of Troy
> With the ribbons on his cuirass nodding the rhythm,
> Glorious Achilles who was the lipless son of Peleus.'

We praised the harper Alphides of Salmydessos long and loud through aching hearts; he had given us a taste of immortality, for his song was sure to live far longer than any of us. I think it was that we still breathed, yet were in the song. The load was too heavy to bear.

When the applause finally ended I wanted to be alone with Odysseus; a gathering of men seemed alien to the mood the harper had inspired in us. I looked across at Odysseus, who understood without having to defile the moment with words. He got up, turned towards the door, and gasped audibly.

Because a sudden silence had fallen on the room, all our heads turned his way. And we gasped.

At first the likeness was uncanny; with the spell of the song still strong on us, it was as if Alphides of Salmydessos had conjured up a ghost to hear his music. I thought, Achilles has come to listen too! But who has given him the blood to allow his shade substance?

Then I looked more closely and saw that he wasn't Achilles. This man was as tall and as broad, but he was many years younger. The beard was hardly stiff and the stubble a darker gold, the eyes more amber. And he owned two perfectly formed lips.

How long he had been standing there none of us knew, but from the suffering in his face it must have been long enough to have heard at least the conclusion of the song.

Agamemnon rose and went to him with arm extended. 'You are Neoptolemos, son of Achilles. Welcome,' he said.

The young man nodded gravely. 'Thank you. I came to help, but I set sail before – before I knew my father was dead. I learned it from the harper.'

Odysseus joined them. 'What better way to learn such awful news?' he asked.

Sighing, Neoptolemos bowed his head. 'Yes. The song told it all. Is Paris dead?'

Agamemnon took both his hands. 'He is.'

'Who killed him?'

'Philoktetes, with the arrows of Herakles.'

He tried to be polite, to keep his features impassive. 'I am sorry, but I don't know your names. Which is Philoktetes?'

Philoktetes spoke. 'I am he.'

'I wasn't here to avenge him, so I must thank you.'

'I know, boy. You would rather have done it yourself. But I happened on the rogue by chance – or with the connivance of the Gods. Who can tell? And now, since you don't know us, let me introduce us. Our High King greeted you first. Next was

DIOMEDES

Odysseus. The rest are Nestor, Idomeneus, Menelaos, Diomedes, Automedon, Menestheus, Meriones, Machaon and
Eurypylos.'

I thought, how thin our ranks have grown!

Odysseus, an ecstatic Automedon and I took Neoptolemos to
the Myrmidon stockade. It was a longish walk, and news of his
arrival had preceded us. All along the way soldiers emptied out
of their houses, standing in the bitter sun to cheer him as
wholeheartedly as they had used to cheer his father. We
discovered that he was like Achilles in more than looks; he
acknowledged their wild joy with the same quiet smile and
careless wave, and like his father he lived unto himself, he
didn't spread his character lavishly on everyone he came in
contact with. As we walked we filled in the gaps in the song,
told him how Ajax had died, told him of Antilochos and all the
others who were dead. Then we told him about the living.

The Myrmidons were drawn up on parade. Not a single cheer
until the boy – he couldn't have been more than a bare
eighteen – had spoken to them. Then they pounded the flats of
their swords against their shields until the noise of it drove
Odysseus and I away. We strolled to the other end of the beach
and our own compound.

'And so it draws to an end, Diomedes.'

'If the Gods know the meaning of pity at all, I pray it draws
to an end,' I said.

He blew a wisp of red hair out of his eyes. 'Ten years ... How
curious that Kalchas was right about that. I wonder was it a
fluke, or if he really did have the Second Sight?'

I shivered. 'It isn't politic to doubt priestly powers.'

'Maybe, maybe. Oh, to shake the dust of Troy from my hair!
To sail the open seas again! To wash away the stench of this
plain with clean salt water! To go somewhere the air is windless
and the stars shine without competition from ten thousand
campfires! To be *purified*!'

444

'I echo all that, Odysseus. Though it's hard to believe too that it's almost over.'

'It will finish with a cataclysm to rival Poseidon.'

I stared. 'You've worked out how to do it?'

'Yes.'

'Tell me!'

'Before the moment? Diomedes, Diomedes! Not even for you! But it won't be long until the moment.'

'Come inside and let me bathe those lash stripes.'

Which made him laugh. 'They'll heal,' he said.

The following evening Neoptolemos came to dinner.

'I have something in trust for you, Neoptolemos,' said Odysseus after the meal was over. 'It's my gift to you.'

Neoptolemos glanced at me, puzzled. 'What does he mean?'

I shrugged. 'How can any man know except Odysseus?'

He came back wheeling a huge tripod, on it spread the golden armour Thetis had begged from Hephaistos Fire. Neoptolemos jumped to his feet stammering something I didn't understand, then reached out and touched the cuirass delicately, lovingly.

'I was angry,' he said, tears in his eyes, 'when Automedon told me you'd won it in debate with Ajax. But I must ask your pardon. You won it to give it to me?'

Odysseus grinned. 'You'll fit it, lad. It should be worn, not hung up on a wall or wasted on a dead man's relatives. Wear it, Neoptolemos, and may it bring you good luck. However, it will take some getting used to. It weighs about the same as you do.'

We got into a few minor skirmishes during the five days which followed; Neoptolemos got his first taste of Trojans, and licked his lips. He was a warrior, born to it and hungering for it. Only time was his enemy, and that he knew. His eyes told all of us he understood that his was to be a minor role in the closing moments of a great war; that the laurel wreaths would be woven for other brows, brows which had endured the full ten years. Yet in himself he was the deciding factor. He brought hope, fury and renewed enthusiasm; the eyes of the soldiers, Myrmidon or Argive or Aitolian made no difference, followed him with doglike devotion as he rode in his father's chariot wearing his father's armour. To them he *was* Achilles. And all the while I continued to watch Odysseus, avid for the summons to council.

It came half a moon after Neoptolemos arrived, from one of the imperial heralds: the next day, after the midday meal. I knew it was useless to try to pump Odysseus, so after we finished supper together I assumed a completely disinterested air as I listened to him pick a subject up and toss it as lightly and deftly as a tumbler his gilded ball. He took my attitude very well, only collapsing into helpless laughter when, very dignified, I took my leave of him. I could have kicked him, but I still smarted from that whipping more than he did, so I refrained; I made do with a pungent description of his ancestors instead.

They all came to Agamemnon's early, like hounds on the leash sniffing fresh blood, dressed carefully in their best kilts and jewels, as if they were going to a formal reception in the Lion Room at Mykenai. The imperial chief herald stood at the foot of the Lion Chair calling out the names of those present to an underling whose job it was to commit them to memory for posterity.

'Imperial Agamemnon, High King of Mykenai, King of Kings;
Idomeneus, High King of Crete;
Menestheus, High King of Attika;
Nestor, King of Pylos;
Menelaos, King of Lakedaimon;
Diomedes, King of Argos;
Odysseus, King of the Out Islands;
Philoktetes, King of Hestaiotis;
Eurypylos, King of Ormenion;
Thoas, King of Aitolia;
Agapenor, King of Arkadia;
Ajax, son of Oileus, King of Lokris;
Meriones, Prince of Crete, Heir to Crete;

Neoptolemos, Prince of Thessalia, Heir to Thessalia;
Teukros, Prince of Salamis;
Machaon, Surgeon;
Podalieros, Surgeon;
Epeios, Engineer.'

The King of Kings nodded to his heralds to leave, and handed Meriones the Staff of Debate. He then spoke to us in the very stilted language of formal pronouncements.

'After Priam, King of Troy, did break the sacred covenants of war, I did commission Odysseus, King of Ithaka, to devise a plan to take Troy by stealth and trickery. I am informed that Odysseus, King of Ithaka, is ready to speak. You are all called upon to witness his words. Royal Odysseus, you have the floor.'

Smiling at Meriones, Odysseus got up. 'Keep the Staff for me.' Then he took a rolled-up piece of soft pale hide from the table in the centre of the room and walked to a wall we could all see. There he flipped the hide open and pinned it securely to the wall with a little jewelled dagger in each of its four corners.

To the last one we stared at it blankly, wondering if we were the victims of a hoax. Admittedly well done in its way, it was a drawing etched thickly on the hide in black charcoal: a sort of a horse done very large, and to one side of it, a vertical line.

Odysseus looked at us enigmatically. 'Yes, it is a drawing of a horse. No doubt you're wondering why Epeios is here with us today. Well, he's here with us today so that I can ask him some questions and he can give me some answers.'

He turned to Epeios, as bewildered as he was uncomfortable in this exalted company.

'Epeios, you're held the finest engineer Greece has produced since Aiakos died. You're also held to be the finest wood worker. Look at the drawing carefully. Note the line beside the horse. The length of that line is the height of the walls of Troy.'

Mystified, we all looked as intently as Epeios did.

'First of all, Epeios, I want your opinion on something,' said the King of the Out Islands. 'You've had ten years in which to observe the walls of Troy. Tell me: is there any battering ram, any siege engine in the world capable of demolishing the Skaian Gate?'

'No, King Odysseus.'

'Very well, then! A second question: using what materials, craftsmen and facilities you have right here now, could you build me a huge ship?'

'Yes, sire. I have shipwrights, carpenters, masons, sawyers and plenty of unskilled labour. And I estimate that there's enough timber of the right kind within five leagues of here to build you a fleet of such ships.'

'Excellent! Now the third question: could you build me a wooden horse the size of this animal on the chart? Note the black line again. It is thirty cubits, the height of the Trojan walls. From which you will see that at its ears the horse is thirty-five cubits tall. And – question four – could you build this horse on a wheeled platform capable of holding its weight? And – my fifth question – could you make the horse hollow?'

Epeios began to smile; evidently the project tickled his fancy. 'Yes, sire, to all your questions.'

'How long would it take you?'

'A matter of days only, sire.'

Odysseus unpinned the hide and tossed it to the engineer. 'Thank you. Take this and go to my house. I'll see you there.'

We were totally at a loss. Our faces must have been studies in bewilderment, apprehension and suspicion, but as we waited for Epeios to depart Nestor began to chuckle, as if he suddenly saw the most exquisite joke of all his long, long life.

Odysseus flung his arms wide and grew in height until he seemed to tower; he was off now, which meant none of us could have either swayed or stopped him. Gesturing magnificently, he made his voice ring around the rafters.

'That, my fellow Kings and Princes, is how to take Troy!'

We sat mumchance and stared at him.

'Yes, Nestor, you're right. So are you, Agamemnon. First of all, a horse that size will hold within its belly, I estimate, about one hundred men. And if the sortie is silent, nocturnal and unsuspected, one hundred men will be quite sufficient to open the Skaian Gate.'

The queries came thick and fast from every quarter of the room. Doubters yelled, enthusiasts cheered, and pandemonium ruled until Agamemnon climbed off the Lion Chair to take the Staff from Meriones and drum it on the floor.

'You may ask all your questions, but in a more orderly way – and after me. Odysseus, sit down and pour yourself some wine, then explain this scheme in every little detail.'

The council broke up as darkness was falling; I accompanied Odysseus back to his house. Epeios was waiting patiently, the hide chart open before him; it now contained several more and smaller drawings. I listened idly as the pair of them discussed technical matters – the things Epeios would need, the approximate length of time the task would take – the necessity for absolute secrecy.

'You may work in the mysterious hollow just behind this house,' said Odysseus to Epeios. 'It's deep, so the horse won't poke its head above the tops of the trees on the far side. No one will be able to see it from the city watchtowers. The locality has other advantages too. It's been off limits to all and sundry for so many years that you won't have any inquisitive sightseers. You'll use the men who live there as unskilled labourers. Every man you have to import to the hollow will be unable to leave until the job is done. Can you cope, working under those conditions?'

His eyes sparkled. 'You may rely on me, King Odysseus. No one will know what's going on.'

CHAPTER THIRTY-TWO

NARRATED BY
PRIAM

Boreas the North Wind came howling down from the frozen wastes of Skythia, dyeing the trees amber and yellow; summer was gone in the tenth year and still Agamemnon remained, a mangy dog guarding the stinking bone of Troy.

Everything was gone. Just before Hektor died I ordered the last of the golden nails withdrawn from doors, floors, shutters, hinges, and threw them into the melting pot. The treasury was bare; all the votive offerings in the temples had been cannibalised to make ingots; rich and poor alike groaned under taxes; yet I still didn't have enough to buy what Troy needed to fight on – mercenaries, arms, war engines. For ten years I had seen no income from Hellespont tolls. Agamemnon collected them from all the Greek ships streaming into the Euxine Sea, from which he had barred ships of other nations. We ate well because our southern and northeastern gates remained open and the peasants were able to continue farming, but what we missed were the items of food our location made impossible to grow. Only a very few of the fabled horses of Laomedon were left to graze the southern plain; I had been forced to sell almost all of them. How true it is that the wheel turns full circle. What Laomedon and I had denied to the Greeks now belonged to the Greeks, for I learned later that King Diomedes of Argos was the chief buyer of those horses. Pride, pride ... It goeth before a fall.

They lit great fires in my chamber to warm my flesh, but there was no fire on earth could thaw out the despair settled like a sucking creature around my heart. Fifty sons had I sired,

PRIAM

fifty beautiful lads. Most of them were dead now. The War God
had culled the best of them for himself, left me the dross to
console my old age. I was eighty-three, and looked as if I would
outlive the last of them. To see Deiphobos strutting, a mockery
of the Heir, made me weep rivers. Hektor, *Hektor!* My wife
Hekabe was crazed, howled like an ancient bitch dog deprived
of sustenance; her preferred companion was Kassandra, even
more demented. Though Kassandra's beauty had grown in time
with her madness. Her black hair bore two great ribbons of
white, her face had fined down to sharpest bones, her eyes were
so big and brilliant that they looked like jet-dark sapphires.

Sometimes I would force myself to make the journey down
to the Skaian watchtower to see the innumerable wisps of
smoke rising from the beach, the ships drawn up rank on rank
along the strand. The Greeks made no assault; we hung on the
brink of an abyss while they accorded us no sop of comfort, for
we did not know what they intended. They simply went about
their mysterious business. The remnants of Troy's army were
concentrated on the Western Curtain; it was here that Agamemnon must attack, as attack he must.

Each night I lay sleepless; each morning found me wide
awake. Yet I was not defeated. While a spirit still dwelled inside
my withering carcase I wouldn't let Troy go. If I had to sell
every person within its walls, I would hold Troy in Agamemnon's teeth.

But on the third day of Boreas's Breath I lay with my face
turned to the window as the dawn crept up over Ida, grey light
streaked with the misty glow of tears. Weeping for Hektor.

I heard a faint shout, shuddered and forced myself out of
bed. It sounded as if it was coming from the Western Curtain.
Go there, Priam, see what the matter is. I summoned my car.

The noise was growing louder and louder as more and more
voices joined in, but it was too far away to learn whether the
racket was caused by fear or grief. Deiphobos joined me,
rubbing sleep from his eyes and pouting sourly.

451

'Are we being attacked, Father?'

'How should I know? I'm going to the walls to find out.'

The head groom came with my chariot, my driver stumbled from his quarters half stuporous; I drove off, leaving the Heir to follow or not, as he chose.

The whole city around the Skaian Gate and the Western Curtain seethed with people; men ran in all directions gesticulating and calling, but no one seemed to be buckling on armour. Instead they were leaping about, screaming to everyone to go up and see.

A soldier assisted me to climb the stairs of the Skaian watchtower; I emerged into the guardroom quietly. The captain was standing clad in a loincloth, tears running down his face, while his second-in-command sat in a chair, laughing insanely.

'What is the meaning of this, captain?' I demanded.

Too possessed by whatever affected him to realise what he was doing, the captain grasped me painfully by the arm and propelled me out onto the roadway. There he turned me in the direction of the Greek camp and pointed one shaking finger at it.

'Look your fill, sire! Apollo has heard our prayers!'

I screwed up my eyes (which were quite good for my age) and peered through the growing light. I looked, and I looked. How to take it in? How to *believe* it? The Greek smoke holes were cold, no scent of burning wood lingered on the air; not a single tiny figure moved; and a swathe of shingle bathed by the rising sun glittered in it. The only sign that ships had ever rested there was the series of long, deep scores running down into the water of the lagoon. The ships were gone! The soldiers were gone! Nothing of an army eighty thousand strong remained save a small city of grey houses. Agamemnon had sailed in the night.

I shrieked. I stood there and carolled my uncontained joy, then my limbs lost their power and I fell to the cobbles. I laughed and I wept, I rolled on the hard stones as if they were thistledown, I babbled my thanks to Apollo, I giggled and flapped my arms. The captain hoisted me to my feet; I took him in my embrace and kissed him, promising him I do not remember what.

Deiphobos came running with face transfigured, picked me up bodily and whirled me round in a crazy dance, while the guards stood in a ring and clapped the time.

No Grecian monster lurked on the beach. Troy was free!

No news ever travelled so fast. The whole city was awake by now, and all of it crowded onto the walls to cheer, sing, dance. As the light spread and the shadows began to lift from the plain we could see more clearly. Agamemnon had indeed sailed away, away, awaaaaay! Oh, dear Lord of Light, thank you! Thank you!

Alert now, the captain still stood protectively beside me. Suddenly stiff with apprehension, he plucked at my sleeve. Then Deiphobos noticed and came closer.

'What is it?' I asked, my spirits sinking.

'Sire, there's something out there on the plain. I've seen it since dawn, but the light's beginning to strike it now, and it isn't the grove of trees beside Simois. It's a huge object. See?'

'Yes, I see,' I said, mouth dry.

'*Something*,' said Deiphobos slowly. 'An animal?'

Others were pointing at it, debating its nature; then the sun slanted onto it and glanced off a brown, polished surface.

'I'm going to see,' I said, making for the guardroom door. 'Captain, order the Skaian Gate opened, but don't let the people go outside. I'll take Deiphobos and examine it myself.'

Oh, the feeling of that wind, cold though it was! Driving across the plain was a panacea for everything that ailed me. I told the driver to follow the road, so we bumped and jolted over the cobbles. A smoother ride than of yore. The ceaseless progress of men and chariots had worn the stones evenly and the fissures between were filled in with powdery dust gone hard in the autumn rains.

Of course we had all understood what the object was, but none of us could credit that we saw aright. What was it doing there? What could its purpose be? Surely it wasn't what we thought! On closer view it must turn out to be something far stranger, far different. Yet when Deiphobos and I approached, some of the Court trailing in our wake, it was indeed what it had seemed to be. A gigantic wooden horse.

It towered far above our heads, an oak-brown creature of huge proportions. Whoever had made it, Gods or men, had adhered strictly enough to equine anatomy to define it as a horse rather than a mule or a donkey, but the body was on such a scale that it was mounted on thicker legs than any horse ever owned, with mammoth hooves bolted to a table of logs. This platform was raised clear of the ground by small, solid wheels – twelve on either side at the front and the back. My car lay in the shadow of its head, and I had to crane my neck to see the underside of its jaws above me. Made of polished wood, it was both stout and sturdy, the joins between the planks sealed with pitch in the manner of a ship's hull; over the pitched seams a pleasing pattern had been painted in ochre. It had a carved tail and a carved mane; as I moved back to take in the head I saw that its eyes were inlaid with amber and jet, that the inner caverns of its nostrils were painted red, and that the teeth open on a neigh were ivory. It was very beautiful.

A full detachment of the Royal Guard had galloped up, together with most of the Court.

'It must be hollow, Father,' Deiphobos said, 'to be light enough to rest on the table without the wheels collapsing.'

I pointed to the creature's rump on our side. 'It's sacred. See? An owl, a serpent's head, an aegis and a spear. It belongs to Pallas Athene.'

Some of the others looked doubtful; Deiphobos and Kapys muttered, but another son of mine, Thymoites, became excited.

'Father, you're right! The symbols speak more eloquently

than a tongue. It's a gift from the Greeks to replace the Palladion.'

Apollo's chief priest, Lakoon, growled in his throat. 'Beware the Greeks when they bear gifts,' he said.

Kapys leaped into the fray. 'Father! It's a trap! Why would Pallas Athene extract such backbreaking labour from the Greeks? She loves the Greeks! If she hadn't consented to the theft of her Palladion, the Greeks couldn't have stolen it! She would never transfer her allegiance from the Greeks to us! It's a trap!'

'Control yourself, Kapys,' I said, distracted.

'Sire, I beg you!' he persisted. 'Break open its belly and see what it contains!'

'Have nothing to do with gifts from the Greeks,' said Lakoon, an arm about each of his two young sons. 'It's a trap.'

'I agree with Thymoites,' I said. 'It's meant to replace the Palladion.' I glared at Kapys. 'Enough, do you hear?'

'At any rate,' said Deiphobos practically, 'it wasn't intended to be brought inside our walls. It's too tall to fit through the gates. No, whatever its purpose, it can't be a trick. It's meant to remain here in this spot, of no danger to us or anyone else.'

'It *is* a trick!' cried Kapys and Lakoon, almost in unison.

The argument continued to rage as more and more of Troy's important people congregated about the amazing horse to wonder and theorise and inundate me with their opinions. To get away from them I drove round and round it, examining it minutely, plumbing the meaning of the symbols, marvelling at the quality of the workmanship. It stood exactly halfway between the beach and the city. But where had it come from? If the Greeks had built it, we would have seen it rise. It must be from the Goddess, it must!

Lakoon had sent some of the Royal Guard into the Greek camp to inspect it; I was still driving round and round when two guardsmen appeared in a four-wheeled car, a man between them. They dismounted at my side and helped him down.

His arms and legs were in chains, his clothing was reduced to tatters, his hair and person were filthy.

The senior guardsman knelt. 'Sire, we found this fellow skulking inside one of the Greek houses. He was as you see him now, in chains. He's been very recently flogged, see? When we took hold of him, he begged for his life and asked to be taken to the King of Troy to impart his news.'

'Speak, fellow. I am the King of Troy,' I said.

The man licked his lips, croaked, couldn't find a voice. A guardsman gave him water; he drank thirstily, then saluted me.

'Thank you for your kindness, sire,' he said.

'Who are you?' Deiphobos asked.

'My name is Sinon. I'm an Argive Greek, a baron at the Court of King Diomedes, whose cousin I am. But I served with a special unit of troops the High King of Mykenai delegated for the exclusive use of King Odysseus of the Out Islands.' He reeled, had to be held up by the guardsmen.

I got down. 'Soldier, sit him on the edge of your car and I'll sit beside him.'

But someone found me a stool, so I sat opposite him. 'Is that better, Sinon?'

'Thank you, sire, I have the strength to continue.'

'Why should an Argive baron be flogged and chained?'

'Because, sire, I was privy to the plot Odysseus hatched to be rid of King Palamedes. Apparently Palamedes had injured Odysseus in some way just before our expedition to Troy began. It's said of Odysseus that he can wait a lifetime for the perfect opportunity to be revenged. In the case of Palamedes, he waited a mere eight years. Two years ago Palamedes was executed for high treason. Odysseus engineered the charges and manufactured the proof which damned Palamedes.'

I frowned. 'Why should one Greek conspire to effect the death of another? Were they neighbours, rivals for territory?'

'No, sire. One rules islands to the west of the Isle of Pelops, the other an important seaport on the east coast. It was a grudge, over what I don't know.'

'I see. Why then are you here in this predicament? If Odysseus could engineer treason charges against one Greek king, why didn't he do the same to you, a mere baron?'

'I'm the first cousin of a more powerful king, sire, one whom Odysseus loves greatly. Besides, I told my story to a priest of Zeus. As long as I lived unscathed, the priest was to say nothing. If I died, no matter from what cause, the priest was to come forward. As Odysseus didn't know which priest, I thought myself safe.'

'I take it that the priest never told the story because you aren't dead?' I asked.

'No, sire, nothing like that,' said Sinon, sipping more water and looking a little less wretched. 'Time went on, Odysseus said and did nothing, and – well, sire, I simply forgot about it! But of late moons the army has become very discouraged. After Achilles and Ajax died, Agamemnon abandoned hope of ever entering Troy. So a council was held and a vote taken. They would go home to Greece.'

'But this council must have happened in midsummer!'

'Yes, sire. But the fleet couldn't sail because the omens were inauspicious. The high priest, Talthybios, finally gave the answer. Pallas Athene was causing the contrary winds to blow. She hardened her heart against us after her Palladion was stolen. She demanded reparation. Then Apollo declared his anger too. He wanted a human sacrifice. *Me!* By name! Nor could I find the priest in whom I had confided. Odysseus had sent him on a mission to Lesbos. So when I told my story, no one believed it.'

'King Odysseus hadn't forgotten you, then.'

'No, sire, of course he hadn't. He simply waited for the right moment to strike. They flogged me and cast me in chains and left me here at your mercy. Boreas began to blow, they could sail at last. Pallas Athene and Apollo were placated.'

I got up, stretched my legs, sat down again. 'But what of this wooden horse, Sinon? Why is it here? Is it Pallas Athene's?'

'Yes, sire. She demanded that her Palladion be replaced by a wooden horse. We built it ourselves.'

'Why,' asked Kapys suspiciously, 'didn't the Goddess simply demand that you return her Palladion?'

Sinon looked surprised. 'The Palladion had been polluted.'

'Go on,' I ordered.

'Talthybios prophesied that the moment the wooden horse rested inside the city of Troy, it would never fall. All its former prosperity would return. So Odysseus suggested that we build the horse too big to fit through your gates. That way, he said, we could obey Pallas Athene, yet make sure the prophecy couldn't be fulfilled. The wooden horse would have to remain outside on the plain.' He groaned, moved his shoulders, tried to sit more comfortably. 'Ai! Ai! They shredded me!'

'We'll bring you in and tend you very soon, Sinon,' I soothed, 'but first we must hear the whole tale.'

'Yes, sire, I understand. Though I don't know what you can do. Odysseus is brilliant. The horse is too big.'

'We'll see about that,' I said grimly. 'End it.'

'It's already ended, sire. They sailed, I was left here.'

'They sailed for Greece?'

'Yes, sire. In this wind, an easy business.'

'Then why,' asked Lakoon, still very sceptical, 'were wheels put on the beast?'

Sinon blinked, astonished. 'Why, to get it out of our camp!'

Impossible to doubt the man! His suffering was too real. So were those whip weals, his extreme emaciation. And his tale fitted together without flaw.

Deiphobos looked up at the mighty bulk of the horse, and sighed. 'Oh, what a pity, Father! If we could get it inside – ' He paused. 'Sinon,' he said then, 'what happened to the Palladion? *Polluted?*'

'When it was brought into our camp – Odysseus stole it – '

'Typical!' said Deiphobos, interrupting.

'She was displayed on her own altar,' Sinon went on, 'and the army was assembled to see her. But when the priests made the offerings to her, she was three times enveloped in flames. After the fire died down for the third time she began to sweat blood – big drops of it oozed out of her wooden skin and rolled down her face, down her arms, from the corners of her eyes as if she wept. The ground shook, and out of the clear sky a fireball fell into the trees beyond Skamander – you must have seen it. We beat our breasts, we prayed – even the High King himself. Afterwards we discovered that the Goddess had promised her sister Aphrodite a favour – that if the wooden horse was placed inside Troy, then Troy would marshal the forces of the world and conquer Greece.'

'Hah!' snorted Kapys. 'Too, too convenient! This brilliant Odysseus thinks of making the horse too big, then sails away! Why should they go to so much trouble only to sail away? Why should they care what size the horse was? They sailed *home*!'

'Because,' said Sinon in a voice which indicated that he was rapidly coming to the end of his patience, 'next spring they're coming back!'

'Unless,' I said, rising from my stool, 'the horse can be brought inside our walls.'

'It can't,' said Sinon, sagging against the side of the car and closing his eyes. 'It's too big.'

'It can!' I cried. 'Captain! Bring ropes, chains, mules, oxen and slaves. It's early morning. If we start now, we can get the beast inside before darkness falls.'

'No, no, no!' Lakoon yelled, face a mask of terror. 'Sire, no! Let me at least petition Apollo first, please!'

'Go and do what you feel you must, Lakoon,' I said, turning away. 'In the meantime, we'll start fulfilling the prophecy.'

'No!' shouted my son Kapys.

But everyone else roared on a whoop, '*Yes!*'

It took most of the day. We attached ropes reinforced with chains to the front and sides of the massive log platform, then harnessed mules, oxen and slaves; with almost infinite slowness the wooden horse moved down the road. Painful,

459

frustrating, exasperating work. No Greek – no man! – could have counted on our stubborn persistence in the face of such a task. At every bend the thing had to be backed to and fro a dozen times to keep it on the cobbles and off the sward, for the wheels were only bolted to the table; there were no axles in the world strong enough to take such a mountain of weight.

By noon we had drawn it to the Skaian Gate, where, sure enough, we could see for ourselves that the head was five cubits taller than the arched roadway above the vast wooden door.

'Thymoites,' I said to my most enthusiastic son, 'tell the garrison to bring picks and hammers. Break down the arch.'

It took a long time. The stones laid down by Poseidon Builder of Walls didn't yield readily to the blows of mortal men, but they crumbled fraction by fraction until a large gap existed above the open door of the Skaian Gate. Those harnessed to the creature drew on the roped chains; the mighty head went forward again. As the jaws crept closer and closer I held my breath, then screamed a warning: too late. The head stuck. We prised it loose, demolished a little more, and tried again. But it would not pass through. Four times in all that noble head jammed before the space was wide enough. Then the gigantic thing rolled groaning and ponderous into the Skaian Square. Hah, Odysseus! Foiled!

To be sure, I decided that the horse must be towed up the steep hill and brought inside Troy's wellsprings, the Citadel. Which took twice as many beasts of burden and what seemed aeons of time, though the cityfolk put their shoulders to it too. The Citadel gate had no arch over it; the horse just squeezed through.

We brought it to rest for good in the verdant courtyard sacred to Zeus. The flagstones cracked and split under its huge weight and the wheels sank into the ground amid fragmented paving, but the replacement for the Palladion stayed upright. No force on earth could move it now. We had shown Pallas Athene that we were worthy of her love and respect. Then and there I vowed publicly that the horse would be kept in perfect condition, and that an altar would be erected at its base. Troy was safe. King Agamemnon would not return in the spring with a new army. And we, when we had recovered, would marshal the forces of the world to conquer Greece.

Came Kassandra's crazed laughter; she ran from the colonnade, her hair streaming unbound behind her, both arms outstretched. Howling, wailing, screeching, she fell to clasp my knees.

'Father, get it out! Get it out of the city! Leave it where it was! It is a creature of death!'

Lakoon was there, nodding grim confirmation. 'Sire, the omens are not good. I've offered Apollo a hind and three doves, but he has rejected them all. This thing spells doom for our city.'

'I have seen it. Father speaks the truth,' said the elder of his two sons, pale and shivering.

Thymoites sprang forward to defend me; my own temper was rising, and the voices around grew afraid.

'Come with me, sire,' said Lakoon urgently. 'Come to the great altar and see for yourself! The horse is accursed! Chop it up, burn it, get rid of it!'

Hustling his two sons before him, Lakoon ran to Zeus's altar, far outdistancing my old legs. Suddenly, attaining the marble dais, he screamed. So did his sons, leaping and shrieking. By the time one of the guards reached him, he was down in a huddled heap and moaning, his arms plucking at his writhing sons. Then the guard skipped backwards very quickly and turned a horrified face towards us.

'Sire, don't come near!' he cried. 'It's a nest of vipers! They've been bitten!'

I raised my hands to the crimsoned depths of the firmament. 'O Father of the Skies, you have sent a sign! You struck Lakoon down in front of us because he spoke against your daughter's offering to the people of my city! The horse is good! The horse is sacred! It will keep the Greeks from our gates for ever!'

461

*

They were over, those ten years of war against a mighty foe. We had survived and we still owned ourselves. The Hellespont and the Euxine were ours again. The Citadel would have golden nails again. And we would smile again.

I led the Court into my palace and commanded a feast; our last misgivings laid to rest, we gave ourselves over to rejoicing like liberated slaves. Shouts of laughter – songs – cymbals – drums – horns – trumpets floated up from the honeycomb of streets below the Citadel, while from inside the Citadel the same noises floated down. Troy was free! Ten years, ten years! Troy had won. Troy had driven Agamemnon from its shores for ever.

Ah, but for me the best sight of all was Aineas! He hadn't gone to see the horse, nor stirred from the palace through all our travail. He couldn't very well avoid attending the feast, however, though he sat with face set and eyes smouldering. I had won, he had lost. The blood of Priam still existed. Troy would be ruled by *my* descendants, not by Aineas.

CHAPTER THIRTY-THREE

NARRATED BY
NEOPTOLEMOS

They shut the trapdoor on us well before dawn, and we who had experienced darkness every night of our lives discovered what darkness really was. Opening wider and wider, my eyes strained to see, yet still there was nothing to see. Nothing. I was struck blind, the world a blackness tangible and unendurable. A day and a night, I found myself thinking – if we were lucky. At least a day and a night crouching in one spot without so much as one pinprick of light – no way to tell the time from the sun, each instant an eternity, ears so finely attuned that men's breathing rolled like distant thunder.

My arm brushed against Odysseus; I shuddered before I could stop myself. My nostrils twitched with the smells of sweat, urine, faeces, malodorous breath, despite the covered pails of hide Odysseus had issued between each three men. I understood now why he had been so adamant about it. To have been soiled by excrement would have been beyond any of us. One hundred men struck blind – how did some men survive a lifetime of blindness?

I thought, I will never be able to see again. Will my eyes recognise light, or will the sheer shock of it dazzle me back into permanent darkness? My skin was tight, I could feel the terror licking all around me in the pit as one hundred of the most courageous men alive were stricken with mortal dread, incarcerated. My tongue cleaved to the roof of my mouth; I reached for the water skin, anything to be doing something.

We did have air, cunningly filtered in through a maze of tiny holes punctured all over the beast's body and head, but

Odysseus had warned us that we wouldn't see light through these holes while there was daylight outside because layers of cloth shielded them. Finally I closed my eyes. They ached so much from trying to see that it came as a welcome relief, and I found the blackness easier to bear.

Odysseus and I sat spine to spine, as did everyone. We ourselves were the only back rests our prison possessed. Striving to relax, I leaned on him and began to recall every girl I had ever met. I catalogued them meticulously – the prettiest and the ugliest – the shortest and the tallest – the first girl I had bedded and the last – one who had giggled at my lack of experience and one who had had barely enough strength to roll her eyes at me after a night in my arms. Girls exhausted, I began on all the beasts I had killed, the hunts I had attended – lions, boars, deer. Fishing expeditions in search of grampus and leviathan and vast serpents, though all we found were tunny and sea bass. I relived my days of training with the young Myrmidons. The little wars I had fought in their company. The times I had met great men, and who they were. I told over the tally of ships and Kings who had sailed for Troy. I thought of the name of every town and village in Thessalia. I sang the lays of the Heroes over in my mind. Somehow the time did pass, but snailed.

The silence deepened. I must have slept, for I awoke with a jerk to find that Odysseus had clapped his hand over my mouth. I lay with my head in his lap, my eyes starting from their sockets in panic until I remembered why I couldn't see. A movement had aroused me, and as I lay collecting my wits it came again – a gentle jolting. Rolling over, I sat up, groped for Odysseus's hands and clasped them tightly. He bent his head, his hair against my cheek. I found his ear.

'Are they moving us?'

I felt his grin against my face. 'Of course they are. Not for one moment did I doubt they'd move this thing. They fell for Sinon's story, just as I knew they would,' he whispered.

The sudden activity broke the suffocating inertia of our

imprisonment; for a long time we felt brighter, cheerier as we lurched and jerked along, trying to work out our speed, wondering when we would reach the walls, wondering what Priam intended to do about the fact that the horse was too big. And for this span of time we rejoiced in being able to speak to each other in low but normal voices, sure that the noise our conveyance made as it groaned along would drown us out. We could hear our progress, though we couldn't hear men or oxen. Just the roaring, squealing turning of all those wheels.

It wasn't difficult to determine when we reached the Skaian Gate. Movement ceased for what seemed like days. We sat praying silently to every God we knew that they wouldn't give up; that they would – as Odysseus had insisted they would – go to the lengths of demolishing the archway. Then we started to move again. There was a grinding, sickening jolt which knocked us sprawling; we lay still, our faces pressed against the floor.

'Fools!' Odysseus snarled. 'They've miscalculated.'

After four such jolts we began rolling once more. As the floor tilted, Odysseus chuckled.

'The hill up to the Citadel,' he said. 'They're escorting us to the palace, no less.'

Then all was silent again. Come to rest with a mighty groan, we were left to our thoughts. The huge thing took time to settle like a leviathan into mud, and I wondered whereabouts exactly we had come to this final halt. The perfume of flowers came stealing in. I tried to estimate how long it had taken them to haul the horse from the plain, but could not. If one cannot see sun or moon or stars, one cannot gauge the passage of time. So I leaned back against Odysseus and wrapped my arms about my knees. He and I were placed right next to the trapdoor, whereas Diomedes had been sent to the far end to keep order (we had been told that if a man started to panic, he was to be killed immediately), and I wasn't sorry. Odysseus was rocklike, unshakeable; just having him at my back calmed me.

When I let myself think about my father, the moments flew.

NEOPTOLEMOS

I hadn't wanted to think about him, fearing the pain, but in the anticlimax of our last wait I couldn't hold out. And was shorn of any pain at once, for when I opened the shutters of my mind to admit him, I could feel him physically with me. I was a small child again and he a giant towering far above my head, a God and a Hero to a little boy. So beautiful. So strange with that lipless mouth. I still bear the scar where I tried to cut off my own lip to be more like him; Grandfather Peleus caught me at it, and whipped me soundly for impiety. You can't be someone else, he said to me. You are yourself. Lips or no lips. Ah, and how I had prayed that the war against Troy would last long enough for me to go there and fight alongside him! From the time I turned fourteen and counted myself a man I begged both my grandfathers, Peleus and Lykomedes, to let me sail for Troy. They had refused.

Until the day when Grandfather Peleus came to my rooms in the palace at Iolkos with the grey face of a dying man and told me I might go. He simply sent me off; he didn't mention the message Odysseus had sent him, that the days of Achilles were numbered.

As long as I live I'll never forget the lay the minstrel sang to Agamemnon and the Kings. Unnoticed, I stood in the doorway and drank it in, revelling in his deeds. Then the harper sang of his death, of his mother and the choice she offered him, of the fact that he considered it no choice: live long and prosper in obscurity, or die young and covered in glory. Death. That was the fate I could never associate with my father, Achilles. To me he was above death; no hand could strike him down. But Achilles was a mortal man, and Achilles died. Died before I could see him, kiss his mouth without needing to be lifted an immense distance upwards, my feet far off the ground. Men told me I had grown to almost exactly his height.

Odysseus had guessed a great deal more than anyone else, and told me as much as he knew or suspected. Then he told me of the plot, sparing no one – least of all himself – as he

explained to me why my father had quarrelled with Agamemnon and withdrawn his aid. I wondered if I would have had the
strength and resolution to watch my reputation marred for
ever, as my father had. Heart aching, I swore Odysseus an oath
of secrecy; some inner sense was saying to me that my father
wanted things to remain as they were. Odysseus assumed this
was an atonement for some great sin he thought he had
committed.

Yet even in the decent darkness I couldn't weep for him. My
eyes were dry. Paris was dead, but if I could kill Priam for
Achilles, I might be able to weep.

I dozed again. The sound of the trapdoor opening woke me.
Odysseus moved like lightning, but he wasn't quick enough. A
faint, dazzling light was seeping through the hole in the floor,
and legs locked together flashed against its brilliance. There
were sounds of a muted scuffle, then one pair of the legs tipped
over. I sensed a body hurtling earthwards; from below there
came a soft thud. Someone from the horse couldn't endure his
incarceration one moment longer; when Sinon on the ground
outside pulled the lever which opened the trapdoor we had no
advance warning, but one of us was ready to escape.

Odysseus stood looking down, then uncoiled the rope
ladder. I moved up to him. Our armour was bundled in parcels
in the horse's head, and we had a strict order of exit; as we filed
to the trapdoor the first parcel a man felt was his own armour.

'I know who fell,' Odysseus said to me, 'so I'll take my
armour and wait until it's his turn, then take his. Otherwise the
men after him won't get the right bundle.'

Thus I found myself the first to tread on solid earth, save that
it wasn't solid at all. Like a man stunned by a blow, I stood on
headily perfumed softness – a carpet of autumn flowers.

Once all of us were down, Odysseus and Diomedes moved to
greet Sinon with hugs, kisses. Crafty Sinon, who was Odysseus's
cousin. Not having seen him before we entered the horse, I was
amazed at his appearance. No wonder the Trojans fell for the

tale he pitched them! Sick, miserable, bleeding, filthy. I had never seen the nastiest slave treated so abominably. Odysseus told me afterwards that Sinon had voluntarily starved himself for two moons to seem more wretched.

He was grinning hugely; I came up to them as he started to speak. 'Priam swallowed every bit, cousin! And the Gods were on our side – the omen Zeus sent was terrific – Lakoon and both his sons perished when they stepped on a nest of vipers, imagine that! It couldn't be better.'

'Did they leave the Skaian Gate open?' asked Odysseus.

'Of course. The whole city is in a drunken sleep – they really celebrated! Once the festivities in the palace started, no one remembered the poor victim from the Greek camp, so I had no difficulty in sneaking out to the headland above Sigios and lighting a beacon for Agamemnon. My fire was answered instantly from the hills on Tenedos – he should be sailing into Sigios around about now.'

Odysseus hugged him again. 'You did magnificently, Sinon. Rest assured, you'll be rewarded.'

'I know that.' He paused, then huffed contentedly. 'Do you know, cousin, I think I would have done it for no reward?'

Odysseus sent off fifty of us to the Skaian Gate to make sure the Trojans weren't given an opportunity to close it before Agamemnon entered; the rest of us stood armed and ready, watching the rose and soft gold creep over the high wall around the great courtyard, breathing deeply of the morning air and inhaling the perfume of the flowers beneath our feet.

'Who fell from the horse?' I asked Odysseus.

'Echion, son of Portheus,' he said shortly, his mind clearly elsewhere. Then he growled in his throat, shifted restlessly; not like Odysseus at all. 'Agamemnon, Agamemnon, where *are* you?' he asked aloud. 'You should be here already!'

At which moment a single horn wound soaring through the sunrise sky; Agamemnon was at the Skaian Gate, and we could move.

We split up. Odysseus, Diomedes, Menelaos, Automedon

and I took a few of the others and trod as softly as we could onto the colonnade, then turned into a high, wide corridor which led to Priam's part of the palace complex. There Odysseus, Menelaos and Diomedes left me to take a side passage through the maze towards the rooms which housed Helen and Deiphobos.

A high, lonely, drawn out scream tore the stillness apart and broke over the head of Troy. The palace passages came alive with people, men still naked from the bed, swords in hands, dazed and stupid from too much wine. Which permitted us to take our time, parry clumsy thrusts easily, chop them all down. Women howled and screeched, the marble tiles beneath our feet became slippery with blood – they didn't have a chance. Few realised what had happened. Some were alert enough to absorb the sight of me in Achilles's armour, and fled shrieking that Achilles led the shades of the dead on a rampage.

Murder in my heart, I spared no one. As the guards tumbled out the resistance began to harden; we had some good fighting at last, even if it wasn't battlefield style. The women contributed to the confusion and panic, made it impossible for the Citadel's male defenders to manoeuvre. Others from the horse followed in my wake; thirsting for Priam, I left them to butcher as they willed. Priam alone could pay for Achilles.

But they loved him, their foolish old King. Those who had woken clear-headed enough had buckled on armour and run through the warren by devious routes, intent on protecting him. A wall of armed men barred my path, their spears held like lances, their faces informing me that they'd die in Priam's service. Automedon and some others caught up with me; I stood still for a moment, considering. The tips of their spears steady, they waited for me to move. I swung my shield round and looked over my shoulder.

'Take them!'

I leaped forwards so quickly that the man directly facing me instinctively stepped aside, unsettling their front. The shield like a wall, I crashed broadside into them. They had no hope of withstanding such a weight of man and armour; as I fell on top of them their line broke, spears useless. I came up swinging the axe; one man lost an arm, another half his chest, a third the top of his head. It was just like cutting down thin saplings. My height and reach unmatchable at close quarters, I stood and hacked.

Bloody from head to foot, I stepped over the bodies and found myself on a pillared colonnade running all the way around a small courtyard. In its middle stood an altar raised on a tiered dais, with a big, leafy laurel tree shading its table from the sun.

Priam, King of Troy, was huddled on the top step, his white beard and hair struck silver in the filtered light, his skinny body wrapped in a linen bed robe.

I shouted to him from where I stood, my axe hanging at my side. 'Pick up a sword and die, Priam!'

But he stared vacantly at something beyond me, his rheumy eyes filled with tears; he neither knew nor cared. The air was charged with the noises of death and mayhem, and smoke was already lowering the sky. Troy was dying around him while he sat on the edge of madness at the foot of Apollo's altar. I believe that he never did realise we came from the horse, so the God spared him that. All he understood was that there was no further reason for him to continue living.

An ancient woman hunched beside him, clinging to his arm, her mouth open on a constant succession of howls more akin to a dog's than to anything human. A young woman with masses of curling black hair stood with her back to me at the altar table, her hands flat on its slab, her head tilted far back in prayer.

More men were arriving to defend Priam; I met their onslaught contemptuously. Some wore the insignia of sons of Priam, which only spurred me on. I killed them until one alone remained, a mere youth – Ilios? What could it matter who? When he tried to attack me with a sword I wrenched it from him easily, then took his long, unbound tresses in my left fist, my shield abandoned. He struggled, pummelled my greaves with his knuckles even as I tipped him onto his back and dragged him to the foot of the altar. Priam and Hekabe clung together; the young woman didn't turn round.

'Here's your last son, Priam! Watch him die!'

I put my heel on the youth's chest and hauled his shoulders clear of the ground, then smashed his head in with a blow from the flat of my axe. Suddenly seeming to notice me for the first time, Priam jumped to his feet. Eyes on the body of his last son, he reached for a spear leaning against the side of the altar. His wife tried to restrain him, howling like a she-wolf.

But he couldn't even negotiate the steps. He stumbled and fell to lie at my feet with his face buried in his arms, his neck presented for the Axe. The old woman had wrapped her arms about his thighs, the young woman had finally turned and watched not me but the King, her face filled with compassion. The axe came up. I judged the stroke so there could be no mistake. The double-headed blade streaked downwards like a ribbon in the air, and I felt in that exalted moment the priest who lives in the hearts of all men born to be kings. My father's axe completed the stroke perfectly. Priam's neck gaped under his silver hair, the blade went through to meet stone on the other side, and the head leaped high. Troy was dead. Its King had died as kings had died in the days of the Old Religion, their heads proffered for the Axe. I turned to find none save Greeks in Apollo's courtyard.

'Find a room you can lock,' I said to Automedon, 'then come back here and put the two women in it.'

I ascended the altar steps.

'Your King is dead,' I said to the young woman – a great beauty. 'You're my prize. Who are you?'

'Andromache of Kilikia, Hektor's widow,' she said steadily.

'Look after your mother, then, while you can. You'll be parted soon enough.'

'Let me go to my son,' she said, very controlled.

I shook my head. 'No, that's not possible.'

'Please!' she said, still in complete control.

The last of my rage left me; I pitied her. Agamemnon would never permit the boy to live. His order was the total extirpation of the House of Priam. Before I could deny her access to her son a second time, Automedon came back. The two women, one still howling, the other quietly imploring to be let see her son, were led away.

After that I left the courtyard and began to explore the labyrinth of corridors, opening each door and peering inside to see if there were more Trojans to kill. But I found no one until I reached an outer perimeter, opened yet another door.

Lying on a bed, sleeping soundly, was a very big and powerfully built man. A handsome fellow, dark enough to be a son of Priam save that he didn't have a Priamish look to him. I entered without making a sound and stood over him with my axe very near his neck, then shook him roughly by the shoulder. Obviously the worse for wine, he groaned, but became abruptly alert the moment his eyes took in a man wearing the armour of Achilles. Only the axe blade against his throat prevented his making a flying leap for his sword. He glared up at me hotly.

'And who are you?' I asked, smiling.

'Aineas of Dardania.'

'Well, well! You're my prisoner, Aineas. I'm Neoptolemos.'

A flash of hope lit his eyes. 'What, I'm not to be killed?'

'Why should I want to kill you? You're my prisoner, nothing more. If your Dardanian people still think highly enough of you to pay the exorbitant ransom I intend to ask, you may yet be a free man. A reward for – er – being nice to us in battle sometimes.'

His face exploded into joy. 'Then I'll be King of Troy!'

I laughed. 'By the time your ransom is found, Aineas, there will be no Troy to rule. We're going to tear the place apart and send its people into slavery. Shades will walk the plain. I think your most sensible course would be to emigrate.' I let the axe fall. 'Get up. Naked and in chains, you'll walk behind me.'

He snarled but did exactly as he was told, and gave me no trouble whatsoever.

A Myrmidon brought my chariot up through the burning, melting streets. I found some bits of rope, took the two women out of their prison and tethered them fast. Aineas held out his wrists for binding of his own volition. All three tied securely, I told Automedon to drive out of the Citadel gates and back to the Skaian Square. The sack was getting under way – not work for the son of Achilles. Someone hitched Priam's headless body to the back of the car, as Hektor's had been; it slid across the cobbles amid the feet of my three living captives. Priam's head sat atop Old Pelion, his silver hair and beard soaked in blood, his dark eyes wide open, transfixed in grief and ruin, gazing sightless over burning houses and mangled bodies. Little children cried vainly for their mothers, women ran dementedly hunting for their babes or fled from soldiers bent on rape and murder.

There was no holding the army. On this their day of triumph they vented all the spleen of ten years of homelessness and exile, of dead comrades and unfaithful wives, of hatred for every Trojan person and thing; they prowled the smoke-palled alleys like beasts. I saw no sign of Agamemnon. Perhaps some of my hurry in quitting the city stemmed from reluctance to meet him on this day of utter devastation. It was his victory.

Not far from the Citadel, Odysseus emerged from a side lane, waving cheerfully. 'Going already, Neoptolemos?'

I nodded despondently. 'Yes, and as fast as I can. Now that my anger's gone, my belly isn't strong enough.'

He pointed at the head. 'I see you found Priam.'

'Yes.'

'And who else have we got here?' He inspected my prisoners, bowing to Aineas with an exaggerated flourish. 'So you actually took Aineas alive! Now he was one I was sure would make it hard for you.'

I flicked the Dardanian a glance of scorn. 'He slept like a babe through the whole business. I found him mother-naked on his bed, still snoring.'

Odysseus roared with laughter; Aineas grew stiff with fury, the muscles of his arms bulging as he fought to be free of the ropes. Suddenly I realised that I had chosen the more galling fate for Aineas. He was far too proud to stomach derision. At the moment I woke him, all he could think of was the throne of Troy. Now he was beginning to understand what his captivity would entail – the insults, the gibes, the mirth, the endless retelling of how he was found dead drunk while everyone else was fighting.

I untied old Hekabe and jerked her forward. Howling. Then I put the end of her tether in Odysseus' hand.

'A special gift for you. You know she's Hekabe, of course. Take her and give her to Penelope as a serving woman. She'll add considerable lustre to your rocky isle.'

He blinked, astonished. 'There's no need, Neoptolemos.'

'I want you to have her, Odysseus. If I tried to keep her for myself, Agamemnon would have her off me for himself. But he won't dare demand her of you. Let some other house than Atreus's display a high-ranking prize out of Troy.'

'What of the young one? You know she's Andromache?'

'Yes, but she's mine by right.' I bent to whisper in his ear. 'She wanted to go to her son, but I knew that wasn't possible. What's happened to Hektor's son?'

For a moment I saw a coldness. 'Astyanax is dead. He couldn't be allowed to live. I found him myself, and threw him from the Citadel tower. Sons, grandsons, great-grandsons – all must die.'

I changed the subject. 'Did you find Helen?'

His chilliness vanished in a huge guffaw. 'Indeed we did!'

'How did she die?'

'Helen, dead? *Helen?* Laddie, she was born to live to a ripe old age and die sedately in her bed with her children and servants weeping. Can you see Menelaos killing Helen? Or letting Agamemnon order it? Gods, he loves her better by far than he does himself!'

He calmed down, though he still chortled. 'We found her in her apartments surrounded by a small guard of men, with Deiphobos prepared to kill the first Greek he saw. Menelaos was like a maddened bull! He took the Trojans on single-handedly and made light of it. Diomedes and I were mere spectators. At length he did for them all except Deiphobos, and they squared up to duel. Helen was standing to one side, head back, chest out, and eyes like green suns. As beautiful as Aphrodite! Neoptolemos, I tell you that there will never be a woman in all the world to hold a lamp to her! Menelaos got ready, but there was no duel. Helen got in first, skewered Deiphobos with a dagger between his shoulder blades. Then she fell on her knees. Chest out.

' "Kill me, Menelaos! Kill me!" she cried. "I don't deserve to live! Kill me now!"

'Of course he didn't. He took one look at her breasts and that was the end of it. They walked out of the room together without one glance in our direction.'

I had to laugh too. 'Oh, the irony! To think you fought a group of nations for ten whole years to see Helen die, only to see her go home to Amyklai a free woman – and still Queen.'

'Well, death is rarely where one expects,' said Odysseus. His shoulders sagged, and I saw for the first time that he was a man nearing forty, that he felt his age and his exile, that for all his love of intrigue he wanted nothing more than to be at home again. He saluted me and walked away leading the howling Hekabe, then disappeared into an alley. I nodded to Automedon and we went onwards to the Skaian Gate.

The team plodded slowly down the road which led back to the beach, Aineas and Andromache walking behind, Priam's corpse bouncing along between them. Inside the camp I bypassed the Myrmidon compound, forded Skamander and took the path to the tombs.

When the horses could go no further I untied Priam from the bar, twisted my left hand in the body's robe and dragged it thus to the door of my father's burial place. I propped Priam in the pose of a suppliant, kneeling over, and drove the butt of Old Pelion into the ground, piling stones about its base to make a little cairn. Then I turned back to see Troy on the plain, its houses spouting flames into the sombre sky, its gate gaping open like the mouth of a corpse after the shade has fled into the dark wastes below the earth. And then, at last, I wept for Achilles.

I tried to envision him as he was at Troy, but there was too much blood; a haze of death. In the end I could remember him but one way only, his skin shining oil from the bath, his yellow eyes glowing because he looked on me, his little son.

Not caring who saw me weep, I walked back to the chariot and climbed in beside Automedon.

'Back to the ships, friend of my father. We go home,' I said.

'Home!' he echoed on a sigh, faithful Automedon who had sailed from Aulis with Achilles. 'Home!'

Troy was behind us burning, but our eyes saw nothing save the dancing sparks of the sun on the wine-dark sea, beckoning us home.

THE FATES OF
SOME SURVIVORS

Agamemnon returned safely to Mykenai, completely unaware that his wife, Klytemnestra, had usurped the throne and married Aigisthos. After welcoming Agamemnon graciously, she persuaded him to have a bath. While he splashed happily, she took the sacred Axe and murdered him. Then she murdered his concubine, Kassandra the prophetess. Orestes, the son of Agamemnon and Klytemnestra, was smuggled out of Mykenai by his elder sister, Elektra, who feared Aigisthos would kill the boy. When he grew up Orestes avenged his father by murdering his mother and her lover. But this was a no-win situation; the Gods demanded vengeance for his father, yet condemned Orestes for matricide. He went mad.

In the Latin tradition **Aineas** is said to have fled the burning Troy with his aged father, Anchises, perched on his shoulder, and the Palladion of Athene tucked under his arm. He took ship and wound up in Carthage, North Africa, where the Queen, Dido, became hopelessly enamoured of him. When he sailed away she committed suicide. Aineas then came ashore for good on the Latin plain of central Italy, fought a war, and settled there. His son Iulus, by the Latin princess Lavinia, became King of Alba Longa and the ancestor of Julius Caesar. However, the Greek tradition denies all of this. It says that Aineas was taken as a prize by the son of Achilles, Neoptolemos, who ransomed him to the Dardanians; he then settled in Thrace.

Andromache, the widow of Hektor, fell as a prize to Neoptolemos. She was either his wife or his concubine until he died, and bore him at least two sons.

Antenor, together with his wife, the priestess Theano, and their children, was allowed to go free after Troy fell. They settled in Thrace – or so some say, in Cyrenaica, North Africa.

Askanios, the son of Aineas by the Trojan princess Kreusa, stayed in Asia Minor after his father left to go with Neoptolemos. He eventually succeeded to the throne of a very much reduced Troy.

Diomedes was blown off course and wrecked on the coast of Lykia in Asia Minor, but survived. Eventually he reached Argos, only to find that his wife had committed adultery and usurped his throne with her lover. Diomedes was defeated and banished to Korinthos, then fought a war in Aitolia. But he couldn't seem to settle down. His last home was in the town of Luceria, in Apulia, Italy.

Hekabe accompanied Odysseus, whose prize she was, to the Thracian Chersonnese, where her perpetual howling terrified him so much that he abandoned her by the seashore. Pitying her, the Gods changed her into a black bitch dog.

Helen participated in all Menelaos's adventures.

Idomeneus had the same problem as Agamemnon and Diomedes. His wife usurped the throne of Crete and shared it with her lover, who drove Idomeneus out. He then settled in Calabria, Italy.

Kassandra the prophetess had spurned Apollo's advances in her youth. In retaliation, he cursed her: always to prophesy the truth, never to be believed. She was first awarded as a prize to Little Ajax, but was taken off him after Odysseus swore that he had raped her on Athene's altar. Agamemnon claimed her for himself, and took her to Mykenai with him. Though she kept insisting only death awaited them there, Agamemnon took no notice. Apollo's curse was still working: she was murdered by Klytemnestra.

Little Ajax was wrecked on a reef while returning to Greece, and was drowned.

Menelaos is said to have been blown off course on his return voyage. He wound up in Egypt, where (with Helen) he visited many lands, remaining in the area for eight years. When finally he arrived back in Lakedaimon, it was on the same day that Orestes murdered Klytemnestra. Menelaos and Helen ruled in Lakedaimon, and laid the foundations of the future state of Sparta.

Menestheus didn't return to Athens. On his way home he accepted the isle of Melos as his new kingdom, and reigned there instead.

Neoptolemos succeeded to the throne of Peleus in Iolkos, but after strife with the sons of Askastos he quit Thessalia to live at Dodona, in Epiros. Later he was killed while looting the sanctuary of the Pythoness at Delphi.

Nestor got back to Pylos quickly and safely. He spent the rest of his very long life ruling Pylos in peace and prosperity.

As his house oracle had foretold, **Odysseus** was doomed not to see Ithaka for twenty years. After he left Troy he wandered up and down the Mediterranean and had many adventures with sirens, witches and monsters. When he did reach Ithaka he found his palace filled with Penelope's suitors, anxious to usurp his throne by marrying the Queen. But she had managed to stave off this fate by insisting that she couldn't remarry until she had finished weaving her own shroud. Every night she unravelled what she had woven the previous day. Assisted by his son, Telemachos, Odysseus killed the suitors. Afterwards he lived happily with Penelope.

Philoktetes was driven out of his kingdom of Hestaiotis and chose to emigrate to the city of Croton, in Lucanian Italy. He took the bow and arrows belonging to Herakles with him.

The sources for the tale of Troy are many. Homer's *Iliad* is but one of them; it narrates the events of some fifty-odd days only out of a war which lasted, all the sources agree, for ten years. The other epic poem attributed to Homer, the *Odyssey*, also provides much information about the war and those who fought in it. The other sources are often fragmentary, and include Euripedes, Pindar, Hyginus, Hesiod, Virgil, Apollodorus of Athens, Tzetzes, Diodorus Siculus, Dionysius of Halicarnassus, Sophocles, Herodotus, and more.

The date of the relevant sack of Troy (there were several) is generally thought to have been around the year 1184 BC, a time of great upheaval around the eastern end of the Mediterranean Sea due to natural disasters like earthquakes and to the migration of new peoples both into the area and from one part of it to another. Tribes were pushing south from the Danube basin into Macedonia and Thrace, and Greek peoples were colonising the coasts of modern Turkey along the Aegean and the Black Seas. These convulsive movements were the successors of earlier migrations and the precursors of others, and were to persist until relatively recent times. They gave rise to much of the richest traditions inherent in the history of Europe, Asia Minor and the Mediterranean basin.

Archaeological evidence commenced with the discoveries of Heinrich Schliemann at Hissarlik in Turkey, and Sir Arthur Evans at Knossos in Crete. There seems to be little doubt that a war was fought between the Achaean Greeks and the inhabitants of Troy (also called Ilium). It was almost certainly waged for control of the Dardanelles, that vital strait connecting the Black (Euxine) Sea with the Mediterranean (Aegaean) Sea, for with control of the Dardanelles (the Hellespont) came a monopoly of trade between the two bodies of water. Some of life's necessities were hard to come by, particularly tin, without which copper could not be made into bronze.

But while trade, economics and the need to survive were probably the roots of the war, no one can dispense with the more legendary trappings, from Helen to the Wooden Horse.

For the most part, the characters bear a Greek form of name. Some, like Helen and Priam, have passed so firmly into English-speaking cultures that I have preferred to give them their English names. A few characters are better known today by the Latin form of their names, as Hercules (Herakles), Venus (Aphrodite), Jupiter (Zeus), Aeneas (Aineas), Patroclus (Patro-kles), Ulysses (Odysseus), Hecuba (Hekabe), Vulcan (Hephais-tos), and Mars (Ares).

Despite the existence of clay tablets (Linear A, Linear B, etc) found at Pylos and other Mycenaen sites, the Aegaean peoples of the later Bronze Age were not literate in our meaning of that word. The ability to write, as distinct from Odysseus's con-temptuous references to 'grocery lists' (the Linear tablets – which were a form of Greek), did not appear much before the seventh century BC.

Coins also belong to the seventh century BC, so money *per se* did not exist, though gold, silver and bronze were used as tools of barter.

To indicate measurement, I chose terms like 'talent', 'league', 'pace', 'cubit', 'finger' and 'dipper'. Though in much later ages a league consisted of three miles, for the purposes of this book it may be assumed as one mile (1.6 kilometres). The pace was a double step measuring five feet (1.6 metres). There are argu-ments as to whether the cubit extended from the elbow to the wrist, or to the knuckles of the clenched fist, or to the fingertips. For the purposes of this book, assume that a cubit

measured fifteen inches (375mm). Smaller lengths were estimated by the breadth of the middle finger (something under
one inch, about 20mm). A talent was the load one man could
carry on his back: about fifty-six modern pounds (25 kilo-
grams). Grain was a liquid measure: assume that the vessel used
to dip into it contained about four American pints (1 litre).
Years were probably determined by the cycles of the seasons,
whereas the month was measured by the moon, perhaps from
new moon to new moon. Hours, minutes and seconds were
unknown.